the wyckham house

OTHER TITLES BY SHARON GERLACH

The Devil's Mansion Series
Malakh (novella)
Condemned (Book 2)

Harper & Lyttle Series
Office Politics
The Secret Dreams of Sarah-Jane Quinn

Sharon Gerlach

the wyckham house

Running Ink Press, LLC

A Running Ink Press, LLC Novel

This is a work of fiction. Names, characters, places, and incidents are products of the author's imagination or are used fictitiously and are not to be construed as real. Any resemblance to actual events, locales, organizations, or persons, living or dead, is entirely coincidental.

Running Ink Press, LLC
1419 N Lee St
Spokane WA 99202

The Wyckham House
Copyright 2007 Sharon Gerlach
ISBN: 0983291276
ISBN13: 978-0-9832912-7-5

www.runninginkpress.com

Cover image ©2011 Joshua A. Gerlach

First Running Ink Press, LLC paperback print: August 2012
Printed in the U.S.A.

ACKNOWLEDGEMENTS

Writing is never a completely solitary venture. Beta readers, proofreaders, editors, formatters – all play a huge role in putting a quality product into your hands.

I have deep and abiding gratitude for everyone involved in this book. My beta readers/fans: Christel; Nikki; Magnolia Belle; my sister Denise, her husband Virgil, and their fantastic kids Jonathan, David, and Kathryn; and all the various readers and reviewers who gave their input on WritersCafe as I was writing the first draft of this book; my proofreaders/editors Nikki & Christel, who keep me from sheer stupidity and correct my mistakes; any lingering typos or awkward sentences remain the fault of yours truly; my formatter, Nikki, who tames the wild beasts my documents become.

Most of all, I thank my family – my husband Gail and my children Valerie, Joshua, Kassandra, and my granddaughter Amélie – whose sacrifice of time with me allows me to exorcise my inner demons and bleed my stories out onto paper.

Lastly, my apologies to the state of Pennsylvania for the audacious liberties I've taken with plunking a fictional town into the middle of the state and for applying my own descriptive of the locale.

PROLOGUE
October 28, 2004 – 10:00 a.m.

How do I get myself into these situations?

The shadowy ceiling offered no answers, not that Kimberly could have read them anyway in the flickering light of the torch. But of course she didn't need the ceiling to point out a few home truths. She was in this situation through her own foolhardiness: a stolen identity, swiped from her best friend, to whom she bore a striking resemblance; a reckless, half-assed plan to find her father, whom she wasn't even sure was missing; and falling in love with the wrong man.

She shifted on the unyielding stone surface, and the links of her chains clinked like chimes. She was caught as surely as a rabbit in a snare; chewing her arm off seemed a drastic step to free herself, although if her bladder wasn't given relief soon it would seem like a fine idea.

He would come for her, of course; nothing would stop him. She wished he wouldn't. He would be given no reprieve this time; they would finish the job they had started years ago, silencing him forever. And what of her? There were worse things than death; he had been right about that.

It was her fault her father was missing as well. Had she begged off gathering his requested research – after all, she had deadlines of her own and little time to spare – perhaps he wouldn't have had the information that led him to his suspicions about this town.

But that was only supposition and a bit of her habit of taking the blame for things that weren't her responsibility. Todd must have already suspected what lay behind the strange animal attacks and unexplained disappearances, or he would not have asked for the particular information she'd collected.

Finally, she had to acknowledge the fact that she'd been warned away. The danger was real, the potential for mortal disaster unequivocal. And yet here she was, strapped to an ancient stone altar in the bowels of the house of the devil himself, lying in a pool of blood still tacky to the touch. The blood of a friend.

Quiet footsteps brought her head around; her hair stuck to the altar, and she fought a wave of nausea as she pulled it free. She'd grown used to the scent of blood over the last two hours, but when she moved, it wafted strong and cloying on the air and coated her tongue with bitter copper, like licking the end of a battery. Her stomach rolled.

He appeared out of the gloom like a violent apparition: her captor, the man who held her fate in his bloodstained, murderous hands. He moved with a fluid grace common to his family, as though he were liquid contained in a human shape. The darkness didn't seem to bother him, and not for the first time she wondered what gifts he'd been given in exchange for his soul.

"How are we doing?" His soulless eyes held a glint of mocking laughter.

"I don't know about you, but I could really use the restroom."

"Just came from there myself, but thank you for your concern." He extended no offer of relief to her, not that she had expected him to. He seemed determined to drive her to such a point of discomfort that she would release her bladder to mingle with the blood on the stone. But damned if she was going to add that humiliation to her already dismal circumstances.

Which brought her to another of her failings: she should have been more cautious, more suspicious of everyone. She'd been bagged easily – too easily, almost as if by complicity she'd been placed exactly where he could catch her.

She turned away, her eyes going back to the dark shadows hovering above her, silently communicating her refusal to beg. He chuckled.

"It's simple, Kimberly. You know what I want: a little bit of truthful information. Then I'll let you go."

Her head came back around. "You won't. You'll keep me captive until it suits you to either kill me or…worse. And I'm sure being in your captivity won't be pleasant. I've already experienced enough to know that much."

Involuntarily, her hand came up and massaged her bruised throat, leaving sticky prints of blood behind. At his widening smile, she damned herself for showing weakness. Yet another of her failings.

He leaned close. He smelled heavenly, like the woods after a heavy rain. How ironic that such an evil man could smell so divine. She tried not to breathe in; his scent clouded her mind with a hellish desire to fling herself at him and satisfy her carnal urges. It would be exquisite, she knew. Exquisite and satiating and shameful and damning. He would be cruel in his passion and passionate in his cruelty, and worse, he would own her then, body and surrendered soul.

His lips brushed her cheek as he spoke. She couldn't stop her shudder, and she told herself it was simple revulsion. But her pulse sped to a wild beat, and her body flared with sudden heat.

"Why did you say it? Who told you to say it? How did you know what she said before she died?"

"I don't know."

It was not the first time he'd asked, nor the first time she had no answer; she hadn't been aware of speaking at all. Her only memory of their altercation was of him catching her by her hair as she bolted for the back door and being pinned to the floor, his elegant fingers around her throat.

She was certain she had died, but perhaps that had been a dream while she had been unconscious. Otherwise, she would have to accept the fact that she had been brought back to life by the breath of an angel – a *real* angel – and that meant she would also have to accept that the driving force behind this man, behind his circle of black magic, was hell itself.

He offered no comment; her answer had been expected. His finger traced an indecent line down her cheek and over her throat, jumping the inadequate barricade of her collarbone, coming to rest in the valley between her breasts and hovering just above the first fastened button of her shirt. Add another of her failings: never dressing appropriately for the occasion.

Her heart galloped like a bolting horse, and his smile grew predatory. His eyes held her paralyzed; she'd never encountered someone who could hold one's gaze so unflinchingly for such a long time. She felt exposed, x-rayed, stripped down and distilled to her core by those cold eyes. She recognized the silent proposition in them and sent back her equally silent answer: *No. Not just no, but HELL no.*

"You might not appreciate the destination, but you will surely enjoy the journey."

"Physical satisfaction isn't everything."

His grin was thoroughly unholy, but he moved away from her, taking with him the tantalizing woodsy scent and his inhibition-erasing sensuality.

"You're taking this rather well, much better than most do. No weeping or begging. Very noble of you to accept your fate so philosophically and matter-of-factly."

"Will fighting you make any difference?"

"None." He leaned in again swiftly, startling her. She pressed back into the stone and instantly regretted it as copper scented the air. "Don't make me kill you, Kimberly," he whispered urgently. "Tell me what I want to know, and I'll let you live."

"As your captive."

"Yes."

"As your consort?" She lifted a brow.

"That goes without saying."

She turned her face away again, forcing her expression to lapse into careful indifference. "I'd rather die."

His rage could not be contained behind his impassive reaction. While he simply straightened from her and squared his shoulders, the very air around them vibrated with his fury. He pressed a finger painfully against her lips and took a step away from the altar.

"So be it."

RECKLESS IS AS RECKLESS DOES
October 3, 2004

It began with a simple delivery from UPS, a medium-sized box addressed to her father. The return address read Los Angeles, but if one knew how to read the shipping company's labels, one could tell this package originated from Pennsylvania.

Her father was in Pennsylvania.

Kimberly Owens spent several hours, collectively, staring at the package as she went about the duties of her day. She sent compiled research for a novelist who wrote historical romances (her client would be relieved); then accepted a challenging request from a compiler of mythology for information on an elusive Hungarian gypsy clan purportedly called *merénylõ*, which meant "assassin" (this client would cheer and then pop a Xanax, which she claimed Kim alone had driven her to with all her waffling about accepting difficult projects). She cleaned her father's Forest Falls cabin where she was currently staying (her possessions littered nearly all of the spacious log structure), and fixed a nutritious dinner (for a change).

Finally tucked into the corner of the sofa, a cozy fire crackling in the fieldstone fireplace and a novel in her hand begging for attention, she glared at the box with undisguised malevolence.

"You're just going to have to wait for him to come home," she muttered sullenly.

The box didn't answer, but simply sat on the floor near the door, shoved beneath the antique drop-leaf table that held her father's mail.

Its very existence called to her, though, as surely as the sirens called to hapless sailors, and she was just as powerless to resist.

Quick work with a utility knife laid the box open for her perusal. At first she could only stare at the contents, perplexed: a Shimano trolling rod, broken down to its smallest form; a Fenwick casting rod, likewise disassembled; a tackle box crammed with fishing lures and spinners of every imaginable brand, bobbers, lead sinkers, floaters, several spools of various test fishing line, half a dozen jars of salmon eggs in Day-Glo colors, and a single white paper drink coaster – imprinted with a drawing of a log cabin structure, the words 'The Watering Hole Tavern' around the edge – taped inside the lid.

Todd Garrett hated fishing.

She detached the paper disk and turned it over. Nothing but an address: 110 Stoneridge Way, Mills, PA – the town her father had gone to research. Her heart hammered in her chest as she sat cross-legged before this tableau, a sense of foreboding catching her breath in her throat. When her arms broke out in goose-flesh, she smoothed them out and tried to push away her troubled thoughts. *I am a professional researcher. I am not prone to will-o-the-wisps or the screaming meemies.*

A headache pulsed behind her right eye: a migraine just waiting for her to let down her guard. Kim scowled. Her migraines hadn't affected her so frequently in many years, but since her divorce – since she'd learned about her husband's mistress, actually – it seemed the headaches were poised on a hair-trigger, ready to flatten her with the slightest provocation.

As a child, she'd suffered frequent bouts of what her mother called "sick headaches." While medication was available, the Garretts couldn't afford it; poor as church mice – possibly poorer – the recommended nutrition and reduced stressors had been all but impossible to attain.

And then Todd had discovered his knack for research. His first paying client, a friend who was trying to juggle grad school, marriage, and a full-time job, had been so impressed he'd sent more students Todd's way. In a relatively short amount of time, Todd had quit his job as a server in a bad Italian restaurant (the smell of garlic would nauseate him for years to come) and opened the doors of his own small research company.

His reputation grew, as did his client list, and by the time Kimberly started high school she wanted for nothing. Her health improved, she blossomed from scrawny weed to graceful flower, and often went a year or more without a migraine.

And then the divorce. At twenty, she had married her high school sweetheart. At twenty-one, she attempted to get pregnant. She'd expected some difficulty – she'd suffered erratic, painful cycles her entire life – but it never occurred to her that it might prove impossible.

Three years and as many miscarriages later, Mark Owens walked out on his young wife, obtained a quickie divorce in Las Vegas, and married his mistress almost before the ink was dry on the divorce decree. His very *pregnant* mistress. He'd placed more importance on having a child than on his relationship with Kim, and that was the killing blow to her self-esteem, the blow that kept her awake at night. He'd thrown her aside as easily as he would a malfunctioning toaster and with as little regret. To be so meaningless to someone who'd once promised her so many idealistic but wonderful things, it was really no wonder the last two years had been liberally punctuated with debilitating headaches.

Pressing the heel of her hand against her right eye to stop the nauseating pulse, Kim chewed her lower lip uncertainly. She could simply text Todd and ask him why he'd sent home fishing gear when he detested fishing. There would be a simple explanation, such as someone had convinced him to go fishing and he'd enjoyed it much more than he had in his younger years; a friend who liked to fish was coming home with him and they didn't want to pay for checking the box on the airline (stupid theory, but it had possibilities). Or perhaps the contents of the box were a message, and the paper coaster a clue. But from whom, and why?

After a while she realized she was sitting on the sofa, staring into the fire, her cell phone open in her hand. She had no recollection of moving, no memory of sending a text, but her sent messages folder showed one placed to her father several minutes earlier. *Box of fishing gear arrived today. WTF?? Did you buy out Cabela's?*

A frown puckered her forehead as she tried to recall composing it, but the memory wouldn't come. With a niggling sense of unease, she went back to the novel, and almost succeeded in putting the incident from her mind.

The nightmare came for the first time that night, blurred images of freezing rain pelting her face; of a broad-shouldered man, dark blue eyes illuminated by the glow of the full moon behind angry storm clouds; of booming thunder drowning out all other sound and flares of lightning blinding her to peril; of a meadow filled with blood and screams and desperation.

She awoke screaming her father's name, a disquieting sense of déjà vu she recognized following her into consciousness. It came only with certain dreams, the kind she hadn't had in more than two years.

Prophetic dreams.

Anxiety had been her constant companion since the day Todd told her he planned to go to New England for a client to research a small town with one of the highest rates of disappearances and wild animal attacks in the United States. She couldn't put her finger on what caused her apprehension, but her best friend Bethany had offered her thoughts.

It's your gift, she'd said calmly, ignoring Kim's skeptical snort. *God gives you a glimpse of knowledge and waits to see what you're going to do with it.*

Yeah, well, Kim had a theory as well: indigestion – the only theory to which she would lend any credence.

That didn't change the fact that her prophetic dreams always came true. Without fail.

She stared up at the ceiling. The frenzied shadows of the wind-blown trees through the weak light of dawn, playing across the ceiling like a frantic ballet, stirred in her a crushing dread.

She considered those indigo eyes, so clear in her dreams that she could have drawn the exact pattern of their green and gold flecks. She considered the dark woods, the snowy sleet that drenched her and her unfamiliar companion, frigid needles that permeated the thin veil between sleep and wakefulness so that her skin felt icy and she shivered even as she huddled beneath a warm quilt. She considered the worst that could happen: her father was in trouble.

And thus, considering the worst, she began to make reckless plans.

STRANGE DAYS
October 4, 2004

The tiny town of Mills, Pennsylvania, sat some forty-five miles northwest of Scranton, just off Rocky Forest Road and down a pitted, potholed track referred to by locals as Old Mills Road. It nestled securely and mostly unnoticed near the banks of the Susquehanna River across from the tiny town of Laceyville.

Shrouded in forest among the rolling foothills of the Allegheny Mountains, Mills seemed shrouded in a supernatural mist – definitely in mystery – much like that mythical Scottish village. No eighteenth century Scotsmen existed here, striking a bargain with God to hide them from witches. Rather, here lived the descendents of a Christian settlement founded around the time of the Boston Tea Party, struggling to survive in a dying town.

Today the whole population buzzed with two subjects, both of which filled Aaron Schaefer with a mild sense of alarm.

The first regarded the apparent disappearance of crusty Mills native Ben Cummings, who worked for Ron from time to time as cook or bartender, whichever he happened to need at the time. Ben provided a constant source of irritation over the years, mostly to the city council and the Historical Society. His scathing letters to the editor in the Mills *Gazette* and his eloquent, demeaning speeches at public meetings served as a source of high amusement to Ron, as Aaron's close friends, family, and – well, nearly everyone called him.

The Historical Society (which his friend Denny often referred to as the Hysterical Society, since it seemed to be made up of nothing more than a bunch of hens squawking in alarm over every insignificant event) had their bones to pick with Ben over the Cummings family home, a town fixture built in 1795. Over the years, however, the Cummings family fortune dwindled away to nothing until the final heir – Ben – inherited nothing but a lifetime of hard work to keep the mansion standing. He had the mansion razed to the ground, revealing fatal termite damage. The Historical Society was outraged and filed suit against Ben for destroying a historical structure. The battle raged for two years until he hired a shark of a lawyer, who managed to back everyone off and get all injunctions lifted.

Ben rebuilt the mansion according to the original blueprints and sued to recoup his legal fees from the Historical Society. The clucking hens retreated to their coop in a stuffy office in City Hall to mutter in privacy, the public squawking over. Just recently Ben befriended a member and rumors abounded that her appointment to the Society faced revocation.

Yesterday afternoon, the constable's office had taken a missing persons report on Ben Cummings, filed by his Historical Society friend.

Ron wiped an imaginary spot off the gleaming surface of the mahogany bar and gazed across the tavern at his clientele, all of which gathered at a few tables across the room by the jukebox, smoking, shaking their heads and clucking in a good parody of the Historical Society.

They didn't talk about just Ben Cummings either. Todd Garrett, a renowned professional researcher, had packed up and shipped out late in the night. Ron could understand; sometimes Mills wasn't to his liking either. But the odd timing, and the fact Todd rented a house from him and hadn't mentioned plans to leave, greatly troubled him. His tenant had been in yesterday afternoon for his daily beer and a dose of "people-watching," and said he planned to go into Philadelphia the next weekend. Not to mention the man had borrowed all of Ron's fishing gear; Ron felt sure he would have returned it had he gone home to California. He'd swung by the rental house on Willow Road during his lunch hour but hadn't found even so much as a lure or a snippet of fishing line.

The door of the tavern opened, letting in a gust of autumn air and a tall man in a policeman's uniform. As the officer slid onto the bar stool directly in front of him, Ron noticed for the first time that more salt than pepper colored Harlan Michaels' hair.

"Ron," he greeted with a nod.

"Harlan," Ron returned the greeting, bending slightly to open the small refrigerator at his feet. He took out a bottle of Miller, uncapped it, and set it in front of the constable.

"So Garrett skipped out on his rent, eh?" Harlan mused without preamble.

"No," Ron said. "His rent is paid up through November. He did skip out with my fishing gear."

Harlan sipped his beer, watching as Ron moved around the bar and across the room to serve the folks gathered by the jukebox. Ron could interpret his look with no difficulty, seeing as Harlan had expressed it once in the lamenting tone of a career police officer whose protégé had utterly disappointed him: Aaron Schaefer would have made a fine police officer, if only he could have passed his psych evaluation.

Ron returned as Harlan finished the beer and set the bottle on the bar. "Want another, Harlan?"

"No, son." He slipped off the stool, dug into his pants pocket, and came out with a dull gold key. "Garrett dropped this in the market a few days ago. Looks like his house key. Couldn't catch him in time, then I forgot all about it. Thought you might want it back, seeing as he's left town."

"I do, thanks." Ron took the key and turned it over, but found nothing to prove it went to his rental. "Any news on Ben Cummings?"

"Not a trace. It's like someone reached down from the sky and plucked him right out of Mills." Harlan gave an eloquent shrug and let himself out the door. Ron stared after him for a moment, and dropped his gaze to the key.

Strange days here in Mills, he thought. First Ben Cummings vanishes without a trace (although for time out of mind, Mills seemed to have a big black hole which sucked unwary citizens into it, never to be seen again) and then Todd Garrett jets on back to SoCal with Ron's best fishing gear. Very strange days indeed.

He pocketed the key, intending to match it to the lock on his rental out on Willow Road. As the day wore on he found himself compulsively pulling it out of his pocket, mulling over the strange circumstances of Todd Garrett's departure, a sense of disquiet blooming in the pit of his stomach.

He closed the tavern that night with relief. The business brought him a good living but he wondered how much responsibility for the townsfolk's over-indulgence and alcohol-induced promiscuity lay with him. After all, he took their money and slung the whiskey their way. He also had to speak and act normally – while feeling like a two-faced jackass – to spouses whose other halves slipped out to the parking lot for a little extramarital activity and hungry families whose breadwinner drank the grocery money.

He himself had indulged in numerous years of no-commitment sex and drunken binges, but there came a point in a man's life where he just had to grow up. Ron had reached that point years ago. Now he watched his peers carrying on with revulsion and a queer sense of pity. He couldn't recall the last time he'd partaken more than a couple of drinks in one sitting, and his last one night stand was more than four years behind him. A whole lot of empty lived in his heart, and his mind dwelled on it more than he cared to admit. Eleven years was a long time to spend alone with his dark thoughts and the shattered remains of his dreams.

Is this how it's supposed to be, Elizabeth? You missing, vanished into thin air, and me alone, barely holding on to my sanity, unable to step away from the abyss? Is this the great plan your loving God – if He even exists – had for my life? What kind of God would inflict this kind of unrelenting misery on a person?

Certainly no god he would trust.

The vacuuming done and the last of the chairs put back on the floor, Ron dismissed his staff, turned out all but the kitchen lights, and sat in front of the slowly dying fire. When he'd first bought the tavern seven and a half years ago, he made the large stone fireplace his priority remodeling project. Constructed from rocks he culled from the Susquehanna River, it became his favorite spot after closing.

He lit a cigarette, one of his remaining vices since he'd given up drinking and meaningless sex, and pulled the gold key from his pocket. He turned it over, letting the firelight glint over the serrated edge. Funny how Harlan, of all people, had just happened to be at the market at exactly the moment Todd Garrett lost his house key. Funny....

Abruptly he rolled to his feet, slid the key under the cash register where it wouldn't get lost because no one ever cleaned under it, and smothered the fire. As he left the tavern through the service entrance at the back of the kitchen, his hand hovered over the light switch beside the door. In the end, he left the light on – he always left one on, no matter where he went – and secured the door behind him.

On the drive home he searched the sky at least four times and once more as he pulled into his garage. He didn't look for foul weather or UFOs.

Aaron Schaefer was looking for a full moon.

DREAM COME TRUE
October 9, 2004

The sun hung just over the tops of the autumn-hued forest surrounding Mills, Pennsylvania, as Kim drove the three blocks from the town's one motel to The Watering Hole Tavern, unsure what populated the woods and unwilling to find out the hard way. The paper coaster from this tavern was stowed carefully in her purse; she'd checked it three times to make sure she was heading to the right place.

Cars packed the parking lot and spilled onto the shoulder of the road in front of the structure. Kim sent a nervous glance at the nearby woods; she'd been forced to park on the shoulder behind an unusual number of battered pick-up trucks sporting gun racks. The western sky glowed a warm, red-orange, and with nightfall came a chill signaling the impending autumn. She shivered a little in her lightweight jean jacket as she crossed the gravel parking lot.

Loud, lively music thrummed from the other side of the heavy oak door, and small neon beer signs glowed and flashed in the windows of the log-cabin structure, which vibrated visibly in time with the music as if in warning. Undaunted, she pushed open the door and stepped inside.

Her five senses were assaulted all at once. She squinted against the flashing lights from the stage in the corner. A live band twanged out country music, and Kimberly mentally winced, hoping a migraine wasn't triggered by the high volume. Heavy with cigarette smoke and the pungent odor of spilled beer, topped off with a hint of frying hamburgers, she could almost taste as well as smell the air. As she made her way to the bar on the right, the crowd jostled and bumped her. Smashed between two staggering drunks, she felt a firm, deliberate pinch on her backside that left her shocked and blushing.

The tavern seemed the most likely place to start her search for her father, and the drink coaster in the fishing tackle box appeared to confirm it. Taverns showed you the pulse of a town, Todd always said, and he spent many hours watching people and becoming an aficionado of various brands of top-shelf scotch. Unfortunately, through his odd brand of voyeurism, he had gained such fabulous insight into the human psyche that recently she found herself uncomfortable under his scrutiny. His advice of late sounded much like it should be preceded by "Confucius say" or succeeded by such legendary names as Sophocles or Plato.

Her text message had gone unanswered for three days before Kimberly had sprung into action. It was not a creditable display of patience that she hadn't taken a red-eye flight to the east coast the day the fishing gear had arrived; she'd had an appointment with a real estate attorney two days later to sign the papers that would finally transfer her and Mark's condo into someone else's hands. No way was she going to miss *that*; it had been more than two years since they'd put it up for sale. The child her ex-husband had conceived with his mistress was already walking and talking.

She supposed – when she bothered to consider it at all – that the three days had given her a chance to really examine the situation at hand and make an informed decision. Ordinarily, she jumped first and looked out below second, which rarely ended well – her broken marriage served as a fine example. They'd also given her the chance to hunt down the return address on the package, which proved to be an abandoned warehouse in East L.A. She hadn't lingered to investigate.

His lack of response had made it evident that Todd was either ignoring her or could not answer her because he had been separated from his phone. He would never do the former, and only force could bring about the latter; Todd Garrett's cell phone was as much a part of him as were his crooked, boyish smile and the almond-shaped, amber eyes he'd passed on to his only offspring.

Once she had made her decision, she had thrown herself into it with no backward glance, no second thoughts, no planning ahead. A short stop in San Antonio to visit her best friend had secured identification; it had occurred to her that going in announcing herself as Todd Garrett's daughter wouldn't do the situation any good if he'd come to harm. She'd taken advantage of a golden opportunity when Beth's purse sat unguarded to slip out her friend's driver's license and social security card, her mind still mulling over Beth's husband's casual comments about their remarkable resemblance to one another. Kim's wild imagination kicked into gear and soon galloped out of control.

Thus, here she was, sliding onto an empty bar stool in this cram-packed redneck country-boy tavern in a hole-in-the-wall Pennsylvania town, not harboring much hope that she could get anything better than Miller Genuine Draft on tap, and hoping like hell that the sandy-haired bartender wouldn't scrutinize the license picture too closely.

The bartender barely glanced at her as he satisfied shouted requests from up and down the bar. Finally, when she felt certain he had forgotten her, his turbulent motion ceased, leaving him standing before her with his hands placed wide apart on the bar. She thought it might be his way of resting, or perhaps he was stoically suffering through a heart attack. But he grinned, lighting up a pair of incredible grey eyes in an otherwise perfectly average face, and she rather doubted he would smile while in the throes of a coronary incident.

"Now you look a lady after one of the best. Let me guess: the darker the better."

"Good guess."

"Guinness?"

"I suppose on tap would be too much to hope for?"

One shoulder lifted in a shrug. "Maybe if I ran an English pub, beautiful, but sadly... How 'bout a Boston Lager? Made by Sam Adams."

"Smooth?"

"Like Kool-Aid, with a bit of hops. I can see you're a very particular woman."

Kim cracked a wry grin. "You've no idea. Bring on the Boston Lager. If I don't like it, you're buying, right?"

He laughed heartily. "Sixteen or twenty-two ounce?"

Kim considered the crowd at her back, the fact that she knew no one in town save her father (if indeed he was still in this town), the possibility of an unknown hostile situation, and decided on a surprising course of prudence.

"Sixteen. I don't relish some stranger having to pour me into my motel room tonight."

"ID?" he asked, his smile twisting a little in apology. She slid Beth's driver's license across the gleaming mahogany. He picked it up, gave it a sharp glance, and handed it back as he turned to draw her beer. She noticed his hands were smooth, unworked, completely unlike what she would expect of a drink slinger in a hunter and logger joint. As though he'd noticed her scrutiny, he scooted her mug to her, keeping his hands carefully out of her line of sight.

"Six-fifty," he said, and she laid a twenty on the bar. She spun around on the stool before he came back with her change; she heard the clatter on coins on the polished wood behind her but didn't turn.

Her eyes fixed on the band with mild interest, not because she enjoyed the music but because the lead singer was quite good. His face, filled with a contagious, frenetic energy and glimpsed only now and again through a break in the crowd, struck her as somehow familiar. She tried to place whom he reminded her of as he signaled to the rest of the band that it was time for a break.

He holstered his microphone and elbowed his way through the crowd to the bar, a task which took considerable time as his groupies hailed him every few feet. The stool next to Kim had been vacated sometime during her conversation with the bartender, and he made a beeline for it. Almost as an afterthought, he glanced in her direction and then away again. Just as quickly he looked back and grinned. Before she could determine just what kind of grin it had been, he swung onto the empty stool.

"Hi!" The word came out with a definite eastern twang.

"Hi," she returned with a frosty smile.

He stuck out his hand, not at all put off by her cool demeanor. "Scott Schaefer. Singer, bartender, and part-time chef extraordinaire."

She grinned in spite of herself. "Is that right?"

"Well, the first two, anyway." He held up a finger to get the bartender's attention and pointed to Kim's beer. A moment later a full mug of Boston Lager slid into place in front of him. Scott took a deep drink and sighed gratefully.

"My cousin owns the bar," he explained, although she hadn't asked. "He's in back cooking, I guess, since Denny's slinging drinks." He made a face. "He does not like to cook, so I'm sure he's not happy."

"Oh?" Kim arched an inquisitive brow. "Did he want to sing instead?"

"Well, he sure didn't want to cook," he replied, cocking his head to one side thoughtfully. "But since he can't sing, I guess we're better off with him at the grill."

"I'll reserve judgment."

He grinned. "You're new," he stated the obvious.

"You're observant," she replied, not meaning it as a compliment.

His grin widened and Kim frowned; he really seemed quite familiar, as if sea-green eyes and chestnut hair had been painted over someone else's face.

"Staying long?"

"Maybe."

"Ever work in a bar?"

"Are you always so nosy?" she wondered in mock consternation.

He laughed. "Only when strange, beautiful women appear in my bar."

"I thought your cousin owned the bar."

"Technicality."

"And how do you know I'm strange?"

He laughed again. "You have a sense of humor, definitely strange amongst the female gender."

"I prefer the term 'different.'"

"You have a quick mind too. You might be over-qualified."

"For what?" she demanded suspiciously.

"If you're staying, you'll need a job. And it just so happens Ron – my cousin – needs another server."

"Does he know this yet?"

Scott Schaefer chuckled. "Even I'm not *that* precocious. He mentioned it himself before the crowd swarmed, as a matter of fact, so you can put your worries to rest. We're running a person short on weekdays days, and on the weekends when the band is playing, there's more work than there are people to do it. It puts Ron in a lousy mood. He could use you."

"If I'm qualified."

"If you can learn how to draw a beer that isn't ninety percent foam, you're a step ahead of the rest of the applicants he's had recently. I worry for the future if this town is any indication of modern intelligence."

Kim broke into laughter, and several heads turned their way. "I'll keep the job in mind."

"You should. Otherwise you end up commuting to one of the nearby towns to work in the five-and-dime for a lousy seven bucks an hour. Woo-hoo." He waved an imaginary flag in a half-hearted cheer, and tipped his beer at her. "I'd mention you to him, but I don't know your name."

She grinned. "You're smooth," she accused, and he nodded without apology. "Beth Fairchild."

He took her hand and shook it with exaggerated chivalry. "Well, Beth Fairchild, I'll put in a good word for you. I wouldn't stay too long tonight or he just might put you to work on the spot."

He grimaced, seeing the bartender open the kitchen door and attach a stack of food orders to a clip mounted on the other side.

"I guess I should go in and help him," he muttered with a distinct lack of enthusiasm. "If you hear a lot of cursing and clanging and see smoke, run in with the fire extinguisher. I'm not much better at cooking than he is."

Leaving her laughing, he slipped around the end of the bar and disappeared through the swinging door. She could see him through the small, eye-level window for a moment before he moved out of sight.

The bartender – Denny, Scott had called him – appeared in front of her with a sympathetic grin. "I see you've been initiated. Another Sam Adams will help you get over it."

Grinning, Kim slid her empty mug into his waiting hands.

Scott Schaefer didn't appear again until he reclaimed the stage for his next set half an hour later. She watched him, nursing her second beer along in the hopes she could make it last through the entire set.

Her eyes scanned the crowd, picking out people who looked interesting and watching for a while, cataloguing the brief flashes of insight into strangers' lives. Over there, by the jukebox – the young yuppie couple. He seemed slouched and defeated; she sat half-turned in her chair, presenting him with her rather rigid profile. Kim guessed he'd just been caught eyeballing some other woman.

Ah, there, by the cozy stone fireplace – the older man wearing the red ball cap. He sat nursing his beer, watching the crowd and smiling at what he saw. A widower, she guessed, missing his wife and needing the human connection.

And the man in the corner by the door – another people-watcher, and a very serious one. Crow's feet lined the corners of his ice-blue eyes as they crawled across the tavern's inhabitants. Silver glinted in his dark hair like streaks of iron ore.

He looked up, his gaze connecting with hers, catching her scrutiny. Kim felt a sudden, inexplicable acceleration in her heart rate, a flood of intense sexual awareness, and then he looked past her. Heart thudding, she watched him watch the crowd until she felt something cold and wet on her leg and realized she had tipped her beer. She swiveled on her stool and set the mug down, reaching to brush away the dark drops of beer before they soaked into her jeans. A dry towel sailed over the bar and landed precisely where she'd spilled. A shadow fell over her.

"Another one, ma'am?" a deep voice drawled, resonating with mocking humor. Instantly her mind supplied a tantalizing vision of a wrecked bed and spent passion to go with that incredible velvet voice.

She flushed and her head came up, her refusal on the tip of her tongue as she looked up into blue eyes. *Indigo* eyes.

The words died on her tongue, and for a moment she could only stare, speechless, dimly aware he had noticed her shock but unable to hide her reaction. Although she had suspected he existed and lived in Mills, she found herself entirely unprepared for proof of the precognitive nature of her dreams. In real life, his good-looks far surpassed her dreams. He would be an easy man to fantasize over but for the cold front she sensed surrounding him like a frigid Arctic wind.

It's your gift, she heard Beth saying, and then his deep voice overpowered the ghost words of her friend.

"Are you all right?"

Her head nodded of its own accord, which seemed to break her vocal paralysis. "Yes, I'm fine. I'm sorry. I guess I'm more tired from the trip than I realized." She pushed away her half-empty mug. "And I think I'm close enough to my limit."

His head inclined slightly in surprise. "Well, you're a step ahead of most of the townsfolk. I've lost track of how many sets of keys I've confiscated." He seemed to be very tired. "Scott tells me you're looking for a job?"

"Ah, you must be his cousin." All at once she could place Scott's familiarity. Strange how an uncanny family resemblance allowed her to recognize Ron Schaefer in the lines of Scott's face when she'd only seen Ron in her dreams. "I guess I'll need a job, as I'm partial to eating."

"Ever work in a bar?"

"My last year of college, when I turned twenty-one."

His blue eyes scanned her face critically. "What, last year?"

"Try almost five years ago," she said dryly, "but thanks. I'll be twenty-six soon."

Still just a baby, his look clearly said, although he didn't look to be a day over thirty himself. "Nine-thirty tomorrow morning. The back service door will be unlocked." He motioned toward the kitchen to indicate on what side of the building she could find it. "I'll be in here setting up tables. Bring your driver's license and social security card."

"I will."

One corner of his mouth twitched as though it wanted to smile. "Goodnight then."

He moved away, effectively ending their conversation. Kim sighed in relief; he possessed an overwhelming presence, and she'd forgotten to breathe through most of their exchange.

She swung off the stool and left the bar, overcome by a strange sense of inevitability that was far less disconcerting than the feel of his eyes on her as the door closed behind her.

THE WATERING HOLE
October 10, 2004

"You came," Ron Schaefer said, surprised, as she pushed through the swinging doors from the kitchen and came around the bar. He sat at a nearby table, one hand holding a newspaper, folded in half, and the other hovering a cigarette over an ashtray. Smoke drifted from its tip, lazily making its way toward the rafters.

Kim's step faltered. "You told me to."

But perhaps she'd misunderstood. It wouldn't be the first time she'd failed to comprehend what a man wanted. She'd wondered, as she hunted up a diner on Main Street, if he would even remember he'd asked her to come in. The diner's delightful blueberry pancakes, filled with huge, juicy berries, had gone a long way toward mellowing her nerves, and she allowed herself to hope that she would find her father today.

"I'm just surprised. What seems like a good idea in the excitement of the evening often seems foolish in the light of day."

She simply stared at him for several seconds, feeling the timbre of his voice vibrate through her: smoky like whiskey, as intimate as a warm, dark bedroom. Her thoughts raced headlong into reckless fantasies. Then he lifted a brow inquiringly, and her cheeks flamed.

"May I?" she gestured to the chair opposite him.

"Please do." His foot on the seat under the table sent the wheeled chair rolling backward. She caught it and slid into it, suddenly nervous. "When can you start?"

"After I'm properly interviewed. And after I fill out an employment application."

"Stickler for the formalities, are you? Very well. Why do you want to work here?" he barked at her.

She blinked. "Ah...to feed myself?"

"Where do you see yourself in five years, Beth?"

"Er...feeding myself and not living on the streets?"

"I'm asking the questions here." He frowned at her sternly. "Can you pull a draft that's not all head?"

"It's been a while," she admitted dryly, "but I think I can manage."

"Okay, then. When can you start?"

"That was an interview?"

"Beggars can't be choosers." He surveyed her through the smoke, waiting, and sighed when she didn't answer. "All right, a moment of truth. I have two servers. One needs to be taken off the busy shifts before she implodes. The other has threatened to walk out if I don't hire some help. If she follows through on her threat, I am well and truly screwed."

"Can't serve tables any better than you can cook?" Kim asked drolly and flushed scarlet, damning her wild tongue to eight kinds of hell. He stared at her in amazement and then threw back his head and laughed heartily.

"Oh, that's priceless. Don't believe everything you hear, especially if it's coming from my cousin. I'll go get the application." He moved to stand up, and she held up a finger.

"Just a moment. I have a question."

"Fair enough."

"Did business suddenly pick up, or did you lose an employee?"

His expression shifted subtly, and he answered almost too casually, "People move on. I'll be right back."

She watched him sidle around the bar and disappear into the kitchen through the swinging doors. He moved like a great cat: fluid, deliberate, an economy of motion that was grace in its simplest form. Something about his reply bothered her, but she couldn't quite define why.

He came back with a packet and a pen, dropping both in front of her. "I'll need to take a copy of your driver's license." She fished Beth's identification out of her purse and reached for the pen. "Would you like a cup of coffee while you're filling those out?"

"That'd be stellar, thanks. I didn't have time for any this morning."

A moment later, a mug filled with the darkest coffee she'd ever seen was plunked down in front of her. She peered into it with a dubious expression.

"Cream or sugar?" He didn't bother to hide his distaste at either prospect.

"Neither. I'm just trying to figure out if this is coffee or crude oil."

"I make it strong. One night of closing and you'll understand."

She pulled the application closer and aimed her pen at the first question as he disappeared into the kitchen again.

He hadn't returned by the time she finished the forms, so she shoved them aside and picked up his discarded newspaper. The front page headline was solemn: *Ben Cummings still missing after six days*. The article explained how the woods had been searched up to the point they became impassable, and the authorities suspected he had fallen into the Susquehanna River while fishing.

Fishing again. Her father had sent home fishing gear a week ago. Ben Cummings had disappeared while fishing a week ago. She didn't need Sherlock Holmes to connect these dots for her.

"All done?"

Ron Schaefer claimed his chair again, and Kim laid the newspaper aside. He flicked a glance at it, his expression tight, and it suddenly became clear what had bothered her about his reply to her question earlier. It had been delivered in a flat tone that matched his flat expression, as though he answered by rote, not because it was what he believed.

"Yes, all done," she murmured. "Just one thing I should mention. I'm allergic to chocolate, tomatoes, and penicillin. I wrote it in the personal information section, but I wasn't sure if you're one of those employers who actually reads the whole application, seeing as you don't really interview prospective employees."

His eyes gleamed at her thrust, but he declined to parry.

"Chocolate?" he repeated with interest, and slanted a mocking smile at her. "How ever do you survive?"

"I have other vices," she assured him.

"As do we all," he murmured. "I won't throw you to the wolves on a Saturday night, so how about you come in tomorrow morning? Sunday mornings are pretty slow, and Taryn and I will have the time to show you the ropes." He paused. "Or do you attend church?"

"No church," Kim said tersely. Her mind instantly flashed up an image of Bethany, who *would* be going to church and who would by now have realized her identification was missing. Would she have put two and two together yet and come up with Kim? Of course she would have, which was why Kim's cell phone was turned off and stuffed in a suitcase, and she'd bought a prepaid replacement at a T-Mobile kiosk in a mall in San Antonio on her way to the airport.

"Uh-huh," Ron remarked, watching what she was sure was a perplexing ebb and flow of emotions playing like a movie across her face. She had never been adept a hiding her thoughts or feelings; "poker face" was not a skill she would ever acquire.

She downed the last of her coffee, wincing as it scalded its way to her stomach. "Thanks for the coffee. I have an appointment to see a house in a while, and I'm navigationally challenged, so I'd better leave myself plenty of time to get lost."

He had already picked up her paperwork and was scanning it. "Who are you meeting?"

"Some fellow named Dennis Wallace."

Kim had the sudden impression of tension coiling up inside him, but his voice almost bored when he replied. "He only has two houses to rent, both on Willow Road. Very secluded. I'd think twice."

"Small town, small crime. Or so I assumed."

He spared her a brief glance. "Your decision, of course."

"Of course," she echoed. "You know this guy?"

A humorless smile curved his mouth. "Small town. I know everyone. And you met him last night; he was tending bar for me."

"Ah, the Sam Adams peddler. So am I safe going alone?"

"Couldn't be safer. But if you're worried, I'll take you there."

"Ha! How do I know you're not planning to gang up on me? I have a fighting chance against one of you, but two? Nuh-uh."

He sighed expressively. "Are you always so mistrustful?"

"Hello, I'm from San B – Antonio. A *lot* larger than Mills."

"Fine." He leaned back in his chair, sliding a hand into his jeans pocket – his very snug jeans, Kim's mind noted with efficient observation – and came out with a cell phone. Flipping it open and pressing a number with one hand, he shoved her mug at her with the other. "More coffee before we go?"

"We?" she repeated suspiciously. "No thanks. God knows when I'll see a restroom next."

"Ten minutes, tops," he replied, and then held up his finger and said into the phone, "You don't need to take Bethany Fairchild to see the cottage; I can do it."

Kim started to protest, but he screwed his finger into his ear to block out her voice.

"It's not a problem, but I don't think it's a good idea." He listened for a moment and then frowned. "Don't go all Kung Fu mystic crap on me. We'll talk about it later. You can go do whatever it is you do when you're not here." The voice at the other end said something that surprised a laugh out of him, and he responded with, "Yeah, whatever" and hung up.

"Charming," Kim remarked, tongue firmly in cheek.

"Yeah, he'd like to think he is," Ron muttered darkly, sending a furtive look toward the kitchen. "Come on; daylight's burning. You can ride with me if you're worried about getting lost."

"Don't we need to get the key from your friend?"

"Got my own." He patted his jeans pocket and motioned impatiently toward the kitchen. She suppressed an eyeroll and followed him through the swinging doors. Scott looked up as they came back through, his hands slimed with tomato juice and seeds.

"Hey there! So when do you star – OWWW!" Not watching what he'd been doing, he'd sliced into his finger, missing the tomato altogether. Ron shook his head, watching his cousin rinse the wounded digit under the faucet. "So are you going to be opening, Beth? You can do the tomatoes from now on."

Kim opened her mouth, but Ron beat her to it. "She's allergic. C'mon, let's go have a look at the cottage."

He didn't touch her, but she trailed after him out the service door as surely as if he had hold of her sleeve. He paused at the driver's side of a dusty red pickup truck and lifted a brow as she stopped uncertainly.

"Hop on in." He swung into the cab of the truck and started it before she had the door open. "I'd wear my seat belt if I were you. I've never been accused of being the safest driver."

She complied with a hint of a grin. What was she doing, anyway? Had she learned nothing in all the years she'd lived in Southern California? She hadn't been in Sticksville for more than twelve hours, and already she had accepted a ride from a stranger to God knew where.

She stole a glance at his profile. Okay, so maybe the possibilities weren't that alarming after all.

Ron Schaefer probably wasn't the safest driver; he did seem to have selective vision when it came to speed limits and stop signs, but she couldn't fault him his skill. He drove with the casual abandon – or was it arrogance? – of an extremely confident man.

Just before City Hall, he turned onto the only road on the right. They'd traveled about half a mile down it when he turned right again, this time onto a gravel driveway. A couple of hundred yards later, he stopped in front of a large English-style cottage. A jumble of brightly colored flowers bordered the curving flagstone walk that wound through the postage-stamp yard.

"There's a courtyard in the back," he said. "No grass, but there's a nice patio and flowerbeds, with a rock wall around it."

"No grass is a good thing," Kim replied.

"Makes it harder to rent."

He popped open the door and slid out, waiting for her in front of the truck. His hand dove into the pocket of his snug, faded jeans again, this time coming out with a key. Kim wondered what else he had in there; she was surprised he could even get his hand in. He took the steps in one bound and slid the key home, and then pushed the door open and motioned her to enter first. Kim stepped inside and caught her breath, immediately charmed.

Decorated with a feminine slant, the cottage stayed true to its English styling. Tasteful floral patterns covered the sofa and matching love seat, the tones picked up in the solid fabric of the wingback chair by the fireplace. The graceful, sweeping lines of the white occasional and coffee tables resembled French Provincial design. Two brass lamps flanked the sofa, topped with pristine mauve shades. Bare wood floors, polished to a glossy sheen and scattered with rag rugs made in complementary colors, invited one to shed shoes.

Kim didn't venture any farther into the cottage before deciding. "I'll take it."

"Don't you want to know how much I'm asking a month?"

She shrugged. "It's either this or the Starlight, I'll bet. I'd much rather have this."

"Five hundred a month, with water and garbage paid. You foot your own telephone and electric bills. You have steam heat, so it's relatively cheap. I'll give you the phone number for you to set up telephone services." He almost smiled. "I'll even let you use the bar phone."

"Gee, thanks."

"Don't mention it. I'll call and have the utilities transferred into your name." He paused. "In case you're wondering," and his tone clearly said he thought it odd she hadn't asked, "I pay eight dollars an hour."

"Nice wage for waiting tables."

"I don't have a lot of turnover, either. Besides, tips can be few and far between in Mills, although I imagine," he added, his gaze sweeping her figure appreciatively, "you'll do just fine."

She turned to hide her blush, cursing her Anglo complexion that showed every nuance of color, and ventured farther into the room, flicking a light switch in the dining room. The furnishings sprang into focus: a large oak table adorned with a vase of dried flowers, the built in china hutch displaying nothing but a few dust-bunnies, and the stenciled paintings on the wall just below the ceiling. She felt as though she had just stepped into a magical cottage straight from a fairy tale.

"This is gorgeous. More feminine than I usually go for, but still..." She trailed her hand over the smooth, polished dining table, liking the feel of the wood beneath her fingers. It was an odd habit of hers, testing the textures of certain items. She loved the smooth roundness of lentils against her skin; the grainy sharpness of rice; the porous roughness of river stones; the cold, slick surface of polished granite.

She glanced up and found him watching her. Her heart stuttered as recognition flashed in his eyes and then vanished, leaving behind a faint confusion. Had she been right to go to the tavern first? Did Ron

Schaefer know her father? Her mouth opened – God knew what she planned to say, because she sure didn't – but he spoke first.

"Come back to the master bedroom. There's a security feature I should show you before you decide whether you're going to rent this."

"It's this or the other house Denny has, I'll bet. I'm not much of an apartment dweller. And it's certainly much better than living at the Starlight Motel."

"Nevertheless," he replied inexorably. He didn't wait for her, but led the way down a short, narrow hallway, confident she would follow.

She bit the inside of her cheek to keep from commenting, and reluctantly gave in. It wasn't that he scared her, but she needed no visions of this velvet-voiced man in any bedroom where she would be sleeping. It would be all too easy to take it from there and envision him in her bed.

He was waiting for her, more or less – mostly less – patiently. One look at the bedroom dispelled any fantasies; this was not the wrecked bed with the twisted satin sheets from her fantasy. No, the mattress was bare, encased in a plastic dust-cover, and the room devoid of any personal touch whatsoever.

"It's pretty safe here, but I don't advise wandering in the woods at night. You can get lost and wild animals have been known to attack. Watch." He pushed the plain drapes out of the way, revealing a metal grid much like that used in a shopping mall to secure a store. A firm tug and the grid unfolded from left to right, covering the sliding patio doors that led into the courtyard behind the house.

"Isn't that a bit of overkill?" She eyed the grid, alarmed.

"Just a precaution," he assured her. "A wild dog chased down a man who lived here several years ago. It came through the glass at him."

Her eyes widened. "Was he hurt?"

His expression was unreadable. "Yes. I'm still working on the second bedroom, so we should probably agree on a good time for me to come over and work when it won't inconvenience you."

"Any time is fine by me. Just let me know you're coming in advance so I don't step out of the shower to find you fixing the towel bar."

"You take all the fun out of everything." His mouth threatened to break into a smile again, bringing shallow dimples to his cheeks.

"So I've been told."

She followed out of the cottage and waited by the truck while he locked the door behind them, an action she thought very odd in such a small town. The drive back to the tavern passed in relative silence, and as she retrieved her car to go gather her things from the motel, she marveled uneasily on how everything had, eerily, fallen in with her plans.

* * * * *

Ron found his cousin in the dining area reading Beth Fairchild's paperwork over a cup of coffee. A frown creased his brow, and he yanked the sheaf of papers unceremoniously from Scott's hand.

"Geez, Ron," Scott remarked, examining his hand for paper cuts.

"Employee paperwork is confidential," Ron reminded him. "And you know it."

"What's the big deal? It's just her job application and – "

"And none of your business."

"Again I ask, what's the big deal? It's not like I don't know everything going on around here anyway. I even know how much everyone makes an hour – "

Ron broke in rudely. "That's because you've known everyone all your life. If they choose to tell you their hourly wage, that's their business, but it's quite another matter going through employee files."

"Hey," Scott protested, taken aback. "You left them out here."

"And you picked them up to read them, which you didn't have to do." Ron, papers securely in hand, headed for his office, his cousin tagging at his heels.

"When does Beth start work?"

"Tomorrow."

"But I'm off tomorrow!"

Ron slid him an amused look. "So much the better for Beth, I think. I want Taryn to train her. Don't give me that look," he warned at Scott's offended expression. "You know Taryn's better at it. You just want to hang around because she's cute."

"I'd say she goes beyond cute." Scott gave him a sly grin. "And I heard she gave you quite a look last night."

"Oh?" Despite his casual tone, Scott's expression was knowing.

"Denny said when she first looked up at you, she just stared at you for a full five seconds. What was that all about?"

"I don't know. She said the trip was longer than she thought and she'd had enough to drink. Maybe she just got dizzy when she spun around on the stool."

But had she? It didn't seem like it. In fact, when she'd gazed up at him, she'd looked as though she'd just seen a ghost. That strange look of shock and recognition still puzzled him; to Ron's knowledge, he'd never met her. He would have remembered. Perhaps she'd felt the same sense of familiarity he'd experienced this morning. Regardless, it had made him quite uncomfortable. He'd been under a woman's open scrutiny before, but usually in much more pleasing ways.

"Yo! Ron."

Ron realized he'd been staring off into space. To cover his embarrassment, he grabbed a bag of onions and a butcher knife, moving to a prep table with a mounted onion slicer.

Scott pulled in a breath and let it out on a sigh. "You sure have been acting weird since old Ben Cummings disappeared and Todd Garrett ran off with your tackle box. What is it with you?"

"Nothing," Ron replied tightly. "Would you please get back to work, Scott? We have a lot to do."

Scott held up a hand to tell his cousin to back off and calm down, and started gathering the tools he needed for his duties. Before he began working, however, he voiced one last thought.

"You're interested in her, aren't you?"

"Don't be ridiculous. I just met her."

"So? You spent half the morning with her. Long enough to form an opinion about whether or not you're attracted to her." Scott paused. "Are you going to one-night-stand her like you do everyone else?"

Ron whirled around, huffing out an impatient breath. "What is your problem? Why do you care *what* I do?"

"You might not be the only one interested in her."

"*You* have a girlfriend." *And I'm not looking for one.*

"Maybe not for long."

"Oh, yeah, right. After eleven years you're finally going to find a backbone? Pardon me if I don't buy it."

"And you're a paragon of virtue, is that what you're saying? Maybe you think I'm whipped, but at least I never swiped your girl."

Don't say it don't say it don't say it, Ron chanted silently, but nothing short of superhuman effort would be enough to hold back the words. And God knew he wasn't that strong.

"Perhaps if you'd been paying attention, I'd never have had the opportunity." Ouch.

Scott flinched. "Sometimes you're a real jerk, you know it?" He stalked off into the dining room.

Ron braced himself against the sink and sighed, closing his eyes. "Yeah, I know, Scotty," he agreed quietly.

He could think of nothing he regretted more than going to the river that day eleven years ago. Had he stayed home, Tiana Michaels would never have confessed what she had, and Scott never would have seen them and formed the conclusions that he did. And no one would have worried about what he knew. His life would be dramatically different.

But he couldn't go back in time and change things and if faced with the choice to do so, he wasn't sure he would. The events of the past shaped them all, for better or worse, and who could say how their lives might have turned out?

Ron's mind turned to Bethany Fairchild, with her honey-colored hair and eyes like a summer wheat field, the scent of lilacs lingering in the air around her. Denying to himself her inexplicable appeal was much harder than denying it to Scott.

STRANGERS BEARING GIFTS

Kim spent the day in Scranton shopping for the household staples she would need to get her by while she was in Mills. She didn't think she would need to stay very long; she was sure she'd unearth Todd within a few days, and her charade would then become unnecessary. She would go back to San Bernardino – or maybe stay with her father in Forest Falls – and forget this whole surreal mess.

On the drive home, she tried not to think about the precognitive dream that had brought her here – the dream of the blue-eyed man she now worked for. It had been nothing more than a means to get her to the one place Todd would have frequented, thus making it easier for her to find him. She was certain of it.

So certain, in fact, that she was willing to discount the fact that, although her visionary dreams always happened in real life, they had yet to be chased by some unknown horror through the snowy woods. That was just a pesky detail she couldn't be bothered with.

She made it home in time to carry her stores into the house by the last light of the day. The sun hovered at the treetops, spackling the yard with weak yellow splotches that danced in time with the breeze. Kim would have danced with them – so to speak – but for her hankering for the Delimax taquitos she'd picked up at the grocery store on her way back into town – and a healthy aversion to the dense woods around her.

Her dinner was half-consumed when her doorbell unexpectedly pealed. She jumped and dropped her half-eaten taquito, splattering sour cream and guacamole across her plate. Her palms broke into a sweat and heart raced unchecked.

"Ridiculous," Kim chided herself. "You didn't come to Mills to get involved with someone. No doubt he's a complete womanizer anyway."

She took a calming breath as she padded down the hallway and into the living room, and yet another as she flung open the door. For a startled moment she simply stared at the man casually lounging against the doorjamb.

It wasn't Ron. It was the intense people-watcher from the tavern. An irrational desire flooded through her, her pulse racing unchecked toward a wild and dangerous rhythm, and then she caught herself. *Good Lord, Kim, you're not a teenager with raging hormones anymore!* She forced a pleasantly neutral expression onto her face to hide her reaction to him.

His mocking expression told her she was too late. "Bethany Fairchild?" She nodded warily. "I'm Caleb Schaefer. Just thought I would drop by and welcome you to town."

He extended his hand, and after a noticeable hesitation, she accepted it. His grip was too firm and personal, and he held on longer than was proper. Kim's face burned with color.

"That's very thoughtful, Mr. Schaefer. I see the grapevine works quite efficiently in Mills." He smiled and waited. After a second her mind processed his name. "Schaefer," she murmured. "The same Schaefer family as Ron and Scott?"

"Ron is my son."

Her sweeping glance took in the similarities between him and Ron: the same raven hair, although strands of silver snaked through Caleb's; identical strong jaw line and sensuous, kiss-me-now mouth shielding even, white teeth; vertical dimples carving deep lines in lean, tanned cheeks. But Caleb's eyes were different – a light wintry blue instead of Ron's indigo, and dangerously hypnotizing. You couldn't look into those eyes without fear of losing all rational thought.

"I can see the resemblance," she remarked, and Caleb's smile slipped a notch.

"Yes," he replied curtly. He suddenly stuck out his other hand, and Kim involuntarily flinched before realizing he held out a decorative, antique-looking emerald bottle with a snippet of ribbon tied around its neck like a silken noose.

"A welcoming gift from one of our senior residents. It's skullcap tincture. She's an herbalist," he explained patiently at her dubious expression.

"I see." She took the bottle gingerly, gazing through the green glass at the liquid inside. "And just what does one do with skullcap tincture?" It certainly didn't sound like anything she would want to ingest.

"It's a mild sedative, antidepressant, good for nervousness. All natural, of course. Sarah thought it might come in handy, since you're new in town. Moving can often cause anxiety and insomnia."

"I'm sleeping fine," Kim prevaricated, although anyone looking at her could see right through the lie. Dark circles ringed her eyes, and weariness dragged at her limbs. But she didn't need a mild sedative; what she needed was something that would put her so deeply asleep that the disturbing dream wouldn't bother her anymore. "Thanks anyway."

She tried to hand the bottle back but Caleb Schaefer politely refused to take it by the simple expedient of stuffing his hands into the pockets of his jeans.

"You might need it."

"All right," she agreed affably. She hoped he wasn't waiting to be invited in; something told her that bringing him into any intimate surrounding was likely to lead somewhere she wasn't ready to go. But it would be terribly rude not to if they stood here much longer.

To her relief, he said, "I'll be going now. A pleasure meeting you."

His parting smile was knowing, almost smug, as though he was perfectly aware of – and pleased with – the effect he had on her. Kim wasn't surprised; she had a terrible poker face and was an abysmal liar. He walked to his shiny black truck with a jaunty stride that belied his years. Her voice stopped him as he opened the driver's door.

"You haven't said, Mr. Schaefer. In what capacity do you serve the town? I mean, besides being the welcoming committee." She forced a smile as she held up the bottle.

He flashed a wolfish grin. "I'm the city manager, Miss Fairchild." His words seemed full of hidden meaning, but he didn't elaborate. He gave her one last nod as he started the truck and aimed it toward Willow Road. Kim wondered exactly what Caleb managed – the city's affairs, or its people.

With a troubled frown, she went back inside, locking the door behind her – no sense in being imprudent – and went back to her dinner.

Light, glorious diamond-like refractions, and a shape at the core, human-like but not human. Otherworldly. Ethereal. Eyes like kaleidoscopes with jewel-tone mists scudding across their surface. A face of breathtaking, alien beauty.

It stopped before her and reached out its hand. Desire like a shockwave slammed through her. Every want she'd ever harbored in her deepest heart amplified a thousandfold, and all suddenly seemed possible, attainable. She was deserving. All she had to do was accept. Take its hand…ask for what she wanted…

"I can make the dreams go away," it said. Its voice caressed her like the finest silk. "Just take my hand and you won't dream of the future anymore."

She shouldn't…but her fingers twitched at her side. It was just a dream, nothing real, nothing harmful. Her hand raised two inches, and then two inches more. Its touch was electrifying, a painful buzz through her hand that burned like fire. A rush of debilitating nausea dropped her to her knees, and she lost her tenuous grip on consciousness.

She came awake in the cold, pre-dawn hours, sprawled on the carpet beside the bed, groggy and confused. For a moment she had a disquieting sense of loss, as though she'd suffered a tragedy she couldn't quite remember.

Rolling onto her knees, she pushed herself up from the floor. Rough fibers ground painfully into her left palm, and it wasn't until she had scooted onto the edge of the bed that she realized why her hand hurt.

Where her hand had touched the being in her dream, her skin was scarlet and blistered.

A BATTLE OF WILLS
October 11, 2004

The morning passed in a flurry of activity. Taryn Ackerlin, her outspoken, auburn-haired trainer, seemed to have one speed: manic. Preparations for the day were completed an hour early – due in no small part to Kim's skill in a bar kitchen – which seemed to please Ron Schaefer immensely.

The tavern's dirty little secret was trotted out, and Kim was inducted into the ranks of nickel poker players. Her name was added to a tally sheet that was prudently kept in a desk drawer in Ron's office.

Now she sat with a crap hand, deciding whether or not to fold.

Taryn perched on the stool next to her, and Ron leaned on the business side of the bar. Not only a crap hand, she reflected sourly, but a wrapped hand as well. She hadn't been quick enough to hide her grimace of pain when onion juice met the raw, blistered flesh of her palm, and before she knew it she found herself yanked away from the rotary slicer and stuffed into a chair in Ron's office, her hand laid out for his perusal like some strange starfish. He'd slathered it with a burn ointment despite her protests that aloe vera with Lidocaine would work better (a tube of which she carried in her purse), and wrapped it in enough gauze to sheath half a mummy.

"Are you gonna fold or are you going to just sit there and scowl all day?" Taryn prodded. Kim grinned. She and her acerbic trainer had hit it off like whiskey and water.

"If I could move my fingers, I'd be a little quicker."

"Your mental acuity is connected to your fingers?" Ron asked dryly. "Why does that not surprise me?"

"Listen, you," Kim said with feigned weary patience. "The jury's still out on whether or not I like you, so you might want to start earning brownie points instead of giving me reasons to take up knife throwing."

"Ha. You like her just fine," and he jerked his thumb at Taryn. "I've known you longer."

"Yeah, but she didn't wrap me up like a Halloween mummy," Kim muttered. She tossed her cards face down on the bar, opting to fold.

He opened his mouth to respond – no doubt she didn't want to hear it, judging from the glint in his eyes – but the phone interrupted him. He laid his cards face down, snatched up the cordless receiver, and disappeared into the kitchen.

"More coffee, Beth?" Taryn was already reaching for her cup, so Kim nodded.

Taryn went to get the coffee pot and came back with a packet of sugar and a small, sealed container of half-and-half. Remembering Ron's displeasure at how Taryn doctored her coffee this morning, Kim smirked.

"Thought he broke you of that," she remarked as Taryn refilled both their mugs.

"So does he," Taryn replied, smiling mischievously, her green eyes dancing. "The secret is to let him think he's in control, even if he isn't. As long as he thinks he's running you, he's easy to get along with."

"Great. A control freak."

"As if you didn't know already. Take this morning, for example–"

Kim grimaced. "Let's not and say we did." She tried to flex her hand, but there was too much gauze. Probably not a bad thing, she admitted secretly, since it hurt like fury to crease her scorched flesh.

"He's got his ways, that's for sure. And he's set in them, too." Taryn tore the top off her packet of sugar and dumped its contents into her mug. She stirred, added the cream, and looked at it dubiously, grinning when Kim snorted with laughter. "I swear," she whispered, "the first cup will put hair on your chest and the second cup will burn it right off."

"When he offered me a cup at my interview, I wasn't sure if he'd given me coffee or crude oil."

Taryn laughed. "And I'll bet you asked!"

"No bet."

"You get used to him," Taryn said, unexpectedly subdued. "You may not like the way he is, but you get used to him. He's very...reserved."

"I like him just fine. But your statement begs the question of any particular reason why he's so reserved." Kim tried to sound more casual than she felt, but Taryn sent her a look edged with caution.

"It's the way he's been since Liz."

The name meant nothing to Kim, but she wasn't surprised a woman from his past caused his sometimes glacial demeanor. Hadn't she been the same way the first year after Mark divorced her? Only she hadn't been able to summon a single flirtatious moment until the last couple of months. Ron Schaefer was obviously an accomplished flirt. More than likely an accomplished seducer as well.

"Who is Liz?"

"*Was,*" Taryn answered quietly. "His fiancée. Three months before their wedding, she vanished without a trace."

After a moment of stunned silence, Kim murmured, "I see." Now she understood the glacier. "How long ago did this happen?"

"Eleven years."

"So now he swears off women."

"Oh, he likes women just fine – too much, truthfully – as long as they don't get involved." Her glance now carried a warning.

"What was that for?" Kim demanded mildly, giving Taryn a sidelong look of her own through narrowed amber eyes.

"What?" Taryn replied innocently.

"That *look*. You mention he doesn't like involvement, and then you give me this look."

"Just some advice, my friend. He'll break your heart if you let him."

"I won't give him the chance," Kim assured her sharply. She started to add more, but Ron came back through the kitchen door, shrugging into a weathered denim jacket.

"Gotta run. My lost case of Lagavulin has been found."

Taryn lifted a brow. "God forbid you go without your Lagavulin," she drawled.

"Yeah, God forbid. Will you guys be all right? I'll be gone for at least an hour." His eyes swung between them as though assessing both Kim's ability to hold her own and Taryn's ability to handle both her and the bar in the event that she couldn't.

"I'm not totally helpless," Kim assured him dryly. "I know how to run the mixology software, and I already know how to make a fair number of drinks without having to look them up. We'll be fine. Go get your fix."

He grinned, the same wolfish curve of his mouth his father had given the day before, and then he was gone.

"You don't listen very well," Taryn complained.

"Shut up. Wanna look at his cards? This game's a bust anyway. I hope I can get my money back."

"Yeah, right. Let's see 'em." Kim turned them over, and they stared at them with morosely. "Good thing the liquor control board called. I don't think I could bear it if he won again. I'm flat-ass broke."

"Yeah, me too." Kim grimaced, more at the lie than at the thought of Ron winning the hand. "I wonder if he'd give me an advance on my salary."

Taryn laughed until she choked, and Kim was more than a little grateful when the ringing phone called her away. Her mind turned almost too eagerly toward the enigma of Ron Schaefer, with his shadowy blue eyes full of superficial come-ons. Come-ons and go-aways all at the same time, truth be told. A girl could find herself confused as to which direction she was going.

"You're not going anywhere," Kim muttered to herself sternly. "At least not with him." And lest her mind think of reckless ways around her resolve, she set off to find something to keep her occupied.

When her shift ended, Kim dragged herself home wearily, unused to being on her feet so many hours at a time. Her hand smarted, sending screaming pain up her arm every time she flexed her fingers, which made it hard to make the pot of coffee she figured would be necessary to keep her awake for the next few hours.

She glanced at the clock over the kitchen sink. In about two hours, Ron would arrive to begin working on the guest bedroom, an event she both looked forward to and dreaded. *A man of a thousand moods, that one*, she reflected wryly, recalling his somewhat moody return. She would have thought the prospect of his newly acquired case of Lagavulin scotch would have had him riding high, but when he returned he was cool and remote. Taryn seemed to find this extraordinarily funny, but she wouldn't explain why except to say that he'd had too much time to think.

She reached an apple out of the fridge, tucked herself into the corner of the breakfast nook and took stock of the kitchen. She hadn't moved since she'd married Mark and left her parents' home; she found her skills in equipping a house sadly lacking. From a nutritional standpoint, she supposed she would have to eventually buy some food that didn't require being frozen and baked on a cookie sheet, which would require a marathon shopping spree in Scranton out of sight of prying eyes. She rather doubted she would need to stay that long, though, so for now convenience food filled her freezer.

The summons of the doorbell – an hour and a half early – brought her out of her reverie. She jumped up, hurrying to the front door, trying to school her suddenly racing heart. Ridiculous. Being plunked down in such feminine surroundings had to be having some weird effect on her.

Any romantic notions fled immediately when she saw the scowling man on her doorstep, laden with drywall tools and clad in baggy, paint-splattered jeans and a tattered t-shirt. She stepped aside, letting him pass, and went back to the kitchen as he vanished into the spare bedroom down the hall. She gripped her apple too hard, wincing as pain zinged through her nerve endings.

A little aloe vera gel would help. She fumbled with the small silver safety pin Ron had used to hold the gauze in place.

"What do you think you're doing?" he demanded severely.

Kim jumped, guilt making her drop her hands and tuck them behind her back. "Nothing."

"Leave it on. You want to make it worse?"

"I was only going to put some aloe vera on it. It hurts like crazy."

"Stop moving it and it won't hurt as much. Better yet, stop using it and it will barely hurt at all. Give the ointment a chance to work." He glanced around the kitchen, taking in the pot of coffee. "Mind if I have a cup of that?"

"Will you get off my back about the burn?"

"Doubtful."

"Figured so. Go ahead, help yourself. "

She gave him no guidance as he rummaged through her cupboards, looking for a coffee mug. He raised a curious brow when he found them – all two of them. Marvin Martian on one, Bugs Bunny on the other. He opted for the alien, poured the coffee, and took an experimental sip, making a face.

"You call this coffee?"

"*Edible* coffee," she agreed. "Unlike the muck you scrape off the bottom of the Susquehanna River and serve in the tavern. Speaking of which… I wonder just what the health department would say about that menu item."

"Ha," he replied sarcastically. "I notice you managed to down three or four cups of it."

"Yeah," she admitted. "It kind of grows on you. And I do mean grows. Just this morning I had to shave hair off my chest."

Ron's gaze dropped from her face to the swell of her breasts beneath her t-shirt. Kim felt her blood heat and silently cursed them both for it. He had no business being able to stir her with just a look. She barely knew him. It was crazy.

"Well," he drawled, his eyes coming back to hers with a glint in them that said he knew exactly what he'd done to her. "As interesting as the thought might be, I have a lot of work to get done." He turned to leave but something caught his eye and stopped him in his tracks. "Where did you get this?"

Kim peered around him to see what he was reaching for: the green glass bottle of skullcap tincture Caleb had delivered to her yesterday.

"Oh, that. Your father stopped by to welcome me to the neighborhood, bearing gifts. Some sort of natural sedative or something."

His eyes had locked on her face as soon as the words "your father" left her mouth. After a moment he looked back down at the bottle in his hand, at the silk ribbon, and then he wrested the cork from the top and upended the bottle over the sink.

"Ah," Kim said, startled. "I believe that was mine." She never would have used it, but she thought it rather high-handed of him to dump it out without asking first.

"It's gone now."

"Would you mind explaining why you did that?"

"Not at all. Never trust gifts from my father."

"That explains everything," she muttered, tongue firmly in cheek. He exhaled impatiently.

"Look, he dabbles a lot in herbal medicine, but it can be very dangerous. Some of the so-called natural remedies out there can be harmful, especially since the field is largely unregulated and haphazardly researched. Someone could inadvertently give you something you're allergic to or tell you to take a dose your body can't handle."

She watched him closely, noting the muscle working in his jaw and the way his hand clenched around the neck of the green bottle like he'd just throttled it and was reluctant to let go in case it wasn't quite dead yet.

He noticed her scrutiny and turned his back, opening the cupboard under the sink to deposit the bottle in the trash. "Don't reuse it."

"I wasn't planning to."

"Good." He set down his mug and left the kitchen without another word. Kim frowned, listening to his footsteps carrying him down the hallway to the spare bedroom, his stride unhurried and full of easy grace.

After a while, she refilled his coffee and took it into the spare room. He pretended not to notice her as he repaired nail holes and gouges in the drywall.

"This isn't a spectator sport."

"Obviously not one that invites participation, either," she remarked dryly. "I brought your coffee."

He sighed expressively. "Will you leave me alone if I drink it?"

"For at least ten minutes. Maybe twenty. I'm easily distracted." She stopped well out of his personal space and handed the mug across. He hesitated before taking it.

"Just be careful. That's all I'm saying."

She shrugged. "I can't promise that. I'm reckless by nature. You never know when I'll drink too much and put on men's clothing." At last he looked at her, his mouth quirking into a reluctant smile. "That's better. I'll be as careful as someone like me can be. How's that?"

"Immensely comforting," he replied sarcastically. He took the coffee, and Kim retreated to the doorway.

"I'll just be in my room reading. Just in case you feel like lecturing me some more on my obvious deficiencies in common sense."

"Will it do any good?"

"None whatsoever, but it's never stopped anyone before," she admitted ruefully.

Her book couldn't hold her attention. Perhaps the intimate setting of her bedroom – the one room she'd personalized – with an attractive man just across the hallway had been a foolish move. She frowned at the wall, thinking back to the dream that had brought her here, wondering if the unrelenting sense of rightness that still guided her actions would eventually leave her drifting and in trouble. That seemed to be how things always ended up.

Her eyes grew heavy, and she let go of consciousness by degrees, reality blending seamlessly with imagination.

So she would never be sure if the object of her indecent fantasies really pulled a blanket over her and pressed a gentle kiss at the corner of her lips.

ANYTHING IS POSSIBLE
October 12, 2004

The town had seen many strange things, the disappearances of Ben Cummings and Todd Garrett not the least of them. Of the former, the priest had no knowledge. Of the latter, however...ah, yes. Fishing could be a dangerous sport, especially when one fished in ponds that were off limits, so to speak.

Ben Cummings, on the other hand, totally mystified him. The squeaky wheel always gets the grease, and Ben definitely qualified as one. He rather suspected Ben had been greased in an entirely different manner than the adage implied, but he couldn't be sure. He wasn't certain he believed Sarah's denial of her involvement, and his trust in her to keep him abreast of all major decisions (such as greasing squeaky wheels) had worn very thin of late. She had her own agenda, of which he knew very little – if anything.

His eyes narrowed slightly as he watched Sarah Bennett, the ruling matriarch of Mills' underworld. She claimed the age of eighty-six, but she didn't look a day over a youthful sixty. Her platinum blonde hair had faded to silver and lay in a braided cable over her shoulder, free of its customary bun. Steady, unlined hands poured the contents of a large brown bottle into a smaller one identical in shape and color. She attributed her youthful appearance to her consumption of the very same herbal concoctions she brewed for various townsfolk.

He placed the blame on deals with the devil. It seemed the old bat would never die; she'd looked the same forty-two years ago when he was thirteen and had first stumbled upon her weathered dwelling deep in the woods. Her genealogy claimed her as the third Sarah in as many generations, but he sometimes wondered if she wasn't, in fact, all three. She never seemed to age and possessed no birth or death documents to support her claim.

From the chamber outside the door of Sarah's large workroom came a dry, hacking cough that erupted into convulsive choking and then faded to a miserable moan. Sarah's hand paused, her brow wrinkled thoughtfully, and she added a little more to the smaller bottle than she originally intended.

"What is it?" he queried, gesturing at the liquid she decanted.

"Syrup made from thyme infusion. Thyme is very good for coughs." She set down the larger bottle and corked it, then hunted through a drawer for a cork for the smaller bottle. Once found and installed, she tied a ribbon with a tag attached to it around the neck of the bottle: identification and instructions.

He had to give her due credit, he mused as her sprightly steps took her from the workroom into the outer chamber she called her "sitting room" where she saw to all of her "patients." She knew herbs. She had more than a passing familiarity with a lot of other, more sinister things as well, which would give pause to a good many of those about to partake of her remedies, had they only known.

The front door of the dwelling closed, and Sarah came back into the workroom, a glint of satisfaction in her eyes. Sooner or later, they all came to her, despite their misgivings. Whether an irritating cough, a particularly heavy menstrual flow, or an unwanted pregnancy – whatever the case, one by one like fallen soldiers, they lay a hand at Sarah's door, seeking her unconventional expertise. And once there, she snared them easily.

His lip curled at the thought. When Sarah noticed his sardonic smile, the glint in her eyes faded. She closed the door and advanced across the workroom purposefully, as if striding across a battlefield to meet her enemy face-to-face. And indeed, in this very room, she waged war against those who would see her into a nice safe asylum somewhere or (better yet, to his way of thinking) into her grave, but neither had determined whether he qualified as an enemy.

"So," she said briskly, climbing with surprising agility onto a stool at her worktable, flinging one leg over the other. "You've come to harangue me about Ben Cummings again, haven't you?"

"Harangue?" he repeated, trying out the word on his own tongue. "No, I don't picture me as *haranguing* anyone."

"You have your own special way of doing it." She sounded weary. "I'm being honest with you, whether you want to believe it or not. I have no idea where Ben Cummings is."

"I thought you had him under surveillance. How could he just disappear without your knowing?"

Irritation puckered her brow, her tone frosty when she answered. "I am not all-knowing, all-seeing." She slid off the stool and began pacing around the table, putting the day's work into a neatly organized, locking armoire. When she had brushed away all but the last few flakes of thyme, she spoke again.

"We have to be united. If we start mistrusting one another, total chaos will ensue, and we can't have that."

"No, we can't," he agreed sardonically. "I know where too many bodies are buried."

Sarah's gaze sharpened on his face. "And your hand sped most of them into their graves."

She returned to her stool and put a hand to her forehead as if trying to relieve a headache. He knew better; he saw this gesture more and more often of late as she tried to control her temper.

"What are your plans for Garrett?" Sarah asked after a moment. Her voice lost its sharpness and she seemed to have regained control over her temper. Still, he clung to his caution a while longer. Just in case.

"We suspect he had some sort of contact with someone from away. He's been very circumspect and uncooperative. Harlan went through the house Garrett rented with a fine-tooth comb and couldn't find a scrap of information about his personal life. We have no idea who he might have contacted or how much he told them. We have to find that person fast."

"Does he have anyone with whom he collaborates in his work?"

"None I know of. It's not so easy to track a professional researcher's affiliations."

"He must have family somewhere." Irritation creased Sarah's

brow, and she shifted impatiently on the stool. "No one is totally alone."

"Some are," he disagreed blandly.

"Do you think he's one?"

"No." He met her sharp-eyed gaze without hesitation. "There is someone out there worrying for him. We'll just have to wait and let that person come to us. They will…eventually." He frowned, and stood up, pacing around the room.

She slid off the stool, came around the table, and put a hand on his arm to halt his pacing. He looked down at her. More than a foot shorter than he, she nevertheless had enormous impact. Standing before her was like standing before a giant sequoia and marveling at its strength and perseverance, its very presence.

"We can only hold Todd Garrett for so long, and we don't dare let his body ever be found. He will have to be taken care of soon, completely erased. But I need to know exactly what he learned and how much he told his confidante."

Her hand fell away and she took a step backward. He let out a breath, just now realizing he had been holding it.

"Another matter troubles me even more than Garrett," he confessed. "This new woman at Aaron's tavern. Beth Fairchild."

"What about her?"

"She seems so familiar. I don't like it. Do you…" He licked suddenly dry lips. "Do they know anything about her?"

Sarah hissed in frustration. "Nothing. It's as though she's hidden behind a black curtain."

"What do you want me to do?"

"Find out what you can. She's from Texas, yes?"

"San Antonio, I believe."

Silent and thoughtful for a long moment, she raised her eyes to his, shocking him with the deep level of concern in her eyes. Sarah could take care of Beth Fairchild – a dozen Beth Fairchilds – barely lifting her hand. Why would she be so worried about a little wisp of a woman?

"Sometimes people are not what they seem," Sarah said softly, as if reading his thoughts. "Something seemingly so fragile can often withstand more burden than you and I put together." Her voice lowered to a whisper, and he had the distinct impression she addressed not him but herself. "She has incredible strength. I can feel it."

"She's just a woman. Do you think it's possible…" He trailed off. "She arrived in town shortly after we nabbed Garrett. Perhaps she's connected to him somehow."

"Anything is possible," Sarah murmured, and without warning spun on her heel and left the room. He was, he thought wryly, dismissed by Her Highness.

Her words followed him out to his truck, and recurred to him throughout the rest of the day as he made his plans.

Anything is possible.

* * * * *

"Will you take this order out, please?"

Kim paused on her way out of the kitchen long enough to let Ron dump the freshly made hamburger into a paper-lined basket with some fries, and then whisked it away, biting back her irritable reply. They clashed badly today. She attributed it to poor sleeping habits: he looked as though he could fall asleep on his feet at any moment, while her dream-interrupted slumber left her feeling slow and torpid.

This morning, he'd subjected her to a cursory examination of her burned hand, unwinding the gauze with a lifted brow. It was obvious she'd replaced the wrapping; it wasn't nearly as efficiently done and the antiseptic scent of aloe vera wafted from the cotton bandage. She wasn't sure if she'd imagined his grunt of surprise and murmured assent that perhaps she had been correct about the benefits of aloe vera, but she secretly hoped his diet today included a substantial helping of crow.

The tavern doors opened as she crossed the room to deliver the burger, and Kim glanced up to see a pair of thirty-something ladies seating themselves at a table near the front windows. She sifted through her memory to place them. The wives of a couple of regulars; she couldn't quite bring up the names, but one of the men imbibed liberally. Ron had pointed him out the first shift she worked and advised her to cut him off at one pitcher or three mixed drinks, whichever he happened to be partaking, as he became surly and often downright violent if allowed more. And for the love of God, don't let him mix hard liquor and beer! Eyeing the fading yellowish bruise on the cheek of one of the women, Kim guessed he imbibed considerably more at home than Ron allowed at The Watering Hole, and decided the drink she'd most like to serve him was poison.

She dropped the burger off and murmured a vague reply to a curt thank you, and crossed the room to take the women's orders. After delivering them to the surly kitchen staff, she set herself to organizing the storage areas beneath the bar. She could just barely hear the women chatting, but didn't pay much attention until she caught a familiar name.

" – Ben Cummings. I personally think – "and the voice lowered to a decibel Kim couldn't make out. Without a single qualm, she edged closer to the end of the bar nearest where the women sat, bringing their conversation into hearing range again.

"Well, I don't think he went fishing at all. I think," and the woman made a sound that immediately brought an accurate mental picture into Kim's mind: a finger being drawn across the throat in pantomime of death.

"Do you think he saw something?"

"Well, you know how he always went on about the Wyckham House...maybe he went there. And saw something he shouldn't have."

"What could there be to see?" her friend scoffed. "It's just an old building."

"If it's just an old building, Melody," the first woman pointed out reasonably, "then why does everyone who goes there disappear or end up dead?"

"They get lost in the woods. And not all of them are missing or dead, Lisa," replied her skeptical pal. "One came back."

"For all the good it did. He can't remember a thing."

The women fell silent for a moment, and Kim began to move casually away when the next comment stopped her in her tracks.

"And isn't it odd how Todd Garrett just up and left, no notice to

Ron, rent paid up through to November. Cleaned out the house on Willow Road; not a trace left behind," Lisa mused.

"If indeed he really did leave." Melody held up her hand to forestall her companion's protest. "I know he hasn't been seen since Tuesday before last and all his things are gone from the house. But no one actually saw him packing up and leaving town. He had some pretty in-depth conversations with Ben Cummings at the tavern, you know. I hope Ben didn't talk him into doing some fool thing like going to the Wyckham House. Men will do the stupidest things."

The women moved on to the more mundane topic of just how sublimely stupid men could sometimes be, and Kim crept silently away because she already knew how stupid men could be.

But she had come away with knowledge she hadn't possessed before, and exactly the kind of information she'd been listening for: her father vanished six days before the fishing tackle arrived at the cabin in Forest Falls. And why would Ron need to be told anything about Todd leaving? She would have to find a way to ask him circumspectly, which would not be easy. Her anxiety for her father would color any casual question, and she didn't think she could easily fool him.

This mysterious Wyckham House...now what could they possibly be talking about? She'd seen no sign of any sinister old buildings, unless the old Presbyterian church across the park counted. And who had gone to the Wyckham House but had no memory of it?

Ron brought out the ladies' orders just seconds before Kim headed for the kitchen door to fetch them, and he delivered them himself. He slid into the booth across from the woman with the bruised cheek – Melody, her friend had called her – his voice pitched so low she couldn't overhear.

Her head lowered and she seemed to have difficulty swallowing. She nodded, and that seemed to be the action he had been waiting for. He pressed something into her hand, and as he scooted out of the booth, her head came up and her hand shot out to grip his for a brief second. Kim felt a swell of unreasonable and unexpected jealousy that didn't quite vanish even when she saw the tears shimmering in Melody's eyes.

The tavern door flew open and Scott came in, looking fresh and alert and much more cheerful than any of his work mates. He took one look at the shadows under his cousin's eyes and his smile faltered.

"No sleep?" he guessed. Ron shot a look at Kim before offering a brief nod. "Dreams?"

"Just didn't sleep well." Ron pivoted away, brushing past Kim without looking at her on his way back into the kitchen. Scott raised a brow.

"Another tense day at the office, dear?"

She sighed, sliding a mug of hot coffee across the bar to him, and turning to get one for herself, replied, "He didn't get enough sleep last night and I got too much. We have clashed badly today."

She turned with her coffee in time to see the priceless expression on Scott's face. Her mouth twisted into a sarcastic smile.

"Not what you're thinking. I am assuming he didn't sleep well, but I have no firsthand knowledge." She paused. "Scott, I want to ask you someth – "

The door to the kitchen flew open and Scott's attention diverted to his cousin, who breezed through the room, donning his jacket.

"Denny is on his way in to cover for me. I'm going home to get some sleep." His eyes skimmed over Kim's face in a fraction of a second, lingering on her lips, and then he focused on her coffee cup. She found herself remembering her dream of a feather-light kiss, and wondered if it had actually been a dream at all. She dismissed the thought, blushing furiously. Why on earth would he even have the urge to kiss her? He didn't even know her.

"Sleep well," she murmured.

His gaze darted to her lips again and then bounced to her eyes, his expression turning critical. "You look like you could use some, too. It's a slow day. When Taryn comes in, go home and get some sleep."

"All right."

Unable to hold his direct gaze any longer, she looked away, only to find Scott watching them with a strangely knowing look. Ron went around the bar, smacking his cousin playfully on the back of the head as he went past, and he disappeared out the tavern door. Kim breathed a sigh of relief at the same time silently lamenting how the room seemed to lose half its light. *You're a fool*, Kim, she told herself, regrettably not for the first time in her life.

"What's that look for?" she demanded when she caught Scott still staring.

"Nothing." Whatever he had been thinking didn't seem to please him, but he didn't enlighten her. Instead went into the kitchen to shed his jacket and don an apron. When he came back out, obviously not intending to do anything more than play cards since he had brought the deck, she idly brought up the topic of conversation she had overheard.

"Scott, I keep hearing obscure little references to some place around here. I wondered if maybe it was some sort of historical site or something, but everyone seems to whisper about it."

If Kim hadn't been watching him closely, she would have missed his suddenly careful expression.

"Oh?"

"Yes. Some place called the Wyckham House. What is it?"

He glanced quickly at the women to make sure they couldn't hear, and then turned to Kim with a look so intense she recoiled in fear. She belatedly remembered the Schaefers were virtual strangers, precognitive dreams notwithstanding, and she had no reason to trust them.

"It's the one place you do *not* want to go, ever. You don't even want to *talk* about it. Now what should we play? Speed? War? Gin-rummy?"

"Gin-rummy is fine," she agreed in a small voice.

Scott blew out a breath, closed his eyes briefly, then said softly, "I don't want to see you get hurt, Beth. I'll tell you about it some other time, but not here. All right?"

"All right."

Kim took her cards and tried not to be impatient for that conversation. As she fanned them out, she cast a surreptitious glance at Melody; the auburn-haired woman was now wiping her eyes and trying not to smudge her mascara while her friend studiously ignored her waterworks.

The twinge of jealousy mushroomed into envy as green as jade.

BEWITCHED, BOTHERED, AND BEWILDERED
October 13, 2004

Finding herself with a day off and nothing to do, Kim followed a footpath from her back gate that led through the woods. About a mile from the cottage, she came upon the Susquehanna River and perched on a large rock, scooped a handful of pebbles into her uninjured hand, and began plunking them into the swift current as though punctuating her thoughts.

She couldn't get Wyckham House off her mind since hearing about it, and wondered what her father knew about it – wondered if he had gone there himself. Despite Scott's promise to tell her all about it at a later time, she couldn't help but think she would have to prod him into it; in fact, it would probably prove difficult to even broach the subject now that he was expecting her to ask.

A twig snapped behind her and she whirled around on her rock, startled. The subject of her thoughts stood behind her, looking vaguely disappointed and a trifle wary. For a long moment she thought he might just turn and leave without speaking, and then his feet negotiated the rocks with careless ease as he joined her, settling near her and staring silently across the river. Kim let him be until she could stand it no longer.

"Bad day?" she wondered, keeping her tone deliberately light.

"Not the best," he admitted with a grim smile. "Fight with my...friend." He shifted uncomfortably and clarified, "My girlfriend." He offered the words so reluctantly, as if embarrassed to admit to having such a thing, that it made Kim laugh.

"Don't worry," she replied with a mischievous smile. "They're not illegal."

"What aren't?" he asked blankly.

"Girlfriends."

He smiled again, but it still seemed grim. "Well, it doesn't matter, because I *don't* have one now, come to think of it. We broke up." He paused. "Again."

"Sounds like a bad habit."

"She is."

Kim meant the breaking up part, but his revealing reply shut her mouth. He seemed so obviously unhappy with this woman – Kim had forgotten her name again; Nancy? Natalie? – that she couldn't understand why he didn't just cut the ties and be done with it. Plenty of other women in Mills would be thrilled to have a man as attractive and talented as Scott Schaefer. Take Tiana Michaels for instance; she positively lit up when he came into the room, although she studiously avoided looking at him. Why were men so blind?

"My ex and I broke up several times while we dated, and once while engaged. The marriage only lasted four years when it finally happened. Just end it now and save yourself a lot of trouble later. Or is she too good in bed to pass up?"

His mouth dropped open, and then he laughed. There was little humor in it, and still he hesitated.

"It won't go past me, Scott."

"Oh, all right." His odd sea-green eyes lifted to stare up at the trees. "In the past eleven years, I've lost count how many times we've broken up."

"Eleven years!" she exclaimed. She hadn't realized they'd been together so long. "You're practically married!"

Scott snorted. "No way!"

"Do you Schaefer men have something against marriage? You're twenty-seven and not married – and obviously avoiding it. Unless I'm way off mark, Ron's not a day under thirty and he's never been hitched."

He shrugged, his face suddenly tight. "He just turned thirty and no, he's never been married. He came close, though." A shadow crossed his face, and then he shook his head slightly. "I want to get married, just not to her."

"So you two are unlucky in love?"

"All it takes is once," he muttered darkly. "This time I'm done with her, for better or worse."

"What does that mean?"

He remained very quiet for a long moment, and then, as if unable to help himself, he blurted, "Do you believe in witchcraft?"

Kim's heart lurched in her chest, and she forced herself to take a deep breath. Her father had asked for research on witchcraft – did his request stem from this town's history? It certainly hadn't figured into the subject of his project. Not for the first time, she wondered why he had asked her to collect information for him when he was a researcher himself.

"Now *there's* an icebreaker," she murmured with a surprised laugh. "I think I'll use it at my next dinner party."

"I'm serious," he protested sternly. "Do you believe in witchcraft?" His green eyes scrutinized her carefully, and she thought he seemed to be placing a lot of importance on her answer.

"I don't know," she answered honestly. "I keep an open mind about such things, you know? I don't want to be caught with – well, with my pants down, so to speak."

Those strange green eyes lit up with sudden and delighted amusement. "Now there's a thought."

"Perish it immediately," she returned loftily. She did not want to encourage his interest in her. While he was quite attractive, something about him turned her...well, completely off, as though he emitted some sort of repellent in place of pheromones. "I allow for the possibility of just about anything."

"That's a very diplomatic answer," Scott accused mildly.

"I'm not trying to be diplomatic. I haven't any proof witchcraft exists, nor have I any proof it doesn't. Therefore I don't have enough evidence to make a determination either way."

"Are you sure you aren't a lawyer?"

"Don't insult me!" she exclaimed, affronted. "I'm just a long-suffering barmaid."

"Just wait until you've been here a year. You'll get a Purple Heart."

Or a broken one. "He isn't that bad," she chided softly, although sometimes Ron could be quite trying. She just couldn't bring herself to let Scott's criticism stand without challenging it.

"Yes, he is. You forget, I live with him." Something very like jealousy flashed in his eyes and vanished. "Back to the subject."

"Witchcraft, yes," Kim said, more than pleased to abandon the discussion of her moody employer. "Why do you believe in it?"

"What makes you think I do?"

"Lucky guess." She slanted him a crooked smile. Scott was very easy to read.

"Did you know Mills started as a Christian town in the late 1700s? Five decades later, the witches took it over. Black magic, disappearances, murders." He paused. "Some say magic is still practiced."

"Do you believe it?"

"Dunno. But rumor has it Nadine's grandmother is – what do you call it – a priestess or something."

Nadine, that was it! "A high priestess?"

"Yeah."

"Do you think it's true?"

Again he shrugged. "I've lived here all my life. I've seen things that would curl your hair – yes, even yours, Miss Been-There-Done-That. Sarah's the one all the girls go to for a convenient miscarriage, and people buy all sorts of concoctions and poultices and stuff from her."

"Herbs and poultices don't make witchcraft, Scott. Anyone knows enough castor oil will make a woman miscarry a pregnancy – anyone who practices folk medicine, anyway."

"Folk medicine. Is that what you call it?"

"What do *you* call it?"

"Me? I call it spells."

She stared at him, marveling. "You really believe it, don't you?"

"How about it, Beth? Have I convinced you?"

He watched her closely, and she managed a negligent shrug. She didn't want to appear too interested or involved or he would become suspicious. She didn't doubt his cousin harbored enough doubts about her already. Ron never said anything outright, but she didn't miss the strange, searching looks he often gave her, the times he seemed about to say something and then obviously decided against it, his avoidance of using her pirated name – not to mention the odd conversations where she suspected he felt her out for information rather than conversed with her.

"All you've shown me so far is rhetoric, which is what caused most of the burnings at the stakes a couple centuries ago. Herbs and spices don't make it Kentucky Fried Chicken, my friend. It could be just folk medicine."

"Then try this on for size. Before I started dating Nadine, I was seeing Tiana Michaels." Ah, *that* explained a few things, namely Tiana's wounded air of tragedy. "Within two weeks of us breaking up, Nadine was all over me, sending me notes, calling me, stopping at my locker and standing too close. I've been with her ever since."

"That's nothing unusual, Scott. Some girls won't let a guy know they're interested in him until he loses the current girlfriend."

"Maybe." He paused. "That doesn't explain why I have such a hard time breaking up with her. I don't love her, so why can't I leave her?"

"Maybe you do love her, but just don't want to admit it."

"No. I don't love her," he stated flatly. "I just can't leave her."

Kim suddenly realized what he seemed so reluctant to say outright. "You think you've been bewitched!" she deduced almost gleefully. He sent her a black look and she quelled some of her enthusiasm. "Sorry. Why would you think so, Scott?"

His voice lowered as if he feared they might be overheard. "If I tell you, you can't ever let him know you know."

"Who?"

Scott didn't deign to answer such an idiotic question; it was obvious he meant his cousin. "He'd never forgive me if he knew I'd told a – a – "

"Stranger?" Kim finished, and he nodded reluctantly.

"It has to do with the Wyckham House."

"Ah," she murmured, satisfied that the conversation had taken this turn. He quirked a brow at her.

"When Ron was nineteen, he was engaged to a girl named Elizabeth. She vanished without a trace. For some reason he was certain she'd gone to the Wyckham House."

"Why would he think that? Had she told him she was going?"

"No, but – "

Kim leaned forward, bracing her elbows on her knees, and interrupted. "What exactly is the Wyckham House?"

He scuffed the toe of his sneaker against a large granite boulder.

"Some decrepit stone mansion in the woods. Long ago I'm sure there was a road to it, but it's been vacant for a couple hundred years and the only way to it is through the woods. It's named after the first Mills resident who disappeared there."

"So people just wander through the woods looking for this place? No wonder they never come back!"

His eyes narrowed suspiciously. "You heard that?"

"I told you I'd heard things."

Scott still looked suspicious but plugged on. "Anyway, Ron went after her, taking his two best friends with him. When morning came and he wasn't at breakfast, my mom started asking around and found out where he'd gone. She immediately filed a missing persons report."

"And they found him?"

"No, he came out of the woods on his own, covered in blood, thirty-six hours after he went in."

Kim gaped for a second. "Blood? Whose blood?"

"His, from all accounts. Same blood type – A negative, which is pretty uncommon – but he wasn't wounded anywhere." He shifted on his rock, looking into the water. A chickadee gave two long-note whistles from a nearby tree. A squirrel scampered in her peripheral vision; Kim turned to watch it while Scott decided if he was going to tell her more. A vague recollection of some of her recent research begged for her attention, but before she could pin it down and think it through, he went on.

"His friends were found in weighted gunnysacks in the pond. In pieces. At first they thought he might have...it was a complicated situation...but they were both O-positive so the blood obviously wasn't theirs. Elizabeth has never been found.

"Whatever happened, he has blocked it out completely. He doesn't remember a thing beyond wandering through the building with Jason and Peter before they disappeared."

"What do you mean, a complicated situation?"

This time his pause was so long she thought he would simply refuse to answer, change the subject, and that would be the end of this conversation.

"Liz was pregnant when she vanished." Kim winced. "But the

baby wasn't Ron's."

"I see. Whose was it, then?"

"Jason's, if my uncle can be believed. He said he saw them together."

"And if he can't?"

"Who knows? Could be anyone's then – Ron was away at University of Scranton and only came home on the weekends. There was some friction about that and about her parents."

She lifted a brow. "He didn't like her parents?"

"He adored her parents. But they were dead, killed in a head-on crash on Old Mills Road almost a year before Liz vanished."

Kim digested this silently. A whole family, extinct within a year. The odds of it happening by natural selection were slim but not unheard of, yet something in the way Scott was meting out the information piece by tiny piece made her think there had been nothing random about it at all.

Almost as if he had heard her thought, Scott continued. "Elizabeth thought they'd been murdered, run off the road and into a tree on purpose. She kept yammering on about the Wyckham House and their deaths, wanting Ron to help her investigate."

"And he wouldn't," she deduced.

"No one in their right minds would. You've heard enough to know that no one ever comes back from there alive."

"Except him."

"Except him," he agreed.

Ah, that was it! Her mind finally coughed up the information she had been trying to recall. Ron had come out of the woods covered in his own blood but with no wounds. It smacked of only one legend she'd ever read about, but to think it was a reality in Mills was insanity itself.

"Strange thing about the blood," she ventured.

"Mmmm. Mom said when she touched his right cheek, he flinched as if it hurt, but they went over every inch of his body and could find no source. No dried blood in his nostrils, so it wasn't a nosebleed. There's no explanation for it."

There's one, Kim thought to herself and dismissed it immediately.

Werewolves? Insanity.

"What is it?" Scott asked unexpectedly, and she looked up to find him watching her closely.

"Nothing. Just a crazy random thought. Never mind. I imagine Ron must have been devastated."

Again he tensed up as though sensing her interest in his cousin went beyond casual. "He spent two years in Meadow Grove, a Philadelphia institution that deals with post-traumatic catatonia. He'd known the guys all his life; he and Liz were to be married within a few months when she vanished. Then suddenly he – wakes up, and it's been a year and a half, and they're all gone."

Words failed her. Whatever she had suspected lurked Ron's past, she had never dreamed it would be so terrible. She wondered what could possibly have made him retreat into catatonia for a year and a half.

Werewolves? In Pennsylvania? She shoved the thought away again.

"He's a lot different now," he continued. "Sometimes I like him better now; he's more focused, more cautious with his decisions. He used to be pretty wild and reckless; I think even Liz would have had a hard time settling him down."

Seems to me she succeeded admirably, Kim thought to herself, wisely not voicing the comment. *She only had to disappear.*

"So this experience had mostly a positive effect."

He thought for a moment, and shook his head. "No. A few positive effects, but something that absolutely cripples a man emotionally can't be a good thing. He has few friends, although the ones he has are very close and trusted. He hasn't had a serious relationship with a woman since Liz."

"Maybe he just hasn't gotten over her," she suggested idly.

"Maybe he's just scared he'll lose the next one too," he countered softly. "He used to love horror novels and scary movies. Now he can only watch the movies during the day, and he reads westerns and mysteries, but nothing supernatural. And he's...he's *darker*, if that makes any sense. Not as fun-loving or light-hearted."

"He gave up everything he liked. Separating himself from the life he had when he was happy, determined not to go through it again."

He gave her a startled look, as though that possibility had never occurred to him. "Maybe."

"That's how I felt for a long time after my divorce. But then I realized I was silly; all that will happen if I choose that route is I'll end up alone all my life – a life I won't enjoy because I gave up things I loved."

"I guess I can't blame him. He lost so much in such a short time. He will probably never have a serious romantic relationship unless he goes through extensive therapy, which he refuses to do."

He hesitated, and then plunged on, obviously trying to keep her from interrupting.

"He's good-looking and he has money – he's not rich, but he's secure financially – and that's a big attraction for a lot of women, but it doesn't get them any farther than he'll let them go. Any emotional involvement with him is entirely out of the question; he'll never allow it."

Kim sat very still for a long moment, her face flaming, and then gave him a brilliant smile as she rose from her rock and stretched.

"Lighten up, Schaefer, for God's sake. I'm not stupid enough to get myself into a dead-end relationship after just escaping one not so long ago. Give me some credit."

"Oh, I give you plenty of credit. You just don't know him like I do."

"Okay," she said, leading the way slowly back to the path. "Number one, I don't want a relationship. Number two, I barely know the man. Number three, I don't think the man in question even *likes* me, let alone gives a rat's sorry butt about getting me in bed. Relax."

"Like I said, you don't know him like I do."

Rolling her eyes, Kim led him down the path to the cottage, and by the time they reached her back yard, she had teased him out of his dark mood and had invited him in for coffee.

"I'd love to, but I should get home and help with dinner."

"Well, another time perhaps," she said graciously, leaving her invitation open.

Scott turned and started away, then turned as he reached the back gate. "Lock your doors. This may be Sticksville, but we have our share of undesirables nonetheless."

"I haven't completely left my city instincts behind," she assured him. He gave a jaunty wave and hurried off down the path to Willow Road, where he'd left his car parked by the shoulder.

She realized suddenly that he had never clarified the connection between Ron's experience eleven years ago and his belief that he might be bewitched.

Troubled, Kim shut the door.

And locked it.

THE WYCKHAM HOUSE
October 14, 2004

"*What* the *HELL* were you thinking?"

Kim winced and held the phone away from her ear. Bethany's voicemail – well, actually the first of eight – was starting out just as bad as she'd expected.

"Don't even *think* of denying that you took my ID. I can't *believe* you would do this! So help me, Kim – "

She didn't wait to hear what Beth would do to her once she was within reach; her best friend was a trifle hotheaded when provoked, and God knew she was provoked now. Kim fast-forwarded through the rest of the message and went on to the next. Beth's anger peaked in message four, and by message six she had softened enough to express her concern for Kim's well-being. By message eight she was genuinely worried, and her anger showed every sign of making a reappearance; Beth detested being worried.

That message had been left last night. Kim bit the bullet and keyed in Beth's number; there was no sense in prolonging the inevitable, and the sooner this was over with, the better. She had to head her friend off at the pass before Beth panicked and reported her missing.

Bethany hit her stride as soon as she answered the phone. "Kimberly Amanda Owens, do you *know* how much you scared me? Are you *aware* that stealing identification is – "

Kim let her rant. Eventually her silence broke through Beth's rage like words would not have. She took a breath and said more calmly,

"Are you all right?"

"Stellar," Kim assured her.

"Are you in trouble? Is that why – "

"No trouble."

"Are you going to tell me where you are?" In other words, *Are you going to tell me where my ID is being used, for what, and will it be attached to enormous debt when I get it back?*

"Umm, no, I don't think I'm going to tell you where I am. I'm sure I can bungle this on my own well enough."

A reluctant chuckle told her Beth was softening; Kim smiled as she reached a bottle of water out of the fridge. A quick twist broke the seal and uncapped it, and she drank deeply. Ron had assured her that Mills drinking water was pleasant, but a lifetime in southern California had trained her to not to trust the tap.

"That's very reassuring. Are you drinking while you're talking to me?"

She swallowed her mouthful and wiped her chin and chest. "Yeah, drinking and spilling down my front. I think this whole batch of bottles leaks. Doesn't anyone practice quality control anymore?"

"Probably not. I can guess where you went: you're in Pennsylvania, aren't you?"

The drink she had just taken gurgled in her throat and bubbled out her nose. She bit back a colorful imprecation Beth wouldn't like and grabbed a kitchen towel to mop her face. Maybe she was just developing a motor skills problem. "I'll never tell."

"I don't know what you think you're going to accomplish, but at least you're out of that condo for a change. Are you at least being careful?"

Kim could picture her pacing around kitchen, bare feet smacking the Mexican tiles, her flashing brown eyes darting from the bright sunshine-gold walls to the cayenne-red cupboards to the bright blue back door – and just the thought of Beth's perpetual motion made a swell of uncharacteristic nausea curl through her stomach. The blueberry pancakes she'd wolfed down at the diner for breakfast didn't seem to be sitting well. She took another drink to settle her stomach.

"Careful as I can be. And what do you mean, at least I'm out of that condo for a change?"

"You can't deny you're somewhat of a hermit."

"I'll have you know I wasn't even in San Bernardino when I decided to come here. I was in Forest Falls."

"Alone?"

"I'm bitterly divorced. Of course I was alone."

Beth sighed. "Look, like Drew and I tried to tell you, you don't even know that anything's wrong. As usual, you jumped to conclusions and made reckless choices."

"Reckless, that's me."

"This isn't funny, Kim!" Beth shouted. Kim held the phone away from her ear. "Reckless got you married to Mark Owens. Reckless got your mother killed. Reckless – "

" – is making me want to hang up on you," she said coldly. "Low blow about my mom, by the way. I was nineteen and the car broke down in the boondocks. I didn't make that drunk driver get behind the wheel on the same highway she took to come rescue me."

Silence for a full minute, and then Beth said contritely, "You're right. I'm sorry. I just worry that there's a lot you aren't telling me, and that even knowing what you aren't telling me wouldn't convince me that you're not being r – "

"I'm dreaming again," Kim interrupted. Beth lapsed into silence again. "In the first one I was running through the woods with a man with blue eyes."

"A man?" Beth perked up.

"Ha! Perish the thought, you shameless matchmaker. It was not a pleasant run. The thing is…"

Her friend waited for the thought to be finished, but Kim's mind had already wandered back to her first night in Mills when she had looked up into those indigo eyes from her dream. She shouldn't have been surprised to see the evidence of her precognition standing before her; hadn't she been expecting it since the first time she'd dreamt of him?

"The thing is what? Do you – oh!" Bethany sucked in a breath. "You mean you found him!"

"I did. I'm working for him right now."

"Working?"

Her mouth twisted. "Yeah, that's not a foreign concept to me, you know."

"I know. It's just been a long time since you worked for someone other than yourself or your father. What kind of work?"

"I'm serving in his tavern."

"Oh, Kim," Beth sighed. "Couldn't you have – "

Again Kim interrupted, grumpy that she had to but not willing to let Beth travel too far down that road of reproach. "My father frequents taverns. This is the only one in town, so I'm sure Dad made more than one appearance there."

"I see."

In her silence she read all the things Beth could see, and all revolved around Kim's impulsive nature. Beth was considering the possibility of Kim's romantic entanglement with her employer, which would be undeniably reckless and would undoubtedly come with a mountain of regret. She was probably also considering the possibility that Todd really was in danger, which then led to the conclusion that Kim's presence in Mills was not only reckless but dangerous.

"Are you super-pissed at me, Bethany?" she asked softly, and her friend drew in a resigned breath.

"More worried than angry now, Kim. If I can't convince you to come home, can I at least convince you to be cautious? As cautious as someone like you can be?"

A sudden wave of homesickness made her dizzy, and she dropped onto the bench at the small trestle table in the corner of the kitchen. "I'll be as cautious as someone like me can be," she promised. Her stomach heaved. "Look, Beth, I gotta run. Breakfast didn't agree with me, and I think it's making a reappearance."

"Kim – "

"Love-ya-bye!" she sang out and hung up.

She barely made it to the sink before the pancakes gave an encore performance. Feeling marginally better – at least until she had to wash it all into the garbage disposal – she got another bottle of water from the fridge and went to lie down for a few hours before her shift.

* * * * *

She slept through the afternoon and awakened from a dream so disturbingly erotic, her conscious mind shoved it into her subconscious with undue haste. No sense going there; that particular recreational pastime with that particular recreational partner would be downright stupid. But…hadn't there been a moment when his indigo eyes had changed, had somehow become a lighter, icy blue? Yes, there had, and she didn't need Freud to tell her that dreaming of making love with a man who morphed mid-stroke into his father was seriously messed up.

The lingering effects of spending most of the day in troubled slumber were a lethargy that dragged at her limbs, making her feel heavy and stupid and slow, and an urgent sense that she *must* go to the Wyckham House. Since she didn't know its precise location, she would have to have a guide.

Today would be the day to approach Scott, since Ron had the day off. Kim couldn't help but be relieved at the chance not only to ask Scott to go with her, but to step back objectively and admonish herself for the way the hours seemed to drag out and the tavern seemed to lose half its light when its owner was not present.

"You're an idiot, Kim," she chided herself aloud in a soft voice. "Didn't you learn with Mark?"

"Who are you talking to?"

Kim jumped at the sound of Scott's voice so close behind her. "Geez, can you Schaefers stop sneaking up on me?" She held a hand over her heart, feeling its rhythm return slowly to normal.

Scott grinned. "Prob'ly not. We're naturally quiet. Who were you talking to? I called your name three times, but I guess you didn't hear." He paused. "Who are Kim and Mark?"

Panic seized her heart, but she managed a stiff smile. "Kim is a friend of mine from back home. Mark is her ex-husband."

"Oh." He paused, then, "Problems?"

"She's getting involved with a man who's probably going to mow her down like road kill," she muttered darkly. "Did you need me?"

"Just thought we could take a break. I poured you a cup of coffee – real coffee, not the sludge my cousin serves."

"Oh, that'd be great." She followed him to the bar, where two steaming mugs awaited. "Although I am getting used to his coffee."

"Mmmph," Scott muttered. She thought she sensed disapproval in that one inarticulate sound. He stirred his coffee – not surprisingly laced with cream and sugar – then looked up at her.

"Do you miss Texas, Beth?"

An easy question at last, she thought with relief. "No."

"Really? I think I would miss Mills if I ever do leave."

"I miss the people. The place isn't all that great, in my opinion." Another truth shadowed by a lie. She didn't miss Texas; she'd never lived there and never planned to, not even to be closer to Bethany. But she felt guilty because he thought it was her home.

"I've always heard Texans are an entirely different breed, that you can never get the Texas out of them."

"I suppose for some. But I grew up mostly in California, and didn't move back to Texas until I'd graduated high school."

"Then you got married. High school sweetheart?"

Kim smiled tightly. "Yeah."

True on both counts: Beth's and hers, only Beth's had turned into Happily Ever After. Bethany had left behind Andrew Fairchild, a grade school friend, when she moved to San Bernardino to live with her grandparents after her parents died. He had been a frequent guest, and when Beth graduated high school, she had promptly relocated to College Station where Drew attended Texas A&M. Eventually they had relocated again to San Antonio where he'd secured a cushy job with an engineering firm.

Kim, on the other hand –

"Hello?" Scott snapped his fingers in front of her eyes, smiling as she jumped. "Where'd you go?"

"Divorce court," she replied shortly. "Do you ever wonder how you ended up where you are in life?"

"Every damn day," he admitted gruffly, no doubt thinking of Nadine Bennett and her possibly witchcraft-initiated snare.

"Scott, I – "

The tavern door burst open, spilling in the first of the evening's drinking crowd, and Scott rounded the bar to fill the first orders.

When her shift ended several hours later, she left Tiana in charge of the floor and Denny watching over the bar, and went in search of Scott. She found him in Ron's office, watching a cheesy sci-fi flick on the small TV Ron kept around for football games and consuming a huge juicy hamburger with all the trimmings. His feet propped on Ron's desk and his face alight with obvious joy, he waved her in, arching a brow when she closed the door behind her and perched on the edge of a chair.

"What's up?" he asked, washing a mouthful of burger down with a big swig of Pepsi.

Kim gripped the edges of her chair tight enough to make her knuckles go white. "I want to ask a favor of you."

"Sure, ask away," he invited airily, taking another huge bite of the burger.

"Would you take me to that place? To the Wyckham House?"

The hamburger dropped from Scott's suddenly nerveless fingers, and his green eyes widened in shock. She thought for a moment he'd choked on the food, and she frantically tried to recall the Heimlich Maneuver. But he managed to swallow, and his face went from an alarming red to an equally alarming waxy white.

"Why would you want to go there?"

"I don't want to." She swallowed hard, her mouth suddenly dry. "I have to."

"Why?" he shouted, and she flinched.

"You don't have to yell at me. I'm sitting right here, and my hearing is just fine."

"Yeah, it's your common sense that's obviously lacking." He slapped his palm down on the TV's power button. In the ensuing silence, he glared at her until she shifted uncomfortably in her seat.

"You don't know why I'm asking!" she blurted before she could stop herself.

"So tell me."

She bit her lip uncertainly. She had to trust someone; she couldn't do this alone. But should Scott be that person? He sure didn't feel like it.

"I can't," she answered finally, bringing another explosive vent of frustration from him.

"Don't ask this of me, Beth. I can't do it. He almost died there and I – "

Whatever else he said fell on deaf ears. Eleven years ago, Nadine Bennett took a baffling interest in Scott after years of snubbing him…*after* Ron had gone in search of his missing fiancée? *After* Ron had become the only person to come away from the Wyckham House alive?

"What is it, Beth?"

"Did you start dating Nadine before or after Ron's…"

"We call it his 'accident,' but I don't think my parents ever thought there was anything accidental about it."

"Certainly not, especially considering what happened to his friends."

"Yeah. As far as Nadine goes, we started dating two weeks before his accident. Off and on while he was in Meadow Grove and ever since he was released."

Her brow scrunched thoughtfully, and when he started to speak again, she held up a finger. "Bear with me for a moment," she requested thoughtfully.

He obediently waited while she followed her train of thought to its destination. She straightened with a tight expression.

"I'm assuming when he came out of the catatonia, he didn't come home right away. There must have been some intense psychotherapy before they would release him."

Scott nodded. "Six months. But when he left the institution, he stopped going. I – " He paused, flushing. "I overheard him telling Mom one day he didn't want to remember what happened."

"I can imagine," she agreed softly.

"What is it? You ask a lot of odd questions sometimes."

"I know, but allow me a few more. After the catatonia but while he was still in the institution, how were you and Nadine?"

"Steady, and then off and on again since he came home. What does this – "

He fell silent as Kim shook her absently, her mind still putting together the timeline. It painted a frightening picture, to say the least.

"Does Ron have –*did* he– have any enemies in town?" He sighed explosively, but she held up her hand to stave off his outburst. *"Please,* humor me."

"All right," he agreed tersely. "I don't know of any except his father. But since everyone knew about that, I can't imagine Caleb would try anything so drastic. Besides, not even Caleb would – "

Kim interrupted, thinking that for someone who detested being interrupted, she was sure doing a lot of it herself. "What do you mean, everyone knew about that?"

He shifted uncomfortably. "Caleb beat Ron's mother until she had a miscarriage in her sixth month of pregnancy. When she recovered, she left."

"She left her son with an abusive man?"

"I'm not privy to the details, but I don't think Caleb gave her much of a choice. All I know is that Ron got hit by a car when he was four and needed a blood transfusion. For some reason, Caleb went completely berserk and beat Belinda into a miscarriage. After she left him, he started on Ron."

"Wow," was all she could manage. How did someone go through all that trauma in one lifetime and not fly apart at the seams?

"I don't know why any of this matters right now, Beth. It has nothing to do with what you asked me to do."

"Maybe it does, Scott." She leaned across the desk, catching his eyes. "Two weeks before his experience at the Wyckham House, Nadine Bennett took a sudden interest in you. Then, during his time in the institution – on again, off again. Until he came out of the catatonia. Then you two went pretty steady until he was released. Then it's been on again, off again for the last nine years."

"So what? It doesn't mean anything."

"Yes it does, and you tried to tell me this at the river yesterday, but you never finished and I didn't get it. Nadine deliberately sought you out to keep tabs on him. They weren't after Elizabeth Peterson or her parents. They were after Ron – she cozied up to you before Elizabeth disappeared. The Petersons must have just been a way to get to him."

He laughed humorlessly. "A conspiracy theory, here in Mills! You've been watching too much TV or something."

"I'm serious, Scott, and I think it's what you believe too. Why else would you think Nadine bewitched you? You made the connection between the two events yesterday yourself; it just didn't hit me until now. She kept tabs on Ron through you. If anything happened they should know about, who else would you confide in but a lover?"

"'They'?" he repeated sardonically. "I knew it wouldn't be too long before the mysterious 'they' were dragged into this."

"Oh, come on, Scott, you don't really believe – "

"I don't believe what you're suggesting, Beth. And if I were you, I would keep it to myself."

"Why, if none of it's true?" she asked archly. He flushed.

"People disappear when they wander in the woods. Does it have to do with witchcraft? I doubt it. Just plain and simple accidents, sometimes frontier-style vengeance. Now if you're done, I have things to do." He looked pointedly at the closed office door.

"You know I'm right, Scott," Kim said steadily, rising gracefully to her feet. "I'll find it myself if you won't take me."

He stood up so fast his chair skidded back and crashed into the wall behind him. His face was white and fearful.

"You're out of your mind if you think you can find it on your own! Promise me you won't even try."

"I can't make that promise."

"Please, Beth, just leave it alone. He's lived with it – we've *all* lived with it for eleven years. We're happy to leave it how it is."

"You don't understand, Scott," she said, her voice steady. "This has nothing to do with Ron."

"Then tell me why, dammit!" he shouted suddenly. "Trust me!"

"I can't afford to." The office door clicked shut behind her, and she bolted for her car.

She wasted no time once she reached the cottage. Moving through the house at breakneck speed as though the devil himself snapped at her heels, she pulled a thick sweatshirt over her head and tugged on heavy socks and waterproofed hiking boots onto her feet. A foray through the pockets of her jacket in the hallway closet produced a pair of Isotoner gloves, and she skipped out the backdoor feeling pretty positive that she could outpace Scott if she walked fast enough.

She struck out on the path to the river, certain somewhere along the way she would come across the branch of the path that would lead her into the woods to the Wyckham House. She kept a close eye on the woods to her right; she doubted she would have to cross the river to get to it; it would be too inconvenient.

About half an hour past the narrow, boulder-filled beach where she'd sat with Scott the previous day, she spied something about a stretch of woods that didn't seem quite natural. She backtracked, coming past it more slowly, uncertain if she should plunge headlong into the fiddleheads and filbert bushes or if she should continue on until she came across a footpath.

A twig cracked behind her, and she jumped straight into the air, turning as she came down. Only a squirrel, scurrying toward the river. Her movement startled it, and it scurried up a nearby tree, where it perched on a branch and berated her for the fright.

Kim caught her breath, chiding herself for being so spooked. The longer she stood here, the better chance Scott had of catching up to her.

She brushed aside the branches, stepped into the forest, and immediately tripped over a thick root protruding from the ground, landing on her knees. Her involuntary cry spooked some sparrows, which chirped indignantly and took flight. When the first eye-watering pain dissipated, she got to her feet and examined her hands and knees. Nothing more than surface scrapes and embedded dirt. She wiped most of the dirt off on her thighs, and looked down at the ground.

Where she had fallen, the leaves had scattered in a cloud of orange, yellow and red, laying bare a line of dirt about a foot wide. She moved forward, kicking the leaves to either side, exposing a defined path. She had found it after all.

With a last nervous glance behind her – after all, this seemed much like the eerie ease with which she'd found the object of her prophetic dreams, a job, and a place to live, all within twelve hours – she entered the thickening forest, exposing the path before her as she went.

It twisted and turned, sometimes turning back the way she'd just come, then taking an abrupt hairpin turn and taking her once again deeper into the woods. What should have taken her about an hour to travel, given the density of the forest and the branches she continually elbowed out of her way, ended up taking nearly twice as long.

She came around one of those hairpin curves into the meadow where it hunched, looming over her like a giant beast about to strike down unwary prey. Her chest constricted. She felt more like the Wyckham House found her rather than the other way around.

Unprepared for its monstrous proportions, Kim could only stare, wide-eyed, open-mouthed, and utterly dismayed. It towered over her, dark, gloomy and silent, built of huge gray stones like something from an evil fairy tale. Towers reached into the forest canopy, and narrow lancet windows gaped like toothless mouths, the glass long ago broken and scattered. The moisture-swollen wooden doors at the front entrance appeared hopelessly stuck shut.

The Wyckham House did not take her breath away in wonderment like Neuschwanstein in Germany. It stole her nerve and held her eyes much as an excruciatingly ugly beast would. It was repulsive but somehow compelling nonetheless. More massive than she had ever anticipated, Kimberly wondered how she would ever find her father – if he was in there. She could wander for days, never finding her way out before hunger and thirst – or worse – overcame her. Maybe Scott had a point; she shouldn't have come.

"I didn't have a choice," she reminded herself resolutely, speaking aloud to overpower the inner voice telling her to run while she still had the chance. "I had to come. Since he wouldn't bring me, I had no choice but to come alone."

She cast a glance at the pond, to the left and about a hundred yards from the building. Large enough to be a swimming hole for the entire town of Mills at once, it gave off a dank, decaying odor that wafted to her on the early autumn breeze. Yellow algae colonies coated the water's surface.

"I'll go in, have a quick look around the main floor, and leave." She patted her pockets, making a face when she realized that, in her reckless haste, she had failed to bring a flashlight. No matter. She would just go in the ground floor and wouldn't wander out of the meager light drifting in through the windows.

She drew in a steadying breath, stepped out of the woods, and started across the clearing. The bushes rustled behind her as something crashed through. For an instant her mind shrieked *Bear!* – no doubt inspired by the stories she'd read of wild animals attacks in forests – and then she was hit hard from behind and skidded face down through the autumn leaves.

REALLY BAD IDEAS

Kim struggled wildly, her panicked mind thinking that a crazed defense might scare away the animal attacking her. When she was abruptly flipped onto her back and her wrists slammed against the leafy ground, it suddenly came to her that the shape was human. She went still, resigned, afraid to open her eyes. She could not deny that she had been warned against coming here.

And then he started shouting, shaking her as though using her for punctuation. *"What are you doing here?"*

Gasping for breath, she stared up into angry blue eyes. "Only...going...just...inside!" she wheezed, and he shook her again.

"It would have been enough!"

"For...what?" she choked out.

"What?" Ron repeated, as if not quite believing she could be so dense. "For *what?"* and his fingers dug painfully into her wrists as though he wanted to shake her again but was restraining himself with monumental effort.

"Stop!" she pleaded. "You're hurting me!"

"Better me than – " He broke off, took a deep breath, obviously trying to get himself under control. "I'm trying to *save* you a lot of hurt."

She stared up at him for a moment, and asked softly, "Would you please get off me? I can't breathe."

He opened his mouth to argue, and realized most of his weight pressed her into the soft earth. His sudden consciousness of the blatant intimacy of their position, of how she felt beneath him, flashed in his eyes. He only had to lower himself an inch to lay fully against her, move his head slightly from there to kiss her... She silently willed him to move away at the same time she prayed he would press his advantage.

His eyes moved abruptly to her lips. She tried to push her hands up from the ground to derail that train of thought. His gaze jerked back to hers, and whatever he saw there made him comply.

He pushed himself away, rose to his feet, and brushed the leaves from his clothes. After a moment, he extended his hand to her, and after another moment, she finally accepted it and allowed him to draw her to her feet. Before she fully regained her balance, he was dragging her by the arm back into the shrubs.

"What are you *doing*?" she protested, beginning to struggle again.

"Taking you home."

"But I haven't gone in yet!"

He muttered something under his breath that she couldn't make out and replied in a louder, implacable voice, "You aren't going to, either. I've half a mind to beat you senseless, but it would take such a short time I would be robbed of the enjoyment."

"Half a mind is probably right," she muttered, returning the insult.

He walked so fast her feet skipped steps, his grip on her wrist so tight her hand went numb. Her flesh would bruise, and she wondered how she would explain it at work tomorrow.

"You can stop with the caveman tactics any time now, Schaefer."

In reply, he stopped, let go of her wrist, and shoved her ahead of him on the path, snagging the collar of her jacket in his hand.

"I can walk by myself," she protested angrily.

"I know you can," he agreed smoothly. "All the same, I'll keep a hand on you, just in case you decide to run the hundred yard dash back the way we came, you understand."

"No, I do *not* understand! You have no right – "

He cut her off, his voice icy. "I, of all people, have *every* right. Pick up your pace, girl; I want to get back before dark."

"Your legs are longer than mine!"

"So take more steps."

"If you would just let go of my collar – "

"In my present frame of mind, I might start beating you, so I believe I'll just keep hold for the time being."

"How did you know I came here?"

"Scott called me. He would have gone after you himself but didn't want to leave the bar unattended."

"No one *needed* to come after me. And why did you, if it's so *dangerous*?" The question came out with more hostility and sarcasm than she had intended. She could almost see his hackles go up.

"You know, sweetheart, it beats the hell right out of me. I suppose it's because you don't look like you could fight off a raccoon, let alone someone hell-bent on causing mayhem and misery."

"I'm stronger than I look."

"Not strong enough to fight off a man."

"That's a stinking macho thing to say."

He shrugged. "Doesn't change the truth of it."

She capitulated to his strong-arming with ill-grace until they reached the riverbank where she'd sat with Scott. He let her wrench her wrist from his grasp, and she ignored his sardonic grin when she smugly pointed out that she'd just freed herself from him with no help from a man. She knew it wasn't true – he wouldn't have let go of her unless he'd wanted to – but damned if she was going to admit that.

"Have a seat." He gestured to a wide, flat boulder.

She crossed her arms over her chest and fixed him with a cold glare. "I'd rather stand."

"Suit yourself." He sat himself, eyes narrowed on the Susquehanna rushing past. When he caught her speculative look toward the path, he said, "Don't even think about it. I'm stronger and I'm faster, and I don't think you could take another tackle today. Just sit and relax for a minute, will you?"

"I could outrun you. I ran cross-country in college."

His eyes gleamed. "So did I." Casually dismissing her poised-for-flight posture, he fished his cell phone out of his jeans pocket, held it up in the air and twisted around until he caught a signal, and punched in a speed dial code. "Everything's fine." He listened for a moment, and a reluctant smile curved his mouth. "Yeah, a few bruises, mostly to her ego... Mmm-hmm. 'Bye."

"Scott?" she asked coolly. She had a few things in mind to say to Scott the next time she saw him, all centering around the sentiment "mind your own business."

"Mmm?" He looked up inquiringly. He hadn't even been listening. Barely suppressing an eye-roll, she repeated her question. "My aunt. I was having lunch with her when Scott called. She was very much against me coming."

"I'd apologize, but it's hardly my fault. I didn't ask you to come after me."

"Be grateful that I did."

He turned away, patting his pockets for his cigarettes. He lit one and watched the smoke drift away on the autumn breeze. His hand shook; she doubted it was from cold since the air, while crisp, was comfortable.

Finally acknowledging that it was childish for her to remain standing out of sheer stubbornness when it was apparent he planned to spend a while by the river, she claimed a flat rock a safe distance out of his reach – ignoring his victorious grin – and followed his gaze upward. The sky glowed a brilliant blue, a hue that seemed to only exist in northern states in the fall. It seemed incredible to her that she had escaped death on a day as fine as this, but that was his implication.

He spoke into the stillness, still watching the sky. "Did you think that Scott warned you for the fun of it?"

"I'm sure he was serious." She didn't ask how he'd known Scott had discussed the Wyckham House with her; she suspected there were very few things the Schaefer cousins didn't share with one another.

"But you didn't believe him."

"I believed him."

"Then…why?"

Kim frowned, looking away as his eyes moved from the sky to her face. He was entirely too perceptive, dammit, and if she didn't curb this conversation right now, his deductive reasoning would logically lead him to suspect she had more than a passing curiosity in the Wyckham House.

Her shoulders lifted in a shrug – not her best dodge, but less incriminating than any verbal answer she could give. She wished she could ask him outright about Todd, but she didn't know that she could trust him.

"I'm assuming you have a reason, which is…?"

"Private, at the moment."

He tried a different tack. "No one who goes there is ever found alive, Beth," he said, with the usual hesitation before her name. "If they're ever found at all."

"You were."

His gaze swept over her, calculating what she knew and how she knew it. "Scott has a big mouth sometimes."

"He wasn't gossiping idly. He was leading up to some advice."

"What advice?"

Kim colored. "Never mind."

"I see," he murmured, and she hoped like hell he didn't. "All right, I was found alive, but my friends weren't. Elizabeth wasn't found at all."

"Do you think she's still…"

"Alive? No. I probably won't ever know for sure, but it's what I feel." He glanced at her and touched his chest over his heart. "In here. She won't be coming back."

He spoke impassively, but it was clear to her that he was still caught in the maelstrom caused by Elizabeth's disappearance. Equally obvious was the vicious circle in which his life turned: Elizabeth's vanishing would haunt him until he let go, he could not let go until he knew what happened, but he did not want to remember even though it meant respite from his unrelenting pain.

"So what do you think is going on there?"

"I don't know," he replied tonelessly. "And I want to keep on not knowing."

Sudden anger flared inside her. "So you just close your eyes and let people die?" Perhaps if someone had done something sooner, people would have stopped disappearing long ago – people like her father.

His eyes flashed with his own anger. "You think I'm a coward? I know what happens when you cross a line. I learned my lesson, and I'm not about to forget it. Am I still scared? *Damn* right I am! And if you had any sense, you would be too. In this town, if you ask questions, if you go places you aren't wanted, you disappear. You die." And almost inaudibly, he added, "Or worse."

She sat a little straighter on her rock. "What could be worse,

Ron?"

He immediately looked as though he wished he hadn't spoken, but he answered her truthfully. "Worse is coming to consciousness to learn your best friends are dead, your fiancée is missing, and you can't do anything about it because it's been more than a year. Worse is not remembering what happened."

"Or not knowing if you're responsible," she added quietly.

He glanced up, eyes narrowed as if wondering if she could read his thoughts. But mindreading wasn't necessary when he wore his guilt like a mantle for all to see.

"And what do *you* know about it?"

She blinked at his sudden hostility. "Just what I've observed myself."

"You know nothing. You see only what I let you see, and that's the way I intend to keep it. So no more trips down curiosity lane." he gestured angrily toward the woods behind them. "No more amateur psychoanalysis. Mind your own business, and we'll all get along just fine."

He looked away from her, back into the sky, his eyes seeking. His tension melted away, replaced by relief. She followed his line of sight to the moon, a mere one-quarter slice of white-yellow in the late afternoon sky.

"We should get back to the cottage before dark," he said. He crushed out his cigarette against a stone, dipped the tip in the river to extinguish any sparks, and pocketed the butt.

The walk back to the cottage was made in virtual silence. Several times she thought of questions she wanted to ask him – *Have you ever considered that what happened to you was intentional?* or *Why were you staring at the moon?* – but his demeanor forbade conversation.

The vanishing wound, bathed in his own blood, and that expression of having been given a reprieve while he looked at the crescent moon...could he possibly think...?

"Here we are. Be sure to lock your door." He had stopped outside the back gate leading to her patio.

She quirked a humorless smile at him, wondering why the Schaefer men were so security-conscious when the rest of the town hadn't locked their doors in so long they probably couldn't remember where they'd put their house keys.

"I will."

"Well, then. Have a good night." He spun on his heel and started to walk away, but stopped when he heard her smothered laugh. "What?"

"You just jumped on me – literally – and treated me like a Shake'n Bake dinner, not to mention dragged me through the woods clutching my wrist so tight I'll probably have gangrene from lack of blood flow, and you tell me to have a good night?"

She chuckled again, but he didn't even smile as he came back. He rested his hands on her shoulders, gently.

"No more questions, no more investigating, no more trips to the Wyckham House. All right?"

"But – "

"I have enough deaths on my conscience," he blurted.

"It wasn't your fault," she said patiently.

"Yeah? Well, I don't want *you* to not be my fault too, y'know?"

She fought back a smile. "That's rather sociable of you. Careful or you'll ruin your image as a misanthrope."

He smiled back. Kim stopped breathing. The smile lit his face like an exploding sun, and she was powerless to move, powerless to hide the sudden flood of reckless desire that washed away her resistance.

Neither moved for what felt like an eternity. He seemed as unable to look away from her as she was from him. Finally he stirred, untangling a birch leaf from her hair. It fluttered away but his fingers wove themselves into her hair, sifting through the fine strands of golden silk with a tenderness she hadn't suspected he possessed. She knew what he was about to do, but she couldn't summon the will to stop him. It would be a train wreck, at least for her; of that she had no doubt. An instant before their lips met, her voice of reason piped up. What did she think she was doing? She needed another heartbreak like she needed another appendix.

And then it was too late. She lost herself in his kiss from the first exhilarating touch of his lips, conscious of nothing but the sensation of intimate contact. Time spun away, became meaningless. Everything ceased to exist but this man and his fervent response to her, her need of him, burning through her blood like fire – potent, overwhelming, devastating.

How long they kissed she couldn't have said. An eternity. Mere seconds. She'd never experienced a stranger connection with a man, as though the very core of her being flowed out and into him, and he into her, until all secrets were laid bare and all emotion stripped raw. For an instant in time, she knew him completely: the edges of his personality and the textures of his emotions, the color of his sorrow and the light of his joy. Their souls intertwined, flowed together until she could not tell what was of him and what was of herself.

He drew away, trembling. His eyes opened, bewildered, panicked. With the breaking of physical contact, she could feel a separation on a deeper level, and the man whose soul she had known so intimately for that blessed moment became almost a stranger again.

Almost.

Ron stepped back abruptly and pivoted on his heel, fishing his car keys out of his pocket as he strode around the house to where he'd parked. Within thirty seconds of ending their kiss, he was nothing but a flash of tail lights and a plume of dust driving down her road.

Kim leaned weakly against the fence post, not trusting her shaking legs to carry her into the house, strangely certain that neither of them had come away from that encounter without irrevocably losing a part of themselves to the other.

NOT GOING THERE AGAIN

"Damn it! You idiot! Why the *hell* did you do that? *Moron!*"

Ron punctuated his verbal self-abuse with some physical abuse as well: a couple of violent punches delivered to his golf bag; a vicious kick to the canvas sheath that held his tent; a mighty shove to a coffee can full of nuts and bolts. The contents spilled across the garage floor; the nuts neatly screwed onto the bolts in matched sets took away from the effect a bit. Splintering pain shot through his hand, and his leg ached fiercely.

But those were nothing compared to his clawing panic. No, no, no

– *no* way he was diving into those shark-infested waters again. He'd already been chum once – chum and chump, if his uncle was to be believed – and he didn't want to be either again. Ever.

"Are you done demolishing the garage?" asked a cool voice behind him, amused.

He jumped and whirled around; his aunt stood at the door leading into the house, leaning against the jamb. She was smirking.

"My garage," he reminded her tersely.

"Mmm," she responded noncommittally. "Want me to heat up your lunch?"

"I'm not hungry." He took a step toward her, skidded on several bolts, and almost fell. He regained his balance by grabbing hold of a seamstress's dress form his aunt kept forgetting to take home with her; his hands landed squarely over its gently rounded bosom, and Renée Schaefer ducked her chin, snorting laughter.

Ron swore violently, shoving the dress form away from him and pushing past her – albeit gently. She was, after all, the only mother he could remember, and his uncle had raised him to respect the ruling female of the house. After all she'd done for him, he gave that respect willingly.

He dropped into a chair at the kitchen table, picking restlessly at the drooping bouquet sprouting from the vase at its center. Renée followed him into the room, shoved a plate into the microwave on the counter, and punched in a code.

"I said I'm not hungry," he reminded her.

She took the chair adjacent to him. "I heard you. I'm heating it up for me; I'm not going to waste homemade lasagna."

"Mmm."

"Are you going to tell me what the trouble is?"

"What's to tell?" he muttered.

He finished plucking a chrysanthemum and moved on to a daisy, and thought darkly about how Beth Fairchild's compact body had felt beneath his, warm and soft in all the right places; her hair, fanned out on the autumn leaves like a sheath of wheat; her eyes, wide and full of desire. Oh, she was trouble, all right – trouble that walked on two shapely legs.

Renée closed her hand over his and pulled his fingers away from the carnation he was attempting to destroy. "That one isn't ready to be plucked, dear."

Ron looked down at the drift of brown-splotched petals that lay scattered in front of him on the table.

"Sorry," he mumbled. He pushed the vase away, and she prudently moved it even farther from his reach. "I just – I don't know what – she drives me nuts!" he burst out. "She's always saying or doing something totally off the wall. I don't get it. I don't get *her*. She hears about…that place…and the first thing she does is go tearing off after an adventure, completely heedless of the warning she was given!" He threw up his hands in exasperation.

The microwave beeped and Renée got up. He didn't notice.

"And then she…none of her business, but she pokes her nose in…it's infuriating!"

Renée silently slid the plate of lasagna in front of him, and he picked up the fork and began eating without thought.

"She just appears out of the blue…thinks she knows everything…" He shoved a forkful of pasta into his mouth, chewing angrily and stabbing his fork in her direction for emphasis. "…she has no frickin' clue…nothing but trouble…"

She watched him passively, reserving comment, until he'd polished off his meal. As he pushed the plate away, he looked down at it, mildly surprised. He hadn't even realized he'd been hungry.

"She's going to get herself killed."

"So you like her." She smirked.

"I do not."

"So you say."

"Whatever." He grabbed his cheese-smeared fork and began tapping it on his discarded plate. Renée tolerated this for a short minute, then snatched it out of his hand and whisked his dirty dishes away to the sink, ignoring the stink-eye he gave her.

"You're really grumpy."

"Yeah, well…" He trailed off.

"I'd like to meet Beth."

Ron skidded his chair back, but she beamed a glare at him that held him pinned. "Uh-uh. No way. Put away your matchmaking hat and get that idea out of your head right now."

"Who said anything about matchmaking? I just said I want to meet her."

"Then go to the tavern and meet her," he growled. "Just leave me out of it."

Renée's smirk returned. "Your behavior the last few days is suddenly making sense. Give her Tuesday night off. That gives me time to plan."

"I'm working Tuesday."

"Who said you have to be here? You've already met her."

"Like I'm going to leave you here with her alone. There's no telling what you'll do." He glared at her, feeling trapped and uncomfortable.

This wasn't the first time she'd wanted to meet a female presence in his life. Thankfully all the others in between Elizabeth and Beth Fairchild had been one-night diversions in other towns. He was a firm believer in not leaving messes where he lived. But the last of those had been years ago; so long ago he couldn't remember her name or what she looked like – or even the town where she lived. Those things hadn't mattered; all that had mattered was not being alone in the darkness, of having a human connection however brief and shallow.

"Aaron, maybe she's – "

"She's not," he said tersely, shutting her down immediately.

He pushed away from the table again, and this time she let him leave. He paused at the door of the kitchen, shooting a glance at the hand-crafted bookcase to the right of the fireplace – or more accurately, at a studio portrait in an ornate frame on one of the upper shelves. The subject of the photograph was indistinguishable from this distance, but his mind provided all the details from long years of perusal: rich auburn hair, laying in waves over her shoulders; porcelain skin with the blush of roses in her cheeks and a scattering of light freckles across her nose; grey eyes fringed with naturally dark lashes. Her lips had been curved in that special smile she reserved for him, and why not? He'd been standing behind the photographer, waiting for her.

Elizabeth.

His mind flashed an image of Beth Fairchild as a comparison, and he impatiently shoved it away as he took the stairs two at a time up to his bedroom. It was unfair to compare them; Elizabeth was a legend in his heart, and Bethany was just an annoyance in his life. Yes, annoying and pretentious and stubborn and beautiful and perfect....

Whoa! He curbed the thought immediately and flung himself down on his bed beside the cat, which slept stretched out, taking up as much room as possible and leaving little tufts of tawny hair on his comforter. Her head lifted when he twined his fingers into her long fur; she yawned, blinked sleepily, and rolled so her back was too him.

He poked her in the back, but she ignored the nudge. "I went there today, Taffy," he whispered. "To the Wyckham House."

The cat stretched and resumed her light snoring.

"I didn't think I would ever be able to do it, but I did. It was easier than I thought."

Still the cat slept. He slid his hand over her back and rubbed her belly. She gave up sleep and rolled over, allowing him easier access. A low purr rumbled through her, making him smile.

"Renée is making me crazy," he grumbled. "I don't what she thinks is going to happen. There's no happily-ever-after for me; two years in a psych hospital aren't exactly sterling credentials for serious-minded females."

Taffy purred on, eyes closed, one paw raking the air until she found his arm. The pads of her foot were warm on his skin, like the touch of human fingers.

"I can't do it," he whispered. "I can't take the chance." He groaned and rolled onto his own back, his hand laying motionless on the cat's furry belly. "But she makes me want to. She's smart and she's funny and she's gorgeous..."

He frowned at that. *Gorgeous* wasn't the word he would have used to describe her right after he'd first met her. Her face was too angular to be classically beautiful, as though a hurried sculptor had carelessly hewed her features in his spare time. But she was stunning, alluring, strangely magnetic: skin tanned to the golden hue of honey; high cheekbones and a smooth, clear brow; eyebrows graceful marks of calligraphy over almond-shaped eyes the color of ancient amber; teeth white and straight behind soft, full lips that made him want nothing more in the world but to spend an eternity tasting them. That brief interlude this afternoon had not been enough.

He had been surprised to find her so responsive; he'd often seen a glimpse in her eyes of a reluctant desire, but behind it there had also been a steely determination not to give in to it. He flirted with her shamelessly and she parried effortlessly, but he could almost see the impenetrable wall erected between them, a wall clearly labeled DIVORCE. She'd been burnt once and was obviously determined not to come close to the fire again.

Since their kiss today, he was oddly certain that it would be remarkably easy to make her fall in love with him. But she deserved better than half a man who was filled with dark phobias and unexplainable aversions – to the forest, the full moon, and Harlan Michaels, who had been a trusted mentor all of Ron's life. He had no idea what had happened at the Wyckham House eleven years ago, but he did know that on the night his fiancée vanished and his friends were brutally murdered, the moon had been full.

Oh yes, it had been huge and colored copper from dust particles in the air, kicked up by the afternoon's blustering winds. At one point it seemed to have turned red, but he couldn't summon more than a vague impression of a crimson orb and excruciating pain before his mind slammed closed the crypt that held that night and the more than five hundred that followed it.

His drifting thoughts carried him off to sleep. When he was deeply unconscious, the crypt door swung open wide, flooding him not with ghosts but with memories too terrible to bear while awake and which colored his dreams dark and unsettling.

THE MODERN WITCH

Mills had always known darkness. It skulked in the shadows and performed its evil deeds under the cover of night.

Sarah Bennett held firm in her conviction that darkness was necessary for some forms of the devil's work, and she had passed that belief on to her granddaughter Nadine. A victim's unshakeable faith in his superstitious fears proved more easily achieved in the still, black hours before dawn.

So during those hours, Nadine Bennett plied her trade and performed her duty to the Circle. With one eye on the darkened window above her – Ron Schaefer's bedroom window – she moved like smoke between the trees scattered across his huge lawn toward the garden around the corner of the house.

Scott's window faced the garden, but she didn't fear he'd see her. He slept conveniently out of the way at her apartment, aided by the sedating effects of crushed valerian root mixed into his bowl of stew. No doubt he dreamt of Beth Fairchild while here across town his cousin lay awake thinking about her, but that didn't bother her. The motivation behind her relationship with Scott Schaefer had nothing to do with love or physical attraction. It helped the Circle keep track of Ron, but Nadine needed no other reason than the reward of pleasing their priest. Over the years, his rewards had become her addiction, and like a crack addict securing her next fix, she did whatever was necessary to gain his favor.

So in the light misting rain, she crept across Aaron Schaefer's land, seeking the talisman that would bind his cousin to her for yet another cycle of the moon. She had thought they'd finished with him and hadn't stayed prepared. When the mysterious Beth Fairchild landed in town, preceded by the secretive and often equally mysterious Denny Wallace, it made the Circle nervous. Unfortunately, information had become difficult to obtain, for on the heels of Beth Fairchild and Denny Wallace came Cody and Renée Schaefer for an unexpected, extended visit. She had to be very careful while Cody was in Mills.

She skirted the deck, slipped between two Rose of Sharon shrubs and into the garden. Garden was an optimistic word; the area consisted of stakes and twine laid out to indicate future raised beds, a few shrubs and clumps of Shasta daisies around the deck, and a hedge of grapevines at the far back of the freshly cultivated rectangle of land. Ron had big plans about which Scott complained in great detail; he dug down the paths to create the raised beds while Ron finished roping off, measuring, diagramming and placing orders by phone and generally avoiding physical labor.

His griping gave Nadine the information she needed. She knelt in the dirt by the path where Scott said he'd been working, careful not to step where she needed to dig and, she thought with wry amusement, careful not to dig where she stepped. She had done so once as a fledgling Caster and spent a full lunar cycle totally enamored of herself. Her grandmother immediately isolated her and gave her a lengthy lecture on the necessity of keeping your collections uncontaminated.

Her admonition came in the stern and acidic tones she used with all the novices under her tutelage who screwed up. But later Nadine heard her and the priest snorting into their brandy snifters, trying to contain their laughter. By the new moon she had been entirely disgusted with admiring herself but completely helpless to stop it, and she'd never felt such relief as when the new moon rose and the spell broke.

Now she scraped the dirt from one booted footprint and popped it into a small plastic container, snapping on the airtight lid as quietly as possible. No clanking pewter chalices for her; plastic containers were almost as essential to her cupboard as her mortar-and-pestle. The modern witch was a practical witch.

Tomorrow she would make brownies and mix a bit of this earth from Scott's footprint into the batter. Once consumed, he would be ensnared. This spell had worked admirably for the last eleven years – although its initial potency had faded – and she had no fear he would be suspicious; she frequently made him brownies when she wasn't bewitching him, and the batch with the spell could be shared with his family and no one would be affected but Scott himself.

She retraced her steps, slipping silently from tree to tree to keep out of sight of Ron's window. Finally she slipped into the woods and trekked along a deer path to the old logging road where she had left her car. She headed for home with a triumphant smile, feeling powerful and invincible.

Scott slept until nine in the morning, giving Nadine plenty of time to do what she needed.

She mixed a small amount of the dirt with essence of orange, said the proper incantation, and incorporated it with a Betty Crocker brownie mix. She smirked a little as she did so; no fancy ceremony, no silly magic wands. This brand of magic was simple, straight-forward.

He woke to the buzzing of the oven timer, and the brownies cooled while he showered. When he came to the breakfast table, he found a hot cup of strong coffee, a plate of fresh fruit, and a brownie.

"Since when do you make me breakfast?" he demanded, but immediately dove into the fresh pineapple slices, eying the mango next to it.

"I haven't done it for a while. I thought you might enjoy it."

He ate with gusto, first the fruit and then the brownie. He left no crumbs. Halfway into his second cup of coffee, he noticed the time.

"I'm late. Ron's gonna skin me."

"Only a few minutes," Nadine soothed. She laid her own fork down and rose gracefully from her chair. She wore only a filmy peignoir, and Scott watched her with the same male appreciation she would have inspired in any man, but nothing more. There would be no indication the spell had worked. As always, she would just have to wait for it to manifest itself in his behavior toward her. In recent months, it took much longer than it had in the beginning.

"Maybe these will placate him," she said now, piling the rest of the brownies onto a paper plate and covering them with plastic wrap.

Scott hesitated only a fraction of a second. Ron was very strange about eating anything prepared by someone outside his small circle of family and trusted friends. Then he shrugged and accepted the plate. Nadine doubted he would tell Ron who had made them; what he didn't know wouldn't hurt him.

He took a last swallow of coffee, and kissed her quickly on the cheek before hurrying out to his car. She watched him go, resigned to another month of being the focus of his unwanted attention.

* * * * *

Kim shot Scott a look of warning as he got his coffee, gesturing at his cousin with an almost imperceptible nod of her head across the room. Thunderheads were gathering on Ron's brow, and Kim watched with amusement as Scott decided to forgo his usual cream and sugar and beat a hasty retreat to the kitchen. She went back to making another pot of coffee, self-consciously yanking the cuffs of her long-sleeved tee-shirt over her wrists.

The door of the kitchen had just swished closed behind him when Ron finished fixing the jukebox and wrangled it back into place.

"That him?" he asked darkly, jerking his head in the direction of the kitchen.

"Yes. He's only ten minutes late, Ron." She paused and then decided to plunge ahead and speak her mind. In for a penny, in for a pound. "It's not like it really puts us behind, you know. You're a little anal about being done early."

The thunderheads on his brow darkened as he crossed the room, stopping uncomfortably close to her. "Oh yeah?"

"Yeah." She reached for a pre-measured packet of coffee grounds and adjusted her sleeves again.

"You're a little feisty today."

"I'm irritable, not feisty."

"Fine line between the two."

"You ought to know."

His mouth twitched. "You're moving a little slow today, Miz Fairchild."

"Not lookin' so spry yourself, genius." She hoped for every muscle ache she sported, he had three.

"I'm supposed to invite you to dinner Tuesday night. Six-ish."

She looked surprised and a little suspicious. "Are we on *Candid Camera*?"

Ron laughed. "I wouldn't put a camera past Renée, just so she can make sure I pass on the invitation."

"Ah," Kim said with a knowing nod.

"Ah what?"

"Nothing."

He struck as fast as an adder, and suddenly she found her hand trapped in his and he was pushing up her sleeve, baring her wrists, where color bloomed on her fair skin like blue-black flowers. She wondered if he was thinking about their kiss, when time had spun out until minutes and seconds didn't matter, when for one soul-searing instant she had known what it meant to trust with every fiber of her being. And how all too soon it disappeared.

She needed to remember that, needed to remember there was no longevity in his sexual entanglements.

"Does it hurt?" He touched the darkest bruise.

"Not much." She steeled herself not to wince as his finger passed over the tender flesh.

"Liar," he whispered. "I'm sorry I hurt you. But I'm not sorry I stopped you." He pulled down her sleeve and let go of her hand, giving her a wicked grin. "Be early so Renée can pump you for information before dinner. Then I can enjoy the meal."

He vanished into the kitchen, still chuckling, and Kim finished with the coffee and moved to the bar to set up the speed rails. Her elbow jostled her uncapped water bottle, toppling it, and water washed over the bar and underneath the cash register.

"Great." She threw a towel onto the puddle and lifted the cash register, setting it down away from the water. It wasn't heavy, but it tended to fritz out when the power cord was jostled; she didn't relish watching Ron's temper ignite as he tried to make it work later.

She grabbed the towel and started to wipe the bar dry. She blinked in surprise: a gold key had lain under the register, and now glittered in the overhead lights.

"Well, hello, sweetheart, where'd *you* come from?"

It looked like a house key; Ron or Denny must have shoved it under there while they were busy and then forgot about it. She pocketed it; she'd give it to Ron when she went in the kitchen to help with prep. Just thinking about turning the crank on the vegetable slicer made her damaged wrists hurt.

"You'd better appreciate the things I'm having to do for you, Dad," she muttered darkly.

There had been no mention of Todd whatsoever; she was starting to doubt her intuition that he'd run into trouble. He probably wasn't even in Mills; he'd probably gone back to California and was puzzling over the box of fishing gear she'd left strewn across his coffee table.

"Hey, Beth! If you're done with the herbs and spices, can you come give a hand with the tomatoes?" Ron poked his head out the kitchen door, a brownie in his hand and crumbs on his cheek, that wicked grin curving his mouth. Her heart stuttered and then galloped full-speed toward her next heartbreak.

"Beth? Tomatoes?"

She turned with a grin fixed to her mouth and her fingers formed in an L on her forehead. "Ron? Hives?"

"Hives?" he repeated blankly.

"Yes, hives. You know, raised itchy welts? Remember – chocolate, tomatoes, and penicillin."

"Ah. Right." He vanished into the kitchen again, and just as abruptly poked his head back out again. "And don't make the Loser gesture at me again. People who live in glass houses – "

"Shouldn't undress before closing the curtains," she finished acerbically. "What else did you want me to do? Other than the tomatoes?"

"Ah...dishes. I got some new dish soap. Tomato extract. Hey, want a brownie?"

"Hey, want a lobotomy?" She followed him back through the doors, and so began the day.

RICOCHET

Nadine Bennett knew the instant the spell backfired. A ricochet on the Caster had a distinct psychic effect, much like being hit by a freight train on a spiritual level. You couldn't avoid a ricochet; you couldn't duck, you couldn't run.

And now she had the insane urge to see – Aaron Schaefer. An urge so strong she actually climbed halfway into her car before she realized to act on it would be lunacy. Ron could smell trickery a million miles away, and witchcraft, really, was nothing more than deception. He had come away from his battle with the Circle with an almost supernatural ability to sniff out his enemies.

Lost in thought, she had actually gotten back into the car and started the engine.

"Enough!!" she raged, pounding the steering wheel. She shut off the ignition and got out of the car, locking it, and then she threw the keys far away from herself. They glinted in the streetlight, limned silver in the moonlight, and she barely heard them clank to earth somewhere on the grassy lawn of her apartment house. She had to physically restrain herself from going after them again, forcing her feet to take her, step by step, back into the apartment, where she went to the phone.

She had dialed Ron's home number three times before she managed to get control of the impulse. In the second or two of sanity she found, she dialed her grandmother.

"Something went wrong." She didn't bother with a greeting. "It ricocheted."

Humor laced her grandmother's voice when she replied, "Impaled upon your own sword, dear? Ah, well. So you spend a month smitten with the man you've been stringing along for nearly twelve years. There are worse things."

"No, Gran, this is serious. Either I misunderstood where Scott had been working in the garden, or Ron went out and worked after him, and Scott didn't know about it."

Silence hummed over the line, pregnant with incredulity. "Are you saying – *you took soil from Aaron Schaefer's footprint?*"

"I think so, Gran."

"And the spell *ricocheted?*"

"Yes, Gran! Can you – "

Sarah interrupted her again. "Don't you know what it *means*, Nadine, when this particular spell ricochets? I'll send the priest over immediately. Do your best for a few minutes, dear; letting Aaron Schaefer witness you under this spell could be disastrous. He's already suspicious enough." She sniffed reproachfully, as though Nadine had been the one to arouse Ron's suspicions.

"Yes, well, I don't suppose *I* had anything to do with it!!"

"No, dear, you certainly didn't. Unplug your phone," she added, and hung up without saying goodbye. Nadine slammed down the receiver, fuming, and had picked it up twice to dial Ron's number before she regained control of herself long enough to unplug it.

It would take her priest ten minutes to get to her apartment, giving her ample opportunity to reflect on the implications of a ricochet when one employed a love spell. This particular one would work only on one who truly hadn't found the love of his or her life. If a witch cast it on a would-be lover who had given away his heart, it would bounce back onto the Caster, often with truly catastrophic results.

It could have been a truly unfortunate occurrence; instead, the Circle had just been given some inordinately useful information. Ron Schaefer had found his heart's desire, which gave them tremendously important information.

Nadine suddenly found herself outside, combing the lawn for her keys. It didn't take her long to find them, and this time she didn't come to her senses until it was much too late for damage control.

WORSE THINGS THAN DEATH
October 19, 2004

Kim didn't drag herself out of bed until two in the afternoon on Tuesday. She couldn't quite believe it when she looked at the clock; she'd never been one to laze the day away in bed, so to find she'd slept eighteen hours straight deeply troubled her. When she tried to reconstruct the hours preceding her sleep, every memory seemed vague and unreal. She only clearly remembered going to the diner and having pancakes topped with blueberry compote for dinner, and then going straight to bed to sleep because she didn't feel well.

Her stomach churned, leading her into the bathroom. She kept it under control until she brushed her teeth and triggered her gag reflex. But she felt better when it was over, although her legs wobbled and her head felt full of cotton. Dinner at Ron's house was going to be excruciating if she felt like this all day.

Equipped with a steaming cup of hot spiced tea and a cool washcloth for her forehead, she collapsed on the sofa in front of the fire, pulled a light blanket over herself, and dozed for the afternoon.

When she woke a couple of hours later, she felt much better although not entirely well. A light dusting of makeup mostly covered the purple half-circles under her eyes and her sickly pallor. She locked up and swung by Mulberry's Grocery for a bouquet of wildflowers and a couple of bottles of sparkling cider, and headed toward Ron's house. Well, she hoped she was heading toward Ron's; his directions had been vague, consisting only of "head left on Stoneridge Way and follow it around the curve. Turn left on the drive between the sugar maples."

Maples did indeed line Ron's long driveway, their leaves turned gold, burnt orange, and crimson. The drive curved slightly to the right, and the house sprang suddenly into sight, a large stone and wood structure facing southeast in the middle of a large clearing. A white vinyl fence, illuminated with spotlights set into the ground every twelve feet or so, surrounded the clearing. The lights lit both the inner grounds and the forest outside the fence.

Three floodlights, each aimed in a different direction, illuminated the majority of the cul-de-sac at the end of the drive, and Kim felt very conspicuous as she took the short walkway to the front porch steps. The door opened before she reached it, and at first Kim thought her reluctant host had been watching for her. But as she drew closer she saw an older version of Ron, silver just starting to thread through his raven hair. He wore gold-rimmed glasses over dark blue eyes and his face bore what she secretly thought of as the Schaefer stamp of break-my-heart good-looks. He looked remarkably like Caleb, with darker eyes and a leaner – kinder – face.

"We're not twins," Cody Schaefer said with a friendly smile, obviously having read her mind. "The family resemblance is so strong we were often mistaken for twins when we were younger."

He stuck out his hand, Kim shook it, bemused. "Cody Schaefer. And you must be Beth Fairchild."

"Guilty as charged," Kim said dryly.

Cody opened the door wider and motioned for her to precede him into the house. She stepped past him, but before she could take in her surroundings, she spied Ron coming down the stairs directly in front of her, rolling up the cuffs of a blood red shirt as he descended. He stopped short when saw her.

"Oh. You're here."

She didn't miss the furtive look he cast his wrist-watch, and she grinned unapologetically. "Yep. I'm early."

If he exhibited any sign of annoyance, Kimberly missed it, for Cody laid his hand lightly on her shoulder to claim her attention.

"Shall I take your sweater?"

She shrugged out of her cardigan and let him carry it away to a coat closet under the stairs. Ron seemed to realize he still stood halfway down the staircase; he came the rest of the way, eyeing her warily.

"Is that a bottle of wine in your hand or are you just happy to see me?" He quirked one dark brow at her.

She flushed and held out the bottles of cider to him. "I don't know if I'd say I'm – *happy* to see you," she rejoined with a fiendish smile, "and no, it's not wine. Sparkling cider. No way am I placing myself under the influence of alcohol when you're around."

"Ah, sparkling cider. And flowers," said Cody, coming back into the room. He had taken the cider from Ron and the flowers from Kim before either could stop him. "Why don't you show Beth around the house, Aaron?" He disappeared into another room, and she turned in time to see the appalled look on Ron's face. She grinned.

"You live to make me miserable," he lamented.

"It's the only joy in my life. Shall we?"

He sighed heavily, but motioned her farther into the house. The whirlwind tour took them through the main floor, and when complete they ended up back at the stairs. Ron stood in front of them as though blocking her way, but Kim didn't mind. Seeing his bedroom seemed almost as intimate as sharing it – a feeling she had every time he entered hers.

Ron herded her into the kitchen, where she found the bouquet already expertly arranged and deposited in a vase at the center of the table. A chestnut-haired woman bustled between the stove and the refrigerator, and she turned with a smile as Ron unceremoniously pushed Kim down into a chair.

"Renée, Beth Fairchild. Beth, Renée Schaefer – my aunt."

Renée wiped her hands on a dish towel and came forward, hand extended. Kim took it, returning the firm, no-nonsense handshake with one of her own.

"I'm very pleased to finally meet you, Beth. I've heard a lot about you."

Kim slanted a look at Ron from the corner of her eye. "I see we need to talk, Renée."

Renée laughed and turned to her nephew. "Dinner will be ready in about twenty minutes. Beth, I hope you Texan girls like Yankee pot roast and the trimmings."

"Love it," Kim assured her, her taste-buds springing to instant life. Hunger gnawed at her stomach, which protested with a sudden wave of queasiness.

"I detest cooked carrots, so nobody gets them," Renée confessed brightly. "I have asparagus steaming and hollandaise sauce to go on top, if you like it."

"Adore it," Kim replied.

The required social pleasantries dispensed with, Renée began to pump her shamelessly for information. Kim fielded the interrogation with good humor and skirted the frank question of why her marriage had failed with an adroitness that surprised even herself. At that point, she looked up to encounter a speculative blue stare from across the table and looked away, flushing.

Ron asked, "You want me to cut the roast, Renée?"

"No, pot roast is easy. Why don't you get everyone drinks?"

"Sure. Where's Cody?"

"He went upstairs to change his clothes. He was splitting wood when Beth arrived. Holler up at him that dinner's on, would you?"

Ron looked loath to leave them alone but dutifully obeyed. A moment later she heard his steps on the stairs, and his voice calling for his uncle.

"Is there anything else I can do to help, Renée?"

"Oh no, dear, I – actually, yes. If you could put the basket of rolls in the microwave and give it a zap, that would help. Thirty seconds or so should do."

While she took care of the rolls, Renée expertly sliced up the beef, then spooned the potatoes from the roasting pan into a serving dish. Ron came back in, followed by Cody and a fluffy, tawny cat.

"I wouldn't have figured you for a cat person," Kim remarked, stooping to ruffle the cat's thick fur. The cat side-stepped her, giving her a baleful glare, and hopped out the cat flap in the back door.

"Well, *you* apparently aren't one," he said with a chuckle.

"Animals usually like me." She shrugged and took her seat, plunking the basket of rolls in an empty spot on the loaded table. Renée came with a gravy boat painted an eye-blistering orange that Kim was sure had been outlawed years ago in the interest of public safety, and she took the chair across from her.

The last to the table, Ron brought everyone glasses of ice cubes and plunked the sparkling cider into an empty place. He claimed his chair to Kim's right. Cody said grace over the meal, and platters, bowls, and baskets passed in every direction. Conversation became chaotic and loud.

If dinner was excellent, dessert was nothing short of divine: a hot peach cobbler topped with homemade French vanilla ice cream, served with fresh coffee in front of the fire in the living room. Ron claimed a wingback chair by the fire after Kim had settled herself in the corner of the sofa adjacent.

"Oh, I'm stuffed," she groaned, setting her empty cobbler bowl on the ottoman and taking up her coffee. "That was outstanding, Renée. Thank you."

"My pleasure, Beth," Renée assured her. She nudged Cody, startling him out of a near-doze. "Let's wash up the dishes real quick and then we can have the rest of the evening to visit."

Cody opened his mouth but a sharp look from his wife brought him to his feet with that enviable Schaefer grace, and he followed her obediently into the kitchen.

"Well," Ron said after a moment of comfortable silence spun out between them. "I'm getting sleepy after so much food. I'm going out to the porch for some fresh air. Care to join me?"

Kim hid her surprise at the invitation, perfectly aware dinner had been Renée Schaefer's idea and not totally approved of by her nephew.

"Sure. I didn't wear a heavy jacket. Is it very cold?"

"I've got a polar fleece you can borrow. Bring your coffee, too," he added as an afterthought. He met her at the door, holding her coffee while she shrugged into the oversized coat he'd retrieved for her.

"I love it when my aunt and uncle visit, but I always eat too much and feel sleepy all the time," he said ruefully as he shut the front door behind them.

Light spilled from the living room windows, illuminating most of the porch. He led her to a darkened corner where a wooden swing hung by stout chains from the sturdy beams overhead. An afghan draped over the back of the swing and an ashtray on the wide porch railing told her this was a favorite spot.

He sank onto the swing and tipped his head to the empty spot beside him, inviting her to join him. With only a tiny hesitation, she accepted; as soon as her backside met the wood he set the swing in motion.

"Your cat doesn't like me," she said when it became obvious he wasn't going to speak first. "Animals usually like me."

"Taryn found her as a stray after Liz disappeared, while I was – away. Taffy didn't make a very good stray. Taryn said she was filthy and starving. She's still very timid."

"How'd you end up with her? Taryn must have had her for a couple of years before you came back to Mills."

"Three years," he confirmed. He shot her a sidelong look. "You know where I went for two of those years, thanks to Scott and his big mouth. Cody and Renée moved to Philadelphia while I was in Meadow Grove, and I went to live with them for a year after I was released. When I came back to Mills and visited Taryn, Taffy took to me. Taryn ended up giving her to me when I moved back."

"I'm surprised you came back here at all."

He shrugged. "I couldn't at first – couldn't even drive the road without getting the shakes so bad I had to pull over." One corner of his mouth quirked up in a humorless smile. "Some kind of brave, huh?"

Kim sighed. "I don't know, Ron. You tried to come; you actually made it into the car and part of the way here. It has to count for something, doesn't it?"

"I suppose," he agreed, but he didn't sound certain.

"Why *did* you move back? I would think, given what happened, you would want to put as much distance between yourself and this town as you could."

He didn't answer for a long moment. He watched the smoke from his cigarette curl into the night sky, wispy swirls of white against cobalt. "I had to prove I could."

"To yourself?"

"To them," he said abruptly and added softly, "And yes, to myself. Tell me, Beth, do you always see the bright side of everything?"

"God, no." She laughed, but like his smile, her laughter held no amusement.

After a moment, he asked, "Why did you get divorced?"

"His version or the truth?"

"Do they differ so greatly?"

"Tremendously, as my lawyer pointed out in court. He claimed I spent all my time with the computer and none with him, that I rubbed his nose in the fact I was the major breadwinner and he couldn't stay with one job for any significant length of time, that I deliberately prevented myself from becoming pregnant in order to punish him, that I did everything in my power to emasculate him. And much, much more." To her credit – and to her surprise – she managed to convey all this with little acrimony.

"Wow. You're really mean." They laughed. "So what is the truth?"

Kim stared out into the indigo night, and for the first time allowed herself to wonder if what she told everyone was really the truth or if she just offered her own version of reality like Mark did. Had she driven her husband so ruthlessly to have a baby that the act of lovemaking had become a chore and not a pleasure? Perhaps she hadn't emasculated him so much as she had relegated him to no more than a stud service.

"He did go from job to job, always dissatisfied with something at work, and it was always someone else's fault, never his. After we'd been married a year, he started spending a lot of time away from the house." She sent him a significant look. "With other women."

He stared back at her, his expression unreadable. "He was a fool." She shrugged, glad the darkness hid her blush at his offhand compliment. "Did you try to emasculate him?"

"The thought crossed my mind." She made a scissoring motion

with her fingers, and they laughed again. "No. If he felt emasculated, he made himself feel that way. I never said anything about his job-hopping; I never said anything about the other women. It all boiled down to my difficulty in getting pregnant and my inability to carry full-term. He believed everyone thought he wasn't man enough to father a child."

"Was he?" All teasing was gone now.

"Yes," she said after a long pause. "He managed with his mistress. He left me the day her pregnancy test showed positive."

She crooked a smile at him, unable to find the will to mask the sorrow and uncertainty that were the lingering legacy of Mark's betrayal. He had shaken her confidence and her self-worth to its very foundation. She was a forever kind of girl, and she didn't know if she could ever fully recover from the brutal breaking of her heart.

"Did you deliberately prevent pregnancy?"

"No." She took in a deep breath and let it out hard. "Severe endometriosis. My doctor says it will take a miracle for me to ever carry a child to term." She looked up, met his gaze squarely. "I'm waiting for my miracle."

"You're involved with someone then."

She shook her head. "No."

Ron looked away, his toe scuffing the porch and stuttering the fluid movement of the swing. "So no one is going to come pound me for kissing you?"

Kim chuckled. "No. Just me."

He sent her a sidelong glance. "That bad, hmm?"

She considered a moment. She wouldn't necessarily call it bad. Strange, perhaps. Disconcerting, certainly.

"Don't answer too quickly," he said wryly. "You'll want to do maximum damage to my ego."

She laughed. "I'm sorry. I'm trying to decide what exactly it *was*. Definitely different."

He pushed against the porch railing to keep the swing in motion. "I thought maybe I imagined – certain things."

"You didn't imagine anything."

Kim found the ensuing silence and the motion of the swing oddly soothing. His voice, when it finally came, startled her.

"So you won't be disappointed if I don't kiss you again."

Her heart constricted, but she replied with humor, "Coward."

Ron snorted, reaching for his coffee cup on the railing beside him. He took a sip, shaking his head. "Maybe. But let me be perfectly frank and honest for a moment, all right?"

"All right," she agreed amiably, although she knew she probably wouldn't like what was coming.

He stopped the swing, jolting her so she almost spilled her coffee. She sent him a reproachful look, which he ignored as he shifted to face her.

"There are – *things* inside my head, images or memories or nightmares, I don't know which. Things I don't ever – *ever* – want anyone to see." She opened her mouth and he shook his head vehemently. "*Please*. We both know what happened when I kissed you. For a moment, I knew everything, and I was afraid you knew everything, too."

"I did."

"I thought maybe you would remember things even I don't remember."

"I don't," she assured him quietly. "And even if I did, I would never tell anyone."

His eyes widened slightly. "I'm not worried about that. But if someone else finds out you know anything about what happened to me…"

"I'm not afraid."

"You should be. If they think you're involved with me – well, you know what happened to my friends and my fiancée."

"I can take care of myself."

He sighed. "That is exactly what she said when I told her to back off and let things go. But she wouldn't listen; her parents' reputations meant more to her than her own life."

"I'm neither naïve nor stupid. I'll be careful."

"Trust me, Beth," he said harshly, "you will never see them coming. You will be another statistic: either one of the missing or one of the dead."

"Why do you care?" she demanded irritably. "I'm nothing to you, just some broad who blew into town unexpectedly and started butting into other people's business."

His mouth tightened into a thin, hard line. "You forget. For a moment, I knew *everything*."

The color drained from her face. "And you remember – ?"

"Nothing. But I do have a sense that something isn't right about what I know about you." He leaned closer to her and cupped her chin in his palm, bringing her a mere inch from his face. His indigo eyes seemed black in the darkness. "I don't know who you are or why you're here, but I do know both might get you killed."

"Or worse," she whispered, baiting him.

He sat still as a statue for a long moment, and then whispered, "Yes. Or worse."

She moved yet closer, and he recoiled, obviously afraid she was going to kiss him in spite of what had happened last time. But she turned aside at the last moment, her cheek brushing against his. The bottom dropped out of her stomach as their flesh touched.

"Have faith in me."

He tipped his head toward hers, his lips against her ear. "I have no faith."

"That's why you're lost," she whispered.

"I'm not lost."

"You've been lost for eleven years, Ron. Everyone knows it but you."

"What I *do* know is if you don't stop whispering in my ear, I'm not going to be responsible for my actions."

She chuckled, foolishly pleased to see him shiver as her breath tickled his ear. She drew away and opened her mouth to reply just as a guttural growl sounded from the darkness beyond the porch.

The blood drained from Ron's face. He barely had time to turn in the direction of the sound when a shape hurtled onto the porch and flung itself at the swing. Kim had a fleeting impression of silver-blonde hair and a pale face fixed in a snarl before the shape hit her full-force, sending the swing crashing into the railing behind it. Ron tumbled to the floorboards and whacked his head with stunning force against a supporting pillar.

Kim fought with everything she had. The shape resolved itself into a feminine, human form – or at least she thought it human; it seemed to have eight arms and eight legs, and she found herself hard-pressed to gain the upper hand in the face of such fury.

Finally she caught her assailant by each wrist and pushed. Her attacker latched onto her jacket, and they both toppled from the swing. Her foe cracked her head hard on the wooden planks of the porch, and Kim finally got a clear look.

"Nadine?"

BLACK ESCALADES AND MEN WHO SAY "SIR"

Kimberly stared, paralyzed with shock. Nadine took advantage of the moment and launched herself again, and they crashed into the side of the house. Dazed, Kim rolled onto her side, trying to get her knees under her so she could stand. Nadine grabbed her around the throat and squeezed. Ron tried to pull Nadine away, but her strength was fueled by rage, and she refused to let go. Spots danced before Kim's eyes as her air supply was cut off.

"He's mine he's mine you man-stealing slut HE'S MINE – "

A dull *thwack!* cut her off mid-shriek, and Nadine toppled sideways to the porch floor, unconscious. Ron knelt behind her, still clutching the stoneware ashtray he had used to subdue her. Cigarette butts and ashes littered the porch around his knees.

Kimberly gasped in huge breaths of air, fighting unconsciousness. Footsteps thundered inside the house and the screen flew open, slamming against the house. It rebounded just as Cody careered through, the handle catching his belt loop and checking his momentum.

He freed himself, his gaze moving over the scene with precision – Nadine prone and silent on the planks, Ron rubbing the knot on his head where he'd hit the pillar, Kim gasping for air and trying to push herself from the floorboards. He shoved his shirt sleeves up to his elbows and waded in, hauling Kim upright. The world spun, and she thought she would lose her dinner all over him. Her legs refused to support her; he half-dragged her back to the porch swing and deposited her into it, wrapping the afghan around her.

Renée stared wide-eyed at her son's long-time girlfriend and then at the ashtray her nephew still brandished as though afraid Nadine might rise and have to be struck down again.

"What in the *world* – ?"

Ron, balanced precariously on his knees, fell sideways, leaning against the pillar on which he had nearly concussed himself. The ashtray fell from his hand; the clatter was deafening in the dumbstruck silence.

"We should call the constable," Renée said, sounding reluctant.

"Not just yet." The quiet authority in Cody's voice stopped Renée in her tracks. Her hand dropped from the handle of the screen. "Are you hurt?" he asked Kim.

"I don't think so." The strangeness of the assault finally sank in. "She tried to kill me!"

He tipped her chin up and angled her toward the light. Red welts striped her neck; they would be bruises by morning. "Do you have any idea why she would attack you? Have you had words with her over Scott?"

Kim stared at him for a moment in surprise. "I haven't had words with her over anything. I've barely ever spoken to the woman."

Nadine rolled onto her hands and knees, still dazed from Ron's blow. "Ah, my head," she moaned, lifting one hand to the knot left by the ashtray. "Ron?" He jumped as though goosed. She wobbled to her feet and turned in a slow, drunken circle, her eyes fixing on her target with unerring accuracy in spite of her possible concussion. "How could you do this to me?"

"You attacked her!!"

She began to cry, and Ron looked rather alarmed. "How could you be with her? How could you let her snuggle up to you and whisper in your ear?"

His mouth opened and closed, but his shock was so great he couldn't form any words. Kim exchanged an apprehensive glance with Renée. This was madness; Ron's loathing of Nadine was legendary – Kim hadn't heard a good word about her come from his mouth – and she seemed to reciprocate it wholeheartedly.

Nadine's eyes did not leave her quarry; she took several steps toward him – and he the same number away from her – before Cody interposed himself between them. Nadine attempted to sidestep him, but he put out his arm to block her, and she found her strength inadequate against his.

"Ron, you were meant to be with me!"

Ron's backward progress brought the backs of his knees into contact with the swing. He sat down hard.

"Let me go!" Nadine snarled at Cody, who remained impassive and implacable in the face of her fury.

A wash of headlights coming up the drive limned the maples in weak light. Scott was home. There was no smoothing over this situation in the few seconds they had before he parked and got out of his car, so they all waited warily, silently. He came up the porch steps, whistling, and barely glanced at them as he headed toward the door.

"Hey guys, how was dinner? Any leftovers?"

When no one answered, he stopped and looked more closely, finally taking in the odd tableau before him. His eyes moved from his father, who physically restrained his girlfriend, to his cousin, who sat in unmistakable retreat on the swing.

"What's going on? Nadine – what are you doing here?"

Kim wished she could simply vanish on the spot; this was going to go over like swearing in church.

Nadine gave him an impatient glare and sent a hateful look at Kim. Her fury broke loose, and she launched herself around Cody.

"I'll kill you for stealing him! I'll kill you DO YOU HEAR ME I'LL KILL YOU!"

"Nadine!" Scott exclaimed, shocked. He took a step forward, but Cody had already caught her around the waist and was carrying her away from Ron. She fought him like a wildcat, kicking his shins and raking her fingernails down his forearms.

"RON! RON, TELL THEM YOU DON'T LOVE HER! IT'S ME YOU WANT! IT'S ME!" She began to cry again. All the fight went out of her; she slithered out of Cody's grasp to the floorboards where she huddled weeping, her head bowed and her face hidden by a

curtain of platinum hair. Scott stared at her for a long, pregnant moment before turning a terrible gaze upon his cousin.

"I didn't do anything," Ron said quietly, his tone calm and conciliatory. His expression was bleak, as though he already knew Scott would not believe him.

"Just like you didn't do anything with Tiana, right?" Scott laughed contemptuously, his lip curling up in a sneer. "You make me sick." He turned on his heel and stormed into the house, slamming the screen door behind him.

Kim slanted a look at Ron and whispered, *"Tiana?"*

She had developed a strange rapport with Tiana, with whom she rarely had to work as Tiana had been moved to less hectic shifts. Tiana didn't have much to say, but she seemed to relax and open up in Kim's presence. Kim rather liked her; she was like a shy kitten she wanted to protect and spoil.

Ron didn't look at her. A muscle flexed in his jaw. "I do not want to talk about it."

"Mmm."

"Are you going to call Harlan?" Renée asked Cody pointedly, her eyes on the livid red stripes on Kimberly's throat.

"Not Harlan, no," Cody murmured distractedly. He looked out into the dark night – Kim was somehow certain he was looking in the direction of the Wyckham House – and finally he took out his cell phone and composed a message, his fingers tapping rapidly. He offered no explanation, and they didn't ask for one. Renée seemed more troubled than puzzled; Ron sat in stony silence.

Kim tried to make eye contact with Cody, but she was the only one at whom he wouldn't look, as though he knew she would press the issue if given an opportunity. But she wasn't brave enough to push very hard; Cody Schaefer emanated authority and power from every pore. She didn't doubt the lines he drew were uncompromising, and she wasn't eager to learn what happened when someone crossed them.

Ten minutes passed without conversation. The swing creaked occasionally as Kim shifted; a breeze stirred wind chimes at the other end of the porch, but otherwise no noise disturbed the quiet. When a car turned down the gravel drive, the crunch of tires was clearly audible all the way to the house. Tension thrummed through Cody like an electrical current, belying his casual posture. He pushed away from the pillar he leaned against and went down the front steps, waiting at the end of the short walk. None of them had even the most fleeting thought of joining him.

A black Escalade stopped beside Scott's car, the moonlight glinting off its polished surface. No dings, scratches, or dents – nothing that could single it out from any other black Escalade. The men who climbed out were dressed identically: charcoal-black slacks, mock turtlenecks of the same shade, and black rubber-soled loafers. She recognized it for what is was: a uniform of sorts for men of some authority. *Covert* authority.

She expected them to be, if not rough, at least indifferent. But they spoke calming words in soothing tones as they each took an arm, lifted Nadine to her feet, and led her to the waiting Escalade. It took several minutes for them to install her in a back seat; Kim suspected they were restraining her. Finally one of the men shook out a blanket and draped it over her, and they closed the door. The driver slid behind the wheel, and the other came back to Cody.

"Anything else, sir?"

"No, that should be – "

"What if I want to press charges?" Kim interrupted. Something about the whole scene seemed sinister, just beyond the boundaries of acceptable law enforcement.

The man turned his unconcerned gaze on her. "That won't be necessary, ma'am."

Her brows winged into her hair. "Excuse me?"

"Nothing more," Cody broke in smoothly. "Thank you."

The man took the steps and the walk in long strides and climbed into the front passenger seat. Kim watched the Escalade through narrowed eyes until the tail lights disappeared from view. Cody came back up on the porch, still avoiding Kim's gaze.

"Maybe I should go talk to Scott," Renée said fretfully.

"It won't do any good. Not tonight, anyway." Cody sent a glance at Ron, who stood abruptly and went into the house. The screen banged shut behind him. "However, you might want to go talk to *him.*"

"Beth, I'm so sorry! I've never had this kind of thing happen at a dinner party."

Kim managed a stiff smile. "Well, you were due for a raucous party then, weren't you?"

Renée's answering smile was stilted. With a last glance at her husband, she slipped into the house, leaving them alone. She turned to grill him, but he spoke first.

"It's probably best that you don't mention that little interlude to anyone." He waved a negligent hand toward the driveway.

"I'm not even sure what I would call it," said Kim sardonically. "Although kidnapping comes to mind."

A ghost of a smile touched his lips, but his eyes were serious. "I suppose it would depend upon one's perspective. But will you trust me?"

"Do I have a choice? I'm sure with another text message you could rustle up another Escalade to haul *me* away."

He chuckled, leaning back against the pillar again and crossing his ankles in a deceptively relaxed stance. "I don't think that will be necessary. The men who took Nadine are with a law enforcement agency. Will you trust me on that?"

She stared at him for a long time and finally said, "A law enforcement agency, but not *Mills'* law enforcement."

"Not exactly, no."

"So how do you justi – "

"My brother is following you," Cody broke in.

"How do you – "

"Be careful, won't you?" he interrupted again.

Her brow creased in irritation. "What is it with all these mysterious warnings? I'm beginning to think there's nothing wrong with this town a little napalm wouldn't cure."

"It's just that my brother has a weakness for much younger women, and he has a bad habit of hurting them."

Her mind provided a clear image of her dream, when Ron's indigo eyes had morphed into Caleb's ice-blue ones in the middle of a decidedly intense physical interlude. "Emotionally or physically?"

He straightened gracefully and held the screen open for her. "Shall we?"

He maddened her with his many evasions, but she recognized that she didn't hold the upper hand in this exchange. She dropped the subject and preceded him into the house.

Ron was nowhere to be seen, but his cat had returned sometime after they had finished dinner. It perched on a high shelf on the bookcase nearest the front door and hissed at Kim as she passed.

"Not an animal person, eh?" Cody remarked with amusement.

She frowned as she repeated what she'd said to Ron earlier. "Actually, yes, I am. Animals usually like me. I even worked in a shelter through most of high school until I was married."

Kim backtracked to the bookcase. The small tawny cat arched its back and tried to squish itself farther into the corner of the shelf. When she reached for it, it hissed again, and swiped a dainty paw at her, claws out.

"Taffy!" said a stern voice behind her.

She jumped; she hadn't realized Ron had come into the room. He crowded in and reached around her for the cat which, in trying to scramble out of his reach, knocked a framed photograph from the shelf and onto Kim's head. She caught it before it hit the carpet, and stared down into the celluloid face of a stunning redhead. Ron froze beside her, the cat forgotten.

"That's Elizabeth."

"She's beautiful."

"She was," he agreed, stressing the past tense. He took the frame from her, reached over her shoulder, and set it back into place, looking only briefly at the frozen color image of the woman whose disappearance had devastated his life.

Kim, however, could not take her eyes from the portrait. Elizabeth Peterson stood against a brilliant, deep blue background the color of a Mediterranean summer sky, her grey eyes taking on a bluish hue as she leaned against a Greek-revival column, her arms crossed over her chest. The camera had captured the rainbow refraction from the pear-shaped diamond on her left hand. Ron's diamond.

An unexpected shockwave of realization slammed through her:

Ron had loved this woman enough to want to share the rest of his life with her, and she had vanished as if she simply had never been. He would probably never know where she had gone or what had happened to her. He had gotten through every day of the last eleven years through sheer force of will. And here Kim stood, breathing in the scent of this woman's fiancé, reveling in his nearness, and she suddenly felt very ashamed. What right had she to feel this yearning for Aaron Schaefer when Elizabeth was still lost?

"Well," she said finally, dragging her eyes reluctantly from the portrait. "I should get home." He took a couple steps backward when she turned, putting some distance between them.

Renée, who had been hovering in the background engaged in silent communication with her husband, came forward with Kim's sweater. "Beth, I'm terribly sorry the evening turned into such a circus."

Kim couldn't help a grin. "Well, at least I can say I was never bored."

Her hostess snickered. "No one has ever accused us of being boring – with the exception of my children, of course." She squeezed Kim's hands. "I adored having you here, and I hope if we invite you again, you won't run away screaming."

"I promise." She wanted to extend her goodbye to Scott, but thought it best she didn't bring up his name just now. She made her goodbyes to the other two men, noting with wry amusement how Ron avoided any physical contact by straightening the cushions of the sofa.

Renée walked her out to the car. Ron hovered at the front door, trying to look casual as he leaned against the jamb, his hands stuffed in his jeans pockets, but he fooled neither of them.

"Look at him," Renée murmured with a snort of what could have been exasperation, amusement, or indigestion. "Like neither of us knows he's really trying to hear what we say."

She raised her voice to a decibel audible to her paranoid nephew in the doorway. "Drive careful, dear, and park close to the cottage. There are wild animals in these woods."

"Yes, ma'am." Kim managed a genuine smile, but as she negotiated the Schaefers long driveway and recounted in her mind the strange events of the evening, her smile faded and a headache began to pulse behind her right eye.

Halfway home she had to pull off to the side of the road. Her trembling legs spilled her into the dirt as she lost the excellent dinner Renée Schaefer had prepared. She rested on hands and knees at the side of the road for several minutes until she remembered the forest around her and Renée's caution about wild animals.

She got back into the car, shaking and certain she shouldn't be behind the wheel. But it was only a little farther, and the thought of spending a few hours in her car on the side of the road at the edge of the woods gave her the incentive to hold the nausea and the headache in check until she could get home.

An hour later she lay sprawled across her bed, trapped in bizarre, elongated dreams exquisitely erotic in nature and darkly disturbing in tone. Her dream-self couldn't move, couldn't speak. Above her, indigo blue eyes turned to winter ice, blazing into hers, possessive, triumphant, full of consuming hunger. In them she saw her reflection: grey eyes unfocused, mouth slack, auburn hair a fiery cloud on the white pillow beneath her head.

That's not me, it's not me! she tried to scream. His mouth crushed down on hers, bringing black oblivion.

The headache throbbed like a base drum out of control until at last her medicine dragged her so deeply into slumber the dream couldn't reach her.

SARAH'S GARDEN
October 20, 2004

"You're late," Ron remarked as Beth dragged herself into the bar the next afternoon. She looked like hell, her face pale and sickly, eyes underscored with purple circles that seemed to get darker every day. Not to mention the faint bruises in the shapes of fingers on her neck.

She winced, casting a glance at the clock as she sank down into the nearest chair. "Yeah, yeah," she croaked, waving a hand weakly in dismissal. "So fire me. Please."

Ron, casting a glance around the bar to make sure Scott and

Denny were still in the kitchen, took the chair next to her and leaned in close. "You haven't accepted any more – ah – *gifts* from my father, have you?" he asked in a low tone.

"Going to tell me about Tiana?"

His mouth tightened. "Are you kidding?"

"You took the words right out of my mouth." She let her head sink to the table, draping her arm over her face. Ron chuckled.

"Can I get you anything?"

"A gun?"

"I was thinking more like a bed."

She cracked one eye open. "No, thank you. I've never felt less in the mood, but I'm very flattered."

He snorted. "I said a bed, not a love nest." She waved a lethargic hand at him in dismissal, and he sighed. "You're no good to me in this condition."

"I just told you that."

He pinched her cheek gently. "I'll have Scott run you home."

Kim groaned. "Have you been in a car with him lately?"

"The alternative is me." Her eyes opened in alarm, and he laughed.

"I can make it. How about I lie down in the break room and come out when we actually have customers?"

"How about you just go find the sofa and stay there? Scott or Denny can work a double shift. Neither will mind."

"Liar. Scott will mind plenty." She opened her eyes cautiously and groaned.

Ron pushed away from the table, a hand under her elbow prompting her to rise as well. "All right, come on. Let's get you prone."

"Oh please. Is that the best come-on line you've got?"

"You're a riot. What did you do, drink a bottle of wine after you went home?" He slid an arm around her to keep her on her feet, and was surprised when she leaned her head against his chest. She must be ill; he doubted she would show any sign of weakness if she weren't.

"No, just a bottle of water like I do every night. I think I'm going to be sick."

Her skin had indeed turned that awful greenish hue that usually preceded a bout of vomiting. "I'll get you a bucket," he promised and hoped she could contain it until then.

He ushered her through the kitchen and to the break room without a word to the rest of his staff. Scott paid him no mind anyway, studiously ignoring him. Denny lifted a brow, but Ron thought it more prudent to get her off her feet without pausing to explain.

A grateful sigh was her only reaction to reaching her destination. He covered her with a blanket and she curled into a ball, eyes shut tightly. She didn't move or protest when his hand covered her forehead, feeling for fever, and his fingers pressed on her carotid artery, checking her pulse. Her heart raced along at a frantic pace from her exertion.

"I'll be back with your bucket in a second. You'd better still be lying there."

"The world is spinning. I don't think I'll be going anywhere."

"Maybe you should open your eyes."

"It's worse then. Go away."

"You want some coffee?"

She made a ghastly face. "No."

"Milk? Water?"

"Go *away*," she repeated firmly, closing her eyes.

He sighed. "All right. I'll be in the kitchen."

Before he had gone three steps out of the room, she called out, "Crackers."

"I'm beginning to think so," he muttered. "What about crackers?"

"Got any?"

"Nope. I'll send Scott to the market when it opens."

She opened her eyes, all trace of humor gone. "Will he do it?"

"He'll do it for you." He left before he was tempted to say more, and this time she didn't call him back.

Scott had left the kitchen while Ron had been in with Beth, but Denny watched him patiently, waiting for an explanation.

"She's ill," Ron said, a little annoyed at the scrutiny – an annoyance that increased as Denny suppressed a knowing smile. "Clammy, nauseated, pulse going wild."

"That'll pass when she gets over you," his friend murmured,

tongue-in-cheek. Ron shot him a nasty look.

"Oh, ha ha. More like the 'flu."

"Want me to take a look at her?"

"I didn't know you were a medic."

"I have many talents," his friend assured him.

"I'm sure. Let her sleep," Ron advised. "When she wakes up, yeah, take a look. If she'll let you."

Denny said with quiet conviction, "She'll let me."

Ron didn't doubt that she would.

* * * * *

Kimberly fought her way through the brambles, stopping often to disentangle her jacket from clutching filbert bushes and her hair from the reach of low-hanging pine boughs. She followed no discernible path through the forest, but she had no fear she would become lost.

Her certainty paid off when she stumbled upon a small stone cottage squatting in the middle of a small clearing, surrounded by an immaculate white-washed picket fence. Herbs and flowers, green and flourishing despite the heavy October chill, threatened to spill over the fence and into the forest. The gate stood open in invitation, but Kim didn't cross its threshold. There seemed to be an invisible barrier that prevented her from taking another step.

The sound of footsteps on gravel reached her before she saw the old woman rounding the corner of the cottage. A wicker basket stuffed with cut plants hung on her arm, and her sprightly step belied her age. She didn't give any indication at first that she'd seen Kimberly, but she suspected the woman had known all along about the intruder at her gate.

And Kimberly felt like an intruder as the woman straightened and slowly came her way, negotiating paths which seemed to crisscross unnecessarily through the garden. She stopped just inside the gate, pinning her with a steady, blue-eyed gaze.

"Have you come to seek my services?"

Kim shook her head. She didn't remember deciding to come or why she had felt it necessary.

"Why are you here?" The old woman asked sharply, her eyes narrowing. Her hands drew the ends of her shawl together defensively. "Who are you?"

"Who are *you*?" Kim countered. "Why do you live in the middle of the woods with no path to your house?"

"There is a path, but it's not yours to tread. Only those who seek my services can find it."

Kim suddenly knew who she had found. "You're Sarah Bennett."

"Yes. But you're not Bethany Fairchild."

Cold fear clutched Kim's heart. "What do you mean?"

"Bethany Fairchild is a mask you wear. But that's no concern of mine. We all wear masks." Sarah Bennett set the basket down at her feet and took a step closer. Kim felt the hairs on back of her neck stiffen in alarm.

"I'm only here to find someone."

"The lost are no concern of yours." Sarah turned without another word and began to wind her way back through the garden toward her cottage. Kim saw that the tiny house had no entrance.

"Your home has no door," she called out, and Sarah turned.

"You're marked. You're prohibited from entering."

"Prohibited? By whom – my *God*?" Kim couldn't help the sarcastic twist of her mouth.

Sarah studied Kim's face for a critical moment. "No. Mine. You have no god."

She disappeared into the cottage, through a door she could see but which Kimberly could not. Kim took a step after her, crossing the threshold of the garden, and exquisite pain exploded through her body like a massive electrical current, flinging her violently backward into the shrubs. Her head cracked against the trunk of a stout oak tree, and the world went black.

She flailed out of the dream, scattering tattered magazines from the coffee table onto the floor and into the bucket Ron had brought in while she was sleeping. Her heart hammered unnaturally fast, and a thumping headache drove waves of nausea through her. The somewhat ratty break room seemed like paradise.

A quiet knock sounded, and the door cracked open a scant couple of inches. Scott Schaefer poked his head into the opening, hesitant until he saw her upright.

"Hey!" he said softly, slipping through the door. He had a large box of saltines in one hand and a bottle of water in the other. Quiet voices just outside the break room drifted in through the open door at a decibel too low for her to distinguish the words.

Kim smiled wanly. "Hey, Scott."

"I got these for you an hour or so ago, but you were out like a light. I didn't want to disturb you." He sat down on the coffee table near her and began opening the crackers. "How are you feeling?"

"I'm not quite sure." Her stomach had mostly settled during her sleep, but she still felt unsteady and disoriented. "Thank you for the crackers; I didn't mean to be a bother."

"You aren't." He struggled with the waxed paper tube the crackers came packaged in, and saltines rained down on their laps. "Well, at least they're open."

Kim picked up a cracker and began to nibble a corner experimentally. Her stomach didn't immediately rebel, so she thought it might be safe to eat a few more. She gathered up the ones that had fallen into her lap, saved back three, and gave the rest to Scott. He stuffed them into the wrapper without looking at her.

"Think you'll be ready to go home soon?"

She nodded. "I think so. Just give me a few minutes to get my bearings."

Scott nodded silently. He glanced up frequently, uncomfortably, unable to keep his eyes off the finger-shaped bruises on her throat.

"Does it hurt?" he finally asked.

She lifted one shoulder in a shrug, swallowed with difficulty, and took a large swig from the water bottle. "Yes. As does my head and my hip."

"You're angry with me."

Kim shrugged again. "Why should I be angry with you?"

"You're angry with me because of Ron," he clarified sharply. "What I said to him."

"It's none of my business." But she burned with curiosity. She had never dreamed Ron was what had happened to Scott and Tiana's long-ago relationship.

"You think I'm being too hard on him."

"I think you're being deliberately blind," she snapped, then closed her eyes and took a deep breath. "I'm sorry. Didn't I just say it's none of my business?"

Scott snorted impatiently. "If you have something to say, just say it, whether or not you think it's your business."

"You were very unfair last night. The situation was exactly what it looked like: Nadine attacked me, Ron defended me, you came home and misread the situation."

"Excuse me?" His voice raised a couple decibels, causing the muted conversation in the kitchen to stumble. "I heard what she said!"

"Yes. What *she* said. You yourself told me you thought you'd been the victim of witchcraft. Perhaps she was, too."

"Nadine? Who would bewitch Nadine?"

"Maybe not intentionally. Maybe something went wrong. Scott, what happens when a witch's spell doesn't work?"

He scowled in irritation. "How'm I supposed to know?"

"I just thought you might." She could see there would be no reasonable conversation with him today; he harbored too much anger. She didn't want it aimed at her.

The door creaked open again, this time letting in Denny and Ron; the latter's expression tied her stomach in anxious knots. The concern he had shown as he helped her into the break room this morning had given way to a deep apprehension. He tried to hide it but didn't manage very well.

"I'll take her home, Scott. Would you mind the place while we're finishing up here?"

Scott's mouth tightened furiously at the obvious dismissal, but he shrugged and stalked away, pushing open the break room door with more force than necessary.

Denny perched on the coffee table in front of her. "I have some basic medical training," he explained. "I'd just like to make sure you're all right before I send you home."

She raised a brow. Before *he* sent her home? "All right. I'm sure it's just the 'flu or something like it."

He grunted his response, took a penlight from his shirt pocket, and shone it first in one eye and then the other. What he saw made him frown and give Ron a sidelong glance that seemed to speak volumes.

"What is it?"

Pocketing the light, he studied the shadows under her eyes while his fingers timed her pulse. Another glance went Ron's way.

"What medications do you take regularly?"

"Just my migraine meds. Maxalt-MLT."

"No birth control? Recreational drugs?"

She scowled. "No to both. What's the problem?"

"Your symptoms are more indicative of medication than of a virus," he replied absently. "That's why Ron asked you if you'd accepted any gifts from Caleb."

"Caleb?" she asked, a little wildly. "What's he got to do with anything?" But Cody's words floated up from her memory: *My brother's following you. He has a weakness for much younger women.*

"He's well-known for spouting the benefits of herbal remedies. Sometimes amateur herbalists misidentify a plant and end up using something harmful."

"I see. Well, to set your minds at ease," and she included Ron in her irritated glare, "I haven't spoken to Caleb since my second day here. And I don't usually take herbal medication regardless of who offers it to me."

"Is there any way your food source could have become unintentionally medicated?"

"I suppose anything is possible, but it's doubtful. Like I said, I don't take anything but my migraine meds. I mostly eat here, at home, or at the diner."

"Do me a favor and keep track of what you eat. We might be able to narrow down what's making you ill. Also, start using tap water, just in case. Mills' aquifer is actually quite clean and tastes good." Denny got up and moved to the other side of the coffee table, effectively making Ron the focus of her attention.

"You ready?"

"I think so. Can you contain yourself and drive like a normal human being for a change?"

"I make no promises." He snagged her purse, slinging the strap over her shoulder, and put a solicitous hand under her elbow to support her. He didn't speak on the drive. Kimberly leaned her cheek against the window and closed her eyes so she didn't have to watch the dizzying speed with which the trees – and the stop signs – went whizzing by.

In what she felt sure was record time, he stopped in front of the cottage. Kim didn't wait for him to come around to open her door and help her out of the truck. She bailed from the cab with undue haste, drinking in the cool, refreshing air. He waited patiently in front of the truck.

"I thought it might be better just to get the drive over with as quickly as possible."

She nodded. "I'll be all right."

He led the way inside, holding the door for her and closing it behind her. When she reached her bedroom, she collapsed with relief on the bed and shut her eyes. She heard Ron rustling around in the kitchen, and a few minutes later he came in with a glass of water from the tap and the afghan from the living room sofa.

"Are you going to tell me what's going on?" Kim asked without opening her eyes. The afghan floated over her, and he tucked it neatly under her chin before answering.

"You said you drank a bottle of water before bed last night, and since you were really sick this morning, I thought maybe you got a contaminated case of water."

"Could be," she murmured. "They all leak."

"All of them?"

"Whole case so far. It's a pain in the ass."

"That's fitting," he replied with a trace of amusement. "I'm going to take the rest of them, have them examined."

Kim opened her eyes now, watching him as he walked toward the bedroom door. "Ron, what does Denny do for a living? Is he a doctor or a paramedic or something?"

"Right now Denny's a bartender. And your landlord."

"Not my only landlord though. You are too, right?" He lifted a shoulder. "That's what I thought."

"He owns a larger percentage of the cottage for various reasons. We own another house together just down the road. I'd have rented it to you – and would have felt more comfortable with you in that one, to be honest – except the last tenant left unexpectedly, and I didn't feel right renting it out from under him in case he comes back."

"He skipped out?"

"Not sure. Borrowed my fishing gear, and next thing I know he's cleared his things out of the house and vanished. He might just have relocated for a couple of weeks; he's a professional researcher."

Her breath caught in her chest and her heart thudded. Her father – he had to be talking about her father!

"I need to get back to the tavern. Will you be all right?"

"Yes." She waited until he was about step out the bedroom door to ask, "Will you tell me what happened with you and Tiana?"

"Oh, c'mon – "

"Please?"

"It's a long time in the past."

"I need to know what kind of man you are."

"That won't tell you."

"Maybe it will," she countered. "I *need* – "

"You *want* to know. There's a difference."

She frowned irritably. "Split some more hairs, will you? After Nadine tried to throttle me and after what happened when you...when we...I think I have a right to know."

His answering smile was both sardonic and bleak. "Maybe it was exactly what Scott thought it was. Did you ever stop to consider that?"

Her smile faded. She closed her eyes and let the silence gather between them. "I don't believe you," she whispered into the silence.

She opened her eyes, but he was already gone.

STALKER
October 20, 2004

"Uncle Ron, you aren't paying attention." Anna Malone tapped her pencil on her math book impatiently, wishing that rather than her reclaiming his attention, the polynomials would vanish from her textbook, thus making his attention unnecessary. She didn't want to talk to him about polynomials; she wanted to talk to him about Jared Olmstead.

"Mmmm?"

His eyes moved back to the textbook with obvious reluctance, abandoning their covert observation of his father, who sat at a table across the room. Anna had not failed to notice how he kept himself between her and Caleb – and how he did not ever put his back to his father.

"Can we finish this? I really need to pass the quiz tomorrow or I might fail algebra."

"Are you going to be an engineer or an architect, Anna?" He arched a dark brow at her, and something in her stomach swooped and fluttered. Oh, he was a handsome man, her honorary uncle. His dark good looks and brooding manner were probably why she had been attracted to Jared, who was equally dark and reticent.

"Doubtful. I want to go to the Culinary Institute of America and then open a bakery."

"Well, you should at least have a firm grasp of algebra. You'll be dealing with math every day."

"Tell me how polynomials are going to help me bake," she challenged, trying to keep the acrimony out of her voice. She'd had this same argument with her parents when she'd asked to drop algebra and take business math instead. She had expected Ron to back her reasoning, not echo her parents' logic.

"I have no idea," he admitted, finally smiling. "But I promised your dad I would try to reason with you."

"Why is it reasonable to make me take a subject I probably won't have any use for in my future? My GPA is going to tank. They should just let me take business math. I'll ace that."

He sighed, flipping the book closed. "They think you want to drop algebra so you won't have to do so much homework and studying, which will then give you more time for boys."

She couldn't stop herself from half-glancing over her shoulder to the large front window and the boy who skulked just outside in the parking lot, waiting for her. Although teens were allowed in the tavern until 9 p.m., Ron didn't allow Jared Olmstead to come in when he was tutoring her. He said it was because Jared was a distraction, but she suspected it was more because he didn't approve of him.

"Well," she said, frowning thoughtfully. "There is that. But seriously, Uncle Ron, I'm only going to be young once. Why should I be constantly studying and never having any fun?"

He turned to look out the window too, pinning Jared with a narrow-eyed gaze that Jared couldn't see because of the reflective treatment on the windows. But the boy shifted as though he could feel Ron's steely-eyed scrutiny, and Ron turned back with a grim smile of satisfaction.

"Perhaps it's who you want to have fun with," he said. He suddenly looked uncomfortable himself, and Anna willed him to shut up before he embarrassed them both. But he pressed on, his cheeks flaming red. "You're very young. I'd hate to see you make a mistake that has lifetime conseque – "

"Uncle Ron, stop! You're embarrassing me." Her blush went so deep it felt like a third degree burn. "I'm not stupid, you know."

His eyes slid toward the window, pulling his head with them. He looked troubled as he glared at Jared Olmstead.

"Will you stop glaring at my boyfriend?"

He asked without looking at her, "Is that what he is?"

"Well," she amended, blushing again. "He hasn't said it in so many words, but he spends more time with me than he spends with…" She broke off as he turned to look at her, cutting her eyes away from his face. "He probably will never ask me if you keep glaring at him all the time. You're scaring him."

"He should be scared," Ron muttered. "If he lays one finger on you in a way I find inappropriate, he'll lose it."

"And that would be why he hasn't asked," she replied with a sigh. She looked across the tavern, catching the icy gaze of Caleb Schaefer. His dispassionate stare stole her warmth and rational thought. Anna shivered but found herself strangely unable to look away. He stared back until Ron noticed and, mouth compressed into a thin line, turned her chair sideways to face him.

"Anna, about this boy," he began gravely. He flicked a glance toward his father. "He spends too much time with my father while his is in here drinking himself into a stupor."

"That isn't Jared's fault," she retorted, the first traces of anger making her sound petulant.

"I know that, but – "

"No one holds it against you that *your* father – "

"Enough."

His clipped tone left no room for argument. He looked angry, and Anna felt a moment's regret. A *fleeting* moment's regret; she was angry too. He, of all people, should know what it was like to have a complete scoundrel for a father – and that it wasn't the child's fault.

She stole another glance at Caleb Schaefer, who still watched her with those cool blue eyes. He was smiling slightly, as though her and Ron's obvious disagreement amused him. Scowling, she slid her math book off the table and into her book bag, shouldering it as she stood up. Ron caught her wrist.

"Anna, please."

"I have places to be."

"And I have your best interests at heart."

"I think you just have your own prejudices at heart." She wrenched her wrist out of his grip and flounced out the door of the tavern with what she hoped was a respectable amount of dignity.

Jared pushed away from the iron railing between the sidewalk and the parking slots – put there to keep drunks from driving through the front of the tavern – and transferred her heavy bag to his own shoulder.

"You look mad."

"Yeah. Uncle Ron…" She made an angry face and sent a smoking glare through the front window.

"I don't think he likes me very much."

"He's just being stupid. Let's go before he comes out here and makes it worse."

She sent another glower toward the tavern as she climbed into the passenger seat of Jared's aging Sentra. No way was she going to take advice on romance from a man who hadn't had one since she was in kindergarten.

Jared headed the car toward the drive-up burger joint near the town square, and Anna pushed aside a rising sense of guilt, turning her attention to the cute boy behind the wheel and the numerous exciting possibilities the afternoon held.

* * * * *

Shadows filled the woods around the house, deepening the late afternoon to near night. Bird calls randomly cut through the hush: starlings sounding their last clicks and whistles before night fell. Off to her left two squirrels chased each other around the trunk of a stout maple, their claws scrabbling on the rough bark. Kim watched them for a moment, smiling slightly, and then turned back to the house. Her sudden movement flushed a covey of quail from the cover of a firethorn shrub, and they ran pell-mell toward the thicket of the woods beyond the clearing, top-knots bobbing frantically.

She approached with a heavy sense of trepidation, crisp leaves crunching under her feet. She should be at home, reading a good book, starting a new research project, checking her inbox for such a project – and not at her home in Mills, either. She should be at her condo in San Bernardino or her father's cabin in Forest Falls. There was no earthly reason for her to be in Pennsylvania; it was obvious Todd was no longer here.

Her numerous calls and text messages to his cell still remained unanswered. She'd even sent several e-mails to him, thinking that perhaps he'd lost his phone but was somewhere he had internet access.

Silence was the only reply, and in that silence her imagination conjured a hundred horrors that could have befallen him. Her common sense told her to get out of this bizarre town while she still could, with both heart and limbs still intact. Her reckless nature, however, refused to let her flee, and it already knew what her mind refused to accept: it was already too late for her heart.

She had awakened just before dusk. The throbbing headache that had followed her into slumber had abated while she slept, enough to let her dream. But something was wrong with her gift; this dream had come in fragments, in flashes of breaking glass and spraying blood, screams and guttural snarls – but she couldn't see the people's faces.

When she had rolled onto her side and felt something sharp poke her in the hip, she'd remembered Ron's earlier words. *We own another house together, just down the road. I'd have rented it to you except the last tenant left unexpectedly.*

Just down the road. And she just happened to have an unidentified key. Could it possibly unlock the other Willow Road house? Her hand had slid into her pocket and brought out the bit of serrated metal; it glinted in the waning light of day. And suddenly it seemed like a very good idea to go to the other house.

She drove because she didn't think she had the strength to walk there, explore, and walk back – not to mention the fact that it would be dark soon. The woods at night were not something she wanted to experience. The house wasn't hard to find; the driveway was clearly visible, about a quarter of a mile from Stoneridge Way and on the opposite side of Willow Road from her own. It sat nearer the road than the cottage, so she had parked around back and was careful to stick close to the shadows.

Surreptitious peeks in the windows assured her the house was empty. She could be in and out without him ever knowing – without *anyone* ever knowing – and back in her house before supper. Yes, it was a fine idea while she'd still been safe in her bed, but now that she was here, her heart pounded erratically and she felt faint with irrational fear.

Nothing about the structure seemed spooky in the slightest; it was a rancher hailing from the 1970's, roomy but nondescript. The classic stucco above the Roman brick had been substituted with lap siding, painted a traditional white, but otherwise this could have been any one of a hundred like homes she had seen in SoCal. Nothing about it screamed Todd's presence.

She inserted the key in the lock anyway and was surprised when the door swung open easily on oiled hinges. A plain white wall faced her; the door opened onto a small entry way. She stepped through and closed the door behind her. The click of the latch echoed. Unlike the cottage, this house was sparsely furnished, the pieces sturdy but unremarkable. No clutter littered the chunky coffee table. Likewise, the dining room table stood empty but for a layer of dust and a handsome, beaten copper bowl stuffed with an artful silk flower arrangement.

Durable brown short shag carpet muffled her footfalls as she travelled through the empty house. White walls faced her at every turn, seeming whiter because of the coffee-brown carpet. Her father must have gone stark raving mad; there wasn't a white wall in his cabin except the bathroom ceiling. He liked vibrant color around him, said it piqued the imagination, which led him to untraditional information. Many people thought research was dry and absolute, like algebra. Todd found it fascinating and knew that creative methods unearthed valuable knowledge.

The kitchen was unremarkable, typical for a rancher: a U-shaped counter with a breakfast bar on the side open to the rest of the room, an old retro 1960's chrome and Formica table lurking behind it. The back door opened to leaf-strewn cement patio. A few paces behind it, close enough that if both were opened at the same time the knobs would lock together, was the basement door. *Cellar*, she thought randomly. *Ron calls it a cellar.*

The door was cheap varnished oak. She stared at it for a long, silent moment, then turned the knob, swung it open, and groped for the light.

The cellar stairs went down halfway to a landing and turned on a switchback. She went down cautiously, peering around the wall as she reached the landing. Her heart thudded a frantic rhythm, but like the rest of the house, the basement was mostly empty and unexceptional. She explored quickly yet thoroughly, but even the storage cabinet built under the stairs yielded no secrets. Todd had left nothing behind.

She went back upstairs, closing the door behind her. Her breath came short and her pulse roared in her ears. The linoleum swam before her eyes as she bent over, bracing her hands on her knees until she regained her equilibrium and a modicum of strength. Nausea rolled her stomach; there was no fighting it off. By instinct Kim bolted for the bathroom. In her haste she dropped her car keys in the hallway; she vaguely heard the clatter of metal on metal before she dropped to her knees and spilled the contents of her stomach into the toilet.

This couldn't continue. She'd rarely been sick in the last ten years – migraines aside – and she didn't understand why suddenly she could barely drag herself out of bed and couldn't keep anything down. Denny had made a vague mention of her symptoms being more indicative to a reaction to medication than to an illness, but she hadn't taken anything except her migraine medicine, and it didn't make sense that her food source – either at home, the tavern, or the diner – could conveniently be contaminated.

The nausea finally passed, and Kim flushed away the evidence, pushing herself off the floor. Her shaky legs carried her into the hallway, where she paused, wobbling, looking for her keys. Nothing lay in the hallway.

"What the hell?" she muttered. She knew she had dropped them in here; there was nowhere for them to go, except... She remembered the clink of metal on metal. The cold air return. "Oh, great."

She dropped to her knees beside the metal grate, which had been painted dark brown to match the carpet. The openings in the grate were large enough her keys could have fallen through; with her luck they would have fallen right into the middle, where the air vent opened to the duct. She'd probably have to dismantle the furnace to get them back.

Groaning, she lifted the heavy grate and set it out of the way. *There'd better not be spiders in here*, she thought darkly, and plunged her hand into the vent opening, groping around. Ductwork usually stretched parallel to the floor until it reached the furnace, which in this house sat almost dead-center in the cellar; she figured she had four or five feet of horizontal duct before it turned downward. Hopefully her keys hadn't rolled to the elbow.

She shifted position to allow her arm deeper access. The duct was amazingly clean but she could still feel a layer of dust on her fingers. A little farther---ah, there they were! Her index finger snagged the tip of a key. She reached in still further to catch the ring, and felt an odd, raised edge.

The keys were of the utmost importance, so she hooked them and pulled them out, stuffing them into her jeans pocket. Then she slid her hand back in the duct, feeling her way to the raised edge. A careful exploration gave her the impression of a large paper rectangle – an envelope, most likely. She lifted the edge carefully so as not to push it farther into the duct and out of her reach, then secured it between her finger and thumb.

It came out easily, crumpling a bit as she wrangled it through the vent opening. It was indeed an envelope, brown manila with a thin layer of dust. Obviously it hadn't been there long. *Why* it had been put there remained a mystery.

She turned it over, but there were no markings on either side. The clasp was fastened and the flap had been sealed. Whoever had put the envelope in the duct had not taken any chances on its contents spilling out. She bent the prongs of the clasp up and slid her finger under the flap to tear it open. The edge of the flap sliced through her skin, drawing blood.

"Damn!" She blotted the wound on her hoodie – grateful that it was red – and emptied the envelope onto the carpet beside her.

The top layer consisted of neat copies of microfiche documents: newspaper articles from the Mills' newspaper, *The Gazette*, and from various other news publications around the state. She thumbed through them quickly, skimming the article headlines. *Mills, PA couple attacked by wild dog; Mills, PA man reported missing; Mills, PA man catatonic after three-day ordeal in forest.* She paused on this one, two words in the article jumping out and grabbing her attention: *Aaron Schaefer.*

The crunch of tires on the gravel drive brought her head up, and she realized she had completely lost track of time. She stuffed everything back into the envelope and shoved it under her hoodie, tucking the bottom into the waistband of her jeans, and then crept toward the back door. The latch snicked shut as she heard the car stop out front and a door open.

She was caught; there was no way to leave without being seen. No way to hide, either, since her car was parked in plain view of anyone who cared to come into the back yard. Her only choice was weak subterfuge, so she crossed the patio, careful to sweep her feet noisily through the leaves, and rounded the corner of the house.

The occupant of the car was coming around the house as well, following the beam of a flashlight. Kim jumped, letting out a startled shriek even though she had been expecting to run into someone, and shielded her eyes as the beam bounced to her face. He stopped dead in his tracks, a suspicious frown his only sign of surprise at seeing her, and he lowered the light.

"Miz Fairchild. Out – ah – seeing the sights?" Caleb Schaefer raised a black brow in inquiry.

She laughed weakly. "Ron mentioned he had another rental house and that it was empty. I thought I would check it out."

"Moving so soon?" His voice was smooth, like velvet, invoking contradictory sensations: fear and revulsion warred with a strange, melting desire. Undoubtedly he would be a consummate lover. She shoved the thought away, but not before her mind had thrown up an image from her dream: his ice-blue eyes above her, the too-exquisite sensation of him inside her. She blushed, glad for the darkness so she wouldn't have to explain herself.

"Thinking about it," she replied, striving to sound casual. "The cottage is a little more remote than I'm comfortable with. I didn't think it would matter, but it does."

His careful scrutiny made her squirm. "A little late to be house hunting," he remarked, and added pointedly, "and without a flashlight."

"I didn't plan to look around for so long. Nighttime caught up with me." She smiled tentatively, relieved when his answering smile came fast and genuine.

"It comes on quickly once the sun goes behind the mountains. Have you been inside?" She shook her head. "I'm sure Aaron would be delighted to show you around."

"I haven't mentioned it to him yet," she admitted, scuffing the toe of her shoe through the leaves. "He'll probably just get annoyed."

"Have you tried the door? Maybe it's unlocked." He started back around to the front of the house, and she had no choice but to follow or appear rude – or shifty. "We don't often lock doors around here. There's no vagrant problem and people are more or less honest."

Her heart hammered out of control as he took the porch steps in two leaps and grasped the door knob. She couldn't remember if she'd locked it again after letting herself in, but she fervently hoped she had. Being alone with him inside a secluded house, with no chance of unexpected interruptions, held possibilities both dreadful and exhilarating. His hand turned, fingers tightening on the burnished brass...and then stopped. He sent her an apologetic smile.

"Ah, well. Aaron's not as trusting as some." He skipped back down the steps to her. "I'll see you to your car."

"That's not necessary," she said, stepping away as he reached out to take her arm. He held up the flashlight with a mocking grin. "Oh...right. Thanks."

She kept careful distance between them, arms hugging herself to keep the envelope from flopping around under her jacket. He held the light aimed at her car door so she could find the keyhole, and held the door as she climbed in. Her foot skidded on a slick patch of mud, and this time she couldn't elude his touch. His hand under her elbow kept her from falling and guided her safely into her seat. His fingers tightened slightly just before letting go, and he took a step back.

"Have a nice evening, Miz Fairchild."

Kim looked up, flushing again when he beamed a smile at her. Damn these gorgeous Schaefer men. "Thanks. You too."

She turned the key in the ignition and at last he shut her door and moved away from the car. Kim turned the car around in an awkward circle and headed down the driveway, pretending not to see his farewell wave.

Finally safe in her own home, she sank onto the sofa and attempted to school her racing heart. Of all people to run into while unlawfully entering a house, it had to be Caleb Schaefer.

It was only as she pulled the manila envelope from under her jacket that she realized Caleb had no reason to be at Ron's rental house.

My brother is following you, Cody had said, and here indeed seemed to be all the proof she needed.

"What do you want, Caleb?" she whispered. "What could you possibly want with me?"

She didn't know if her shiver was of dread …or anticipation.

PRISONER OF AN UNHOLY WAR
October 21, 2004

In an effort to ward off the numbing chill in the cell, Todd Garrett rubbed his frigid hands vigorously over his arms. It didn't offer much relief; his hands weren't any warmer than the arms he tried to heat up. He drew in a deep breath; bitter air filled his lungs and he coughed it out, watching his breath jet out in long, white plumes.

He knew he could not survive many more nights in this degree of cold, perhaps not even one more. By his best estimate, he'd already been awake for nearly two full days trying to avoid what could be a deadly, hypothermic sleep. He ate whatever they brought him, no matter how foul it looked or smelled, knowing he had to feed his inner furnace to stay alive.

This was their latest form of punishment. Positive Todd had family somewhere who might raise a ruckus if he vanished, they had first attempted to beat the information out of him. They wanted no loose ends – or loose cannons – once they'd dealt with him.

When the beatings failed to produce the desired results, they had taken away his blankets, coat and gloves, and the small propane heater that had kept him warm during his incarceration in the Wyckham House. Meals came once a day in meager quantities, and he had to eat quickly; they only gave him ten minutes to choke down the pig slop they passed off as cuisine. He would have died of thirst days ago if not for Tiana Michaels sneaking in water.

At first they had been unfailingly polite, and while the Wyckham House could be considered nothing less than a prison, with its massive stone walls and heavy oak doors dead-bolted on the outside, he had at least been kept warm and fed. His captor had even been downright apologetic: *I'm sorry, Todd, but if you hadn't been snooping around, I wouldn't have had to bring you in. You understand.*

Well, Todd did understand. He didn't like it, but he understood. This was a war, and he had been taken its prisoner. He supposed he should be grateful they hadn't shot him outright, but he knew it would have been more of a mercy than anything they might have planned.

He cast a glance at the tiny window in the door of his equally tiny cell, seeing nothing but blackness beyond. Held somewhere underground in the labyrinthine passages of what could only be called a dungeon, Todd knew he had no chance of escape. He had been unconscious when they brought him in, and even if he could manage to free himself from the cell, he didn't fool himself into thinking he could find his way out before they caught him.

The icy stones had numbed his back and buttocks; he didn't generate enough body heat to warm them. To keep his mind off how cold he felt, he thought back to when his scant amenities had been confiscated.

It had been at least five days ago, if he could still count on his internal clock to accurately track time. Their black magic priest himself had come to see him for the first time since Todd had been abducted, and he was *not* a happy man. He had interrogated Todd for hours, punching him hard in the gut or the kidneys or delivering a knuckle punch to the large muscle of his thigh when Todd gave an answer he didn't like.

The questions had all been centered on family, friends, and business associates. By the end of the evening's festivities, Todd had begun to suspect that something had happened to cause a high level of nervous tension within the Circle, as they called themselves. When his interrogator had left the cell, Todd had been black and blue from ribs to thighs, unable to put any weight on his left leg, and he had pissed blood for a long while.

But he hadn't given them what they wanted, no matter what they had done to him.

He closed his eyes briefly, bringing them much needed relief from the cold air, and offered a silent prayer to God, who seemed to be his only friend of late: *Keep Kimberly safe. Keep her safe and away from Pennsylvania!*

* * * * *

He awoke from treacherous slumber at the sound of the deadbolt rattling. Keys jangled together as the lock fumbled open, and he recognized the light touch with relief. Tiana Michaels. Funny the things you became familiar with: the feel of a lover's body, the tread of a trusted friend, the rumble of a familiar car's engine. The different sounds of your various jailers.

His limbs were stiff, numb with cold as he braced his back against the wall to help him stand. He didn't want to be caught at a disadvantage if anyone came in with her, but he couldn't make his legs support his weight. There was nowhere to hide in the cell; it barely measured seven feet by five feet, and the only niche was a small fireplace where his propane heater had been before they had confiscated it.

The door creaked as it opened, and Tiana's petite form slipped inside behind the dim glow of a propane camp lantern. Todd squinted against the light, momentarily blinded. She lowered it to the floor and stepped back toward the shadowy doorway.

"Are they going to give me back my blankets?" Todd asked.

"Yes. I have some things for you." She reached back into the dark corridor and dragged in a large box. Todd made another valiant attempt at rising, dismayed when he failed again. "I can manage," she said gently.

She rummaged through the box's contents, tossing badly needed items to him as she came across them: gloves, a scarf, a hat, hand and feet warmers. These items landed in his lap, but he couldn't do anything with them; his hands refused to obey his brain's commands. He looked at her in bleak resignation.

"I'll help," she said simply. She knelt beside him and pulled the gloves onto his hands, then cracked a hand warmer for each hand to help speed the thawing process. "I brought your heater back, with plenty of propane for both it and the lantern. Be sure to keep it in the fireplace so the fumes vent out through the flu."

"Does he know?"

Tiana didn't ask whom he meant. "No. It's been five days, and you still haven't told him anything. It's pointless to torture you for information that you refuse to give."

She pulled his goose-down winter jacket out of the box. Todd almost cried with relief as she slung it around his shoulders and helped him guide his arms into the sleeves.

"He's going to be angry with you," he said. A shudder racked his body as he began to warm.

"It won't be the first time."

She left the rest of the items in the box; once warm enough, he would be able to rifle through it and take what he needed. He could even break down the box and use it as a pallet, providing another layer of protection between him and the cold stone floor.

"Thank you." The words galled him; after all, if she was not outright in league with them, she certainly did nothing to oppose them. But perhaps it was not her fault; she seemed to be as much a prisoner as he, albeit one who was free to move about the town at will.

She stood in obvious retreat by the door, reluctant to leave but visibly afraid to stay. "I thought you might like something to read." Her foot nudged the box closer to him; there was a paperback book on top of several folded blankets. He gave it only a cursory glance; he couldn't make out the title in the gloom.

"It gives some meaningful information in chapter twenty-four," she said persistently.

"Why don't you just let me go? You have a key, you know the way. You could come with me. I can keep you safe."

Tiana laughed bitterly. "No one can keep me safe, Todd. But being safe is not my lot in life."

"I have money, a lot of money. I know people who can give you a new identity – "

"A new identity that will be sold to the Circle for the right price," she replied, a hard bite to her voice. "You don't understand, Todd. I have tried to leave more than a dozen times. They always find me. *He* always finds me."

"It was bad luck. He's just a man," he said resolutely.

"He's just a man, and he's more than a man," she said inscrutably.

"What have they done to you?" he murmured, more to himself than to her. They had become larger than life to her, and she saw no escape. They couldn't be that powerful and long-reaching...could they?

"Why can't you just let me escape? You don't have to have any part in it but leaving the door unlocked."

"I can't let you go. You're dangerous now."

"No one would believe what little I have to tell," he said dryly. "And I'm not dangerous to the Circle if I don't know anything of value."

"It's not what you know; it's what you are." She yanked the book out of the box and opened it, shoving it under his nose. He saw with hopeless irony that she had brought him Alonzo Stafford's *Witch's Moon: Legends of the Werewolf* – the book he had been anxiously awaiting when he'd been kidnapped. She had highlighted a passage in yellow.

There is no cure for the werewolf who has been cursed by a witch's spell.

"Werewolf? But – I'm not – "

"They've been monitoring your mail, you know. He thought this book might give you too much information, so he made sure it never reached you. The moon isn't full yet, Todd. When it is, they will release you, but you will be in no position to appreciate it. And if it suits him, they will make sure she is where you can find her easily enough because she's already making them nervous."

"Who?" he whispered.

The word fell from her mouth with terrible finality, and in it Todd saw the end of his hope. "Kimberly."

He gained his feet and came toward her in a lurching, hitching gait. She stumbled backward to the door, preparing to run. But the cold had taken its toll; he staggered and dropped to his knees before he reached her. He hit the hard stone with a resounding crack and cried out, not with pain but in horror and helpless desperation.

"How?" he rasped. "I protected her! *How could you people find her when I took precautions?* "

Tiana stepped forward, her hand held out in supplication. "The Circle doesn't know! As soon as you were abducted, I alerted someone who could help. He arrived in Mills shortly before she did, and – "

He lifted his head, terror stamped on his face in sharp relief. "She's *here?*"

She gave a jerky little nod, still eying him warily. "In Mills, yes."

His strength fled, and he huddled on the floor, head bowed, his eyes on the shredded knees of his jeans. His panic was so great he was numb. She didn't try to soothe him, and he was thankful; her comfort would be of no use to him. She stood between him and freedom, and at this very moment he was afraid if she came too close, he would do whatever was necessary – even kill her – to escape his prison and protect his daughter.

"She's going by the name of Bethany Fairchild," she said when the silence became heavy and unnerving. "She's working for Ron Schaefer. We believe she's here looking for you."

"Of course she is," he said, exasperated. "Why else would she come? And she dragged Bethany into it, too. What explanation did they give for my disappearance? Did I fall into the river and drown? Wild animal attack?"

"You went back to California unexpectedly. Ron Schaefer is a bit miffed you took off with his fishing gear. When the Circle cleaned out your house, they didn't realize the fishing tackle wasn't yours. I sneaked it out and Fed-Ex'd it to your home."

"Why would you do that?"

"No one knew anything about your family, but I knew there had to be someone who would miss you. I sent that person clues."

"You mean you lured her here!" he snarled.

She bristled. "I did the only thing I could. Had I just called your home phone number and gave whoever answered an anonymous tip about your kidnapping, that person would have called in the authorities. The Circle would have slit your throat at the first opportunity, and then they would have gone after her. They don't like loose ends. How was I supposed to know who would get the box, or that she'd be rash and come here herself? I thought at the very most a private investigator would show up."

Todd just closed his eyes, shaking his head back and forth over and over again as though denial would erase everything. Of course she couldn't have known. No one but he and Bethany could have predicted Kimberly's impetuous actions.

"Let me go. The moon isn't full yet – I can get far away from Kimberly."

"What about other people, Todd? They have a right to live, too."

"I'll take care of it."

"I've no guarantee."

"I'm an honorable man."

"Honorable or not, your instinct to survive will mar your judgment. You might think you can control it, that you can be locked up during dangerous times and otherwise still lead a normal life. But the longer you're under the curse, the more animalistic you will become, until every shred of your honor is corrupted beyond redemption.

"You're a dangerous man now, Todd. I can't let you go. Had I known what they had planned – " She sighed and shook her head. "But you can't outrun a spell, and they would have had you anyway."

"This doesn't make any sense! Werewolves don't even exist!"

"Don't they?" She raised a brow. "You know how a chemist experiments to perfect a formula to make the best product?"

"Yes, but – " He broke off as her meaning became clear. "They're perfecting a spell?"

"Yes."

"But…a *werewolf?*"

"They've been trying for decades to achieve immortality. The goal is to create an immortal being that retains its ability for rational, human thought. So they decided to start with a being that's already immortal: the lycanthrope. Unfortunately, it's also unstable and the growing list of missing persons and people attacked and killed in the woods has attracted unwanted attention. Not to mention the loss of humanity as time goes on doesn't leave much room to enjoy everlasting life."

"And they're going to use this spell on themselves? Immortality at the expense of your soul and a few bodies left in your wake?"

Silence spun out between them, laden with her sorrow and his revulsion. Her lack of answer gave him all the answer he needed. Men had been lusting after immortality for centuries, unconcerned with the cost.

But this time Todd Garrett's soul – and his daughter's life – were the price. He vowed that if he ever escaped, there would be a day – a very bloody day – of reckoning.

FREEDOM

Tiana didn't know how he found out so quickly, but she didn't have time to dwell on it. It didn't matter anyway.

What mattered now was how badly he was going to beat her.

He had been waiting for her, standing just inside his room and out of sight from the hallway. She hadn't seen him until she was three steps past him and there was no avenue of retreat – no time to even recognize the danger. His fingers twisted into her hair and his other hand at her back, he drove her into the rough stone wall with bruising force, knocking the breath from her lungs and his ring of keys from her hand.

That was a problem. She had learned ways to ease the pain of the beatings – if she relaxed enough and regulated her breathing, the blows didn't hurt quite as much. Not that she would ever tell him that. He had given her a ghastly thrashing once when she'd forgotten herself and had failed to react to the sting of a willow switch on her bare buttocks. Blood had been shed that night – a lot of it and all hers. He had been forced to take her to Sarah Bennett to have splinters dug from her raw flesh, and she'd been unable to lie on her back for a week. The experience had left shiny silver scars from her shoulders to her buttocks.

But when he knocked the wind from her, her muscles tensed and the pain from the blows tripled – like now.

His fingers tightened in her hair, gripping closer to her scalp. "I asked a question."

Tiana concentrated on the texture of the rough stone millimeters in front of her face, trying to gasp in enough air to respond. "I answered," she squeaked.

Although she had been prepared for it, the swiftness – and forcefulness – with which he shoved her into the stone wall stole her breath again. Tears of pain scalded her eyes and rolled down her cheeks.

"Want to be flippant with me again? I'm sure I can break every bone in your face next time."

His question was a trap; to answer that she hadn't been flip was to fan the flames of his wrath. To apologize for being flip would ignite his temper just as quickly. So she remained silent, her tongue exploring her cheek, which was already swelling. Her teeth had left a ragged gash in the soft lining, and she tasted blood.

He pressed closer, seeming to envelop her. His voice was a seductive croon in her ear – another trap. Seduce her and make her think the time of violence had passed, and when her guard had been lowered he would beat her until she lost consciousness. There was no point in crying for mercy; he would simply ask her why she insisted on driving him to hurt her even as he delivered the vicious blows. It was always her fault. Always.

"Who told you to give him back his things? What made you think you could act without my express permission?"

"You were going to kill him while making your point. What good would he be then?"

He yanked her head back so hard than pain radiated through her scalp and down through her neck and shoulders. "You stupid cow. He can't die unless silver comes in contact with his blood. He's under the lycanthrope curse."

Play stupid, she chanted silently. *Play stupid and maybe it won't be so bad this time.* "How was I supposed to know? It's not like I'm told anything." There was a trace of impatience in her voice that he did not miss.

"Oh, I'm sorry, I must have missed your initiation ceremony." His sarcasm told her the beating was going to be very bad tonight. The two things about him she feared most were his sarcasm and the eerie calm that claimed him just before a killing rage. "I wasn't aware you were entitled to privileged information."

He flung her away abruptly, and she hit the wall with stunning force, bounced off, and crumpled to the flagstone floor. Dazed, she tried to crawl into the corner – the beatings weren't as merciless if she could protect part of her body – but he delivered a violent kick to her ribs that sent her sprawling short of her destination. She curled into a wheezing ball, her tears coming in earnest. One day he would go too far and kill her. Sometimes Tiana thought that day wouldn't come soon enough.

His foot caught her in the shoulder, and she wondered if perhaps that day had come. *Tell him! Tell him you're pregnant before he beats the baby right out of you!*

But that was a trap too. Letting him know she was pregnant wouldn't stop him from killing her; it would only bring about her murder that much sooner. She hadn't forgotten Elizabeth Peterson.

Oddly, she found herself remembering her thirteenth birthday – the day dread and terror became the ruling factors in her life. Nothing could have stopped what the black magic priest had set in motion. Her father had seemed sick at heart as he ushered her through the ruins of the Wyckham House, but he hadn't stood as a barrier between her and his vile Circle. Never had he once intervened in the thirteen years since, and for that she could never forgive him.

Here in this very room, she'd learned the horror of catching a madman's eye. With the breaching of her virginity and with every violation that followed, the priest had taught her of cruelty and anguish until her life became nothing but a blur of unrelenting abuse. Her heart had died that night, but he wasn't satisfied with that. Every year he took another piece of her spirit, and she feared that soon nothing would remain but the madness to which he had driven her.

He came to her frequently, usually with brutality and violence, yet there were odd times when he would slide silently into her bed, his passion tender, his touch gentle. Even while her mind recoiled in horror, desire flared in her traitorous body like gasoline thrown on flames. Those nights, after his desire had been slaked, he would fall asleep spooned against her back, his fingers linked loosely with hers. Tiana would lie awake, bewildered and sickened at how absolutely she'd been imprisoned by his twisted libido and mercurial, soulless passions.

She couldn't confide in anyone; she'd done so once and it had nearly been fatal for her confidante. There had been other reasons for the Circle to target Aaron Schaefer, but she had been a major one. They feared what she had told him and had taken steps to ensure his enduring silence. It was truly unfortunate Ron had chosen law enforcement as his career; it virtually ensured that the Circle would consider threats and intimidation inadequate control over him. Removing him permanently gave them the only real assurance he would not blow the whistle. Dead men, after all, tell no tales.

"Scream, damn you!" he roared. "Scream or by everything unholy, I will beat you dead!"

"I don't care." She felt a wild – and totally unexpected – bubble of hysteria well up inside, too huge for her to fight. She started to laugh and couldn't stop.

Enraged, he grabbed her hair and dragged her across the rough stone floor to his bed, where he snatched up the willow switch that was propped between the wall and the night table. His arm rose and fell in a frenzied blur with such strength she feared the switch would whip through her skin to the bone. When it broke, he tossed it away and used his fists.

A long time later he threw her onto the bed and unleashed his fury in the only other way he knew.

The brutal assault brought the screams he wanted, but even then she couldn't stop her laughter. Between her shrieks of pain, it rang through the room, feral and uncontrolled, something his rage could not touch.

Finally, in all the ways that truly mattered, she was free.

THE EVIL CASTLE

Kim spread the contents of the envelope across the bed and began sorting into small piles: copies of articles, handwritten notes, and correspondence. There were only two letters: one from a research colleague in Los Angeles, and one from an Alonzo Stafford; the name rang a bell, but she couldn't pinpoint why. But both letters confirmed these papers belonged to her father, and that he had secreted them away in a heating duct showed he had felt sufficiently threatened by what he had learned.

She decided to start with the articles, which would give her a good idea of what Todd had been researching on his own, and she could compare it to what he had asked her to look into. The headline on the topmost article seemed to validate her aversion to the forest surrounding the town: *Mills, PA couple attacked by wild dog*. A good enough place to start.

MILLS, PA – A Mills couple was attacked in their home in the early morning hours of October 28, 1994. Rodney Solomon, 38, and his wife Emily Solomon, 34, were found after neighbors reported hearing gunshots and screams from their secluded house just off Willow Road in Mills. Both were pronounced dead at the scene.

Willow Road. It had to have been at either the cottage or the other rental house. She didn't think there were any other houses on this relatively short stretch of road.

Authorities are trying to piece together events but it is unclear exactly what happened in the Solomon home. Mills constable Harlan Michaels ventured that something came through the sliding patio doors at Rodney Solomon, which he tried to fend off with his shotgun. Apparently his wife came in to help, where she also was attacked. Michaels said there have been reports of a couple of wild dogs in the area.

Emily Solomon had wounds that were hours old, according to Scranton Medical Examiner, Charles Wiggins. Michaels speculated that the couple, nature lovers, had come across a wild dog in the woods while on a nature walk, were attacked and managed to escape. The dog apparently tracked them by the scent of Emily Solomon's blood and jumped through the glass patio doors.

It *had* been her cottage! Ron had never said anything about someone dying here, although if she were honest, his lack of answer when she had asked if anyone had been hurt in the attack should have been answer enough.

Canine blood found at the scene indicates at least one of Rodney Solomon's shots found its target. Both Michaels and Charles Wiggins declined to comment on inconsistencies of the blood with that of a domesticated breed of dog. Neither did it appear to match that of a wolf, which have been seen with increasing rareness in the area.

Constable Michaels has issued a curfew in the township of Mills, for all residents to be off the streets by sundown. Mills residents appear to be eager to comply. None have forgotten the vicious attacks just a year ago that left one person missing, two dead, and one wounded and catatonic. Aaron Schaefer, now 20, remains in Meadow Grove Rehabilitation Center, a psychiatric institution in Philadelphia that specializes in severe mental and emotional trauma. His condition remains unchanged.

"I'm gonna kick his ass for not telling me someone died here," Kim muttered. She had adhered to his stern advice about using the metal grid. In fact, she left it closed all the time, and if she wanted to go out onto the patio, she went via the back door.

The rest of the articles were more of the same: deaths, disappearances, the vanished found dead after being missing for months, if not years. The last couple of pages weren't articles but had been photocopied from a book; the header across the top read *The Evil Castle*. She suddenly remembered where she'd heard Alonzo Stafford's name; he had written couple of the books on myths and legends she had recommended to her father. This title had not been among them, as it hadn't dealt exclusively with witchcraft or werewolves.

Her eyes scanned the page, looking for any handwritten notes Todd might have made, but there was only the copied text from the book.

Everyone knows the story of Lycaon, who, after serving Zeus a meal of roasted human child, was transformed into a wolf as punishment. This appears to be the basis for all legends of the werewolf.

The myth is perpetuated in such stories as that of the mad Countess Mariska of Gizellatelep, Hungary. Rumored to be of the Árpád dynasty matrilineally, Mariska was suspected of witchcraft and consorting with Lucifer himself. However, Béla IV, King of Hungary (1235-1270) was reluctant to execute one who commanded such power, fearing she might return after death in a more terrifying form. He exiled her to a dilapidated ancestral holding, officially known as Gizellatelep Castle.

After Countess Mariska had occupied the castle for some time, the surrounding area was plagued by disturbing events. The locals began to call the castle *ördögöt kastély*, or "evil castle." There were reports of missing persons, of mutilated bodies, of strange beings sighted in the Visegrád Hills. The villagers in Gizellatelep petitioned Béla IV to take action and remove Mariska from the castle, but the king was preoccupied with the Mongol invasion and turned a deaf ear.

The turning point came when Mariska took an unsuspecting lover, Dezsö Szilvasy from Buda (now Budapest). Dissatisfied with the countess's odd behavior and jealous rages, Dezsö began a secret relationship with Mariska's body servant, whose name is unknown.

The legends say that Mariska was bitterly hurt and furious when she learned of his affair. She called on her black magic to curse him with lycanthropy. With each full moon he would be destined to transmogrify into a wolf and stalk innocent victims, eating of their flesh, until slain with silver. Furthermore, he would transform throughout the whole month of February, part of the natural mating cycle of wolves, and would be able to mate only during this time and only with a female wolf.

She frowned at the wall as her imagination kicked into high gear. Say, just hypothetically, that Ron Schaefer had been attacked by a werewolf eleven years ago. Who had died and released him?

"Oh, for Pete's sake." She gave herself a mental kick. *Werewolves?* Impossible.

Idly, she picked up the next paper, this one a printout from a website. She flattened it and felt her breath stop in her throat. The caption under the drawing of the huge stone mansion read: *Ördögöt Kastély, Gizellatelep, Hungary.*

Kim had seen this castle somewhere else. Here in Mills.

The Wyckham House.

She snatched up the letter from Alonzo Stafford. Her eyes couldn't seem to read fast enough for her frantic brain.

September 28th, 2004

Dear Mr. Garrett,

I have not heard from you as I requested in the note I enclosed with the copy of "Witch's Moon: Legends of the Werewolf," which I sent you a couple of weeks ago. I had hoped to speak to you about a few things, to "pass the torch" as you might say from one who hails from an old and superstitious world to one who dwells in a relatively new country without the old myths and legends. Oh, I know America dabbles with them. Even I have seen An American Werewolf in

London and Wolfen.

But these legends are not woven into the fabric of your history and your very existence as they are mine, and I cannot let you go forward unprepared. It is that imperative you contact me. I have the feeling your research is for personal reasons, not for a client. My home number is (360) 555-2819.

Kind Regards,
Alonzo Stafford

That had been five days before she had received the box of fishing gear. She wondered where the book had gone, and if Todd had called Alonzo Stafford. There was only one way to find out.

A soft, European-accented voice answered the phone at the other end midway through the third ring.

"Alonzo Stafford, please," Kim asked crisply.

"Who is calling, please?"

"He won't know my name. I'm calling from Pennsylvania, on behalf of Todd Garrett, at Mr. Stafford's request. My name is Kimberly Owens – Kimberly *Garrett* Owens."

After a minute pause that would have gone unnoticed had she not been expecting it, he said, "What can I do for you, Miss Owens?"

"There's no easy way to put this, Mr. Stafford. My father – it appears he – " She broke off, choking on the words, and Stafford broke in before she could go on.

"Something has happened to him, yes?" A delicate pause. "Is he dead?"

Kim closed her eyes, trying to swallow her rising panic. "No. I don't *think* so, anyway. But...I believe he's gone missing in Pennsylvania. It's just – just a feeling I have...deep down inside."

"That is good enough for me," Alonzo Stafford said gently. "How can I help?"

"Your book – the one he requested a copy of. I didn't find it among his research items, but he had some photocopies of a couple of

pages of another book. I need to ask you about… Ördögöt Kastély."
She stumbled over the pronunciation and he corrected her gently,
turning her O sounds to U sounds, as in the word *fur*. She tried it a
couple of times until she came close.

"It is called the Devil's House or the evil castle," Stafford said.
"But it is not advisable to talk about the devil too much."

"Why is that?"

"We have a saying: *nem jó az ördögöt a falra festeni, mert megjelenik*.
Talk of the devil and he will appear."

Kim chewed her lower lip for a moment. "Well, I don't have
much of a choice but to talk about him, or his Hungarian castle at
least. The drawing in your book – is it really from the 1300s?"

"Oh yes. It has been handed down through my family for
centuries. We are…the keepers of the knowledge, you might say."

"What knowledge?"

"The knowledge of the evil castle. May I ask your interest in
Ördögöt Kastély, Miss Owens?"

"I've seen it."

"You have been to Hungary, yes? How did you find it? Most
people go to Visegrád to see the Fellegvár and the Visegrád
strongholds. A very interesting specimen of the double castle method.
Few people find their way to Ördögöt Kastély." His tone had an edge
to it now.

"Not in Hungary. I've never been to Hungary. I've seen it here in
Pennsylvania." Absolute silence claimed the line. She couldn't even
hear him breathing.

At length he asked with urgency, "Are you sure? It is the same
house?"

"I'm positive. They call it the Wyckham House, named after the
first known person to have disappeared there."

"And you found it with ease?" Now he sounded suspicious.

"Not exactly," she said dryly. "I knew the general direction, and it
took more than two hours. It wasn't an easy trail. But I'm not the only
one to have found it. People disappear there with amazing frequency."

Again Alonzo Stafford was struck speechless. "This is highly
unusual," he murmured. "Please, tell me everything that you know

about this house."

And perhaps because she didn't know him and might never come face to face with him, Kim found herself telling him everything, even her suspicions about werewolves and the bizarre kiss she had shared with Aaron Schaefer. He remained quiet while she spoke, breaking in only for clarification. She finished with finding the packet her father had hidden before vanishing. "You say this Aaron Schaefer, he is afraid of the full moon? And he was attacked eleven years ago?"

"Yes. I – I think he might have been bitten by a werewolf." Her tone came a little more defensively than she intended. "He doesn't remember anything. His cousin said they found him covered in his own blood, but he had no wounds. He remained catatonic for nearly eighteen months and came out of it unexpectedly and suddenly. I'd bet it coincided with a hunter killing a wolf in the woods around Mills."

"I do not believe in coincidences, Miss Owens. But from what you've told me, I believe there very well may be bigger problems than werewolves in that town, and you are not prepared to take them on. You spoke of witchcraft. Americans are relatively skeptical of old magic, but it does exist, and it is terribly dangerous."

"Mr. Stafford – " She paused, feeling foolish for what she wanted to ask. She almost changed her mind, but her need to know overruled her pride. "Have you seen a werewolf? A real werewolf?"

His voice was world-weary and deeply afraid when he spoke. "You must stay away from that house at all costs."

"It's just a house, Mr. Stafford. It's the – the coven that makes it dangerous."

"It's not just a house. It's a conductor of evil, a device of transportation. There are many things in my native Hungary to which we give the name *szörnyeteg*. It translates to English roughly as monstrosity. We use it for the *farkasember* – the werewolf – and the *vámpír*, demons, practitioners of black magic – for anything that is linked to Lucifer. These things imperil your very soul, and if you go to fight them unprepared, there will be terrible consequences. There are worse things than death."

"That doesn't precisely answer my question," she said sharply. He didn't reply; he simply waited patiently. "But never mind. What do I need to do to prepare?"

"You don't understand, Miss Owens. *You* cannot fight them. It takes deep spiritual commitment and belief, intense preparation. You must be cold and calculating, totally emotionless. You must not care who is the werewolf. You must be prepared to commit what the authorities will call murder. Are you prepared to commit murder, Kimberly Owens? Are you prepared to commit murder if it is, say, your father who is the *farkasember*?"

The question haunted her long after she had turned in for the night. She lay sleepless and troubled, afraid to close her eyes. At last she fell asleep counting – not sheep, but the days until the full moon.

TALL TALE
October 22, 2004

She had been given two days off to recover from her illness, but instead of staying in bed where she belonged, Kim rose early the next morning and drove the nearly two hundred miles to Philadelphia. Once there, she easily found Meadow Grove Rehabilitation Center, and she sat in the parking lot for a good half an hour, debating with herself.

Ron was apt to blow a gasket if he ever found out she'd come here, but she couldn't shake the certainty that what had happened to him held the key to rescuing her father. She'd already deceived him about her identity; it seemed a bit late to worry about integrity now.

She climbed out of the car and left behind any indecision.

The lush gardens had been carefully put to bed for the winter, although a few late roses bobbed in the gusting wind. She barely glanced at them as she stepped through the automatic door, which had swished open at her approach. A perky receptionist at the round reception desk looked up and smiled.

"I'm Maggie. May I help you?" Kim didn't doubt her chirpy tone disguised an iron will.

"I hope so. I'm looking for a certain doctor who worked here in 1994 and 1995."

"There were several. Do you have the name?"

"No. This one had a patient named Aaron Schaefer."

Maggie's smile slipped. Her hand went subconsciously to her perfect blonde coiffure to pat an imaginary stray hair into place, and she rose from her chair a bit too fast.

"You do realize we can't discuss a patient without a release of information signed by the patient?"

"I understand," Kimberly said evenly. "But it's urgent I speak with his doctor."

The chirpiness vanished, giving way to the suspected iron core. "Please wait in the guest area." Maggie motioned Kim to a cozy seating arrangement out of earshot of the reception area, and disappeared down a hall behind the desk.

She returned a few minutes later with a tall, dark-haired man in tow. She tipped her blonde head toward their intruder, and the man strode across the lobby to the guest area, an uncompromising set to his jaw.

"Are you the one inquiring about a patient?"

"Yes." Kim rose and stuck out her hand, which he ignored.

"I'm afraid I'll have to ask you to leave."

She had expected as much. "Please. I *must* speak with you."

"Doctor-patient confidentiality. I cannot discuss a patient without express permission from the patient. I can't even tell you if this man was indeed a patient here."

"You don't have to. I told you."

He didn't relent. "I don't want to have to call security to escort you out."

Kim yanked up her sleeve and showed him the fading purple bruises circling her wrist. "Do you see these, Doctor – " She checked his name tag. " – Hansen? Aaron Schaefer gave me these a week ago when he stopped me from going into the house where his friends were murdered. There are things I *have* to know. *Please.* "

He turned on his heel and walked away. She trotted after him, fighting down a sudden wave of nausea and a disorienting second of vertigo.

"Please, Doctor Hansen. My father has disappeared in the same town. I need your help, *please!*"

He vanished down the hall behind the reception desk. Maggie stood as sentinel between them, the phone in one perfectly manicured hand. The other hand hovered over the keypad, waiting to dial security should Kim prove to be uncooperative.

"Before you sic security on me, will you please let me leave my name and phone number in case he changes his mind?"

"He won't," Maggie replied frostily. But without further remark she pushed a pad of paper toward her, and handed her a pen. Kim scrawled her name and cell phone number and pushed it back across the desk.

"Please don't throw it away."

"I won't. I promise. But he won't call you."

She sat unmoving behind the wheel of her car for several long minutes, uncertain what to do next and paralyzed by a growing sense of panic. She had to know what had happened to Ron. He had been inside the Wyckham House. Did he know the way in? Could he find where they might be holding her father?

She wasn't likely to find the answers to those questions here, so she started the engine and headed toward the highway.

She had just merged onto I-76 West when her cell phone rang. Plucking it out of the cup holder, she glanced at the caller ID but didn't recognize the number. It could be no one but the good doctor. She was surprised and pleased; had she been a betting woman, she would have laid odds that she would never hear from him.

"Hello?" she greeted tentatively.

"Miss Owens." Hansen's voice came across the line, terse and unfriendly. "This is probably a very bad idea. In fact, I *know* it's a very bad idea. But we need to talk. Where are you?"

"Heading back to Mills. I'm almost to the exit to merge onto I-476 North."

"We call that the Schuylkill Expressway. Take Exit 332 at Conshohocken, follow Matsonford Road to Front Street and hang a left. There's a diner called Molino's on the right-hand side of the street. I'll be there shortly after you."

"I'm on my way."

"Call this number back if you can't find it and I'll give you directions."

Without further ado, he hung up. A few miles farther, Kim veered off the highway at the Conshohocken exit.

She took a wrong turn and had to stop for directions – and then fight her way back through traffic to the correct route – so Hansen had already been seated by the time she walked in. He nursed a cup of coffee that strongly resembled what Ron served in the tavern, and when she approached the table, he looked up with haunted eyes and silently poured a mug for her. She slid into the booth and cupped her hands around it, savoring its warmth.

"I'm glad you called."

"Like I said, this is a bad idea, and I'm probably going to regret it. Don't think my motives are completely altruistic; this has been like a poison inside of me for the last decade. If I can't completely extract it, I can at least dilute it by passing it on."

Kim digested this wordlessly and finally decided that, if not entirely philanthropic, it was at least honest.

"I can accept that," she agreed.

He slanted a wry smile at her. "Where do I begin?"

"The beginning, I suppose. When Aaron Schaefer came to your institution."

"Rehabilitation center," he corrected kindly.

She sipped her coffee. "Is that what you did – rehabilitated him?"

Hansen gave an ironic, humorless laugh. "I don't delude myself into thinking we helped Aaron Schaefer one iota other than making sure he didn't succeed where others failed."

"Suicide, you mean."

"Yes. When he recovered from the catatonia, he had no desire to live. We had him on suicide watch for three months. I doubted he ever would be emotionally stable again."

"He's not." At Hansen's quirked brow, she elaborated. "He's emotionally crippled, scared to death of anything resembling commitment. I'm sure there have been one-night stands, and many of them over the years, but nothing that has lasted. He doesn't want anything to. I believe he still blames himself for the deaths of his friends, and even though he can't remember what happened to her,

I'm sure he blames himself for Elizabeth."

'So his memory has never returned?"

"No."

Robert Hansen regarded her speculatively over the rim of his coffee cup, his scrutiny so thorough Kim felt almost naked under his practiced observation. "There's more to this than just finding your father, isn't there? Where Aaron Schaefer is concerned, I mean."

And because she sensed it would make the difference in how much he told her, she gave him an honest answer, blushing furiously. "Yes."

"All right, then. I'll tell you what happened. It's an incredible story and I won't blame you if you don't believe a word. But I swear it's true, although if you ever told anyone, I wouldn't admit to any of it. Do you understand?"

"Completely."

"He came to us in late October 1993. I remember watching from the Admissions entrance when the ambulance stopped outside. My colleague, Olivia Jarvis, kept fidgeting and chewing on her lip. She never displayed anything but competence and confidence when taking a new patient, so I asked her what was wrong. She said – "

* * * * *

"Bad vibes," Liv said, and then looked as if she regretted her words. Her brow furrowed beneath her blonde bangs as she watched the raven-haired young man being wheeled toward them. He lay motionless on the stretcher, eyes open and unblinking despite the rain the blustering wind drove underneath the carport. She shivered.

"I know what you mean," Hansen murmured, his voice pitched low so the admitting nurses couldn't hear.

The doors swished open, and both Olivia Jarvis and Robert Hansen put their personal doubts behind a professional guise. For the next two hours, they helped the Schaefers complete intake forms, settled their nephew into his room, and explained the route of therapy they would initiate to help him recover.

Long after the Schaefers left, Olivia appeared at Hansen's office door, troubled. At his invitation, she sank into a cushy leather arm-chair near his desk and sighed expressively.

"Have you examined Aaron Schaefer yet?"

He lifted one shoulder slightly. "Yes, when they took him upstairs to his room. His vitals are to be expected. Why?"

"Did you look at his eyes?"

"Yes. It's very odd. It's almost like he's aware sometimes but deliberately not responding." He frowned. "Do you think he's faking?"

"With classic catalepsy? It's doubtful. Botulism, schizophrenia, and autism have likewise been ruled out."

"But not post-traumatic stress disorder," he pointed out.

"A diagnosis of PTSD does not mean the catatonic state is not real." He didn't miss the bite in her voice. "His friends are dead; Cody Schaefer is fairly certain Aaron saw them die. The girlfriend is still missing. Whatever happened out there in those woods, it was bad, and he is determined not to remember it to the point he's disengaged from the world."

Olivia chewed on her lip; he didn't chastise her, although he knew tomorrow she would be lathering it with lip balm.

"He's from Mills, isn't he?" she asked, and he nodded. "Maybe that's all the answer we need."

"Say again?"

"You've heard about that town. You've even treated a person or two from it. You know what goes on there."

He laughed incredulously. "No, Liv, I know what rumors *claim* go on there, and I don't buy a word of it. Besides, I'm a psychiatrist, not an exorcist."

She shifted in her seat and turned her gaze to the wet, windy day beyond his office window. Dusk had smothered out the last embers of the sun, and the wind in the trees moaned ominously.

"After Cody Schaefer called, I researched that town. Since 1970, there have been seventy wild animal attacks, many of them resulting in death. Remember that girl we referred to a sexual abuse counselor a few months ago, the one claiming to be the constable's daughter? The things she had to tell – witchcraft, curses, murder, rape…"

Hansen's mouth drew down in his effort to keep from smirking at her silliness. He didn't want to tick her off.

But Olivia had seen the laughter in his eyes and knew it came at her expense. She stood abruptly, her skirt swishing around her legs as she walked to the door. There she paused, one hand gripping the door jamb.

"I'm not wrong, Rob. There's something weird here, you mark my words."

She left then, and for a long time Hansen stared at the doorway where she'd been. His scientific mind refused to indulge in the belief of witchcraft. He didn't know what had happened to Aaron Schaefer, but witchcraft hadn't put him here.

Over the next three weeks, Olivia Jarvis didn't mention her unorthodox beliefs, and Robert Hansen assumed she had dismissed them herself. She found hypnosis had an alarming effect: his blood pressure dropped dangerously, and he lapsed into an almost comatose state. She tried it twice, and when CPR was required to revive him the second time, she didn't dare try again.

As dusk fell the evening of his twenty-fourth day in Meadow Grove, Olivia came skidding into the cafeteria where Robert Hansen ate dinner, her hair disheveled and her eyes bright with excitement.

"Come *on!*" she insisted, dragging him from his chair by the arm. He followed her out of the cafeteria with a glance of regret at his meal growing cold on the tray.

Olivia didn't wait for the elevator. She bounded up the stairs two at a time, and he didn't catch up with her until they reached the door of Room 227 – Aaron Schaefer's room.

She had posted a nurse to watch Aaron, who now took his pulse and frowned at the chart on which he noted the result. "Pulse erratic, blood pressure high. He's agitated."

Their patient moved restlessly on the bed, his face pulled into a tight mask of pain. He tossed his head violently from side to side as though to escape physical discomfort. Once he rolled onto his side and pulled himself into the fetal position, and then straightened just as quickly.

Olivia approached the bed, Hansen beside her, and placed a cool hand on Aaron's cheek. He burned with fever, his skin beaded with sweat.

"Look at his eyes," she murmured, and held her patient's head still while Hansen flicked on his penlight. He lifted a lid, revealing a huge pupil ringed with a thin circle of indigo, full of intense suffering. He clicked off the light immediately.

"He's in pain," he said to Olivia, and she nodded "For how long?"

"Since about four o'clock."

Since dusk, Hansen thought silently. "Keep a watch on him. Will he swallow capsules?"

"No."

"Have Eric prepare an IV push. Diazepam, 10 milligrams via IV every three hours. We don't have time to wait for intramuscular injections; he's in too much pain. I want to be informed immediately of any further change."

Olivia nodded, looking to the nurse to make sure he'd heard the instructions, and she set about carrying them out.

Hansen went back to the cafeteria, unaware he'd just made a decision that saved at least four lives that night. Maybe more.

Shortly after eight o'clock, while Hansen put away the last of his files and prepared to leave for the night, his phone burred insistently on his desk. He picked it up, and could barely hear Olivia through the commotion at the other end.

"Get up here!" she shrieked. A sharp cry of pain in the background and what sounded like the room being upended made him wince. *"I need you stat! 227!"*

Hansen had run halfway up the stairs before he remembered who occupied room 227.

He skidded into the room, hurtling into Eric, whose eyes were saucer-like in his face. Hansen didn't ask questions but rushed over to the bed where two burly orderlies tried to hold Aaron still. Olivia attempted to administer more diazepam to the IV drip line, but Schaefer's thrashing sent the IV drip swinging wildly. Just when she thought she'd managed to insert the needle, the tube swung away.

Hansen did the most expeditious thing he could think of. He simply sat on the patient's chest and immobilized Schaefer's arm with his knee. Olivia administered the injection quickly, barely withdrawing the needle just as Aaron threw Hansen off with a surge of superhuman strength.

Hansen grabbed an arm again and felt the flesh shift beneath his fingers. He let go immediately, backing away, staring in horror at the bizarre metamorphosis taking place on the bed.

The orderlies, feeling bones buckling in their hands, released the patient and backed away nervously, glancing from Olivia Jarvis to Robert Hansen, waiting for orders. Seconds later, they recoiled against the wall in horror.

Aaron Schaefer began to change.

His joints popped like champagne corks as his bones dislocated and shifted position and shape. His skin turned an unnatural gray, and coarse hair sprouted with a shimmery sound that made Hansen's skin crawl.

Olivia made a terrible, keening noise beside him, but he didn't dare take his eyes from the fantastic tableau before him. He groped for her hand and she held on tightly, grinding the fine bones of his fingers painfully against each other.

Stitches exploded as Aaron's clothes strained at their seams. Chambray ripped and fell away in faded blue shreds, showing the skin beneath stretching to cover the new bone structure. He groaned, tears of pain spilling from eyes pulled into animalistic slants.

When his ears lengthened into points and his lower face pushed out into a snout, Olivia Jarvis could stand it no longer. She screamed, and at last Hansen pulled himself out of his surreal disbelief enough to notice the razor-sharp fangs growing in his patient's mouth.

"Get him out of here!" he bellowed, and the orderlies, jammed against the door and about to make their escape, looked at him as if to say *Who, us?* "Get him to the basement! THE BASEMENT NOW!"

They gingerly reached into the melee, not wanting to touch him, not wanting to be near him, but they each gamely grabbed a side and hoisted Aaron Schaefer – now more beast than man – from the bed. His feverish, squirming muscles gave them all the encouragement they needed to move as quickly as possible. They careened out of the room and down the hall toward the service stairs, Hansen hot on their heels.

Partway down the last flight of stairs, the beast gave a guttural snarl and snapped half-heartedly at one orderly, barely missing his arm. The man dropped his half of the burden and ran, sobbing hysterically, never to be seen at the clinic again. Hansen quickly stepped in, although his stomach quailed at the thought of touching Aaron Schaefer.

The diazepam had worked nicely, however, and the man-wolf didn't snap again. Hansen suspected that had he not been able to administer that last dose, they would all be dead.

They man-handled him down the last stretch of stairs, sliding and tripping and falling more than running, laid Aaron Schaefer on the floor, and ran. Halfway back up the steps, he heard another throaty growl behind him and turned to find a wolf – but *not* a wolf – pulling itself clumsily onto the second stair. Its tongue lolled out of its mouth, and its eyes, deep-set in its massive head, glowed green. Hansen watched, too petrified to move, as it collapsed and lay panting, eyes half-closed, on the stair below his.

Hansen escaped through the door at the top and threw the bolt, securely locking the horror on the other side. He slid to the floor, his head reeling, and laid his cheek against the cool tile floor, trying not to vomit.

He heard a sigh and a rather loud thump, and raised his head to see Olivia Jarvis sprawled on the floor in a dead faint.

CIRCLES

"We built a room in the basement of the facility, large enough to be comfortable for man or beast. Concrete walls two feet thick with an iron door that cost more than I care to remember." Hansen clutched his coffee cup like a life preserver.

"And – " Kim croaked. She stopped and cleared her throat. "And when did he stop changing?"

She barely heard his reply. Although she had been expecting a story just like this, her mind was clamoring *Oh my God, he really* was *a werewolf!* And what happened after one was cured? Did the wolf continue to shadow the human, coloring instincts and habits?

" – man named Richard Boyd was shot in the woods. A hunter

mistook him for a wolf."

She started. "I'm sorry, what was that?"

"April of 1995. A hunter in Mills was being stalked by what he thought was a wolf. But when he killed it, it was actually a man who had been missing for more than two years. Mills authorities claimed the man was living in the woods – some survivalist thing – and had been wearing a wolf fur for warmth. After what I experienced with Aaron Schaefer, I didn't believe it."

"No," she murmured. "I wouldn't have either."

"We kept him for another six months, until we felt he was stable enough to be reintroduced to the world. We had hoped he would continue therapy after his release – his aunt and uncle had moved to Philadelphia, after all, so he would still be in the city. But he adamantly refused."

"What did he remember?"

Hansen laughed, a sound as bitter as the coffee going cold in their mugs. "We'll never know. He refused to confide. He dreamed poorly and suffered acute insomnia in the form of what we call middle insomnia, or middle-of-the-night insomnia. He would wake prematurely and not be able to go back to sleep.

"We worried about the consequences of sleep deprivation in a patient suffering from a severe emotional and biological trauma like his, but what could we do? We tried any number of sleep aids. Opiates gave him nightmares and made us fear a relapse. Natural sleep remedies like chamomile and valerian allowed him to sleep a couple of hours longer, but still he only got five or six hours sleep at the most. After a while, those stopped working. We tried melatonin, which seemed to have no effect."

"Nightmares," she repeated. "Or memories?"

He shrugged helplessly. "He talked and screamed in his sleep as well, but nothing ever made any sense."

"Such as?"

"Such as 'the devil took her' and 'she's in the cat.' I'm sure he was just shouting about things in his nightmares, not about specific actual events. Nightmares are usually symbolic of the traumas we've been through."

"Did you try hypnosis to take him back to that night?" It's what she would have done. Perhaps remembering while he was in a safe environment would have made a difference.

"Twice while he was catatonic. Once more when he'd recovered. We didn't dare try it again. As a defensive mechanism, he would stop his heart before we could take him back to his time in the woods. I've read of this phenomenon in popular novels, but assumed it was fictional. I've never had a patient attempt it."

Hansen fiddled with the handle of his coffee mug. He didn't reach for the decanter to refill, but simply stared into the dregs at the bottom of the cup.

Kim pushed her own coffee away. It was cold by now, and not that good anyway. "Did he believe you about his lycanthropy? I imagine he would have had a hard time accepting it."

"We never discussed his lycanthropy," he replied, looking up at her from under lowered brows. "We thought it best to leave that whole subject alone. He didn't remember any of it. Do you understand exactly what he did regarding his experience in the forest? He shoved it behind a wall he built in his mind, and then he set traps around that wall in case anyone tried to breach it. That is phenomenal in itself. But add to it what he did regarding his lycanthropy. He systematically blocked his memories pertaining to changing, blocked them so completely that he may as well have erased them."

"You mean he did his own brainwashing."

"Yes. And because he did it himself, there is probably nothing that will make the memory block crumble. It is too dangerous to force him to remember. I'm afraid if it's even tried, even this many years later, he will kill himself before he remembers."

"By stopping his own heartbeat."

"Yes." Hansen leaned forward across the table. His hands tightened convulsively on his mug. "I don't *want* him to remember, Miss Owens. I'm afraid that if the people who did this to him don't come to finish the job, the memory of what he became will do it for them."

Robert Hansen's analysis of the strength of Ron's psyche bothered her for some reason. She stared across the café in the ensuing silence, trying to pinpoint why. Their server gave her a nervous glance, studiously avoiding eye contact. Kim shifted her gaze; she wasn't sure what the young woman had overheard, but it obviously was enough to make her dread approaching them.

And speaking of dread...what was it that Ron dreaded so much? Yes, discovering you'd become a werewolf would be quite the shocker, but there was more...there had to be more... He was stronger than the past. He had even moved back to the town where his life had been destroyed. What he had become during his lost months would not concern him as much as any possible after-effects. No, his subconscious would worry that he still had the potential to shape-shift, and perhaps that if he still had the ability, he would transform again if he remembered that he could.

"Miss Owens?"

With reluctance she pulled her attention back to him. "I don't think it's about what he became," she said. "I think subconsciously, he's worried that he can still transform. So if he doesn't remember doing it, he won't know that he can."

Hansen looked horrified. "Do you think he can?"

"I doubt it," she assured him quickly. "The legends are very specific. Once cured, always cured. Or dead, if you're the first of a bloodline – that is, a werewolf-created by a spell. He won't transform again unless he's bitten again."

"And yet he moved back to that damned town."

"Yes. It boggles the mind, doesn't it?"

"Has he told you why?"

"He said he had to prove that he could – to them and to himself. But I think it's more than that. I think he has unfinished business there."

"Elizabeth," Hansen murmured. "He asked about her only once. Liv dodged the question and changed the subject. He never asked again."

The doctor reached across the table and covered her hand. "I am sympathetic to your plight, Miss Owens. I hope that you find your father, but I pray that you do it without involving Aaron Schaefer. He's been through enough."

"I will do my level best, doctor, but I can make no promises. Thank you for talking to me. The information is invaluable, even if it doesn't necessarily pertain to my father." She frowned at a sudden thought. "It seems that Olivia Jarvis was his attending psychiatrist. Wouldn't she speak with me? Is that why you came instead?"

Hansen closed his eyes. "Olivia Jarvis has been dead for more than eight years. Car accident, shortly after Aaron moved back to Mills." He slanted a sardonic smile at her. "Of course, I never really believed it was an accident."

"But no attempt was made against you?"

"I wasn't his attending doctor," he explained, his tone bland. His gaze swept her face, taking in the light stippling of sweat on her brow, her pallor, her dark-smudged eyes. "Are you all right? I'd be remiss in my professional capacity if I didn't point out that you don't look well at all."

"I've been ill. I'm well on the way to recovery," she prevaricated.

"Mmmm. What are you going to do now, Miss Owens?"

"I'm going to do some research, find the name of the man who killed the wolf that bit Ron. Maybe he's still alive."

He looked surprised. "Oh, I can tell you that much," he said, surprising her. "There was an article in *The Philadelphia Inquirer*. Liv cut it out and put it in Aaron's file. I read it before I came, just to be sure I remembered correctly. The man's name was Andrew Malone."

Kim contemplated circles as she travelled in one through Mulberry's Grocery, picking on impulse ingredients for dinner. A werewolf bit Ron; Andy Malone killed a wolf; Ron recovered. Andy Malone's daughter Anna was dating Jared Olmstead, the son of one of Caleb Schaefer's pals; Caleb hung with Sarah Bennett, who was a renowned herbalist and suspected witch; werewolves were created through a witch's spell. Which brought them back to the wolf that had bitten Ron.

A headache pulsed behind her right eye; she'd popped a Maxalt when she hit the town limits. By the time she picked up a few things at the store and prepared her evening meal, the medicine should have banished the headache and she would be able to sleep.

She stopped in front of the cake mixes and pressed on her temple, easing the pain slightly. It wasn't until he spoke that she realized she was not alone in the aisle.

"I find it very hard to decide sometimes. No matter which you choose, it presents a lost opportunity to sample another. And if you choose poorly, it's a lost opportunity to enjoy the delights of dessert."

"I usually just buy lemon bars," she said. She didn't know why.

Caleb Schaefer chuckled lazily, reached in front of her, and plucked a box from the shelf. "Devil's food cake. My personal favorite. I'd be delighted if you'd join me for a slice."

She raised her eyes to his, and his smile was replaced with a look of concern. He opened his mouth to continue, and she cut him off before he could ask her if she was all right. She was, quite frankly, tired of the question.

"I'm allergic to chocolate."

"Lemon bars, then." Caleb smiled engagingly. Her headache pulsed, and her stomach rolled slowly over. "Aaahh," he murmured. His expression was knowing. "Migraine. May I?"

He didn't wait for her permission, but lifted her right hand and laid it across the palm of his left. Her heart raced, making the headache pulse harder. She hoped he didn't notice the sudden acceleration while she mentally kicked herself for it.

The thumb and forefinger of his right hand pinched down on the sensitive webbing between those fingers of her captive hand. His skin was almost feverishly warm. The headache immediately abated, and she stared up at him in thankful surprise.

"My headache's gone."

"A temporary fix, for as long as the nerve cluster is compressed."

"That's amazing!"

His smile widened, and Kim suddenly remembered Cody telling her that Caleb liked much younger women – and that he was following her. His expression was frankly appreciative, and he *did* stand a trifle too close to her, a habit he shared with the rest of his family, as though they had no sense of personal boundaries. Close enough that she could see every detail of the odd, six-sided buttons on his black shirt.

But it was his eyes that confirmed Cody's warning. Their ice-blue depths held a glow that was just a fraction too intimate. He would have no trouble getting much younger lovers; his face belied his years, with only the slightest trace of crow's feet at the corners of those arresting eyes. His skin was still smooth and supple, tanned from the summer, his jaw darkened with the day's growth of beard. Many men on the expressway to sixty had edged toward paunchiness, but he was still trim and muscled, his black shirt clinging to his chest in a way that invited feminine hands to explore.

She tried with difficulty to mask her sudden confusion – what had they just been discussing? – and tried to withdraw her hand. He let it go with a show of reluctance. The headache pulsed to life again.

"We were discussing lemon bars," he reminded her softly.

No we weren't, she thought narrowly. *We were discussing sex.*

It wasn't a far stretch of the imagination to see beyond the pretense of sharing lemon bars. Alone, in an intimate setting, the delights of dessert sending an almost sexual pleasure through them both, it was a short reach to put them in bed together, both willing and eager participants.

She backed away a step, fighting the urge to stammer what was sure to be an embarrassing explanation for her sudden confusion. "I'm afraid I don't feel very well, Mr. Schaefer," she managed. "I'll have to decline, but thank you for the invitation."

He was unperturbed. "Very well. And please, call me Caleb. Can you make it home all right?"

"I took my medication. I should be fine by the time I have dinner ready." She wiggled her hand basket. "Have a good evening."

"Likewise." He stole a look at her purchases and took his leave, smirking slightly.

She didn't understand the smirk until she was home and unloaded her bags onto the kitchen counter. Her dinner tonight would consist of a yellow bell pepper, a package of beef jerky, eggs, and buttermilk, which she detested and had no recollection of selecting from the cooler.

Suddenly, lemon bars sounded delightful.

DEADLY NIGHTSHADE

October 23, 2004

"What do you mean you found nothing?"

Denny arched a brow. "Well, thought I was pretty clear. I chose words of few syllables, just in case."

"Oh, ha ha." Ron frowned at him. "Are you a hundred percent sure her illness is drug-related?"

"There's no way to be a hundred percent sure without doing a tox screen, but I'm convinced. I even have a culprit in mind."

"Really." Ron slid onto the stool in front of Denny, alert and expectant as though it wasn't almost two in the morning, and flicked a finger at the back bar. Denny poured them both a couple of fingers of scotch over a cube of ice and came around to sit down.

The night had flown by, and this was the first chance they'd had to be off their feet. He really missed Ben Cummings at times like these – Tiana hadn't shown up for her shift, and Taryn had absolutely refused to work another double, which left both him and Denny covering. With Beth out sick, having Ben to fill in somewhere would have eased things considerably.

Denny was curiously anxious about Tiana's no-show. He had tried phoning her no less than four times an hour. But despite the tension that made him pace in between his phone calls, he had stayed to work an extra four hours with no complaint, although Taryn had plenty on his behalf. No doubt she was fuming now, building up a head of outraged steam, and Denny was going to get an earful when he got home. The tension between them as their long-distance relationship foundered had a palpable presence that set Ron on edge.

"Let's consider her symptoms. She's complained several times about a low-grade but chronic headache and dry mouth, her pupils are often dilated, she loses her balance frequently, and her heart rate was going wild when I checked her pulse."

"Okay. That could be any number of things."

"True," Denny conceded. He sipped his scotch and swirled the ice cube around his glass. "Then there's the nausea and the fatigue. I think that's a separate issue. That could be anything – lack of sleep, change of water quality, pregnancy – "

"She's not promiscuous, and she has female problems."

His friend flicked him a curious glance. "I'm not even going to ask how you know that. The first set of symptoms indicate a drug. A likely culprit is *atropa belladonna.* "

"Belladonna? Why belladonna?"

"Actually, the dilation of her pupils set me on that trail. The symptoms match. Since the root and leaf are quite fatal, I'd have to assume she's ingested the berry form. Ten to twenty berries in an adult at one time can be fatal, so it's obvious she hasn't been given that many at once."

"What do you mean by *given?*" Ron's brow lowered ominously. "You think someone's poisoning her?"

"Ron, it isn't likely she could ingest belladonna berries by accident – she's a city girl, but she's smart. No way would she pick something and eat it without first checking with someone to make sure that she should. Now my first thought was Nadine – God knows she went a bit weird about you. But she's not been around and Beth is still sick." He tapped a finger distractedly against the side of his nose.

"No other suspects?"

Denny shook his head. "My mind is going in circles. I'm dead tired and not thinking clearly. Too many long hours working."

"I know. And Taryn's very unhappy about it."

"That wins the Understatement of the Year award," Denny muttered. "All right, I admit it's reaching to assume someone else is giving her belladonna. I came to that conclusion because this is Mills, after all."

"So what?" Ron's reply was sharper than intended. His fingers tightened around his rocks glass, and he glared into it. "What is this?"

"Laphroaig," Denny responded absently. "Good, eh? Nice and peaty. Anyway, you have to admit the town's reputation lends itself nicely to poisoning. Belladonna is often used in witchcraft, you know. And it wouldn't be the first time someone's been poisoned here."

"Oh? Who else?"

"Lorna Mulberry's daughter all those years ago."

Ron scoffed. Denny *must* be tired if he was beating that dead horse. Everyone knew that Lorna's six-year-old daughter Marianne had eaten a fatal dose of death cap mushrooms, mistaking them for paddy straw mushrooms. An easy mistake, and more common among children than any other age group. It had not been an easy death; excruciating abdominal pain and renal failure, followed by coma and cardiac arrest seven days later. Had Lorna known sooner that Marianne had eaten the mushrooms, the child might have lived, but she had been in the care of a babysitter who hadn't realized she'd ingested anything out of the ordinary.

"Marianne Mulberry was an accident, not murder."

"Keep telling yourself that. You, of all people, should know better."

With a derisive snort, Ron downed the last of his scotch in two gulps. "So what is your theory about the rest of it?"

"The fatigue and nausea? I'm thinking a sedative she's not reacting to very well."

"Okay, say you're right. How are the mysterious 'they' getting it into her system? It would have to be through a food source."

"I was banking on the bottled water, but it's clean." Denny slanted a crooked smile at him. "I would say it's been put into her other food or some other prepared beverage."

Ron considered this and found a fatal flaw in Denny's theory. "Say you're right about that, too. It begs the question of why."

Denny's answer was too careful. "Perhaps it's just an accident that she's ended up with the tainted food. Maybe it's meant for someone else."

"But you don't believe that."

"No. I believe it's meant for her, meant to slow her down physically and mentally." Denny glanced up from his scotch and saw Ron's next question in the taut lines of his face and his death grip around his empty glass. "A long-term, slow-acting roofie, if you will."

Ron thought back to the first night she'd come into his tavern and drew the gaze of every man with a heartbeat. One gaze – besides his own – still followed her obsessively. A strange panic clawed at his insides like a trapped rat digging its way out, a panic that had no reasonable, identifiable origin but which threatened to consume him. An overwhelming need to protect her eclipsed every other thought in his mind, and he couldn't tell if it was fear for her safety or fear of her turning her affections toward another man – a man who might be slowly poisoning her – that most alarmed him.

After a long time he said, "Belladonna is *Solanaceae* family – nightshades. The family includes eggplant, potatoes, chili peppers." He spun his empty glass on the bar, watching until the revolutions ceased. "And tomatoes."

Denny looked puzzled. "Your point?"

"That might explain the nausea. Some people who are allergic to penicillin have trouble with foods containing the *penicillium* fungi, which can cause nausea and diarrhea just like any other food intolerance. It's not common, but it's possible."

"Thanks for the education on *penicillium*, but did you have a particular point to make?"

"She's allergic to tomatoes."

"So you think someone's slipping her tomatoes?"

"You're dense tonight. Say you're right and someone is slipping her belladonna. It's part of the nightshade plant family – a plant family to which she's already shown an allergy. Perhaps she's having an allergic reaction to it."

"I hadn't thought of that. Of course, I didn't know she was allergic to tomatoes."

"Guess you're not all-seeing, all-knowing, eh?" He grabbed both of their glasses and tipped his head toward the kitchen. "I'll clean up. You go home and try to mend things."

"Not so easy to do." But his friend slid off his stool without argument. "Don't stay too long."

"Not planning to." He waited until Denny had reached the swinging doors to the kitchen before posing his next question. "So are you gonna tell me who you really work for now?"

His friend paused. "Right now, I work for you." He slipped through the door, and Ron let him go.

He cleaned up in short order and locked up the bar on his way out. It took monumental effort to turn the truck away from the cottage and head for home.

IF IT WEREN'T FOR BAD LUCK
October 24, 2004

Tiana woke in the dark hours of early morning and lay silently in her bed, listening for sounds of movement. When she was certain she was alone, she crawled out of the cozy bed, pulled on her clothes and began hunting for her shoes. The room held a slight chill but not overbearingly so. He allowed the fireplaces to be used; since she didn't sleep well; her frequent wakeful times allowed her to keep her fire burning constantly. The wood was replenished daily; she never asked how or by whom.

Finally locating her shoes under the dresser, she slid them on, grabbed her flashlight, and crept out into the hallway.

The Wyckham House had undoubtedly seen its glory days many centuries ago, but present day found the thick stone walls scraped and chipped, darkened with age. The hallway temperature was much cooler than her bedroom. She shivered but didn't go back for a sweater; she was afraid she would lose her courage. She crept to his door and pressed her ear to it for several minutes, and then stooped to press an eye to the keyhole; a candle burned beside his bed, shielded by a glass hurricane shade, but the bed was empty.

She breathed a sigh of relief. He was busy elsewhere. The hinges creaked as she eased the door open; she froze but no one came.

He kept the key in a dish on his dresser, and Tiana wasted no time. She streaked across the room, snatched it up, and shoved it into her pocket. A simple matter then to make her way to the dungeons.

In the quiet hours just before dawn, the Wyckham House was deserted. She passed through the Casting Room – where eleven years before both her and Elizabeth Peterson's lives were devastatingly altered – to another set of stairs. This rough-hewn passage was narrow and a damp chill emanated from the dark opening.

She negotiated the staircase cautiously and made her way down a long passageway to a remote cell. The faint flicker of firelight came from under the door, no doubt from Todd's lantern. She let herself into the cell, slipping to the side of the door to stand with her back against the wall.

Todd lay on his back on his pallet of blankets, arms folded beneath his head. His eyes watched the patterns of firelight play across the stone ceiling; his face held no interest in what he saw. The cruelest thing the Circle had done to him was not the lycanthrope curse; it was confining him so absolutely that he could not protect his daughter. He didn't look around to see who had come.

"Todd," she said softly. "I've come to let you out."

Now he looked at her. The propane lantern gave a warm glow to one side of his face while throwing the other into shadow. Not a drop-dead gorgeous man like the Schaefers, Todd had nevertheless possessed a California beach bum charm that had lost its boyishness and taken on a haunted cast.

"It's not right to keep you here."

"You can't let me loose, Tiana. I don't know how long I've been here – it's hard to keep track of the days when I can't see outside – but it has to be getting close to a full moon by now. You don't dare let me out."

"I don't dare leave you here. If I do, they will turn you loose in the woods at the turning of the moon. What if Kimberly is in a vulnerable place? If I let you out now, you probably have enough time to get someplace where you can be restrained. My recommendation is to hitch a ride to Philadelphia and go to Meadow Grove Rehabilitation Center. I don't know for sure, but I suspect they had to take some measures of restraint with Ron Schaefer while he was there."

"A werewolf attacked Ron?"

She gave him a measured look. "You can't tell me you haven't given it some thought yourself, Todd. You've heard what happened to him, I'm sure. You researched the town."

"I didn't get far enough into my research to form any concrete conclusions. The Circle nabbed me too quickly."

She nodded. "I suppose they did. They're always so quick to assume the worst that they actually make their own trouble."

The contempt with which she said this made him lift a brow. "I thought these were your people, Tiana."

Disgust contorted her delicate features but she made no comment. "Now you have to get moving. We don't have much time. Stay off the main roads as much as you can; walk along the shoulder near the woods so you can hide quickly if a car comes."

He said softly, "I can't make it on foot out of this town. I've been locked up here for a month, fed on rations." He paused. "You'd've done better to bring me a gun."

"You can't shoot your way out of here, Todd," she said reprovingly. "There are too many of them."

"Not for them. For me."

She straightened. "Oh Todd, you can't do that! Your daughter would be devastated!"

His mouth tightened to a grim line. "You think she won't be devastated if I kill her? Or worse, what if I wound her and she lives? Do you think she'll thank me for sharing this curse?"

"Good point, but that's what I'm trying to keep from happening. Please, Todd, let me release you."

"You've already said there is no cure for what they've done for me, that I'll eventually lose my humanity as time passes. Why would you let me go, knowing I can't ever live a normal life? Knowing I might not be able to find suitable sanctuary and I'll end up killing someone?"

"I'm giving you two days to find that sanctuary and get your affairs in order. I think if you can make your way to Meadow Grove, you will find someone who can help you. Maybe a cure can be found. At least you'll be alive and able to have visitors; it's only three days a month, and the month of February."

Todd sat up, his eyes blazing. "A half-life in captivity because of what they've done to me," he spat bitterly. "That's a miserable kind of life."

"Yes, but there's hope in biding your time in relative freedom." Impulsively, she delved into her jeans pocket and brought out a key. "My spare key to my apartment. How familiar with the streets are you?"

"Fair."

"It's on Manor Drive, four blocks behind Town Hall. Apartment 8."

After a brief hesitation, he took the key from her outstretched hand. "I can't stay there."

"No, but you can get my car. Red Toyota Celica, the only one in the lot. The keys are hanging just inside the apartment door on a letter rack."

"Do you think they won't be suspicious when they see your car driving out of town?"

"Just be discreet, Todd. Now are you coming or not?"

She didn't need to ask again. He followed her out into the passageway hesitantly and found courage when no one else appeared. They went up a flight of stairs and down hallways filled with stygian darkness, and finally up another set of rough steps. She cocked her head and listened carefully before leading the way into what looked like a ruined kitchen.

Tiana grabbed him by the front of his coat and pulled his ear down to her mouth to whisper, turning him toward a glassless window on the exterior wall. "Go out that window. There is a little-used path leading to the road just west of the tavern. Take it. Go directly to my apartment to get the car."

"Does it have a full tank? I have no money. They took my wallet."

"There's a set of canisters on my kitchen counter. I keep flour in the largest one in a plastic bag. Pull the bag out; there's some emergency money underneath it."

"I can't take your – "

"*This* is an emergency, Todd. Now go."

She released him. Todd looked down at her for a brief moment. She had turned off the flashlight and now stood limned in silver moonlight that poured through the glassless kitchen window. He didn't know what impulse moved him to it, but he leaned in again and kissed her gently, full on the lips.

"Thank you, Tiana."

She reached up and cupped his cheek for a second, and then shoved the flashlight into his hand. "It's the very least I can do, Todd. Now go!" She gave him a shove toward the window and he needed no further prodding.

He climbed through the window and dropped into the weedy yard outside, free at last.

She waited with bated breath, but when she heard no obvious signs of capture, she sighed in relief. Her mission accomplished, she turned her mind to her own predicament. It would be a dark journey back to her room on the third floor, but she was intimately familiar with the Wyckham House and would have no trouble returning.

But why? Here she stood with the open windows and concealing woods before her. Why not liberate herself as well? She hadn't considered it when she had decided to free Todd; if they both were discovered missing at the same time, the Circle would know she had betrayed them. Now she wondered…perhaps she should have gone with him. Freedom was intoxicating, and it lay only a few feet in front of her…

In the end, she decided Todd's need was greater tonight. She had made her own arrangements for liberation, which would require suffering through her own captivity until Scott got the message she had scheduled to be delivered today. There was more than one way to skin a cat, and Tiana thought she had found hers.

She turned and headed for the dilapidated staircase in the main entry which would take her back to her own prison, her way lit by a shaft of moonlight coming through the broken front window.

She never saw the figure detach itself from the shadows and slink silently up behind her. A hard and heavy blow to her skull, and Tiana Michaels knew no more.

* * * * *

If she had forgotten to give him the flashlight, Todd knew he would never have made it out of the woods. As it was, his progress seemed haphazard and fitful. At times he could move rapidly along a well-defined deer path; other times he had to fight his way through closely spaced pines and overgrown filbert bushes, certain his escape could be heard all the way to Scranton.

Finally he reached the edge of the woods and poked his head cautiously out of the shrubs, looking to his right. The Watering Hole was just visible in the orange glare from a sodium-arc streetlight. Darkness shrouded its windows, giving him a vague sense the time.

After two but before five in the morning. The late October air, crisp and sharply scented with decaying autumn leaves, seared his nostrils. Vapor from his breath wafted away from him, curling lazily in the light from the nearly full moon.

He felt a momentary panic; could this really be happening to him? Could he *really* be standing here along this edge of road in an unfriendly forest, fleeing one life of imprisonment to embrace another? Was the life he had known a short seven weeks ago truly out of his reach now?

It seemed too incredible to even consider. Wasn't it just yesterday he'd opened that letter from an author who wrote nonfiction naturalist books, asking him to research the high rate of wild animal attacks in Mills?

Now he hovered at the edge of an unfamiliar wood, frankly terrified to cross the road because it would take him out of the cover of the trees, and he felt a million miles away from his California cabin. He would have nowhere to hide until he could make his way to the residential neighborhood behind Town Hall.

"Get a grip," he finally muttered. "This isn't getting you out of town."

He drew in a deep breath, closed his eyes briefly, and took the plunge. He dashed across the road and slunk into the shadows of the dark businesses lining Stoneridge Way. Town Hall sat just short of a mile up the road from the tavern, and when Todd reached it, he could have felt no less relief than did Odysseus at the end of his epic journey. He tucked himself into a shadowy shrub and rested for a few minutes, trying to calm his hammering pulse.

The four blocks to Tiana's apartment took only a few minutes. He kept in the shadows as much as he could, although now he desperately wanted to gain entry to the apartment simply for its warmth.

The apartment complex parking lot was lit like an airport runway at midnight; there would be no sneaking up to her door. Deciding it would be best just to pretend like he belonged, Todd strode from the shadows into the light and boldly crossed the lot. He took the outside stairs to the upper level without bothering to be overly quiet, fumbled the key into the lock, and let himself into the apartment.

Blessed warmth washed over him, and Todd's nose immediately began to run. He made his way into the tiny kitchen and snatched a paper towel off the roll sitting on the counter to wipe it with. He glanced around the room, taking stock of his surroundings.

What he could see of the apartment through the gloom seemed pretty much in line what he would expect for a small-town bar employee: a shabby-chic décor, light on the chic. A tiny, one-butt kitchen, great for the single life but dreadful when giving a dinner party. No dining room, just a couple of barstools on the other side of the wide counter, which overhung the other side and served as a buddy bar. Shadows lurked in the living room, the curtains drawn over the paned windows. A sliver of orange glow from the sodium-arc streetlight outside filtered between the curtain panels but did nothing to dispel the darkness.

Dismissing his surroundings, he opened the flour canister, took out the bag of flour, and retrieved the money Tiana had told him about. He counted it quickly, making a mental note of the amount so he could eventually return it. He was privately astounded to find she had amassed better than a thousand dollars in her emergency stash. Todd took it all, not fooling himself with false nobility; he knew even a thousand dollars might not be enough to get him where he needed to be.

Now the car keys, and freedom. Well, not freedom, he amended, but at least an imprisonment of choice. On the letter rack inside the door, she had said. He slipped out of the kitchen and into the entryway again.

Only one set of keys hung on the letter rack, and he pocketed them. Time to go; he felt like too much time had already passed. The possibility of his escape having been discovered grew greater with each passing minute.

He laid a hand on the doorknob and stopped. Something didn't feel right. He didn't know what alerted him but he ducked just in time. A club smashed into the door over his head. Todd flung himself backward and collided with his assailant's legs. They both crashed to the floor in a tangle of limbs.

Todd drove his head backward, connecting with his attacker's face, and felt something crunch. A strangled scream like a squawk, and the club fell away. Todd snatched it up, brandishing it at the man who still sat on the floor, cupping his broken nose. Blood pooled in his hands and spilled over onto his jeans.

"A cricket bat?" Todd marveled. "You were going to bash in my head with a *cricket bat?*"

The man glared at him. "You broke by dose!"

"I'm going to break your head!" Todd threatened, rage boiling up inside him. He was so close to freedom; he didn't need this asshole messing it all up. "How did you know I'd be here?"

"You're nod doo smard, are you?" The man reached into his jacket pocket, and Todd raised the bat a fraction. But the man's hand came out holding only a cell phone. "No reception in da house, bud oudside…" He shrugged and managed a bloody smile.

"You knew?" Todd felt a fatalistic sense of defeat. Of course they knew. There seemed to be no keeping secrets from these people. They were everywhere; they heard everything.

"Can'd dalk aboud anything in dere withoud him finding oud," the man confirmed.

"Now what?" Todd demanded. "Cricket bat versus cell phone? I'd say I have the distinct advantage."

"How about gun versus cricket bat?" said a new voice behind him. "Kind of like rock, paper, scissors, only the stakes are higher."

Todd closed his eyes as he felt the cold end of a gun barrel against his temple. "Fred."

"Mr. Garrett," Fred Olmstead replied. "Fancy meeting you here."

"Well, I didn't exactly plan it this way."

"I thought not." Fred chuckled. "Drop the bat. I can pull a trigger faster than you can swing that."

"But you won't, will you?" Todd challenged. "It defeats your purpose."

"Ah, there is that. I suppose I'll have to do this instead…"

Todd didn't wait to find out what constituted "this instead." He ducked and swung. The butt of the gun grazed Todd's shoulder instead of his head, and Todd's cricket bat connected with Fred's ribs. Fred dropped the gun. Todd took advantage of his momentary upper hand to deliver another vicious blow to the other man's ribs. Fred crumpled to the hallway floor, gasping for air.

Not wasting a second, Todd stepped over his prone opponent, wrenched open the front door, and flew down the steps. He found Tiana's car without difficulty, slammed the key into the lock, and swung into the seat, slamming the door behind him.

Fred staggered out the apartment door onto the balcony, his face a lurid vision of wrath. Todd smacked the lock down, jammed the key into the ignition…and nothing happened. He tried again. Not even the idiot lights on the dashboard came on.

"*No!* Come on come on *come on this can't be happening!*" But he knew he would not be escaping in this car. He fumbled for the door handle, and froze, staring into the barrel of a gun.

Fred tapped the glass with the gun and motioned for him to open the door and get out. Todd didn't think he'd be given another opportunity to attack, but he stayed on guard anyway as he climbed out of the Celica.

"Now Todd, I don't see why we can't do this civilized. Where do you think you can go? Unless you're locked up, you're a danger to society. We can't let you run loose on an unsuspecting public, now can we?"

Todd swallowed hard. "Why did you do this to me? I didn't bother you! You could have just left me alone. I didn't know anything!"

"You knew enough and suspected more. But it's not just what you knew, Todd, but who you knew. Pardon us if we're a bit paranoid when it comes to Aaron's friends."

Todd considered the ramifications of acquiescing when the thought *suicide by cop* occurred to him. He was doomed no matter what; he just wanted it to end before he had the opportunity to hurt – or kill – someone. Could he provoke Fred Olmstead into shooting him – and if he did, would Fred's gun be loaded with the appropriate bullets? He didn't know for certain. Olmstead was furious but he rather doubted he'd waste all their hard spellwork in one fit of rage.

"How many people have you killed as a result of your misguided paranoia, Fred? Aaron's just – Aaron. A man like any other, no more special than anyone else."

"Misguided?" Fred cocked his head and smiled a little. "I do believe you're baiting me, Todd. Now if you don't mind, it's late, it's cold, and I have business to attend elsewhere. It's time for us to be going."

Todd allowed Fred to take him by the arm and went with pronounced docility. When Fred's grip eased a fraction, Todd drove his elbow deep into the man's injured ribs and took off running across the lot. If he could escape into the shadows, he just might be able to lay low until he could find his way to Ron's house. On one of her many visits to his cell, Tiana mentioned Cody Schaefer was in town. A capable man, Cody would know what to do.

The shrubs and shadows within reach and Fred Olmstead hurt, Todd thought for a thrilling moment that he might actually make it. He wagered he'd broken several of the man's ribs and running would be no joy and no easy task.

But then an object struck him in the back of the head. As he tumbled painfully to the blacktop, Todd couldn't help being grimly amused that Fred had thrown his gun at him.

TÊTE-À-TÊTE

Kim met Taryn at the Main Street Diner for breakfast before their shift. As Taryn came across the parking lot toward her, she thought her friend's eyes looked red-rimmed and swollen, as though she'd been crying. But the smile she offered was warm and genuine, and Kim thought she just must have slept poorly.

"You didn't have to wait for me outside." Taryn linked her arm through Kim's and drew her inside the diner. "You've been ill; you should've come inside."

"Quite frankly, I'm sick of inside. I'm gonna have eight hours of it today, so I thought I'd get some air while I could." She surveyed her friend and said with a hint of censure, "You don't look so hot yourself. Sleep bad?"

"Sleep? What's that?" Taryn asked, tongue-in-cheek, but her answer was sharp and bitter.

Kim was greeted warmly by the hostess – the woman who had been with Melody Olmstead the day she'd come into the tavern with a bruised cheek – who lamented her two day absence and assured her that her favorite table was available. This elicited an amused look from Taryn, who murmured "Come here much?" out of the corner of her mouth as they were seated. Coffee and cream were banged onto the table, and the hostess gave Kim's shoulder a squeeze as she left.

"Do you often have insomnia?" she asked after the hostess was out of earshot.

Taryn snorted. "No. But I often have man trouble," she muttered darkly. "Enough about me. How are you feeling?"

"I'll be better with some blueberry pancakes in me," Kim confided with a grin. "I came here at least every other day until I got sick. I haven't felt much like eating for the last few days."

"Well, don't hurl on the table. It will ruin my appetite, and like every other woman in the world, I eat when I'm stressed. I'm really jonesing for a chicken fried steak."

Kim gave her a sympathetic grimace. "So what did he do?"

"Works too much. Plays too little," her friend replied shortly. "Loves too selfishly," she added in an undertone. She blew her fiery bangs off her forehead with an impatient breath and snatched up her coffee, hiding as best she could behind the mug.

"Pretty typical for a guy, don't you think? A leopard can't change its spots, and face it, they're all leopards."

"Oh yeah? Not everyone still has on their just-fell-in-love rose-colored glasses, Pollyanna."

"What do you mean by that?" Kim scowled at her.

"Oh please. A blind man could see how you feel about Ron. If it's any consolation, I think he feels the same way about you, but good luck getting him to admit it. More luck on getting him to commit."

"I believe you've already made that point once." Kim lifted her own mug to hide her irritated frown.

Taryn covered her eyes with one hand and sighed deeply. "I'm sorry. I'm really snappy today. It's not your fault, and I have no right to be jealous. It's just…"

Their server appeared then, and in the flurry of ordering the conversation was lost. Kim rather thought Taryn was glad of it.

When they were alone again, she said, "Why on earth would you be jealous of me? You can practically watch my heart break right before your very eyes."

"Maybe it won't be like that."

"I'd rather be realistic than hopeful."

"You never know."

"We both know how this one will turn out. I'd rather talk about you and Denny and how you've made a long-distance relationship work this long."

Taryn's hand dropped from her face. "You call this 'working?' I was excited for him when he got into Quantico. I supported him through it all, even when he had to move to Philadelphia because that was the only opening in the Bureau."

Kim gaped at her with sudden comprehension. "He's FBI!" The bureaucratic hands, the capable, unflappable demeanor, the rudimentary medical training – all of it suddenly made sense…except why he was here in Mills, working in a tavern.

"He *was*. Not anymore, at least that's what he says. He poured most of his money into real estate – has several rentals in Philly along with a few here besides the ones he co-owns with Ron. It's enough to keep him busy and in Philadelphia most of the time – except I know he has a property management company looking after them. Quite honestly, Beth, I don't have the faintest idea what he really does or from where he really earns his income."

"And he's not talking," Kim deduced.

"Only to tell me I'm being silly." Taryn poured more coffee from the carafe and stirred a creamer into it. "When he went to Quantico, he promised that as soon as he was placed we would get married. Do I look like I have a husband?" She thrust her left-hand ring finger in Kim's face to illustrate her point. "I asked him last night if he ever plans on keeping that promise. He got angry and said 'Now is not the time to discuss it, Taryn.'"

"I'm sorry."

"And I realized last night that he's already married. He's married to whatever he does when he's not with me. I'm just a mistress – no,

I'm not even that. I'm just a benny."

"Benny?" Kim queried. It wasn't a term she was familiar with.

"Friend with benefits," Taryn clarified glumly.

Their food arrived, and in between bites Kim tried to cheer her friend by roundly abusing men in general. She finally managed to wrangle a couple of laughs from Taryn, and the conversation turned to lighter topics. Kim ate with relish even though she couldn't manage more than a third of what was on her plate; she liked the spurt of the giant blueberries as she crushed them between her teeth. A couple were intensely sweet, and she dug through the cakes looking for more.

As they walked to their cars after paying their tab, Taryn stopped suddenly and gave her a brief hug. Just as suddenly she let go and hurried to her car, speeding away without another glance, as though embarrassed by her uncharacteristically emotional behavior.

Kim followed at a rather slower pace, but her mind wasn't on her friend's relationship issues. She was wondering why the FBI – or whomever Denny Wallace actually worked for – had sent him to Mills mere days after her father had vanished.

* * * * *

Hours later, she glanced up from her task of straightening the back bar, hoping for a distraction in the form of poker when Scott came out of the kitchen. Business was slow and playing cards made the time pass quickly and enjoyably.

But Taryn had disappeared into the kitchen to give it a thorough cleaning, something she said she did at least once a month because she knew the men wouldn't. Kim suspected she was regretting confiding her troubles and was hiding lest she be tempted to tell more.

Scott had been abnormally withdrawn as well; he had pleaded a headache when he came in, but she wondered if it was more to do with Nadine's sudden attack of devotion to Ron. Not for the first time she wondered where Cody had sent her and under what authority. Another enigma, that man; she wondered idly if he were somehow connected to Denny in profession.

"Beth, I have to go home. This headache is killing me. I can't even think straight." Scott stopped beside her, rubbing his temples and squinting in the light. Pain drew his mouth into a tight line and sweat beaded on his pale face.

"Do you need a ride home or can you make it?"

"I can make it." He smiled wanly, but it looked more like a grimace to Kim. "Do you want me to send Ron in early? He's supposed to be here in a couple hours."

"I'll be fine," Kim said, and hoped she hadn't lied. She knew how to run Ron's mixology software, but that didn't mean she was any grand bartender.

"I'll see you later." He walked back toward the kitchen, and for a moment it seemed he staggered slightly as he went through the swinging door. Being prone to debilitating headaches herself, she could sympathize.

Her own illness had made coming in today an iffy proposition, but her guilt over being gone at the same time Tiana decided to skip two days without notice had dragged her from her warm, cozy bed. Once she'd ventured out of the house into the cold rain, she'd regretted her decision but figured she could fake her way through the day despite the waves of nausea that frequently gripped her. This morning's blueberry pancakes sat heavily in her churning stomach, and she doubted much more time would pass before they were ejected. Business would be slow until evening, though; Ron would be there by then, and she would be able to go home.

But Ron didn't show up for his shift. Kim paced, worried, while Taryn tried phoning the Schaefer household and, in turn, all Schaefer cell phones. No one answered, and Kim's concern grew. Taryn also began pacing after she had called Denny in to work the bar, and they circled each other like a couple of edgy tigers in a too-small cage.

"I can't imagine what could have happened," Taryn said over and over.

"It's probably Scott," Kim said for the hundredth time. "His headache might have been so bad he had to go to the hospital."

"But Ron would have – " The phone rang, and Taryn vaulted over the bar in a remarkable feat of gymnastic skill just as the door of the tavern blew open. Kim turned with a smile of relief, expecting Denny.

Her smile froze when she saw Caleb Schaefer instead.

"Good evening, Miz Fairchild," he greeted smoothly.

"Mr. Schaefer," she returned. "What can I do for you?"

"A private word with you, if you don't mind." He nodded his head toward Taryn, who listened to the caller on the telephone with single-minded concentration.

Kimberly didn't want "a private word" with him, but she couldn't see how to refuse without being rude or awkward. Denny would be here in a matter of minutes, and while his hands seemed to be those of a bureaucrat, she had no doubt he could handle Caleb with efficiency.

"Certainly." She motioned for a booth by the fireplace that would afford them a measure of privacy but was within full view of the bar and Taryn's watchful eye.

He slid into the booth across from her with catlike grace, resting his hands on the table and gazing at his linked fingers with a troubled frown. To Kim, his scrutiny seemed contrived.

"I wanted to talk to you about my son." He looked up, pinning her with those mesmerizing eyes. Kim forgot to breathe.

"I don't think that's a good idea." She gripped the edge of the table, poised to slide out of the booth and leave him sitting there with his unwelcome advice. But she couldn't make herself move; lethargy held her rooted to her seat even while nausea made her want to bolt for the restroom.

"I'm trying to save you a lot of heartache," he said kindly. *Or save me for yourself*, she thought cynically. "Aaron has experienced a lot of tragedy in his life. He'll never have anything more than brief, dysfunctional, and ultimately failed relationships."

"Maybe I'm not looking for anything permanent," she replied blandly. Her eyes skated over his without lingering; his steady gaze made logical thought impossible, and she had the feeling she would need her wits about her in this conversation.

"There are other, better – " He broke off and drew in a breath. "There's a lot about his past that you don't know."

"You mean what happened eleven years ago."

"He told you? I'm surprised, to say the least. He doesn't even talk about it with family. But Beth, you're misplacing your trust. He went into the woods with two friends and came back out again alone, covered in blood. His friends had been cut to pieces and thrown in a pond. How do you think they got there?"

"Do tell."

"My best friend is the town constable; a cover-up is entirely too easy. I have a strong sense of family, estranged though we are. Do you think I'd let my own son take the needle for something he did out of a sense of private justice?"

Kim finally let her eyes lock on his. Taryn, now fully facing her, still talked on the phone although her face bore an expression of suspicious concern. Denny had arrived sometime in the last minute and, quite expressionless, perused the Old Mr. Boston guide she had left on the bar, positioned so he could keep them both in sight.

"We only have his word that he and Elizabeth had a date and that she never showed up. But one of the friends he took to help find her had betrayed him, and Aaron knew it. So into the woods goes the faithless fiancée – and mysteriously vanishes. And into the woods goes Aaron and his traitor best friend – and only Aaron comes out alive."

"He would *never* – "

"Wouldn't he?" Caleb countered, his voice, pitched low to induce trust, now grated with impatience. "His fiancée slept with his best friend and became pregnant. Did he tell you?"

"No. But I heard as much."

"Then you have to agree, what better way to get rid of them both – and the child – and make it look like the mysterious 'coven' did away with them? There is no coven, Bethany. There are no witches – well, there *are* Wiccans, but they're harmless."

"It seems to me you're spinning the truth to make it fit your desired end result."

"And that would be?" Kim flushed to the roots of her hair. "I see," he murmured, amusement – and interest – laced heavily through his velvet voice.

"Regardless – " she began, but the words stopped when he dipped his hand into his jacket pocket and slapped it on the table. Metal clattered, and she stared down at three bullets tipped with a strange, yellowish metal that rolled on the table between them.

"Silver," he said. "From Ron's personal stash. I want you to understand how deep is his emotional scarring. He has convinced himself that some black magic cult killed his friends; it's the only way he can deal with what he did. The moon was full that night; he's associated that with the werewolf legend even if he won't admit it out loud." He nudged the bullets, and they rolled toward her.

Her heart, already racing, picked up pace. The world swam out of focus for an instant. She lost the thread of conversation. When she gained control, she found herself staring down at a diamond solitaire lying amongst the silver bullets. For a crazy moment she thought he must be some sort of magician. *Watch me pull a rabbit out of my hat!*

The light refracted through the diamond, sending rainbows glimmering across the dark mahogany table. She stared at it, utterly numb. Her hand floated out and picked it up. The inside of the small circle of gold was engraved with an inscription: *M.E.P. ∞ A.E.S. 1993.*

"Mary Elizabeth Peterson," Caleb explained softly. "Aaron Evan Schaefer. The sign of infinity, supposedly how much he loved her. Infinity lasted until she slept with his best friend."

Her stomach churned. She hadn't expected *this*. Her lips were numb when she whispered, "Where did you get this?"

"I know where Elizabeth Peterson's body is buried. I've known all along. He showed me where he'd killed her, and we buried her together. The others – sweet Jesus, Beth, he'd hacked them to pieces. We weighted the pieces in gunny sacks and threw them into the pond, never dreaming it would be dragged and the bodies found.

"Then he ran into the woods, and I couldn't find him. I didn't think I'd ever see him again. To be honest, I was sure he would commit suicide. I believe his emotional collapse was real; the enormity of what he'd done must have been a tremendous burden."

Kim lifted her head suddenly, her eyes narrowed. "The blood on him was an uncommon type."

"Possibly. But he's one of six or seven in town with A negative blood." He paused for effect. "Jason Kent had it too."

That seemed to contradict something she'd already heard, but she couldn't quite put her finger on it. She remained silent for a long time, staring at the ring Aaron Schaefer had put on the finger of the woman he intended to marry twelve years ago. It was entirely conceivable that events had unfolded just as Caleb claimed – except that Caleb was unaware that Ron had been attacked by a werewolf after fleeing the murder scene. One event did not necessarily preclude the other.

Her mind coldly considered the veracity of Caleb's version while her heart desperately denied it. She couldn't have been so wrong about Ron. After that kiss in her cottage, there was no way would she trust him if he had committed such heinous acts. She had known all of him for those brief, extraordinary moments; known every nuance of his soul. If murder had been a facet of it, wouldn't he repulse her?

She pushed the bullets back across the table to Caleb but kept the ring. He didn't object.

In her peripheral vision, she glimpsed Taryn talking to Denny, her hands gesturing spiritedly. The time had come to tilt the world back to a sane position.

"I'm afraid I have no more time to spare," Kim said, somehow finding a steady voice.

"Of course. You're at work. I understand," Caleb said smoothly. "Please think about the things I've told you."

"Oh, I will." Kim clenched her jaw to hold back what was sure to be a flood of humiliating admissions, all in defense of Ron's innocence. Without further word, she slid out of the booth, shoving the ring into her jeans pocket. Her pulse roared in her ears. She took two wobbling steps and crumpled to the floor.

FROM BAD TO WORSE

Reggie Spaulding, one of Mills Memorial Hospital's five regular doctors, had just left the waiting room when Ron's cell phone chimed. He made no move to look at the incoming text message; his mind still reeled from Reggie's news: *We don't know what's wrong with Scott. He hasn't responded to any of the migraine medications we've tried, or to any of the painkillers. We're taking him for a CT scan to look for tumors or swelling in the brain. I'll be honest: his vitals are not good. If we can't stop whatever is happening…*

Cody stared into the corridor as though he could will the physician back with good news. He too made no move to check his cell phone when it vibrated in his pocket, but with monumental effort dragged his eyes away from the empty hallway when Ron's phone buzzed, indicating an incoming call.

"You should get that."

"What about you? Yours is ringing too."

His uncle lifted his shoulder in a careless shrug. Ron stared down the hallway for a moment more, then dug his phone out of his jeans pocket, glancing at the display. One missed call: Denny. And one text message: again, Denny. He opened the text message, finding the command: *CALL ME!!* He gazed at it but made no effort to reply or to obey.

As though sensing his dawdling, the phone vibrated in his hand again. Cody sent him a censuring look, and Ron got up, answering the call as he left the room.

"Can't this wait? I'm a little busy right now."

"Any news?"

"No change whatsoever."

"Then I think we have time to talk about Caleb and Beth."

"What do you mean? Where are they?" The thought of her with his father made his stomach clench in dread. Caleb liked young, attractive women – liked them very much.

"He left about ten minutes ago. Against my advice, she's on her way to you as we speak. She won't tell me what he said, just that she had to talk to you about it immediately."

Ron was puzzled; Denny was making no sense. "What was he doing there talking to her to begin with?"

"I don't know. That's not the point of my call. She passed out, so when she gets there, take her car keys away. She should not get back behind the wheel."

"Whoa, wait! She passed out?" The admitting nurse shot him a glare as his voice rose. He made a grimace of contrition and headed out the emergency rooms doors. The frigid air burned his lungs and made his eyes water, but he had relative privacy. He shivered as he paced under the portico, trying not to think about the nearly-full moon hanging portentously in the night sky – and his coat hanging in the waiting room.

Denny had said something that Ron missed, but he didn't ask his friend to repeat himself. His brain latched on to Denny's next words, and he forgot about anything else as an icy trickle of fear chilled his blood.

"She had been talking to Caleb pretty intensely. Then she stood up and down she went, out cold. He was the epitome of concern, of course." Sarcasm dripped from Denny's voice. "I gave her a cursory exam – Ron, she hasn't improved at all in the last four days. Whatever she's being drugged with, she's still getting it from somewhere."

"Great. What do you suggest we do? Short of forcibly stuffing her into the hospital for tests…"

"While that's not a bad idea, I'm working on a safer plan."

"Your people want to take her? Will I ever see her again or will she be classified?"

"Ha ha. It's probably best you keep an eye on her. In fact, I don't think it's a good idea for her to be at the cottage alone anymore."

"Yeah, well, *you* try convincing her of that. She's not going to listen to me. Why the hell didn't you stop her from leaving the tavern? Don't tell me you had to pass PT tests at Quantico but you can't outrun a girl who's ill."

Denny chuckled ruefully and – Ron thought with a bit of malicious glee – a trifle embarrassed. "I admit she's quicker than I thought. A lot more clever, too."

"And yet you think I'll have more success than you," Ron marveled. His eyes picked out headlights coming up the street. The car slowed and turned, bouncing into the parking lot, the sodium arc light turning the dark blue paint to gun-metal grey.

"Well, she *is* willingly coming to talk you, whereas she wouldn't tell me squat. She should be there by now."

"Yeah, I'm watching her park. Rather," he went on with a grim smile, his eyes tracking the sedan as it made an awkward U-turn and backtracked to an empty spot closer to the ER doors. "I'm watching her circle the parking lot like a drunken vulture. I'd better go."

He closed the phone and stuffed his hands in his pockets, watching her get out of the car. She stumbled slightly as she swung the door closed and started across the parking lot. Even from this distance he could see the determined set of her shoulders and jaw as she battled exhaustion – tenacity and vulnerability bound up in one damned attractive package.

Her step faltered when she noticed him leaning against the stone pillar of the portico, and then her mouth flattened into a grim line, which was regrettable because she had a rather lovely mouth.

Frowning, he pushed that thought away. It didn't matter how lovely her mouth was, or that her eyes were like polished chips of clear, fine amber, or that her small frame packed delightful layers of firm muscle and soft, silky skin, or that her hair – good Lord, her hair! He suppressed a smile.

"What?" She frowned irritably at the look on his face, stopping just out of his reach.

He didn't know whether to laugh or give in to apprehension. "What the hell happened to you?"

She put a hand to hair, trying to straighten her ponytail, which had migrated toward the side of her head. Her hair, in fact, was in total disarray and stood up in sweaty spikes. He thought the look went rather well with her sickly pallor and the purple circles under her eyes.

A scowl darkened her brow. "I need to talk to you."

"Obviously. Can it wait for a while? This is a really bad time."

"I know. There's not going to be a good time for this."

He sighed. He had been afraid of that. "Let's go inside." Her eyes drifted to the sliding doors of the ER with a fair amount of suspicion. "Woman, I'm freezing my ass off."

"You're not going to try to stick me in the hospital, are you?"

"How'd you guess?"

"It's a gift," she muttered, and for some reason her scowl deepened. "Let's just stay out here."

"No way. You wanna talk to me, you have to go inside. I'm moments away from dying of hypothermia." He put a hand toward the small of her back to guide her to the door. She moved away from it as soon as they were inside and stood just out of range of the electronic eye of the automatic door opener.

"Your – "

"Let's have a seat." He didn't wait for her, but moved to the hard plastic chairs that made up the short-term waiting room décor and simply watched her from his chair until she relented – with ill grace – and joined him. He might not be able to stick her in the hospital, but he could make sure she got a marginal amount of rest while they talked.

"If you're done playing games," and she sent a smoking glare at him, "your father came to see me at the tavern."

He considered several responses, discarded them all, and opted for the fairly neutral, "I didn't realize you two knew each other on a social basis."

"We don't, which made the visit even odder. He wanted to talk about you."

"Me?"

"Warn me away from you, actually," she responded frankly. "You aren't going to like this. Caleb claims he knows what happened to Elizabeth."

"There's been a lot of speculation about what happened to Elizabeth," he replied, barely managing to keep his voice even.

She closed her eyes. "He implied that you murdered Elizabeth because she slept with your best friend and became pregnant."

He gaped at her. His brain seemed capable of churning up only profanity, so he clenched his teeth to keep back a violent stream of swearing. After a moment, he managed to say, "I can't deny that Elizabeth was pregnant when she vanished. I also can't deny that there was plenty of evidence that the father was one of my best friends. Neither of them could remember anything, but Jason was convinced they hadn't been intimate. He was going to pay for a paternity test."

"To get out of child support?" she asked, her voice slightly acidic.

"No." He shook his head to emphasize his answer. "Not at all. Supporting the child wouldn't have been a concern. He'd have done it even if she'd told him it wasn't necessary. And it *wasn't* necessary; I'd have married her no matter what. The baby would have been treated well."

"I have no doubt," she said, her tone softening.

"But she vanished three days before she was scheduled to have the test done. And by the next morning, Jason was dead as well. Since Elizabeth was never found, no DNA comparison could be done even though they had Jason's body. Thus...no proof."

And none had been needed. Liz was gone, Jason was dead – as was Peter, who'd perhaps known more than he'd ever let on but had played it close to the vest in his usual manner, not wanting to color someone with suspicion unless it was warranted. Pete had never voiced his suspicions; they had died with him at the Wyckham House. The only thing Ron knew for sure was that Pete had believed Jason.

"There's more," she went on with some reluctance. She seemed to be working up the courage to continue. When she suddenly rose, he thought she was leaving and grabbed her wrist. One delicate brow, arched slightly, was enough to make him let go. Her hand slid into her pocket and clenched into a fist. As she struggled to extricate it, he was forcibly reminded of the story of the monkey and the coconut. Then her hand broke free, still curled around her treasure, but she made no move to hand it over.

"Well?"

"Ron," she began, and stopped abruptly, closing her eyes for a moment. She drew in a steadying breath. "He told a very convincing story."

He couldn't have been more shocked than if she'd sucker-punched him. "Did he now? Well, I'll grant you he's a charmer. More sophisticated women than you have fallen for his lines." She winced. "I'm sor – "

"Then how did he get this?" She smacked her hand down on his and opened it. A warm circle of metal poked into his flesh and then eased up as she drew away. He stared down at the ring that lay in his palm like a gold and gemstone accusation. The world titled at a dizzying angle. He hadn't seen this ring in eleven years, but he had no doubt that it was the one he'd slid onto Elizabeth's finger the day he'd asked her to marry him.

"Is it hers?" she asked. He nodded convulsively. "I have to ask you – no, don't shake your head, I *have* to know – did you have anything to do with her death?"

He was shocked that she would ask that. Didn't she know? Hadn't she seen him – all of him – in that glorious moment when every nuance of his being had been laid bare to her? How could she even think it?

Something niggled at his memory, a truth waiting to be remembered, long suppressed and buried under denial and evasion. Something was wrong with his perception of events; he knew he had believed Elizabeth had gone to the Wyckham House, but he couldn't remember why he'd believed it. And he couldn't remember how Jason and Peter had become involved. He'd obviously not wanted to go alone, but he couldn't recall asking them to go with him. Repressing the memories now would be of no help, but he had done it for so long he didn't know how to get around his memory block.

"Dr. Jarvis," he said suddenly, making her jump. "I need to talk to Dr. Jarvis." She shifted uncomfortably in her chair, her expression stricken and – guilty? "What?"

"Olivia Jarvis is dead, Ron." She bit her lip nervously and went on in a rush, "She died right after you moved back to Mills."

"How do you know that?" He turned sideways in his seat so fast that she started, flinching backward. "Didn't I tell you no more investigating?"

"I had to know!" she burst out, her cheeks reddening and illustrating how far her health had deteriorated in a few short weeks. Denny was right; she couldn't be allowed to drive home tonight, and she couldn't be allowed to stay at the cottage alone.

"Had to know what?"

"I found a picture in a book – a picture of the Wyckham House. But the drawing was from the 1300s and was of a castle in Hungary. They call it the Evil Castle. I called the author of the book and he said…he said…" Her rush of words withered under his glare. She seemed to shrivel a little in her chair.

"He said what? Go find my shrink?" Worse than annoyed, he was embarrassed. And worse than embarrassed, he was fearful. What had she learned about him that he himself didn't know?

"No. It doesn't matter what he said. The point is Olivia Jarvis is dead and her colleague doesn't think it was an accident."

"Colleague? What colleague?"

"Robert Hansen. He worked at Meadow Grove with her. He thinks she was murdered."

"Why would he think that?" But his heart hammered in his chest, obscuring her reply. He was grateful; he didn't want to know. Knowing meant facing what had happened, perhaps remembering the events of eleven years ago. He didn't think he could face that.

What a fine shade of yellow you are. He covered his eyes, pressing lightly to stop the throb of a tension headache.

"Look," he began, his hand falling away. But the words died in his throat. Reggie Spaulding beckoned to him from the doorway of the waiting room, his expression grave. Ron shot a look at Beth, who had gone, if possible, paler than before.

Reggie waited to impart the news until Ron had joined Cody and Renée. Beth, who had been hot on his heels all the way across the lobby, hung back just inside the room. Reggie flicked a glance at her and then at Cody, who nodded slightly.

"Nothing we do makes any difference," Reggie said gently. "Scott's gone into a coma. We can find no reason for his illness, which means we have no cure." He looked from one to the other of them. "If you know anything – *anything* – that will help, please let me know now. If the rate he progressed into a coma is anything to go by, he doesn't have much time."

CONFESSION

Silence had fallen over the waiting room after Reggie Spaulding left to continue his rounds. Renée rested against the wall, her eyes wide and terrified. No one seemed to want to move – or perhaps they were all afraid to lest their one simple action break the fine thread tethering Scott to life.

Cody's cell buzzed, and again he made no move to answer the call. But the sound broke Beth's paralysis; a look of grim determination claimed her expression as she navigated menus on her own phone. Ron couldn't summon the energy or push aside his fear long enough to ask her what she was doing.

"No," she murmured, barely audible. "No, they wouldn't do *that*."

But her brow creased, and she looked worried.

Ron opened his mouth to ask what she was doing, but Beth's breaking the silence seemed to have ended Cody's paralysis as well. He checked his phone, blinked, and checked again.

"What could Harlan possibly want?"

"Maybe you should call him back," Renée murmured.

"Later." He shrugged and avoided his wife's eye.

Ron couldn't help but think they were afraid that what they waited for now was the news of Scott's death. He glanced at Beth again, but she now stared blankly at her phone, her moment of avid interest gone. Elizabeth's ring seemed to burn a hole in his pocket, begging him to do something about its existence.

"Why are you so fidgety?" Cody asked him. He sent a glance at Beth, who gazed back impassively for a second before closing her eyes. He interpreted that to mean the information she had given him was his to do with as he wished.

"I need to talk to you. Is there somewhere we can do it privately?"

Cody stared at him silently for a long moment, then took off his gold-rimmed glasses, polished them on his fleece jacket, and slid them into his shirt pocket. "We'll be in the chapel, Renée."

Renée opened her mouth, and Cody shot her a quelling look. She clamped her mouth shut and nodded once, looking scared. Ron followed his uncle down a short hallway to the chapel. A quiet hush hovered in the room; he was loath to break it, but he needed answers that he suspected only Cody could give him. He scooted farther down on the pew to make room for his uncle.

"My phone call earlier was from Denny."

"Trouble at the tavern?"

"You could say that. Caleb showed up today to speak to Beth."

Cody arched a brow but didn't seem surprised. "Hurricane Caleb. He has a knack for timing."

"Or he simply took advantage of me being occupied elsewhere," Ron ventured sharply.

Cody nodded. "I told Beth that he has a taste for much younger women and to watch out for him. I hope she heeded my advice."

"She doesn't like him much." Ron lifted a shoulder in a half-shrug.

"She didn't invite him; he went all on his own to warn her about me. About my past."

That sparked Cody's interest. He half-turned on the pew to face Ron, his arm stretching along the back. "Is that right?"

"He said that I murdered Elizabeth because she slept with Jason and got pregnant."

"That seems like a pretty specific charge," Cody admitted, pursing his lips. "And his evidence?"

His hand dove into his pocket to retrieve the ring, and for a moment he had difficulty pulling it back out. He smiled faintly, thinking of Beth doing the exact same thing not half an hour earlier. Then his hand came free and with no dramatics he let the ring drop into his uncle's hand. Cody went very still, staring at the gold circle.

"Caleb had this?" At Ron's curt nod, Cody turned the ring over to peer at the inscription inside and frowned. "I see."

Ron drew in a deep breath . "If Caleb had her ring – Cody, he had to have seen Elizabeth before she disappeared."

"Yes," his uncle replied, reluctant to follow that thought through to the obvious conclusion.

"And if he saw Elizabeth before she disappeared, it stands to reason he probably had something to do with her disappearance."

"Are you saying you think Caleb killed her?"

Ron thought about it for a long minute, his jaw clenching and unclenching as he considered the ramifications of admitting his suspicions. "I don't know. Something's bothered me about the timing of…of everything. Elizabeth conveniently vanishes three days before Paul was going to draw the samples for the paternity test."

"What exactly are you saying, Aaron?"

He kicked his toe against the kneeler and it swung down, barely missing his foot. The muted thump on the thick carpet made them both jump.

"I'm saying that the more I think about it, the more I think Jason was telling the truth and the baby wasn't his. I think maybe they both died to keep the identity of the real father a secret."

Cody digested this silently, brow furrowed. At last he asked, "And Peter?"

"Whatever Peter suspected, he took to his grave. All I know is that he believed Jason when Jase said he didn't think he and Elizabeth had ever actually been intimate. There seems to be more to it, reasons Pete believed him, but I can't remember."

Cody squeezed his shoulder. "It will come, Aaron, don't worry."

"Say Caleb killed her. And say the timing was no coincidence."

"I don't believe in coincidences."

"Nor do I. So the question then becomes…did Caleb kill her because he didn't want anyone to know who fathered her child? Which then begs the question…"

"Was it him?" Cody finished.

Ron flipped the kneeler back up; the bang as it hit the pew echoed in the small sanctuary made Cody flash him a censuring look. "Why would he do that? Of all the young women he could pick from…why mine?" His uncle didn't answer, and after a moment Ron continued, sliding a sidelong glance in Cody's direction. "It makes a man wonder if it was a personal vendetta."

Cody sighed and shifted in his seat as though uncomfortable. "You have no idea what you're asking me to explain. But I'll give it my best shot.

"There's been a lifetime of animosity between Caleb and me, almost from the time I was born. I don't know if it's just sibling rivalry or if he'd already started down his twisted path by the time I came on the scene, but I *do* know we never had the kind of relationship you and Scott had growing up together.

"Everything remained more or less civil – meaning Caleb more or less ignored my existence – until I graduated from high school. I met this young woman in college." His mouth curved in a reminiscent smile. "I fell head over heels in love. I asked her to marry me, and she said she would. We began planning our wedding, and I brought her home to meet my parents.

"During that weekend, Caleb was obviously taken with her. He made no attempt to hide it. It made her very uncomfortable, but when the weekend ended and we went back to school in Philadelphia, I thought that was the end of it."

Ron titled his head a fraction. "But it wasn't."

Cody closed his eyes and said wearily, "No, it wasn't. He openly pursued her. She emphatically rejected him. But by the end of the month...by the end of the month, she had given me back my ring and had accepted his."

Ron felt the color drain from his face. "You were engaged to my mother, weren't you?"

"Yes, it was Belinda. She married him, and I didn't see them for a year and a half. By then you'd been born, and his abuse of Belinda had become a routine occurrence. I met Renée, and by the time you turned two, we'd gotten married.

"And then two years later you were hit by that car. Things got really, *really* bad." Cody's voice lowered to almost a whisper. Ron leaned in closer to hear him. "You lost a lot of blood, and you needed a transfusion. Belinda was pregnant again and having difficulties; the doctors didn't want to let her donate, so they typed Caleb's blood to make sure it was compatible. The results determined Caleb's blood type combined with Belinda's could not have produced yours. Caleb couldn't donate."

Ron stared at him blankly, unable to completely absorb what Cody had implied.

"Do you understand what I'm saying, Aaron?" Cody prodded. "Caleb is not your father."

"But..." He couldn't finish. His face bore all the trademarks of Schaefer blood. Which meant...

Cody settled his shoulders straight. "I'm your father. Belinda and I had one night when things...went too far, just before she ended our engagement. One night was all it took." His smile was ironic.

Ron felt an invisible hand squeezing his throat. He and Cody stared at each other, their identical eyes a testament to the truth of Cody's claim.

"Did you never wonder why it had been so easy for us to take custody of you after Belinda left Caleb?"

Ron tore his gaze away from his uncle's – no, his *father's* – with difficulty. "I did, but I always assumed the abuse gave enough reason."

"It did, but the case would have dragged out much longer. We had a paternity test done, and gaining custody of you went smoothly and quickly. We were in court only one day."

"Why didn't you take me sooner? And why didn't you tell me this years ago? I've spent all these years thinking that man was my father, thinking I had the potential to be like him!"

"Ron, how *could* we tell you?" Cody replied helplessly. "We had our hands full for the first couple of years undoing what Caleb had done to you. I can't imagine the hell it must have been living with that man and his tyranny. We certainly saw the aftermath of his rage at Belinda when he found out she'd been pregnant with you when she married him." He gave an expressive shudder. "Oh, he was brutal. She stayed in the hospital for a week and a half. She almost didn't make it to the hospital; he'd beaten her so badly she miscarried her child and hemorrhaged badly. When she was released, we took her to her house to get her clothes and you, but you weren't there. Caleb had hidden you."

A chill raced through his veins. "Where?"

"The Wyckham House," Cody confirmed.

Ron nodded silently. He'd had dreams since he left Meadow Grove about running down deserted hallways. Did they stem from his stay at the Wyckham House as a child…or from his venture there as an adult?

"Belinda…left before we got the results of the paternity test, but she'd already told us that I was your biological father," Cody continued quietly. "We filed the court papers to take custody of you. Caleb was forced to present you at a Social Services interview, and he couldn't put it off without going to jail. When he produced you with bruises all over, you were taken immediately into custody. You never went back to him.

"As for why we didn't take you sooner – well, Aaron, how could I take you from your mother? You were the only bright spot in her life, and she was a good mother. She took the bruises for you more often than you'll ever know."

"If she was a good mother, she would have taken me and left before all this happened. She wouldn't have raised me in a house with a violent man."

"Do you honestly think she didn't try? He has an almost

supernatural ability to find people. Why do you think Tiana has never been able to leave?" At Ron's shocked look, Cody smiled cynically. "Did you think we didn't know?"

"How *could* you know? She's never told anyone except me."

"I found out through – other means."

"Where is my mother?"

"Alive, but I don't know where. It was deemed safer that way."

"By whom?"

Cody examined his fingernails with undue interest. "We should get back. I don't want to leave Renée alone for long right now."

"I have just one more question," Ron said, remaining seated as his father rose. "The rumors of witchcraft...they're true, aren't they?"

"Do you believe in that sort of thing?"

"That's not an answer."

Cody lifted on shoulder in a slight shrug. "I'm just trying to assess how much you'll believe. It's real, Aaron. I've seen enough strangeness to know it's real."

"Caleb and the Wyckham House – they're at the center of this, aren't they?"

Cody slid his hands into his slacks pockets and rocked back onto his heels. "We believe that Caleb is the coven's high priest."

"We?" Ron asked sharply. His eyes narrowed on Cody's face. "What do you do for a living? I know what you used to do and I know you put a lot of money away to live on so you could retire early...but what do you *do*?"

Cody smiled blandly. "This and that. Now is not the time to go into it. While we walk back, I think we should talk about finding a way to get Bethany admitted for observation. That girl doesn't look well."

Ron chuckled. "Yeah, go ahead and mention it. It'll serve you right."

But when they reached the waiting room, Beth Fairchild was nowhere to be found.

BLOOD LINK

Kimberly waited as long as she dared, not wanting to leave Renée alone in her vigil. But after twenty minutes of her fidgeting and rereading the information she'd looked up on her phone, Renée said without opening her eyes, "Go do whatever it is you need to do. I'll be fine."

"You don't want to stuff me in the hospital like your nephew does?" she asked acerbically, and a ghost of a smile curved the older woman's mouth.

"While the thought is tempting, I've got enough to deal with as it is. And more on its way from the chapel, if my intuition serves me right. Leave while you can; you know you won't be going anywhere if he's here to stop you."

So she went, even though she rather suspected Ron and Denny were right in wanting to admit her to the hospital. She was exhausted to the marrow of her bones, and nausea rolled in her stomach like tumbling surf onto a beach.

It had started raining since she'd gone inside the hospital; the frigid drops splashed her face as she circled Ron's house to the back deck, and took cover under the eaves by a stack of vinyl-shrouded Adirondack deck chairs, shivering and looking out into the rain-drenched yard.

She had no illusions that the spell could be hidden inside the house; Ron's security system was more than they'd want to bypass. So it had to be hidden outside on the property, and if they'd used the spell she suspected they had, it would have to be hidden in an item of Scott's clothing.

It was a long shot, she had to admit, thinking that Scott's sudden illness was caused by anything other than natural means. Even believing in witchcraft to start with was a stretch, but she could think of nothing else, and she couldn't leave Scott's fate to chance.

"Think, Kim!" she admonished herself. Needing to sit, she perched on the edge of a sturdy wooden planter that sat under the shelter of the eaves and let her eyes wander around the grounds.

They would want a hiding place that no one would come across easily, so she doubted the spell had been placed in an item of clothing he normally wore; the chance of it being discovered was too great. She supposed they could have hidden the item in a tree; there were so many dotting Ron's back yard – not to mention those still on his property but outside the cultivated area around the house. But again, that seemed wrong. The ones in the yard were well-cultivated, and someone hiding something like that far up enough in a tree to avoid notice might have attracted the attention of the Schaefers. No, it had to be something else, something simpler to do and virtually undetectable.

Movement in the garden caught her eye, a flash of light against dark. Kim froze, but it was only Taffy, digging in the dirt. Even through the gloom Kim could see mud caking her short legs and the fur on her chest. Ron was going to be furious.

"Hey, knock it off!" she called out. The cat jumped, startled, but when it saw it was only Kim, it went back to digging, dainty paws frantically scrabbling through the muddy soil.

"Fine. If you don't mind becoming a plate of almond chicken, why should I care what happens to you?" Dismissing the cat, she took out her phone and started the web browser, ignoring the call that flashed Ron's number on her screen. Right now she didn't have time to explain. She went to the page she had bookmarked at the hospital and read the information again, hoping for some sort of clue to help her find the spell she suspected they had used.

Called the Witch's Ladder, its deadliness lay in the fact that there was no counter for it unless one could convince its caster to undo it. It caused sudden, severe illness that became progressively worse as the spell ran its twenty-four hour course, and as the clock struck the last second, the victim died instantly. There were anomalies with Scott's illness, however, that made her worry she was wrong. This spell had come to mind only because she'd researched it for a client several months ago. Witchcraft wasn't an exact magic despite what people thought; the only way she could be sure of what had been done was to read this particular witch's grimoire – and then only if the witch in question had written it down. Some didn't.

She glanced up, realizing she could no longer hear the cat's frantic digging. Taffy had her teeth in something, her little face smeared with mud, and was trying to pull it from the wet ground.

"What are you into now? He's gonna be mad if you're digging up his plants." She pocketed her phone and stepped out into the rain.

Taffy didn't run way as she approached; instead, she planted her little legs more firmly into the slippery mud and began pulling again. The object came free a few inches, and Kim stopped in her tracks at the flash of red plaid. She recognized the shirt; Scott had been wearing it under his sweater the day they'd talked at the river.

Her phone rang again. She didn't look at it; she knew by the insistent tone that it was Ron. She dropped to her knees in the garden beside the cat, scraped away the mud anchoring the shirt in the soil, and lifted it free. Something fell from the pocket and rolled across the dirt. Taffy hissed, arching her back, and edged closer to Kim.

It glittered in the back porch light, the small glass cylinder sealing Scott's fate. To know she had been right didn't give her any relief. Instead a dark despair washed through her, because she knew there would be no making them take this back.

She picked up the vial, fancying she could feel its evil intent, and held it up to the porch light. An oddly folded square of paper that looked as though it had been soaked in dark ink, dirt, and a knotted piece of twine had been mashed into the glass tube and sealed in with a thick wax plug. The twine confirmed their choice of spell; it was indeed the Witch's Ladder. But the dirt and the ink-soaked paper were a mystery.

"Oh, Scott, you're in really big trouble," she whispered, horrified. For the first time she allowed the thought to take hold that Scott Schaefer was going to die – and soon. She had to, so she wouldn't curl up in a closet somewhere and hide from these people for the rest of her days. The things she'd read in books, the research she'd done for her father – all of it existed here in this town, not just as academics, not an illusionist's shell-game but *real*, and deadly.

Headlights washed the driveway, and with a sigh of relief Kim scrambled to her feet and started around the house before she realized the car didn't belong to any of the Schaefers. Harlan Michaels' police cruiser. She stopped, uncertain what to do; it was too late to run across the grounds and hide in the forest – not that she wanted to anyway, not in this town. Harlan would be sure to see her tracks through the grass if he didn't actually see her, and her car sat in the driveway as a silent testimony of her presence.

Taffy mewled and darted across the space between them, winding through her legs and nipping her calves. When Kim didn't immediately respond, the cat clutched her pants leg in its sharp teeth and tried to drag her backward.

"It's just Harlan Michaels," she whispered. "Why are you freaking out? He's the..." Her voice trailed off as she remembered Caleb's words. *My best friend is the town constable; a cover-up is entirely too easy.*

The cat pulled again. Kim reached down and picked her up, tucking her inside the open flaps of her jacket, and edged into a dark shadow outside the reach of the porch light. The soaked animal trembled in her arms. Kim trembled too.

Harlan pounded on the front door and shouted, but the skies suddenly opened and let loose a deluge of rain that clattered on the steel roof of the house, masking his words. Thunder boomed in the distance, drowning out the sound of his footsteps on the gravel walk until it was too late. She pressed herself more deeply into the shadow, but it was only a matter of seconds before he saw her.

He stopped at the bottom of the deck steps and cupped his hands beside his mouth, shouting Ron's name out across the yard, and then whirled to come up the step to the back door. For a moment he just stared at her as though not believing his luck.

"Miss Fairchild," he said uncertainly.

"Constable," she returned coolly, raising her chin a scant inch. Taffy issued a low growl from the back of her throat, and even Kim's sheltering embrace and soothing caress wouldn't calm her.

"Ron's not here? I've been by the tavern but I didn't see his truck."

Kim shook her head. "He's still at the hospital. I came to see him also. Instead I found Taffy locked out of the house." She watched Harlan's eyes closely, but he didn't seem suspicious.

He took a step closer to get out of the rain, and the cat went berserk. Kim could do nothing but try to extricate herself from the panicked ball of fur, claws, and pain. Her car keys fell from her pocket and clunked on the deck, and the vial holding the spell dropped from her hand and rolled toward Michaels. The cat's yowls shrieked in her ears as the animal made its way over the top of her head and down her back and then off into the dark sanctuary of the yard. Kim smothered an expletive as she felt her scalp wounds and her fingers came away with smears of blood.

"Are you all ri – " Harlan didn't finish. He saw what she had dropped. The glass vial lay squarely between them. Kim closed her eyes, but when she opened them again, the spell still lay in a puddle of water between them.

Harlan lifted his gaze from the ground to her face, all cop now. "I think we need have a chat, Beth."

He closed the distance between them, grasped her firmly by the elbow before she could bolt, and bent to retrieve the spell and her car keys. His step was brisk as he guided them to the cruiser and shoved her into the passenger seat.

"Stay there." He shut the door and crossed the front of the car to the driver's side. Kim stayed; she wasn't walking, not in this town after dark. Not all the animals came out only at the full moon, and not all of them were the four-footed variety.

Don't panic. You're not out of options, and you can't be certain that he's the enemy.

The driver's door chunked closed behind him, and he turned the key in the ignition. The heater poured warm air into the car. She shivered when it hit her wet clothes. He backed up until he could turn the cruiser around and headed it down the long driveway to the road. When they bumped onto the blacktop and Harlan stomped on the accelerator, bringing the cruiser's speed to forty miles an hour with no effort, Kim found her voice.

"Where are we going?"

Harlan blinked as though surprised. "The hospital, of course."

"The hospital? I thought – "

"Thank God you didn't open it," he interrupted, taking one hand from the wheel to hold the vial up to the dashboard lights. The engine rumbled with power as Harlan accelerated. Kim clutched the edge of the dashboard as the cruiser topped fifty.

"What would have happened?"

"They would have died instantly."

"They? I thought this spell targeted only one individual."

He flashed her a surprised look. "You know about this spell?"

"I've read about it. I can't believe it's real. Can this be undone?"

"It's real. And yes, it can be reversed. But like many things in this particular branch of magic, it requires certain safety measures and a sacrifice."

Kim took her eyes off the road only long enough to send him a sharp look. "A *human* sacrifice?"

"Yes," he said, his tone level. "But not in the way you're thinking. This magic is unlike anything you've studied. And you *have* studied, haven't you?"

"Yes," she admitted reluctantly.

"Much of what is done in the Circle is experimental. We've moved beyond traditional witchcraft, moved beyond voodoo or hoodoo, even. It's walking with the devil now, and it's lethal."

"Why are you here with me, on the way to the hospital, telling me all these things, if you're a part of this Circle?" Kim demanded angrily. "You're part of what's happened to Scott, part of what happened to Ron all those years ago."

"I won't lie; I'm part of the Circle. But I didn't do this to Scott. I don't have time to explain to you my change of heart, and I doubt you would be convinced of it anyway. This is a twenty-four hour spell, performed last night at midnight. I only found out about it an hour ago or I would have taken action sooner. I can reverse it, but it has to be within the next few hours. It will take some preparation, and I have no time to lose."

"Who else was named? How was it done? I've never heard of anything like it."

"It's called a blood link," he replied tersely. "The second person named is not affected at all, while the first person becomes inexplicably ill. At the end of the twenty-fourth hour, they both die instantly."

"Who else?" she persisted.

"Tiana." He scrubbed a hand across his face. She understood his panic now – and his change of heart. It stops being acceptable when it happens to you.

"Why? Why would they do that to her? You're one of their own."

"She told Scott something. I don't know what or when she had the opportunity, but I've never – *never* – seen him in such a rage. I'm not even sure how he knew. But he took action against both of them immediately."

"Who are you talking about?"

He didn't answer. "I can undo it," he assured himself. "But the Circle is going to know what I did. Reversing the work of a fellow of the Circle is a betrayal of the Circle as a whole; I'll be marked for death. I don't know when or how it will happen, but it *will* happen."

"How will they know you reversed it?"

"Didn't you hear me?" he said impatiently. "I'll be *marked*."

"I thought you meant it figuratively."

"No, literally. They'll know, and they *will* kill me."

She was silent as he wheeled the car into the hospital parking lot. His strides were long as they crossed to the building. Kim had to jog to keep up. Once inside, he fell in behind her, and she led the way to the waiting room across the lobby.

Cody Schaefer watched them approach with an impassive, hooded expression. Ron stood as though ejected spontaneously from his seat, thunderclouds forming on his face. A slight cough from his uncle was enough to make him hold his tongue. Kim wondered again about the black SUV that had carried Nadine Bennett off into the night, and what kind of agency granted the kind of power needed to make such a thing happen with just a phone call.

"Harlan?"

"We've got no time for chit-chat, Cody. I have to work fast. We should do this in Scott's room."

"He's been moved to ICU. I think it's best we involve Paul Jacobs. Aaron, please go find him. I saw him about an hour ago."

Ron left with an obvious show of reluctance and a smoking glare of betrayal sent Kim's way. She was torn between running after him to explain and hearing the rest of what Harlan Michaels had to say.

"What are you up to, Harlan?" Cody asked once Ron was out of earshot.

"Restitution."

Cody's lips pursed thoughtfully and he asked, "Reversal?"

"Yes."

Renée sucked in a breath; her husband squeezed her hand comfortingly. "It's a spell then, not an illness. A bad one?" Worry swam in his cobalt eyes, the only indication that Harlan's presence had rattled him.

The constable shrugged. "I've seen worse, but this is in the top ten, Cody."

"Are you sure you want to do this, Harlan?"

"I'm sure."

"But – "

"I'm *sure*, Cody," Harlan snapped irritably. "I would do it no matter what – I owe Aaron – but there's a blood link to Tiana."

He broke off as Ron came back across the room. Kim realized she still stood next to Harlan Michaels, and she moved farther into the room, taking a seat on a small sofa. She shrugged out of her jacket and used it to wipe the remaining smears of dirt from her hands. Her shirt was filthy.

"They paged Paul; he should be here shortly."

Cody waved a hand at the empty chairs in the waiting room. "Then why don't we all sit down and have a civilized discussion about what needs to be done?"

Kim was vaguely amused to see everyone – Harlan included – instantly comply with the obvious command. She was surprised when Ron came to sit next to her.

"They will kill you, Harlan."

"D'you think I care anymore, Cody?" the constable asked wearily.

"And who will take care of Tiana then? Who will protect her?"

"You."

"But – " Cody broke off, shaking his head, and abandoned what he had been going to say. "There's no taking it back once you've done it."

"You've learned a lot about it."

"It's my duty to know. What do you need from me?"

"A small amount of blood from you and Renée both," Harlan said. "And from Scott."

"The blood link," Cody began.

"You're going to have to act fast," the constable replied circumspectly. "Once he realizes she's not going to die – " He broke off. "I won't be around to help her. I need your promise."

"I'm ready. But Harlan, undoing witchcraft with witchcraft isn't the answer," Cody began. "Prayer, trust in God – "

"I have to be sure, Cody. This is the only assurance I know."

"But – "

"Ahem."

At the polite cough from the doorway, everyone stopped talking and looked up. Paul Jacobs, the attending physician of the evening, looked rumpled and tired and more than slightly ill-tempered.

"You rang?" he asked Ron, who tipped his head at Cody.

Cody wasted no more time arguing with Harlan. "We need a favor, Paul, with as few questions asked as possible."

Paul Jacobs' gaze ticked from one face to another, gauging their expressions. "Will it help your son?"

"Yes."

The doctor perched on the arm of the small sofa Ron shared with Kim. Ron edged over to give him some room. "Name it."

Harlan said, "I need three vials with a small amount of blood. Scott's, Cody's, and Renée's."

Paul opened his mouth, shut it with a snap, and swallowed his curiosity. "All right. How soon?"

"Five minutes ago."

Paul rose. "Time is clearly a concern. If all relevant parties will come with me, we'll handle this out of sight of prying eyes."

An awkward silence descended on the room after the older adults left. Kim became acutely aware of Ron's left side pressed up against her right. His voice vibrated through her when he spoke, setting her body humming in reaction.

"You shouldn't have been driving."

"Don't I know it," she admitted. She closed her eyes, leaning her head against the back of the sofa, trying not to think about anything but the reversal. It had to work.

"You knew what you were looking for before you left here."

"I suspected. I would still be looking if your cat hadn't already found it. She's going to need a bath."

He flicked a glance at her mud-stained shirt but didn't comment. "What made you go to Harlan?"

Kim turned her head to look up at him, finding him – as always – closer than she expected. His eyes were shadowy pools of cool blue water, fixed on hers with tongue-tying intensity.

"I didn't. He came to your house looking for you. I happened to be there. We bumped into each other at an opportune time."

He swallowed with difficulty and said with obvious effort, "Thank you."

"Don't thank *me*. Taffy found the spell, Harlan's the one who knows how to reverse it and is willing to do so. Thank *him*."

A granite mask slipped over his features, and she mused that perhaps Cody's eyes weren't the only things Ron had inherited from the Schaefer bloodline. They all seemed to share an exasperating ability to mask all emotion.

"That'll never happen."

Unable to understand the cold anger that burned in his voice, she lowered her gaze. After a moment he covered her hand with his, twining their fingers together. She didn't understand this either, but his skin warmed her cold flesh and his touch anchored her there, giving her a solid reason to share in his family's vigil, so she didn't pull away. Her cheek pressed against his shoulder, Kim closed her eyes and slept.

REVERSAL

The syringe quivered in Harlan's hand, and he took a steadying breath. When he felt he could control his trembling, he held it over the contents of the glass vial, dimly lit from the flickering flame of a blood red candle.

He had said his prayers over the spell; only with spiritual protection could the vial be opened and the contents removed without the target dying instantly. Arrayed on a silver tray liberated from an incomplete tea service, the components of the spell seemed innocuous: a length of twine, knotted thirteen times; a small scrap of parchment, folded around snips of hair from both Scott and Tiana; a teaspoon of dirt, taken from Scott's footprint in the mud. By themselves, each meant nothing, but under the manipulation of magic, infused with evil, death was served on antique silver.

And it waited for one last elemental ingredient: blood. He had worried that the blood he had taken from Tiana's mother long ago would no longer be viable, but his concern had been unnecessary. The Vacutainer with citrate had kept it from coagulating; he had feared that one day he would desperately need it. It need not be fresh; it just needed to be liquid.

His hand steadied, and he lowered the syringe, pressing the plunger with an oddly delicate touch.

Three drops of blood from each of the targets:

One drop on the folded square of paper, binding the target and the Caster.

One drop on the witch's ladder, identifying the spell to be reversed.

One drop on the dirt from the targets' footprints, nullifying the binding of the spell to the target.

He sealed and laid aside the vials of blood and the used syringe, reaching for a clean one, thoughtfully provided by Paul Jacobs.

Three drops from each of the targets' mothers:

One for the labor of bringing a new life into the world.

One for the sacrifices made to nourish that life.

One for the fierce and tender love of mother for child.

Again he sealed and set aside the vials of blood and used syringes. He filled two clean ones with Cody's blood from a vial, and his own from a freshly poked vein.

Three drops from the targets' fathers:

One to seal paternity.

One to bind the family as parts of one.

One to cover those parts in patriarchal protection.

He laid the blood and used syringes in a silver tray, so no more spilled near the spell. After the next step, there would be no turning back. He held the sharpened edge of the silver knife to his right palm, and sliced from upper right to lower left. Blood welled and he cupped it in his hand, gritting his teeth against the stinging pain as he squeezed the wound to make the blood flow freely. He poured it in a line over the spell components to mark the reversal as authorized by one of Power. It pearled on the silver tray and ran into the engravings. The blood correctly split, he wrapped his hand with a length of gauze he had ready so that he didn't corrupt the reversal.

The candle had been burning steadily for the last hour. Harlan carefully poured melted wax over the ingredients of the vial, covering it entirely except for one end of the witch's ladder poking through the center. Harlan set it aside and waited for the wax to set. When it had hardened, he lit the exposed end of the ladder and watched it burn. As each knot in the witch's ladder met the flame, he tossed a small amount of blessed thistle into the flame to break the hex and offer protection to the targets. As the fire flared with each addition, Harlan murmured, "Undone."

As the last knot was engulfed in flame, Harlan began to tremble and waited for his mark. Darkness leached into the room, grabbing with hungry fingers the meager light, until he sat in utter blackness. The Power gathered, thickening the air until it hurt to breathe. The world seemed poised on the brink of chaos, the anticipation unbearable. Every hair on his body stood at full attention, his nerves humming with dark energy.

The Power hung ready to strike. Petrified, he shook like a palsy victim, for he knew from whom the Power came and what he had sold to have even the tiniest use of it. He didn't fool himself into thinking he'd ever had any control over it. Perhaps Cody had been right; he should have turned to prayer, to repentance. *Sorry, so sorry, for my failures, for my sins, for my deceit and my duplicity, for my stupidity and my faithlessness…*

Sudden warmth flooded through him, and his fear bled away like a bad dream. The Power dissipated – slowly, reluctantly, shrinking back into the shadows to sulk at another lost opportunity.

Drifting like a breath on the still air came one whispered word that seared Harlan Michaels to his soul: *"Forgiven."*

* * * * *

He sat in his den, sipping scotch and soda, listening to Fred Olmstead's whiny exegesis about his wife. His mind, however, had drifted more pleasant avenues of thought involving a woman, pain, blood, death. And Power.

Ah yes, Power, the core of his existence – and the curse of it, too. The betrayal of the whole human system of morals for the seductive control of darkness.

Fred fidgeted and began to sweat profusely. His rambling, whining complaint halted as he uncharacteristically lost his train of thought.

"Something the matter, Fred?" he asked, idly swirling the ice around his rocks glass.

Fred shook his head, wiping a calloused hand across his brow – the same hand that had a nasty habit of striking his wife's face.

"Hot in here all of a sudden," Fred muttered. "Anyway, as I was saying – "

"Yes, Fred, you said something about your wife being a meddling inconvenience." Those weren't precisely the words Fred had used, but they served to sum up the main point.

"She snoops. I know she's been in the room where I keep my things. And she's been talking, whining outside my home about how bad she has it."

"Perhaps, Fred, if you would attend to your family's needs before your own – desires," and he cast a look of distaste at the number of rocks glasses on Fred's side of the cocktail table, "there would be no need for her to carry tales to outside ears."

Olmstead's eyes goggled. "You're taking her side?"

"I'm taking the side of caution," he said wearily. "You have to get your drinking under control; sloppiness in your private life will spill over into the Circle, and we cannot have sloppiness in your magic. It is too dangerous."

Olmstead clunked his rocks glass down on the expensive teak table. The black magic priest mentally winced.

"Look, you just butt out of my family. I've got … you've … never…"

"Ah – say again, Fred?" he said, startled.

Sweat poured in rivulets down Olmstead's face, which now slacked oddly on the left. The priest watched, puzzled and fascinated, as his colleague seemed to suffer a stroke before his very eyes.

It ended as suddenly as it started; Fred Olmstead hovered upright for three full seconds before toppling from his chair to the handsome Turkish rug, dead.

He sat frozen for what seemed an endless moment, his scotch and soda halfway to his mouth. Finally, when it became apparent Fred wouldn't be getting up, he flung the rocks glass toward the cocktail table – barely aware of it missing and bouncing across the rug, or of the scotch and soda spraying the leather chair Fred Olmstead had occupied – and fell to his knees beside his colleague. He could detect no pulse when he pressed his fingers to Olmstead's carotid artery, not that he needed any confirmation of death beyond the man's staring eyes, slack mouth, and unmoving posture.

Shock pulled a woolen shroud over his ears so he could only hear the thudding of his heartbeat. When the telephone rang he jumped to his feet, startled, wondering how long it had been ringing.

The caller didn't identify herself; he didn't need her to. This was a private, unlisted number, and only three people had it. One was dead at his feet, and the other was male. Her voice was crisp as she delivered the second shock of the night.

"Scott Schaefer suddenly regained consciousness about five minutes ago. I thought you should know."

"He should be *dead*."

"I know," came the smooth reply. "It was instantaneous. You can start looking for the mark."

Reversal. His mouth tightened, a cold mask of anger slipping over his features. "Who has been at the hospital with them?"

"Beth Fairchild."

"Anyone else?"

And came the reply he half-expected: "Harlan Michaels."

He hung up without another word, his hand clutching the receiver so tightly his knuckles went white. He picked up the phone to dial a number that would launch a retaliatory strike against Michaels, but the doorbell rang first. He closed his eyes, drawing in an impatient breath.

The last thing he needed was a visitor when a dead man lay sprawled on the floor of his den.

He put down the phone and strode out into the hall, pulling the pocket door shut behind him. A peek out the eyehole in the door gave him the third shock of the night. Harlan Michaels stood on the stoop, writing in the small notebook he used to record information when interviewing witnesses and suspects.

"A moment of sanity would be quite nice right now," he muttered. He unlocked the door and stood in the opening, blocking the constable's entrance.

"I swung by the hospital a while ago to see how things are progressing," Harlan said in the clipped tone that identified him as a cop. "It's not looking good for Scott Schaefer; the doctors of course can't find anything wrong, and they don't give him very long to live. I don't think Cody suspects anything, but it's hard to tell with him." Harlan shook his head, drew in a breath to keep going, and looked up from his notebook, taking in the priest's expression. "What's wrong?"

He stood silently for a long moment, scrutinizing his henchman, before stepping aside and letting Michaels into the house.

"You'd better come with me, Harlan." He pushed past the other man and led the way down the hall to the den. "We have a problem."

The constable lifted a brow but didn't question. He flipped his notebook closed and tucked it into the breast pocket of his shirt. "Do I need a weapon?"

"Not unless you're into shooting dead men." He pushed open the door and stepped aside.

"*Oh,*" Michaels said when he saw Fred Olmstead laying dead on the floor. "What happened? Heart attack?"

"It looked like he had a stroke or a heart attack," he said, watching Michaels' face carefully. "He became confused and just fell over dead."

Both brows lifted now, Michaels stepped over Olmstead's body, knelt down, and pressed his fingers to the carotid artery. "Definitely dead. Should we call Doc Hamilton? And what about Melody?"

He didn't answer immediately, and as the silence spun out to the point of awkwardness, Michaels finally looked up at him.

"You need to stand up and undress very slowly, Harlan. I'll take your gun for the moment."

The constable's brows shot up into his hairline. "Are you kidding me?"

"I'm serious as – well, serious as a heart attack," he replied, his gaze flickering to Fred Olmstead's body.

Harlan stood slowly, his movements measured, his eyes wary on the priest's face. He offered no hesitation in handing over his weapon. "What the hell are you implying?" he demanded quietly as he unbuttoned his shirt and shrugged out of it. He held it uncertainly for a moment, then tossed it gently onto a chair.

"Scott Schaefer recovered, Harlan, minutes before you arrived, just about the same time Fred Olmstead dropped over dead. He was the Caster."

Michaels' eyes popped open wide. "You're looking for a mark of reversal? On *me?*"

"I'll look on everyone until I find who did it. Get moving, Harlan. You're making me nervous."

Harlan shot him a look that clearly said he thought his priest had lost his mind, but he complied without further argument. When he stood in just his boxers and socks, he straightened and with as much dignity as he could muster said, "Are you satisfied?"

"Hardly. Socks and shorts, Michaels."

"Oh, come on!"

"I'm losing patience."

With a sigh indicating he was losing patience as well, Michaels stripped off the rest of his clothes and stood, naked and fuming, before his priest, who circled around him, sometimes bending embarrassingly close, inspecting every inch of visible skin, and even inspected the soles of Harlan's feet in turn. Finding nothing, he finally relaxed.

"You can get dressed. It obviously wasn't you."

Scowling, the constable yanked his clothes back on. "That's humiliating."

"It's necessary."

Harlan shot a look at the man on the floor as he took back his weapon. "Now that you can see I haven't done a reversal, will you let

Tiana leave the Wyckham House?"

"Tiana is quite content."

"I rather doubt that."

A muscle twitched in his jaw. Harlan Michaels was coming dangerously close to insubordination, and he'd obviously forgotten his complicity in Tiana's predicament. He exhaled sharply through his nose.

"Fine. I'll deliver her to you at the station tomorrow." Michaels opened his mouth to protest. "Right now we need to deal with Olmstead's body. It can't sit in here all night."

Harlan's mouth shut. "Quite right. I'll call Doc Hamilton."

He laid a restraining hand on the constable's arm. "Make sure Doc understands Fred had a heart attack or a stroke. Melody is too close to Aaron, and Cody is in town; this has to look one-hundred-percent like an accident."

One shoulder lifted in a shrug as he dialed a local practitioner who also served as the town's coroner, the constable said, "In a way, it was."

He stood by the window, monitoring Harlan Michaels as he made the disposal arrangements, watched as Doc Hamilton hauled Fred Olmstead's body away. Very little of it registered; in his mind he was making contingency plans.

Aaron had always been on guard for another attack on him, even though he didn't consciously realize it. Now he would be on guard for another attack against Scott. The Circle's magic didn't work on Cody or Renée.

But Nadine's ricocheted love spell gave him one other avenue of opportunity – a very pleasant avenue. Yes, there would be pain and blood and death.

And sweet, sweet retribution.

TREASURE HUNT
October 25, 2004

"No, I don't need to go home and lay down. Who's got my phone? Mom – stop messing with me!" Scott ducked out from under

Renée seeking hand, patting his jacket pockets for evidence of his cell phone.

"I think you left it at the tavern," Ron replied. "There's one on the desk in the office, and Beth said it's not hers. It was dead; I threw it on the charger."

Scott swore under his breath, eliciting a sharp look from his mother.

"Maybe we should have left him in the hospital another night," Ron murmured in an aside to Cody. But the look he gave his cousin – his *brother* – was one of wary concern. One didn't just come out of a comatose state after an excruciating, witchcraft-induced headache and waltz nonchalantly into the sunset.

"They don't let you sleep!" Scott said in his own defense. "I think I got two hours of sleep total. They kept waking me up to take my temperature, or my blood pressure, or to shine a light in my damn eyes." And he cast a smoking glare at the weak sun peeking out from behind a huge black storm cloud.

Cody hid his smirk lest his wife's sharp look turn in his direction. For some reason, this made Ron remember the two different versions he'd heard of Cody's stay in the hospital ten years ago after being knifed in Chicago, as told by each of his parental figureheads. Cody laughed off much of the experience, saying he'd been in the wrong place at the wrong time and he was just glad the guy had missed both spleen and kidney. He seemed relatively unconcerned with the scar that, as it healed, strangely resembled the state of Florida, and joked about the nurses poking and prodding him until he'd shouted at them to not bother him for a full eight hours.

Renée, on the other hand, had told Ron an account of the injury (as Ron had been confined in Meadow Grove Rehabilitation Center at the time it happened) that he rather suspected was closer to the truth – but still not all of it.

Cody had walked out of a Burger King in Chicago, right into the middle of a serious altercation between two fellows of dubious character, unfortunately just as one jabbed a knife at the other. The blade went through Cody's Burger King bag and into his abdomen, just below the spleen and barely missing the kidney. Both men scrammed, leaving Cody lying in a pool of his own blood, his Whopper with cheese smashed between his hip and the asphalt, a pickle and a ring of white onion stuck to the back of his hand.

By the time the paramedics arrived, he had lost a fourth of his blood volume. That in itself wasn't alarming; he didn't need a transfusion and the knife had missed all vital organs. But the wound had become infected, the infection had spread through his blood stream, and Cody had spent a good amount of time in ICU.

Ron had never learned, despite asking bluntly, why Cody had been in Chicago in the first place.

He watched Cody covertly over the rim of his coffee mug, wondering what story he might get if he asked about Chicago now. He rather doubted much of it would change; telling a man you were his father didn't entitle that man to all the secrets of your life, and Cody Schaefer definitely had his secrets – such as the black Escalades that came to do his bidding at a single text message, and the men inside them who called him "sir."

"I'm going to the tavern to get my phone and then to the diner for some onion rings."

"I don't think – " Renée began, and lapsed into silence without finishing her sentence. Had he not been watching, Ron would have missed the fleeting glance Cody had flicked at her, a glance that, in its nanosecond of life, carried the distinct message "Back off."

Scott escaped out the back door, jingling his car keys. Renée huffed out a breath and left the kitchen in quick strides, her irritation with both her husband and her son a palpable force that lingered over the room in her wake.

"Women," Ron ventured, remembering with a mental grimace Beth's reaction an hour ago when he accompanied her into the cottage and started gathering her few possessions to relocate her to Taryn's. She hadn't just left behind a cloud of anger; she had fired words at him like pointy little darts, each hitting a vein of guilt until the urge to apologize nearly overwhelmed him. But the violet smudges beneath her eyes told him he was making the right decision regardless of her impatience with him. His need to see her safe obscured his desire to please her.

"What's on your mind, Aaron?" Cody asked, his finger tracing the rim of his own mug.

"Chicago," he answered without thinking and winced at his bluntness. But blunt didn't faze Cody one iota.

"Chicago," the elder Schaefer repeated softly and chuckled. "Been stuck in your craw a while, hasn't it?"

"What has?"

"Chicago." Cody took off his gold-rimmed glasses and folded them carefully, setting them by his mug.

"I guess so. Something didn't seem quite right about what you told me."

Cody pushed his chair away from the table. Ron sighed in resignation. But his father was only going for the coffee pot to refill their mugs.

"I *did* get knifed. A mission went south; an adversary got the jump on me. I lay in a puddle of my own blood and managed to call for my own ambulance. The entire mission was compromised, my cover was blown, and the bad guys are still at large."

Ron considered this for a long moment. "Incredibly, that tells me very little that I didn't already know. What mission, for whom, against whom?"

Cody sipped his coffee with apparent nonchalance. His face above the collar of his black mock-turtleneck appeared serene. It was impossible, as always, to tell what his father was thinking; he seemed to have cornered the market on poker faces.

Ron prodded a little harder. "I need for something to make sense. Nothing does lately."

"Need often sparks desire, and desire often has nothing to do with need," Cody replied inscrutably.

"Did Confucius say that?"

"No, that's all Cody Schaefer." His father grinned. "All right. How about this: I work for a covert agency that shall go unnamed. My team is called the Omega Team, because we are truly the last resort. We extract people from the clutches of dangerous cults."

"What people?"

"Anyone deemed important."

"By whose standards? Wealth? Renown? Public figures?"

"All of the above, but not exclusively. Wealth, fame, and public office need not be qualifiers to come under our protection."

"I thought you worked for the government."

"I do. Our funding comes secretly, approved in bills as art endowments and social programs. We offer our own brand of witness protection. Only the man at the top knows our witnesses' identities and where they live. He escorts them personally – well, all but one, that is – and he's good. Not a single one has been found, including your mother."

"Who's the man at the top?"

Cody pointed at himself. "I place witnesses in safe houses personally – hence all my travel – and I'm the only one who knows where they all are – well, again, except your mother. My second-in-command placed her."

"And who is he? Or she?"

Cody bridged his fingers together, studying them with a slight frown. "Let's just say Benjamin Cummings didn't fall into the river and drown. My third-in-command is in town as well."

"Yeah, well, Denny is a little easier to peg; I had no idea Ben worked for you."

His father chuckled again. "You're too smart by far. Anything else you need to know?"

"Nadine Bennett?"

"Quarantined and under observation until the new moon."

"What happened to her? Why was she so...weird?"

Cody rubbed a finger along his upper lip; Ron thought he might he suppressing a smile. "You could say she shot herself with her own gun. And there are unique problems with Nadine Bennett that we didn't anticipate when we quarantined her."

Whatever that meant. He had a more pressing question to ask. "Beth Fairchild – who is she really?"

"Do you have some reason to believe she's not who she says she is?"

"Just a hunch."

"Can't help you there," was the indifferent answer. Ron wondered if that meant he didn't know or wasn't going to tell. Before he could ask, Cody pushed away from the table again. "Now I'd better go see to your stepmother before I end up divorced."

Ron snorted. "Not likely. She knows how lucky she is to have you."

His father smiled. "I'm the lucky one."

His soft footfalls carried him up the stairs, and Ron mused that he could use some of that luck himself.

* * * * *

The tavern had been closed until all of the staff were healthy and accounted for, but Scott had a key. He let himself in the service entrance and made his way through the kitchen to the office. Ah, there it was! His cell phone lay in the center of the desk on top of the inventory sheets he'd been trying to work on before his headache exploded. And just as he'd suspected, there were voicemails and text messages. Before he could press the button that would dial his voicemail, he heard the service door creak open.

"We're not open!" he hollered, snapping his phone closed and tucking it into his pocket. He poked his head out of the office door and blinked in surprise. "Melody? What the hell happened to you?"

Melody Olmstead stood with her back against the service door, which had swung closed behind her. Her arms hugged her torso as though she thought she might be sick, and she quaked from head to toe. But it was her tears that caught and held him riveted. They flowed in a steady, dirty stream down her cheeks and off her chin, dislodging yesterday's mascara and eyeliner as they spilled from her eyes.

"Where is he?"

Scott didn't need to ask who; he had seen the lay of this land years ago, although Ron himself was either blissfully oblivious or was simply refusing to acknowledge what stared him in the face.

"He was at home, I think, but he might have gone to Taryn's by now. What's the matter? What happened? Did Fred hit you again?"

She wiped her face on her sleeve, leaving streaks of black cosmetics smeared across her blotchy skin. "How did you know about that?"

"Small town."

"Fred is dead." The rhyming words struck her as funny and she giggled. More tears poured incongruously from her eyes.

"Holy crap! How? What happened?" He took a step toward her but stopped when she shrank against the door.

"He had a heart attack last night." She drew in a steadying breath and let it out, finally gaining some control over her wild emotions. Scott saw, with the clarity that comes from sudden illumination, that the emotion etched sharply upon her face was relief. Which, in turn, told him why she was here, of all places, mere hours after her husband's untimely demise.

"Melo – "

"I need to talk to Aaron."

"Shouldn't you be – "

"Don't you see what's happened?" she barked, surprising him into silence. "You're suddenly well, and Fred is dead."

"Well, yeah. It's just a coinci – "

"There are no coincidences in Mills. But never mind, I'll go find him myself." She inched forward and eased the door open.

"He'll probably be with Beth Fairchild at Taryn's. Beth is ill." A muscle twitched in her cheek as she clenched her teeth. "You're wasting your time. He's in love with her."

Her eyes narrowed slightly. "Often what a man desires one day, he finds he no longer needs the next."

She slipped out the door, and as it banged closed Scott found himself thinking about his discussion with Beth about witchcraft, about his inability to leave Nadine behind despite their wholly unsatisfying relationship, and her words took a more sinister meaning in his mind.

He'd best let Ron know Melody was on her way so he had time to disappear before she got there.

He dug his phone out of his pocket and flipped it open, and saw he had voicemails. He scrolled through his missed call list: Taryn, Taryn, Ron, Denny, Renée, Taryn again; he could safely skip his voicemails. He clicked his way into his text message folder, surprised to see one from Tiana.

His surprise turned to bafflement when he opened the message: *Your copy of Mystic River is on the bookshelf in the break room.* For one, he'd never read *Mystic River* and didn't own a copy. She must have selected the wrong person from her contacts list when she sent the message; perhaps she'd meant to send it to Ron, in which case he could ignore this.

He went out the service door and was about to lock it behind himself when he thought twice. Even if she meant it for Ron, it wouldn't hurt him to take the book home, save Ron the trip if he'd been expecting it.

It lay on a mostly empty shelf beside a box of Cheez-Its. As he whisked it up, an envelope slipped from between the pages and dropped face-down on the floor with a soft thud. He stooped to pick it up, and ran his fingers over a lump with serrated edges. The flip side of the envelope bore his name, scrawled in a hurried hand.

He ripped it open, wincing as the gummed flap sliced into his forefinger, and dumped the contents into his palm: a small square of paper, folded around a battered gold key, "under the bandstand" written on one side. Scott's unease blossomed into real fear. Tiana had done no more than exchange greetings and farewells with him since they'd broken up eleven years ago. In the intervening time, she had not once reached out to him for help, for advice, not even for small talk. To find she had laid an inexplicable treasure-hunt for him made him distinctly uneasy.

He threw the envelope and the scrap of paper in the trash, pocketed the key, and headed for the bandstand in Town Square Park.

THE RIGHT HAND OF GOD

In the ceremony room deep under the Wyckham House, the priest lifted his head, brought out of his introspective reverie as the young woman on the granite altar moved her head. He had thought her dead – had feared her dead, actually, if he were to be honest with himself. It would be regrettable. Where she found the strength to defy him was a mystery, one that kept him enthralled. Yet despite the years of his abuse, she had refused, to the last, to surrender the core of herself.

He rose from his chair – an ancient, rusty, folding relic liberated from the Town Hall many years ago – and leaned over her. Blood matted her blonde hair, seeping copiously from the skull fracture he'd given her after she'd released Todd Garrett into the forest. He hadn't meant to hit her so hard, but it didn't matter now. He would have had to silence her in a matter of days anyway; her hysterical outburst after giving Garrett back his amenities had shown his control was, inexplicably, slipping.

What Harlan might do now was anyone's guess, but this didn't trouble him much either. Hers wasn't the first body he'd had to dispose of without the constable's help. Harlan would only have suspicions, and his own days were numbered. As the high priest of the Circle should, he was keeping a close watch on *that* one; he had a feeling the Michaels' family had morphed into loose cannons. Despite the fact that Harlan didn't bear the mark, he couldn't help but believe the constable had been involved in the reversal that killed Fred Olmstead.

Tiana groaned, a faint, eerie sound in the nearly silent room. He almost didn't hear it over the spitting torch in the wall sconce even as close as he sat. Her eyes opened, dark brown pools of confusion and pain.

"Tiana," he said quietly, his hand reaching stealthily for her throat to finish what he'd started. Incredibly, she smiled. A bubble of blood burst from her lips, leaving crimson splatters on her alabaster cheek.

"He sees," she murmured in a faint, otherworldly voice.

All the hairs on his body stood on end as her head swiveled toward him. Her eyes locked on his with sudden clarity; despite her initial disorientation, despite the more than twenty-four hours she'd spent in a comatose state, at this moment she knew him and what he was to her.

"Tiana, don't try to – "

"Jesus sees you."

He took a fearful step away from the altar.

"I'm free," Tiana Michaels whispered. A smile of beaming brilliance lit her wan face, and a low chuckle of astonishing delight escaped her

lips. *"Free,"* she repeated, and said no more.

* * * * *

He sat in the shadows, watching Harlan chase the small beam of a flashlight across the ceremony room. When the constable reached the head of the staircase going to the dungeons, he cleared his throat and stood up.

Startled, Harlan whirled around. The beam of light hit him full in the face, and he threw up a hand, shielding his eyes.

"Cut the light and come on over here. We need to talk." He moved around the altar to light to torch on the wall. Harlan's eyes traveled to the stone slab, where a still figure lay covered with a sheet.

"Another mess?" Harlan said with a distinct bite to his voice. "I'm done cleaning them up. Too many people die or disappear; it's already attracted notice. No more killing."

"You've had yourself a change of heart, have you," the priest rejoined. He didn't pose it as a question, and Harlan didn't answer. He removed the torch from the bracket to another holder closer to the altar, throwing glowing light over the white sheet and illuminating the dark stain at its head. "Well, isn't that great. Is that how you escaped the mark of reversal? You switched sides?"

"It's not a matter of 'switching sides' as you so simplistically termed it. It's a matter of perspective. My perspective has changed."

"You don't say." He laid a hand on the inert figure beneath the sheet, and noted the anxiety that suddenly pinched the constable's expression. "There was an accident earlier, Harlan. I had nothing to do with it except for the fact I came on the scene too late." His hand twitched the sheet, and he looked up with a serious, concerned expression. "You may want to brace yourself."

Like an illusionist performing a magic trick, he swept back the sheet to reveal Harlan's only child. A strangled gurgle came from Michaels' throat, and he seemed unable to tear his eyes away. The priest understood; Tiana –*his* Tiana – with skin like marble and eyes like cocoa, lay without breath or movement, her eyes clouded and her mouth slack. She looked as beautiful in death as she had in life.

"How did – how – " Harlan stammered. He reached toward his daughter and drew back his hand before he touched her, shying away from the undeniable proof that she was gone.

"I found her at the bottom of the first floor stairs. She wouldn't use the back steps; she kept trying to go up those ruined ones. I brought her down here when I found her – colder down here, you know. I knew her injuries were fatal. I had no time to get medical help."

"What did she do to you? Did she try to leave? Did she threaten to go to – ?"

He looked down at the still form of his latest victim, and then slanted an unreadable look at Harlan. "The situation is what it is, Harlan. Believe me or not, it doesn't matter. The fact remains we must make arrangements for your daughter."

Harlan's mouth tightened into a thin line. "You dirty bast – "

"Do you know what she said to me just before she died?" he cut in as though Harlan had not spoken. "She said, 'Jesus sees you.' Now what do you think she meant by that? And where do you suppose she found Jesus, Harlan?"

"AT THE RIGHT HAND OF GOD, YOU SON-OF-A-BITCH!" Harlan bellowed, taking a menacing step closer. The priest held up a cautionary finger but didn't cower in the face of Harlan's rage.

"You might want to rethink your decision to kill me. It wouldn't sit well with your new boss."

Harlan stopped, his jaw clenching. "You're right. I can do something even better." Quicker than he could blink, Harlan had drawn his service revolver. But he didn't aim it at his former priest; instead he slid out the cylinder, emptied the bullets from it, and reloaded it with ammunition he took from his jacket pocket, bullets that had a slight yellowish sheen to them.

"Silver bullets, Harlan?" he asked, suddenly careful.

"I hear they're good for what ails this town."

"You've got to be kidding me." The priest began to laugh. "It's just a legend. I can't believe you fell for a myth."

Harlan leveled a look at him. "Then you have nothing to worry about, do you? Why don't you go make some more deals with the devil and get out of my hair? I've got some things to do." He wheeled around on his heel and headed determinedly toward the steps to the dungeon, where he paused and sent a look over his shoulder. "By the way, silver as a talisman is useless. But silver as an allergen is quite effective. It reacts with the altered blood chemistry and attacks the lycanthropic cells. Death is unavoidable and fast. I ought to know."

Rage slammed through him, a finer high than drugs, more intoxicating than alcohol. He rode on its wave, knowing where it would carry him: to another dead member of the Michaels family. "You've killed our lycanthropes? Are you crazy? You know how much work went into that magic. Lycanthropes don't die – we're so close to immortality!"

"It's a false promise of immortality, a flawed magic that curses instead of benefits. It hasn't escaped my attention that you've declined to join the ranks of the lycanthrope set. And transference – how's *that* coming along? Been able to transfer human-to-human without killing the host? You're a cheap huckster, a two-bit magic show, and I'm done watching your flash and fire and convincing myself it's magic."

"What the hell bug crawled up your ass? Last week you were fine. Now suddenly you've grown a conscience?"

"Last week you didn't kill my daughter."

Harlan's eyes flicked to the still body of that daughter and then back to the priest. Cold, calculating vengeance lurked in the constable's eyes, more concerning than his grief-stricken rage. The priest shifted position, bringing his weight to bear on the balls of his feet, bracing for an attack.

"I've cured seven of your victims in as many years, and when Andy Malone went into the woods nine-and-a-half years ago to kill a wolf for Aaron, I tracked him to make sure that wolf died, either by his hand or by mine."

"Wolf? What are you talking about? Aaron was never bitten – I would have known!"

"Not as all-seeing, all-knowing as you'd like to think, eh?" Harlan replied with a nasty bite in his voice. "You knew he was like a son to me. Is that why you did it? Your twisted sense of power has warped my entire life. I sold out Aaron and Tiana both. I gave my daughter into slavery – I gave *myself* into slavery. But I'm done, and I won't stand by and watch you condemn an innocent man to a less than human existence."

"You're bluffing." He narrowed his eyes and came slowly around the altar toward the stairs.

"Care to make a wager on that?"

Harlan wasted no more words. He started down to the dungeons, appearing supremely unconcerned when the priest charged after him like a raging beast. Down the dark hallway to the last door on the left, key at the ready to spring the lock, Harlan completed his last journey through the shadowy corridors of the Wyckham House. He stopped at the door to Todd's cell, the priest hot on his heels, and jammed in the key.

The lock tumbled and the door swung inward as he hit Harlan at a run. They spilled into the cell and across the cold stone floor, startling Todd Garrett out of a troubled sleep. Harlan's flashlight spun across the floor like a crazy disco light. His revolver flew in the opposite direction. Their captive sat up and turned up the propane on his lantern, throwing their shadows onto the walls. Legs flailed and fists swung as the fight burned furiously, forcing Garrett to keep dodging out of the way as the two-headed, eight-limbed raging beast battled through his cell.

The priest was unaware of anything but his bloodlust. Harlan gained his feet and rushed him, crashing them both into the far corner of the cell. His head rapped the stone wall with considerable force, stunning him so that he lost his grip on the constable. It didn't matter; Harlan sprawled on the floor nearby, knocked senseless.

It was then that he noticed Todd Garrett pressed against the wall, edging toward the door. He staggered to his feet and lumbered after him, but had only taken two steps when something snagged his foot and brought his momentum to a screeching halt. He hit the stone floor with a bone-jarring thud. As pain sang through his body, he twisted around to see what he'd tripped over. Harlan Michaels, his face filled with grim determination, had snaked the fingers of both hands around his ankle and pulled his foot out from under him. Michaels grinned victoriously.

He spun back around as fast as his injuries would allow, but Todd Garrett was already gone.

"Judas." He kicked his foot free of Harlan's grasp and rolled onto his knees.

"Pot calling the kettle black." Harlan pressed his back to the wall for support to push himself to his feet. He patted his pockets as he did so, alarmed.

The priest had already found it. "Looking for this?" he inquired coolly, emptying the silver-tipped bullets from the cylinder and onto the floor. They clattered around his feet.

"That was kind of stupid." Harlan's lip curled. "Now you have an empty gun."

"Waste not, want not. I may need those rounds later." His hand dove into his pocket, coming back out with five ordinary bullets. He chambered them by feel, his gaze on Michaels. "Boy Scout motto: Always be prepared." Slapping the cylinder into place, he leveled the cold steel weapon at his traitorous right-hand man, thanking Ruger for the double-action beauty in his hands.

Harlan closed his eyes with a fatalistic smile. "You're really gonna shoot me with my own gun?"

"The thought has crossed my mind. You're really just going to stand there while I shoot you?"

"Are you kidding?" Harlan launched himself away from the wall but not at his nemesis; three strides to the left lay the flashlight, and he kicked it out into the hall in a move that would have made Beckham proud.

The priest squeezed the trigger, and Harlan fell with a bloody smile of triumph.

ODYSSEUS FREED

As he slipped unnoticed from the cell, Todd Garrett realized he stood in a pitch-black hallway with no hope of finding his way out without a light. It was too risky to go back in for the lantern; he didn't want to chance his captors noticing his escape. Without a light, though, he could wander for days in the darkness until starvation and thirst killed him. Or something worse did.

And then, like manna from heaven, Harlan Michaels's flashlight spun out of the cell and stopped at Todd's feet. A quick glance heavenward to offer his surprised thanks, he snatched up the light and headed away from the cell. Down four corridors and up a narrow flight of steps that he almost missed, they were hidden so well, he found freedom: a door to the outside, and the forest a hundred feet away. And no one in his way.

He came out into bright sunlight that hit him like the white flash of a nuclear explosion. His eyes protested the bright autumn day, but Todd didn't stop. He made a break for the trees, and as he stepped into the forest, a gunshot echoed from the open side door through which he'd just escaped. He paused only for a moment before plunging headlong into the thicket, not caring which of his nemeses had survived.

RETRIBUTION AND REGRET

Scott followed Tiana's trail from the tavern to the bandstand, but instead of finding her waiting, as he'd expected, he found nothing but a frosty drift of autumn leaves and a squirrel that hastily scampered away at his approach. It ran up a nearby tree and scolded him as he swept his foot through the leaves, hoping to unearth another clue.

Finding nothing, he hunched down and looked under the railings, then stood on them to look up in the eaves. Nothing. He sat on the frigid floorboards for a long time, stumped, toeing the metal ring that lifted a trap door in the floor. After a moment he stopped, considering the thick ring. Tiana didn't like closed spaces, and she was deathly afraid of spiders, but it was still conceivable that she might have hidden something underneath the bandstand – that *she* might be hiding there.

He scooted onto his knees, grabbed the ring, and eased the trap door open, peering into the blackness. The space beneath the bandstand was protected from the elements by chipboard skirting covered with lap siding, making it fairly snug but blacker than the center of hell. He was reasonably sure there was a light, with a switch located within reach, but rather doubted it would work without running the generator, which powered the electrical outlets.

"Tiana!" he whispered, and his voice was swallowed by the thick darkness below. No answer. No surprise there. After a moment of contemplation, he dropped into the space and crouch-waddled around, following the weak beam of light from his cell phone flashlight.

He found it stuffed between the generator and the bandstand skirting: a cloth-bound journal tucked inside a gallon-size Ziplock bag. Unzipping the bag, he upended it, and the book drooped into his cold-numbed hand. He flipped it open and stared down at the words she'd written on the first page: MY CONFESSION. Confession? To *what*?

He turned another page and his name screamed out at him from the paper: *I can't stress how important it is that this be kept safe. The key fits a storage unit rented by Fred Olmstead. Read and then give these to Denny Wallace. He'll know what to do.*

Scott frowned, sending a suspicious look at the trap door as though expecting mysterious enemies to have crept up on him as he read. *I can't stress how important it is that this be kept safe.* Which probably meant that trotting out of the bandstand carrying it out in the open would be foolhardy. He stuffed it into the inside breast pocket of his jacket and waddled back to the trap door, hoisted himself out, and closed it behind him.

He took the journal to the only place he could be assured uninterrupted time to read: the tavern.

And read he did, through the lengthening shadows of late afternoon, through the sunset that licked orange and red flames through the small patches of sky between puffy rain clouds, through the soft blue twilight and the supper hour – it didn't matter; after what he'd read, he didn't think he'd ever be hungry again – through the witching hour and beyond into the early hours of morning. He read slowly and carefully, absorbing every word, sometimes stopping to rage through the empty tavern or weep for the woman whose heart he had betrayed.

At last he sat with the book closed in his lap, the fire he'd built in the fieldstone fireplace faithfully pumping out BTUs that failed to warm him, his eyes red-rimmed and gritty with weariness, his heart hollow with sorrow. He'd been wrong all those years ago – so very wrong – and Tiana had paid a terrible price for his unjust condemnation.

He opened the book to the beginning and read the first pages again, a self-flagellation he couldn't seem to stop.

I have to tell you many things in a short time, and I don't know if I'll remember them all. So I'll start with the most important one. Don't hate Aaron for something you misinterpreted. He told you the truth; he was simply listening and comforting. There was nothing but brotherly affection and concern on his part, and I certainly had no designs on him. I loved you, Scott. I've loved you my entire life, since we were in kindergarten and you gave me your blue crayon when Billy Weatherby broke mine and stuffed it down the back of Margaret Hansen's pants. And now, what I told him that day, I'm telling you.

The pages that followed were a horror story, the kind shown on channels like Lifetime. It occurred to him that, after what had been done to her, the very fact that she'd ever looked at him in a romantic way spoke volumes on the strength and endurance of her childhood love for him.

The Circle took my life and gave me back nothing but a miserable existence. I am nothing but a slave, body and soul, to the Circle's High Priest. He may kill me tonight after what I do – I have to stop the craziness in this town – but I've been dead for years, so what does it matter? My body just didn't realize what my mind had already accepted.

Nadine Bennett has been using magic to keep you with her so she can monitor Ron through you. I won't call it witchcraft, because this magic is blacker than that; this magic is straight from the fallen. But it's not about the Circle's fear of what I told Ron that day by the river. At all costs he wanted to keep that paternity test from happening; it would have been disastrous for him if the biological father of Elizabeth Peterson's baby was revealed. He could never allow that to happen; it would have begged a lot of questions, which he would not have wanted to answer – such as why he wanted to father a child on Elizabeth in the first place.

His motives are not paternal or familial in any sense; there is pure power in the unborn, in a life and personality yet to be molded, and he uses that – has used it countless times. So steeped in evil…I don't know if he's beyond redemption. How far do you have to run away from God before you're lost beyond salvation?

There's no easy way to say this. I'm pregnant. He is the father. I hate saying that – he's no father. But what do you call a rapist who makes you pregnant? When he finds out, and he will, I will be no less doomed than Elizabeth Peterson. No matter what I do, I'm not going to make it out of this alive.

He closed the book with a snap, anxiety clutching his heart in an unshakeable grip, the need to exact justice on her behalf seizing him and springing him from his chair. Perhaps she was at her apartment, waiting for him to find her scavenger hunt and follow its clues. Waiting for liberation. Waiting for that justice.

He would find a way to give her both.

She didn't answer his knock at the apartment. He peered through the front window, unable to see anything in the predawn gloom inside. The door was locked, but he was able to jimmy the window, push the screen in, and climb through.

He secured the window and pulled the drapes closed, made sure the door was bolted, and turned on the light over the stove. In the meager glow, he surveyed the disarray around him with a puzzled frown. While Tiana wasn't a neat freak, she certainly kept the destruction to a minimum – unlike what he faced right now.

Blood-splattered towels lay discarded in a heap on the kitchen floor, a large stain in the carpet in the living room haphazardly cleaned. A cricket bat had been flung to the floor in the entryway, which perplexed him – cricket? Tiana played no sports, although when she had been younger she had shown promise in gymnastics.

He had a moment of anxiety that she had attempted a do-it-yourself abortion; that would explain the blood. But he knew Tiana better than that – at least, he thought he did – and he rather doubted she would do such a thing despite the mind-blowing identity of her baby's father.

And *that* – he still couldn't bend his mind around it, couldn't reconcile the man he thought he knew with the man described in Tiana's journal. He had tried calling his father, but Cody and Renée had gone to Scranton, and neither was answering their calls or texts.

So he turned up the heat in the little apartment and sat in the battered easy chair she had strategically positioned by the heat vent, waiting for her to come home, waiting to be the knight in shining armor he should have been years ago. His fingers absently stroked her journal through the layers of his winter coat as he lost himself in thoughts of vengeance and retribution. And regret.

FALLING

Across town, Ron Schaefer awakened from a nightmare so horrible his conscious mind pushed it deep below his memory banks as fast as possible, leaving him with nothing but the vague sensation of *changing*, as though his body twisted into strange and unnatural shapes.

And hadn't Elizabeth featured at some point? Yeah, she definitely had.

Now he sat awake, smoking silently by the open window, curled up on the padded seat and staring out at the dark forest beyond his yard. Cody and Renée had gone to Harrisburg and would be back day after tomorrow. Scott had stayed the night elsewhere; he hadn't said where. In fact, he'd been gone since being released from the hospital that morning. He had the house to himself, and silence filled it, broken intermittently by the rumble of the ice maker in the fridge dropping its bounty into the bucket; the hum of the furnace; the wheezing snore of the fluffy cat sleeping on his abandoned bed. Wind buffeted the windows, and the rumble of distant thunder sounded like a far-off war.

He closed his eyes, trying to conjure up an image of Liz, but her features wouldn't come in spite of her framed photograph that had lived the last eight years on the living room bookshelf. He couldn't remember the feel of her skin, or her scent, or the sound of her laughter. Instead, another image forced its way in: a spill of brownish-blonde hair over a drift of autumn leaves; golden eyes the color of ripe wheat fields, wide and startled in a striking, sharply-angled face. He could feel her against him as though she'd just left his arms, slender and fragile but firmly toned, strong for her size and gender. And her scent, earthy and fresh like lilacs left out in the scorching sun, hung heavy in his nose, a psychic fragrance that made his head spin, his stomach drop, and his groin ache.

His eyes popped open abruptly, cutting off the mental image with finality. No sense going there. No sense dreaming about things that he would never allow himself. Really, he should stop giving Scott such a hard time about it and step out of the way. He rather suspected she would not indulge in a casual affair, and Ron could not – would not – offer anything else.

If only the thought of her with his brother didn't disturb him so much that he wanted to break something, preferably Scott's face. No, he didn't want to commit to her himself, but he sure didn't want to see her commit to someone else.

He rapped the back of his head against the wall several times, annoyed at himself for his hypocrisy. What did he expect, anyway – that they would dance around each other indefinitely, sending looks and making innuendoes, and both would be satisfied? He must stop being unreasonable. They both would want more, and she would want more than he did.

He pressed his cheek against the cool window. Rain battered the other side of the glass and thudded on the metal roof, creating a soporific mood in the room that lulled him toward sleep. And he was almost safe in slumber when he thought he heard a car coming up the drive – Scott, coming home after all, probably. Then thunder boomed and drowned out the sound.

Pulling a t-shirt over his head, he moved quietly down the dark hallway to Scott's room, which faced the front of the house and overlooked the driveway. He peered out the window and blinked in surprise. Not Scott, but what in God's name was *she* doing here at this time of night?

She rapped softly on the front door as he stepped off the last stair into the living room. He squinted out the peephole before opening the door, and he didn't like what he saw. She stood with her arms wrapped around herself, shivering, her hoodie not thick enough to ward off the icy rain. Exhaustion pinched her face; she stared at the door knocker as though it alone kept her on her feet. He couldn't believe she'd gotten behind the wheel in her condition…especially since he'd hidden her car keys.

But the caustic admonishment he had ready faded when he opened the door. She looked up, her gaze raising no farther than his chin, seeming lost, forlorn. His annoyance melted away, replaced with something that suspiciously resembled concern. Damn it.

"I'm sorry to wake you. Can I come in for a minute?"

He wondered what she would do if he said no. Get back behind the wheel and try to drive herself home, no doubt. She'd end up in a ditch by the side of the road, or worse. He sighed.

"You'd better. You look like you're about to fall down. Are you okay?"

When she didn't immediately move, he took her arm and gently drew her through the door, closing and locking it securely behind her. He didn't let go of her until he had pushed her into a wing-back chair in the living room. She stared into the dark fireplace, still hugging herself.

"You're ill," he said sternly. "You should be at home asleep."

Her eyes flashed to his, darting away again instantly – guiltily. "I couldn't sleep."

"So you thought you'd come wake me and share the misery?"

She shrugged, a ghost of a smile touching her lips. "You said you often have insomnia. I figured I had a sporting chance at catching you awake."

He huffed out an impatient breath, frowning. He didn't like the odd swooping in his stomach every time he looked at her, or the rush of desire that flooded through him and made coherent thought all but impossible. It didn't matter that she was closer than not to collapsing from exhaustion; if she made one move toward him in that way, he wouldn't be able to hold the floodgates closed.

It didn't *appear* that she was making a move toward him, if he could judge by her posture. She hadn't moved an inch since he'd shoved her into the chair. In fact, she looked as though she had fallen asleep sitting up. But her hoodie was halfway unzipped, and he caught a glimpse of exposed honey-toned flesh and an edge of lace. A sudden suspicion made him wonder if wakeful company wasn't the only reason she'd come.

He perched on the edge of the raised hearth and tugged the legs of his shorts down. He felt too undressed, as though his bare legs and feet were somehow indecent. "You could have woke Taryn if you wanted to be entertained. She would have gotten up for you."

Hot color flooded her cheeks, and he watched the ebb and flow with more interest than was wise. So he'd been right. She had decided on this course of action with a specific end result in mind. That end result was exactly what he'd been avoiding since he'd kissed her.

"I should have just stayed home."

She stood abruptly, swayed on her feet, and waved him away when he moved to steady her. Her exhaustion went deeper than she'd admitted; he could see it clearly in the purple circles under her eyes and the pallor of her face. He stepped closer and crooked his finger under chin, forcing her to look up. Her eyes were wary, embarrassed.

"*Why* are you here?" His tone was harsh, and he mentally kicked himself when she winced. But he didn't want to encourage her foolish ideas; she needed to think about this before they went too far and had cause to regret this night.

"I...don't..." She stopped, closed her eyes, and took a deep breath. "I'm going to get myself a drink of water, and then I'm going to go home. I shouldn't have bothered you."

Her legs wobbled in protest as they carried her to the kitchen. Cupboard doors opened and closed, and the tap ran. He gave her a moment to compose herself before following. She stood at the sink, staring out the kitchen window, her hand cupped around a full glass of water. Feigning thirst had been her way of saving face.

The words he had ready – *Look, we both know this is a bad idea. Go home and I promise I won't ever mention this* – died on his tongue. Her posture spoke of worry, desolation, weariness. She tightened her fingers around the glass when she caught his reflection in the window.

He stopped behind her, intending only to comfort, but the scent of rain mixed with lilacs wafted on the air, enticing him, seducing him. He buried his nose in her hair, inhaling. She stopped breathing.

"If you're going to leave, now would be the time," he whispered. She shivered as his breath soughed over her damp skin.

Neither moved for what seemed like hours. Then her hand fell away from the glass, and her head tipped back and to the side, exposing her neck. Her skin was impossibly soft against his lips, the rain salty on his tongue. She sighed and turned around in his arms, relaxing against him, her lips seeking, finding his, drawing him into the enigma of her.

And for the first time in eleven years, Aaron Schaefer let himself fall.

BLUEBERRIES WITH A KICK
October 26, 2004

She was still asleep when Ron left the next morning to have breakfast with Taryn, her hair fanned out on his pillow in a golden cloud. Sleep had flushed her cheeks, leaving them rosy with deceptively healthy color. But the shadows under her eyes were still there, despite the seven hours she'd spent deep in slumber.

The corners of his mouth tugged into a reluctant smile. The first woman he'd brought to this bedroom, and he'd done nothing but watch her sleep. The surprisingly sensual journey to his room had left him with a raging libido and no fulfillment in sight – and, amazingly enough, a blush in his cheeks as he remembered last night's anticlimactic events.

When she would have tugged him down to the kitchen floor and had her way with him, he had resisted, dodging her seeking lips because her kiss – and what happened between them when they each surrendered to the other – made him completely unable to think straight.

"I'm not going to make love to you on the kitchen floor."

She tried to pull him closer. "Why not?"

"Because it's not…it's…well…" He scowled. "This isn't open for discussion." He stepped away and took her hand, drawing her out into the hallway and up the stairs. She swayed once or twice but kept her feet, although her breath came short by the time they reached the landing on the second floor.

Down the hall and through the door at the end. She displayed no normal womanly curiosity about his bedroom; her eyes remained locked on his, trusting him to lead her to the bed without mishap. She stopped when he did and simply waited until he moved first.

He dropped her hand and slid her hoodie from her shoulders. The lace-edged tank top she wore underneath was scant, not nearly enough armor to hold temptation at bay. His fingers stole under the hem and headed north across her back. He was delighted to discover she hadn't worn a bra; her skin was satin and her muscles smooth and firm beneath his fingers.

The side of her nose grazed his chin as she leaned into him. She didn't flinch away from his five o'clock shadow. More like midnight o'clock shadow; he hadn't shaved before bed and his reflection in the kitchen window had resembled a pirate with more than just mayhem on his mind.

She was slim but not skinny, her body layered with the muscle of a light weight trainer. Her breasts pressed against his chest with satisfying firmness. He found her chilly skin intoxicating against his warmth, the opposing sensations exhilarating.

Her hand at the back of his neck pressed him closer, urging their kiss deeper. The other slipped from his chest and up under the back of his shirt. Her touch was electric. She was fire in his arms, a molten river of desire the depth of which staggered him. He'd known there was passion in her and that she held it in check, always under tight control. He'd never expected to be the catalyst that turned it loose, had not *wanted* to be that catalyst until this moment.

He surrendered coherent thought, throwing control to the wind and letting desire reign. It happened then, like a spiritual counterpoint to their physical symphony, the strange force that persistently drew them out and wove them together, forging two souls into one.

Neither recoiled from it this time, and the binding begun with the first kiss consummated in the second: unwavering, undeniable, and irrevocable. Something inside him fell into place at long last. She was the completion of his being, what his soul had been seeking even before Elizabeth.

He lifted her with one arm, the other bearing their weight as he eased her down onto the bed. Her leg snaked around his, anchoring him against her. Her response to him bordered on savage and destroyed his last ounce of emotional resistance. No turning back; he was hers, body and aching, tattered soul. If she left, if she stayed – it didn't matter. He would love her to his dying breath and then beyond.

An errant shaft of moonlight fell across her eye as he broke their kiss to shrug out of his tee-shirt. Her pupil didn't dilate; it spanned the breadth of her iris, leaving a sliver of amber circling the dark void. He crossed the boundary from worry to fear with a healthy dose of self-disgust thrown in for good measure; he couldn't allow her to do this while she was ill and not thinking rationally.

He deepened their kiss, let his caress become slow and deliberate. Slowly her frantic passion devolved from a raging inferno to a slow burn. At length he broke away, pulling her more firmly against him, his cheek pressed to hers, his fingers sifting through her silken hair, their breath ragged in each other's ears.

Her heartbeat slowed. Her grip loosened. He breathed a sigh of relief and with considerable reluctance drew away from her, his hand hovering over her hair to smooth it from her face – and found her eyes closed. Her breathing came deep and rhythmic through slightly parted lips.

She had fallen asleep.

He couldn't help but laugh. Some kind of Romeo he was, when his would-be lover fell asleep in the middle of a seduction.

It wasn't easy, but he managed to maneuver her under the blankets and pulled them up to her shoulders. She settled in with a sigh, pressing her face into his pillow. Chastely settling himself on top of the comforter, he pulled the extra blanket from the foot of the bed over himself. Sleep had been a long time coming.

He stared down at her now, at her hand curled under her chin, at her tousled hair. The grey light of day brought with it a moderate amount of sanity. He would have to find what was making her ill, or by God he'd see her into the hospital before nightfall.

Taryn was waiting for him just inside the café, her face pinched and irritated.

"Am I late?" he asked, and she jumped. She hadn't even noticed him come in.

"No. I got here early." Her critical gaze swept him up and down. "Well, you don't look any different."

He scowled. "Why should I look different?"

She smirked. "I woke this morning to a note left by a certain young woman who snuck out to pay you a midnight visit. I sincerely doubt she wanted to play checkers."

Painful color flooded his cheeks. "Damn right she didn't, but she was in no condition for what she had in mind. She's currently sleeping in my bed, as unmolested as the day I met her."

"Aren't you the gentleman."

"Taryn," he admonished. "What kind of man do you think I am?"

A sheepish smile curved her mouth, and she linked her arm with his, hugging it, as the hostess –Melody Olmstead's friend who always came into the tavern with her – bustled toward them. "A better man than you think you are."

"What, no Beth today?" Lisa chirped at Taryn before Ron could respond.

"No. She's not feeling well so she's having a sleep-in. Can we get a table away from the windows? I'm cold." And indeed Taryn's fingers were chilly around his as she took his hand and followed Lisa.

He waited to speak until Lisa had brought them coffee and menus, then leveled his own critical look at his childhood friend. "You don't look like you slept much. How could you have missed her leaving your house?"

"First, I didn't miss her leaving, but I knew where she was going. Since the general consensus amongst your friends and employees is that you dearly need some sexual release, I thought it counter-productive to stop her."

"So you guys sit around discussing my sex life?" His fingers curled around the mug, reveling in its warmth.

"*What* sex life?" she countered. "And no, we don't, but it *has* been discussed in passing, especially when you're grumpy. Second, I did sleep, just not very well and not very long."

"What's wrong?"

"Just couldn't sleep."

"Usually there's a reason," he prodded.

"Yeah, there's a reason all right," she muttered, setting her mug down with enough force to catch the attention of the patrons at the nearby tables. "And it's leaving in a week."

"Where?"

"So he hasn't mentioned it to you?"

Ron shrugged. "We had other things to talk about the last time I spoke with him."

"He hasn't said where — he never does, does he? — but he has a flight out of Scranton on November second."

He drew in a breath, but their server — another person he'd known most of his life — appeared at his elbow before he could speak. Taryn ordered Eggs Benedict with a waffle on the side — stress eating — and he asked for blueberry pancakes.

"Giant blueberries, or wild Maine blueberries?" Jayne asked.

"Maine."

She beamed. "A good thing — your friend Beth has cleaned us out of the giant ones. She's in every couple of days. I'll turn this in and bring you more coffee."

She touched his shoulder fleetingly as she left, and Ron suddenly remembered that he had dated her once in high school. They had never repeated the experience — no chemistry. Funny how you just clicked with some people, whether or not they were good for you. Like Anna and that Jared Olmstead...

"I'm going to break up with him."

Taryn's quiet admission brought his head around, and he speared her with searching look. She wasn't looking at him; she was fiddling with her coffee mug, watching the steam rise up and fade away. He felt torn. Denny was his friend too, had been his friend as long as Taryn, and Ron knew things that would make this situation better — at least for a time — but he had no right to divulge that information. He felt a flash of irritation at them both.

"Are you sure that's what you want to do?"

"Of course it's not what I *want* to do," she snapped, "but what else *can* I do? I can stay with him and feel like crap indefinitely, prolong the misery, have a few more arguments to add to the bitterness — or I can end it and feel like crap for a while, and then go on with my life."

"You're assuming that he'll just let you go without a fight."

Her mouth twisted. "Why wouldn't he? He barely notices me now."

"That's not fair. "

She held up a hand. "You and I both know it's the truth. Stop trying to defend him. Anyway, it'll probably take months to work up the courage to actually do it."

"He loves you."

"He loves his job more."

"You can't even compare the two."

"I have to be more important than the job or this will never work."

Jayne saved him from having to reply by bringing their meal. He ate his fill and then sat picking through the three giant, fluffy cakes for more blueberries, contemplating his friends' predicament. There were things Denny couldn't tell Taryn because she wasn't his wife, but things were so strained between them that Denny was afraid to propose because he thought she would refuse. He knew Taryn loved him, he'd told Ron, but sometimes loving someone became a wearying burden and it was simply easier to stop; he suspected she had reached that point.

"You're as bad as Beth," Taryn remarked with amusement. "She picks through looking for these ginormous berries that are so purple they look black. She says they're the best ones, really sweet, but she doesn't always get any."

"I don't remember any almost-black giant berries in any of my pancakes."

"You got the Maine blueberries, remember?"

"No, I mean other times when I've been in here and ordered the giant berries. Are they a new kind?"

"No clue. Never had any myself; I'm not partial to blueberries, actually." She laid her fork down. "Look, Ron, I'm sorry to have put you in the middle of all this. You're his friend too – "

"Stop it." He frowned sternly at her. "I'm always here to listen. It's the least...I..." His voice trailed off what she said penetrated his brain. *She picks through looking for these ginormous berries that are so purple they look black.*

The berries of *atropa belladonna* were so purple they were almost black, and were intensely sweet.

"Ron?"

He cut her off, digging in his pocket for his cell phone. "Is he home?"

"I think so. But he didn't answer when I called him a while ago."

Ron he was already dialing. He held a finger up to tell her to wait a moment, and turned away from her as Denny answered. "Hey, I need to see you right away. I think you're right about the belladonna, and I think I know where she's getting it." He explained his hunch quickly, with a minimum of details.

Denny didn't waste time with useless questions. "I'll meet you at your house in an hour."

"Yeah, see you then." Ron hung up and turned back to Taryn, finding her seat empty and her half-full juice glass anchoring a ten-dollar bill to the table.

THE CYCLE BEGINS
October 26, 2004

"It could be any one of them," Ron muttered, pacing around his kitchen. In contrast, Denny stood quite still, leaning against the counter by the sink, his arms crossed over his chest.

"Seems plain to me. Lisa Bernard is Melody Olmstead's best friend. Melody's husband is – was – a known member of a black magic coven."

"Was?" Ron's pacing paused. "He's not a member now?"

"Haven't you heard?" Denny asked in surprise. "He died of a heart attack night before last. Conveniently around the same time your cousin miraculously recovered."

"I hadn't heard. I can't say I'm sorry; he was a complete ass." Ron began to pace again. He had to surmise that Fred Olmstead had been the one to cast the death spell over Scott, although he was still having trouble believing that kind of magic was real. He stopped again.

"Is there anything we can do to counteract the belladonna?"

"Common folklore advises a glass of warm vinegar or mustard and water taken as soon as possible after ingestion, which won't help her now. The modern medical information I've read name two commonly used antidotes: physostigmine salicylate or pilocarpine, although pilocarpine can have side effects that can be permanent, such as chronic epilepsy. Physostigmine has side effects as well, but they're temporary as long as the patient isn't overdosed, and they're along the lines of what she's already experiencing."

"So she remains sick longer?"

Denny replied mildly, "Isn't it better that she be sick for a while because we're countering the toxin? And while we're on the subject of symptoms, do you know if she's been hallucinating? Any trouble speaking?"

Ron shrugged helplessly. "Neither that I'm aware, although she has said she dreams vividly. I should be so lucky for her to have trouble speaking." He slanted a rueful smile at his friend. "Won't her system flush the toxin as long as she's not ingesting more?"

"It should. Just make sure she doesn't eat any more blueberry pancakes from the café. I'll send someone to deal with that situation."

"More black SUVs and men who call you sir?"

Denny just smiled blandly. "I'll be leaving in six days. I've been reassigned to a case in Wisconsin."

"Why? The situation here hasn't resolved itself."

"You don't even know why I'm here."

"I can hazard a guess that is has something to do with Todd Garrett."

The bland smile never slipped from Denny's face. "It's not too late to consider a career in law enforcement."

"I degreed in horticulture," Ron reminded him. He had changed his major when his guidance counselor at the university had told him it was doubtful anyone would hire him as a cop after he'd spent two years in a mental trauma center - and then he'd bought a bar, rendering his education virtually useless.

Denny shook his head. "Somehow I just can't see you cultivating pansies."

"Hey, pansies are tough flowers."

"Next you'll be wearing tights."

Ron grinned. "You say that like it's a bad thing."

"Whatever happened to you definitely knocked a screw loose. But I don't have time to worry about you growing tulips and wearing tights. I have to call some men who drive black SUVs and call me sir."

He pushed away from the counter and clasped Ron's hand. "Be safe, bro."

"What could possibly happen to me in Small Town USA?" Ron countered, tongue-in-cheek. Denny was laughing as he left, and Ron sincerely hoped Taryn didn't find her courage today.

Ron kept busy with various errands for the next two hours before the siren song of the woman sleeping in his bed became too much to resist. She was curled under his blanket when he came in, her breathing deep and even. "Her side of the bed" seemed to encompass most of the middle (as well as the side he was accustomed to sleeping on), leaving him a narrow sliver of comfort, but he didn't mind. He kicked off his shoes, scooted in as close as he could without disturbing her, and pulled some of her blanket over him.

On impulse, he turned on his lamp and cautiously lifted her eyelid. When the light hit her pupil, it contracted, though a bit sluggishly. He released the lid and watched it slip closed, some of his worry easing. The drug was wearing off.

He turned off the lamp and drifted into dreams.

* * * * *

Kimberly watched him sleep, his face mere inches from hers. She'd awakened this morning to find herself in a cozy albeit unfamiliar bed, surrounded by cider-colored walls and tasteful, masculine furniture. She didn't have to wonder where she was despite her initial sleep-induced amnesia; the pillow on which her head rested smelled like Ron. A glance at the digital alarm clock on the far side of the bed told her she'd slept through most of the morning.

He'd left a note, a pointed message she imagined was full of annoyance: *Running some errands. Left some things for you in the bathroom. Chicken soup in the thermos on the dresser. Since hiding your car keys does no good, I took them with me.*

That had made her laugh. The soup had energized her enough to manage a shower – and she had been surprised to find a clean towel and most of her toiletries waiting for her in his private bathroom. The shower had made her feel better – amazing how being clean refreshed one even when one was ill – but it had taken the last of her reserves. She had curled up on the bed, wrapped herself in a thick blanket that he'd obviously slept under, since it was balled up on the other side of the bed and smelled like him, and slept away the rest of the day.

She'd awakened again as dusk threw blue light across the walls. Ron lay beside her, a respectable two feet of space between them, his breathing deep and even as he slept, a corner of her blanket tugged over his chest. That was hours ago. She dozed again and awakened to his troubled mutterings. Whatever he dreamed disturbed him, but she didn't rouse him.

Instead, she watched him, studied him, committed his slumbering face to her memory. A light sheen of sweat stippled his upper lip, glistening on his five o'clock shadow. Long, black lashes fanned out on his cheekbones and his eyes moved rapidly beneath his lids as he dreamed. He presented a stern countenance when he slept. She wanted to reach out and touch his cheek, offer whatever solace she could, but she held herself in check. She had no claim on him to justify such contact, and he had made it clear in days past he had no interest in being claimed.

That was before you tried to seduce him last night. Things have changed now.

Perhaps they had – she had felt his capitulation last night on an emotional as well as a physical level – but she wasn't banking on it. A kiss didn't constitute a vow any more than sex implied love.

Gradually she realized his breathing had changed and his eyes no longer darted back and forth beneath their lids. He opened them, blinking slowly for a moment before fixing her with a sleepy gaze.

"Hey there," he murmured.

"Hi," she whispered back.

"What time is it?"

"Sixish."

"How are you feeling?"

Kimberly slanted an ironic smile at him. "Amazingly better. Sleeping all day has its benefits." Her smile faded abruptly, and color flooded her cheeks. "Listen, about last night – I'm sorry."

Ron reached up to touch her cheek. "You *should* be sorry," he whispered. "You shouldn't do that to a man my age."

She snorted, her blush deepening. "You weren't arguing much," she parried gamely.

He chuckled, moving closer to her. His fingers slid from her cheek to tangle in her hair.

"I need to tell you something." She rushed out the words before he could close in.

He was a breath away now, giving every indication of taking that breath just before he kissed her. Kim planted her hand against his shoulder, no match for his superior strength in her weakened state but determined to stop him.

"I lied to you."

He blinked lazily but didn't seem shocked. "Ah. Have we reached the moment of truth?"

"The moment of *what* truth?" She frowned at him crossly.

"The moment when you tell me why you sometimes don't answer to the name you gave me, why sometimes you seem anxious and worried, why – "

"I'm not who I said I am."

Ron simply stared back without expression. "I figured that much out myself."

"I came here looking for someone, using my best friend's identity because we closely resemble each other. I didn't know what I would find when I arrived, so I thought it best I not come using my real name."

"Which is?"

"Kimberly Owens."

"And who are you looking for? Maybe I can help."

"You've already told me as much as you know. I'm looking for Todd Garrett."

He pulled back, stunned. "Todd isn't here. He went home to California."

She shook her head vehemently. "He never made it. A box arrived full of fishing gear – he hates to fish – with a paper coaster from your tavern taped inside a tackle box."

"*My* fishing gear," he muttered. "So the first night you came into the tavern, you were looking for him?"

"Yes." She was dismayed when he moved even farther away from her.

"And who is he to you?"

She gaped at him for a second before realizing she'd left out important details. "I didn't explain this very well. He's my father."

"That's a relief. Well, mostly a relief – I'm not sure how thrilled Todd would be to find his daughter in my bed."

"Not very." She swallowed over a lump of anxiety in her throat. "Are you really angry?"

"I knew all along something wasn't right with what I knew about you. I even said as much when you came to dinner."

"You could have asked." His quirked brow clearly said *Would you really have told me?* She closed her eyes. "Good point." When she opened them again, she found him nose-to-nose with her.

"The only thing I'd like to know right now is, would you have told me before…ah…"

Hot color blazed in her cheeks again. "I'd like to think so."

"Then we can talk about the rest later."

His arm snaked around her waist, drawing her against him. His kiss was much like the first time: leisurely, exploring, demanding nothing she wasn't willing to give. She relaxed in his embrace, returning it in kind.

A long while later he drew slightly away, resting his forehead against hers and settling the blanket over them both. The blue light of dusk had grown murky and dark. Moonlight limned the slats of the mini blinds and threw bars of light onto the back of the curtains.

Tonight began the cycle of the full moon. She wondered where her father was, and prayed he was safely indoors.

THE UGLY WOLF

The sun had set when Scott awoke, indicating that he had slept the whole day through to evening. He rubbed the bleariness from his eyes and stretched his cramped limbs. Still no Tiana. He doubted she would go to Taryn's with Beth staying there – she was too private a person to air such dirty laundry around someone she barely knew – so when he left, he aimed the car toward The Watering Hole.

A preternatural quiet hovered in the tavern, a hush that spoke of rooms that had lain vacant for an extended period of time. The tavern had not been closed a single day since Ron had purchased it, not even when winter snowstorms had slowed the town to a crawl. His cousin had simply attached a plow blade to his truck and blazed his own trail to work.

The dishes from the last shift had been washed and were sitting, dry, on a metal counter. Scott bypassed them and went into the dining room to see if Tiana had sought solitude in the closed building.

He found the dining room empty and two tables that had been missed in the last cleaning. He wiped them down, filled salt and pepper shakers, and grabbed the coffee pot – full of cold, sludgy coffee with an oily sheen on top – on his way back to the kitchen. Just as he started to push through the door, he heard the clatter of the prep pans near the sink. He stopped, cold chills walking across his body. The pans were laid flat, so he knew they couldn't have shifted on their own.

The door opened from the left side, so Scott stood to the right side by the hinges, holding the sloshing coffee pot in his left hand. He slowly moved so he could peer with one eye through the small window, and breathed a sigh of relief. Taryn stood at the sink, stacking the pans to put them away on a shelf above her head.

Scott slipped through the door, making a lot of noise so he wouldn't startle her too much. She jumped anyway as she turned, smiling when she saw him.

"You're feeling better, I see. I saw your car and thought I'd stop in. Ron said I couldn't be here alone, but he didn't say anything about being here with you."

"I just thought I'd clean up a bit." He gave his friend a one-armed hug and set the coffee pot in the sink. Taryn dumped the contents and sprayed hot water in it, peering dubiously at the coffee ring around the center of the pot.

"I think we'll have to leave it soaking."

"You didn't leave Beth alone, did you? That's kind of the point of her staying with you – so she's not alone."

She sent him a puzzled look. "Didn't you just see her? She left me a note; she's at your house."

"Well," Scott said, and surprisingly felt little rancor. "If she's there, she ought to be safe."

"Any idea how long Ron plans on the tavern being closed?"

"Dunno. But I doubt he plans on reopening until there's some resolution in the…situation."

"Situation," she repeated thoughtfully. "Now there's a diplomatic way of referring to murder, Scott."

She turned off the water and wiped her hands on a towel. She placed her hands on either side of his face, turning it up toward the light. Her scrutiny made him uncomfortable but he knew better than to pull away: Taryn was a younger, fiercer clone of Renée.

"Well, you *seem* to be all right," she remarked, and was about to continue when the squeak of the service door carried down the hallway to the kitchen. Her hands froze midway between Scott's cheeks and her side, her eyes startled.

"Did you lock the door behind you?" he whispered, and she shook her head silently. He motioned her to stay put and tiptoed to the end of the bank of sinks. He peered cautiously around the corner and down the short hallway, off which branched the break room on the right and the storage room on the left. The service door capped the hallway, leading to the side lot where staff parked.

The door bumped closed. A moment later something scratched at it, as though a large animal begged entry. The door, which never had latched correctly, bounced open a little farther with each scratch. The creature outside slipped a huge paw inside. Scott's breath stopped in his throat. The door bounced closed, and the animal withdrew quickly, growling.

Scott took a step backward and found Taryn directly behind him. "I told you to stay back!" he whispered.

"I'm scared. Can we make it into the office?"

The door bounced again, and this time the creature got a leg in up to the first joint. Scott couldn't see the rest of the animal; darkness shrouded everything beyond the door because he'd forgotten to turn on the parking lot lights.

"We'd better do it now, if we're going to." His hand groped for and clasped hers, slick with sweat. He twined his fingers with hers so he wouldn't lose his grip. "On three. Ready? One...two..."

Huge black claws gained purchase on the door, flinging it open with such force that it bounced against the building and tore from its hinges. A nightmare stepped into the hallway, a wolf of monstrous proportions and excruciating ugliness, freezing them in a bestial glare. A bracelet of thick gold links circled its left front ankle. Scott's eyes fixed on this incongruity desperately so he wouldn't have to admit he stood face to face with his own death.

"*Scott!*" Taryn moaned, nearly crying. Her eyes had locked on the bracelet too, her terrified expression shifting to recognition and then, oddly, to utter horror.

The beast curled its lips back, growling deep in its chest. Its flattened snout wrinkled as it voiced its warning and hunkered down, preparing to pounce.

Scott didn't think twice. He whirled around and pushed Taryn in front of him in one smooth motion, propelling her toward the dining room. They slammed through the swinging door and ducked to the right a mere second before the wolf charged through behind them. Unable to stop as quickly as they had, it skidded on the tiled floor, sliding beneath the flip-up section of the bar and into the main room. Chairs clattered and a table overturned as the wolf crashed.

Jerking Taryn back through the kitchen door, he bolted at top speed toward the service entrance, dragging her behind with such force her feet barely touched the tiles. The door itself lay alongside the building. Scott didn't waste time marveling at this feat of superhuman strength. Silently thanking God he'd left his car unlocked, he and Taryn ran to opposite doors and jumped in. He slammed the key into the ignition just as the wolf careened out the door behind them.

"*SCOTT!!*" Taryn screamed.

"*I KNOW I KNOW I KNOW!!*" he bellowed back. He wrenched the gear shift lever into reverse, stomped on the accelerator, and the car shot backward just as the wolf pounced toward the windshield. The wolf just missed the hood and landed in the gravel. Scott shifted into drive and gained the road as the wolf rolled three times and found its feet. He sped down Stoneridge Way toward home, his foot jamming the accelerator to the floor.

He checked the rearview obsessively as they bounced down the gravel driveway to the house, nearly driving off the road several times. Taryn moaned each time the tires lost purchase in the weedy shoulder. He thumbed a button on a small black box clipped to his sun visor, and the garage door swung upward slowly. Scott brought the car to a screeching halt, pushing the button again barely before he'd completely pulled inside. He waited with bated breath as the door took an eternity to shut, craning around wildly to search the bright fluorescent-lighted garage for four-footed intruders.

But nothing had followed them inside.

The garage door completed its slow journey to the floor, and Taryn began sobbing hysterically, her hands clapped over her eyes, rocking back and forth in her seat.

"Hey! *Hey!* We're safe now." Scott pried her hands away from her face. "Taryn, we're all right."

"Omigod…omigod…" She lifted her stricken eyes to his face. "Scott, that wasn't a wolf!"

"It looked like a wolf to me. A big one and kind of ugly, but a wolf."

"No. No no no. You don't understand. Scott – I've seen that bracelet before! I know who it belongs to. Omigod…*omigod*!"

"You aren't making any sense!" he shouted.

"That was a werewolf!" she yelled back. "A *werewolf*! And I know who it is! That bracelet is Todd Garrett's!"

* * * * *

From the shadowy edge of the forest, it watched the car skid into the bright rectangle, and then watched the rectangle slowly disappear. It waited just out of the reach of the perimeter lights, watching for any sign of human movement outside the structure.

But no one came outside, and the beast's nature was not patient. It slipped through the forest, searching, senses on alert for a scent traveling on the air like a homing beacon: the scent of a human. Over fallen trees rotting on the forest floor, under deadfalls snarling with grasping tangles of branches, past boulders the size of Buicks and a creek that masked its footfalls, it trotted on, sniffing the air until it caught the scent of food.

It found them on the shoulder of the old logging road, in a tiny car it could peel open like a sardine tin. Furtive movements caused the car to rock on its frame. A blonde head mashed up against the glass for a brief moment. The beast hunched down, lips curling over its teeth in a silent snarl. The car door popped open, and the flood of tantalizing odors was like ringing a dinner bell. The wolf salivated as supper climbed out into the chilly night.

"I don't care what she said. My uncle had nothing to do with your father's death. Your mother's just a bitter, jealous bitch!"

"She is not a bitch!"

"Yes, she is. And you're a jerk for believing her, Jared."

The girl took another step away from the car, her foot brushing the scrubby grass that lined the shoulder of the road. She didn't hear the sound of the stalks rustling together, but to the wolf it was a symphony of whispering sounds. Dinner music.

"C'mon, Anna. Get in the car. I'll take you home." The boy leaned across her seat as far as his seatbelt would allow, his eyes scanning the dark woods along the road. His unease made his blood pump thick and salty in his veins, sparking a wild, primal hunger in the wolf's belly.

But the girl was easier – if less tantalizing – prey. Outside the car, it would be quick work to take her down and drag her into the forest. To get the boy, it would have to jump inside the car, into close confines, where retreat would be difficult if not impossible. It settled into position, eyes on the girl, and froze, waiting.

"I'd rather walk. I can make it to my uncle's house in half an hour." She took another step from the car. Now she was away from the open door, and the wolf had a direct line of attack.

"He'll have my hide, Anna! He already doesn't like me – you saw how he was the other day at the tavern while he was tutoring you. I'm sorry, all right? Just get back in the car."

"Now you're sorry?" Her temper rose, flooding her blood with an interesting, mouth-watering scent. "Too late. I don't want to ride with you."

"Be reasonable. He's going to chew your ass too when he finds out you walked through the woods after dark. C'mon, it's only – OH MY GOD!"

The boy's eyes had drifted over her shoulder, scanning the woods uneasily, and somehow had picked out the wolf's crouched form. He lunged across the seat, grabbing for her arm again. The seatbelt jerked him to a halt, and the girl danced another step away from the car, laughing coldly.

"I'm not going to fall for cheap tricks."

"GET IN THE CAR, FOR GOD'S SAKE, ANNA, GET IN THE CAR RIGHT NOW!" The boy fumbled with his seatbelt, searching frantically for the release. His panic penetrated the girl's anger, and she whirled around just as the wolf launched itself from its crouch.

It hit her in the chest, driving her backward against the car, its jaws wide open to close around her throat. At the last second she jerked to the side, and its fangs found her shoulder instead. Her shriek of pain rose on the air. Sweet, rich blood flooded its mouth, triggering barbaric instincts. It shook its head, teeth sinking deeper, rending tissue, bringing a torrent of blood.

The boy found the release button on his seatbelt and spilled into the passenger seat, grabbing something from the floor. A metal cylinder. The wolf released the girl's shoulder and dropped to all fours, seizing her ankle, dragging her toward the edge of the forest. Her head smacked the car's frame; the blow stunned her, and she stopped fighting for a few precious seconds.

Blinding light hit it squarely in the eyes. The girl was tugged back toward the car. The beast growled savagely, clamping its jaws tighter around her ankle, freshets of blood squirting into its mouth and across its muzzle, the wild craving for her blood – for human blood – eclipsing all other instinct. It yanked hard on her leg, wresting her from the boy's grasp. Her howl rose into the night again, her song like wolf-song, only hers sang of pain and terror and imminent death.

And then the light hurtled toward it, and something hard and cold crashed onto its muzzle. Shocking pain made its jaws open, releasing the girl's ankle. The bright light swirled away into the ditch. It shook its head violently, droplets of blood flying from its muzzle, and pounced toward the girl again.

But she was gone. The car door thunked closed, muffling the voice inside – *"Oh God it burns Jared IT BURNS IT BURNS!"* – and the wolf hit the door with a thud. Both the girl and the boy screamed. The engine rumbled to life. The beast jumped onto the roof as the car rocketed forward, and it lost its balance, rolling onto the dirt road. Tires squealed as the boy made a U-turn to head back toward town. The engine screamed as he floored the accelerator, pushing the tiny car to its extreme limit.

The wolf watched the headlights coming back toward it, spearing the night like tiny suns. An instinctive calculation of angles and trajectories made it leap into the air at precisely the right moment. It hit the driver's window, shattering safety glass that rained in chunks on the shrieking occupants of the car. Its jaws closed over the boy's throat and it gave a vicious twist, cutting off his scream abruptly. Blood sprayed the windshield and the girl's face. The car careened off the road and into a shallow drainage ditch, dislodging the wolf from the window. Glass shattered as the windshield popped free of its frame and hit the ground.

The boy's blood had only whet its appetite. The girl had been thrown halfway out her seat; she lay against the dashboard, unconscious, bleeding from a dozen wounds, scenting the night with a smorgasbord of olfactory sensations.

A sound carried on the night breeze, bringing with it the scent of human life. More prey, in the forest to the northeast. Large, healthy, rich-blooded prey.

With no backward glance at its abandoned meal, the wolf bounded off into the forest.

PAST CURFEW

Ron had just gotten out of the shower when he heard the clatter of the garage door and the rumble of the Dart's engine. A moment later the door from the garage into the kitchen banged open and closed, and the sounds of a muted argument carried up the stairs. Muttering imprecations under his breath, he dressed quickly and went back into his bedroom. The room was dimly lit by a small lamp on his dresser, but he could see that Kimberly's eyes were open, although she still looked very tired.

"What's going on?"

"Dunno. Scott's home, from the sound of it. Go back to sleep; I'll go shut him up."

She smiled and closed her eyes, snuggling deeper into the blankets. For a moment he was tempted to ignore the disagreement downstairs – Scott could fight his own battles – and crawl back under the blanket and bask in her warmth, but the rising volume of the voices downstairs said he'd have to intervene eventually to regain peace and quiet.

Ron followed the auditory trail into the kitchen, where he found Scott and Taryn in animated disagreement. Tears sparkled on Taryn's cheeks, and Scott's expression was mutinous.

"What's all the commotion? We were trying to sleep."

"Who's we? Are Mom and Dad home?"

"No, 'we' is Kimberly and me." They met this information with blank expressions, although Ron could almost read Taryn's dismay and knew she was wondering where this left Beth Fairchild. "Kimberly Owens is the woman you know as Bethany Fairchild. She came here to find Todd Garrett. She's his daughter."

A look of horror contorted Taryn's face, and she shot a glance at Scott. He made the connection more slowly and sent his own uncomfortable glance toward Ron.

"What?"

"Nothing." Scott frowned at Taryn, shaking his head slightly. She subsided into a chair but could not contain her outburst any longer.

"We were just chased by a werewolf!" she blurted, and started to cry.

"A *what?*" Werewolves again! Would he never be shut of that idiotic subject?

"I told you I recognized that bracelet!" she shouted at Scott.

"What bracelet?" Ron asked.

"The *werewolf* we saw earlier"—Taryn's chin jutted out stubbornly as Scott rolled his eyes—"had a bracelet around its ankle."

"The left ankle? Large gold links and an engraved ID plate?" asked a new voice.

They all jumped; they had been so immersed in their conversation none of them had noticed Kimberly in the doorway. She had wrapped a fleece blanket around her shoulders and she jerked it tighter in a convulsive movement as she stepped into the room, her eyes burning into Taryn's, her question hanging in the air.

Taryn replied hesitantly, "Yes."

"Can you...can you describe it?"

"Large chunky gold links, set with diamonds. The ID plate had a foreign phrase on it, Latin, I think."

"Da mi basia mille," Kimberly quoted numbly. "Give me a thousand kisses," she translated and continued in English, "Then a hundred, then another thousand, then a second hundred. It's a love poem by Catullus, quoted in a novel my mother loved. She had the bracelet made for my father the year before she died." She swayed on her feet, her eyes heartsick. Ron grabbed her shoulders and guided her into a chair.

"Kimberly, we have no proof Taryn and Scott saw your father," Ron soothed, shooting a nasty glare at Taryn. "I mean...werewolves? Seriously?"

"The bracelet is all the proof I need," she said simply. "My mom's best friend designed it. It's one of a kind, no mistaking it." She raised her head. "I don't understand how you had time to see it clearly, Taryn."

"When the...the *wolf* "—and she sent her own smoking look back at Ron—"jumped toward the car, I saw it long enough to recognize it. Todd – he used to come into the bar all the time and chat with Ron and me. And then he just...stopped coming. Harlan Michaels said he'd left town."

Kimberly bowed her head again. Ron squeezed her shoulder, but she sat lost on the fog of her despair and didn't respond. When the phone rang a few minutes later, shattering the silence that had descended on the kitchen, she didn't jump like the rest of them; she didn't even raise her head. Scott answered and passed the phone to Ron.

"It's Andy Malone. He says it's urgent."

"Great. Now what?" he muttered but took the call. "Andy? What's up?"

"Been better. Anna hasn't come home from her date."

His stomach dropped. "How late is she?"

"An hour and fifteen minutes. I've been calling Harlan, but I get no answer, not even on his cell phone."

Ron sucked in a breath and bit his lip uncertainly. "All right. What do you need me to do?"

"Be ready in five minutes. I'm on my way to your house. Do *not* wait for me outside."

"Awww, Andy, are you on a werewolf kick too?"

"Stay inside and be ready when I pull up. We'll talk as we drive." Andy broke the connection and Ron stared at the phone as though it offered a sane explanation to the sudden insanity that had descended on his town.

"Ron?" Taryn prodded anxiously.

"Anna," he said faintly. "She hasn't come home from her date."

"You're going *out?*" Taryn said incredulously. "Did you not hear what we told you? There is a *werewolf* out there, Ron!"

"And there is also a sixteen year old girl out there, almost an hour and a half late coming home. That's more important than your belief in a myth."

Taryn's lips compressed into a thin, angry line; her hands gripped the edge of the table as though it could stop events from spinning out of control. Kimberly raised her head, fixing him with her blazing stare. She didn't protest, didn't offer any arguments against him going, simply accepted what he had to do. Something in the look she shared with Taryn froze his blood. She believed Taryn about the werewolf.

He snagged a warm hunting jacket from the closet under the stairs and came back into the room just as Scott set cups of brandy-laced coffee in front of Kimberly and Taryn. Given enough time, the entire household would probably be gripped in an alcohol-induced calm, but he could deal with that better than he could deal with hysteria.

He glanced at Kimberly; no hysteria there. He didn't think she was prone to it, but the detached calm that now ruled her frightened him more.

As if sensing his worry, Kimberly rose from the table, letting the blanket fall from her shoulders. The sweatshirt he had given her to wear brushed her knees and her bare feet tread silently on the tiled floor as she crossed the distance between them. Her eyes, the only things alive in her face, smoldered like hot coals as she stopped before him and cupped his face between her icy hands.

"I'm fine, Aaron. I'm not a quitter." Stretching up on tiptoe, she kissed him hard and quick, fierce, her cold lips burning like ice. "I'll be here. You'd *better* come home."

Ron nodded numbly, aware of Taryn and Scott watching with avid interest. He brushed a strand of hair out of her eyes as a horn blared twice outside.

"He's here," he said unnecessarily and took a reluctant step away from her. He turned and left without a backward glance, sure he'd be unable to leave if he looked at her again.

The car sat as close to the porch steps as possible, engine throbbing; Andy Malone was taking no chances. In the three seconds it took to cross the distance and climb in, his skin had prickled into gooseflesh.

"Where are we going first?" Ron asked as Andy floored the accelerator. The car spit gravel behind it as the tires sought and gained purchase.

"Don't know. They went to a movie in Scranton. That should have been out by eight-thirty. Her curfew was ten-thirty. She called me from her cell phone about nine and said they were going to the park to hang out with friends and she'd be home by curfew."

"Have you gone to the park?"

"No, Aaron, I thought I'd panic first and call you."

"Okay, you've checked the park. Are you sure they went to the park in Mills? They like to go to Sugar Run and play tag in the cemetery there." Andy raised a brow. "Hey, don't look at me. You hung out there too when you were a kid – especially this close to Halloween."

Andy didn't respond; in fact, he didn't say much over the next hour as they drove to each location where Ron thought Anna might be, despite telling Ron they would talk on the drive. Finally he stopped the car in front of Town Hall, shoved the gear shift into Park, and turned halfway around in his seat to look Ron squarely in the face.

"Where do the kids go to neck these days?"

Ron held up a hand. "Whoa, buddy! Anna's a good girl. I don't think – "

"I'm not asking you to think, Aaron, I'm asking you a question."

Ron sighed, resigned. "They closed Weaver Road a couple years back, so now the kids all go to the old logging road just off SR 4004. There's a clearing at the end of it where the kids have their keggers."

"You're saying my daughter went to a kegger?"

"No, Andy, I'm saying other people's daughters are going to keggers. Yours, however, may be down that road necking with her date, according to you. I don't want to think so, because I don't really feel like being arrested tonight for murdering the little creep she's with."

Andy, a man of few words in normal times, spared none now. He straightened in his seat, put the car back in gear and headed toward the logging road. The route took them past Ron's driveway; through the trees he could see the distant lights of his house, and he prayed this was just simple rebellion about a math class.

SHADOW OF THE WOLF

Hunting other prey proved fruitless. It followed the scent of the men along a beaten track that spanned half a mile from the road to a cabin, where their trail ended. Lights glowed behind small curtained windows. The whole cabin was a pulse of heat and light and sound – laughter, music from a slightly out-of-tune guitar, conversation. It waited; perhaps one would come out to get water from the stream nearby, or to relieve himself. But no one came, and eventually the wolf followed its own scent back through the forest to the old logging road, back to the girl with the fear-rich blood.

Headlights approached, tires crunching, engine revving at a pace too fast for the pitted dirt road. The wolf retreated to the safety of the forest's edge, watching, head lowered, eyes unblinking, as the new car skidded to a stop in the middle of the road beside the wrecked car in the ditch. Two men spilled out. One ran toward the wrecked car, shouting, "Anna! *Anna!* " Close…so close… It could take down this man and go after the other before either realized what was happening.

Then the second man jogged after the first – "Andy, wait! We have to call an ambulance!" – and the wolf backed farther into the trees with a low whine. The shadow of the wolf lay upon this man; he smelled like all the rest of his species, but with the underlying musk of a predator in his blood.

The man's eyes searched the woods around them even as he caught up with his companion at the wrecked car. Both stopped in their tracks at the bloodbath before them.

"Sweet Jesus in heaven," said the man with the wolf-shadow.

The other man gave a strangled moan of grief and stumbled down into the ditch, tugging on the passenger door, which was wedged shut against the side of the embankment. Close…so close the wolf could smell his fear, his sweat, the scent of blood on his breath from the rare steak he'd eaten earlier. Saliva flooded its mouth. It hunkered down, low to the ground, edging closer.

The other man hopped into the ditch, catching his friend as he fell to his knees, sobbing. The wolf waited, watching as he reached into the shattered window, touching the girl's neck. It didn't want to attack this man. It didn't like his scent, the scent of a rival, a challenger.

"Andy, look – I can see her breath. She's alive!"

The sobbing man lurched to his feet, flinging himself at the car, shoving his friend aside. "There's a blanket in the back seat of my car. Hurry!"

The wolf-man scrambled up the embankment to get the blanket. The wolf in the trees prepared to pounce. But the man returned swiftly, something in his hand making tiny bleeping noises as he came back down into the ditch.

"We need an ambulance on State Route 4004, on the old logging road just past Sturdevant Road. About a mile down the road. We're setting flares for visibility. It looks like an animal attack."

The beast in the shadows edged backward, under the cover of the sweeping branches of a hemlock, as red fire light the night and was dropped to the ground. As though sensing its unwavering gaze, the wolf-man turned his eyes toward the woods again, spearing the shadows with an intense gaze. At one point it seemed he locked gazes with the wolf, but then his eyes moved past.

His companion hung halfway into the broken passenger window, murmuring in a low voice to the girl. But the wolf-man set his back against the car, his gaze constantly sweeping the tree line.

When the unearthly wail of sirens sounded in the distance, the wolf acknowledged this prey was out of its reach. It crept deeper into the forest with barely a sound, away from the girl, away from the grieving man, and – with relief – away from the wolf-man.

* * * * *

They waited in silence to hear whether Anna would live or die. The hospital waiting room – where Ron seemed to have been spending an abnormal amount of time of late – was all but deserted at this late hour, Ron and Andy the only ones inhabiting it aside from the occasional nurse who poked her head in to reassure them. Andy stared stone-faced at the wall. Ron couldn't begin to fathom the thoughts racing through the older man's mind. His own traveled guilty roads of regret for the argument he'd had with Anna the last time he'd seen her.

Reggie Spaulding hurried through the waiting room door, his step faltering when Andy stood abruptly, expecting bad news. Reggie glanced at Ron, who stood up beside Andy and laid a steadying hand on his shoulder.

"It's all right, Andy," Reggie assured him. He motioned them back into their chairs and pulled up a third chair to join them. "She's resting comfortably. I won't lie; she lost a lot of blood and she has a dangerously high fever. We've piled ice-packs around her to bring it down. We're short on compatible blood type; can you donate?"

Andy shook his head, dazed, helpless. "She's A negative, I'm O positive. I can't donate."

Reggie turned to Ron. "Aaron, you're the same type. Are you

willing?"

Ron stood up again, rolling up his sleeve. "You don't even have to ask."

He followed Reggie out of the room, sending one last backward glance over his shoulder at Andy. The older man stared at the wall again, his jaw set and his expression tortured.

Andy's wife had arrived while Ron had been drained of as much blood as he could safely give. He hugged her and claimed the seat on the other side of Andy, who sat hunched in his chair, looking as though he'd just spent a season in hell. He thought Andy's burning gaze should have scorched a hole through the plaster by now.

Andy suddenly squared his shoulders, his voice shattering the silence and startling them as though he'd shouted.

"We need to talk, you and I, but I don't want to do it in here. Chapel?"

Ron wondered fatalistically if all disconcerting information would now be given to him in the hospital chapel. But he nodded and said, "I'll tell the nurse where we'll be."

The chapel was empty, the silence rich and soothing after the sterile, bleak sounds of the emergency waiting room. Ron watched silently as his friend knelt on the knee rest and pled to the heavens on his daughter's behalf. He added a silent *Amen* as Andy scooted back onto the pew; Ron had said his own prayers while watching his life-saving blood flow from his vein into a plastic bag.

His thoughts hovered again around mythology and legend but had refused to seriously contemplate the idea that a werewolf roamed the town. If he allowed that possibility to take hold, he would then have to wonder whether he had suffered a high fever after he had been attacked, and then he would have to speculate about what might have happened during his time in Meadow Grove.

"I need to tell you what happened eleven years ago."

"Andy, I *know* what happened eleven years ago. Peter and Jason were murdered, and Elizabeth vanished. That's all I *need* to know."

"I have great loyalty for your family," Andy went on as thought Ron hadn't spoken. "When I was sixteen, I'd gotten in deep with a bad group of people, and Cody rescued me. I made some powerful enemies that day, and if they'd known what I'd grow up to do, they probably would have killed me. But they didn't. And because they didn't, you sit beside me today, a whole man."

Ron's mouth twisted cynically. "Is that what I am – whole?"

Andy fixed his bloodshot eyes on Ron's face. "Your missing piece isn't lost in the Wyckham House; she's slinging drinks for you at your bar. If you stopped looking back at the past and started looking ahead to your future, I bet you'd see she's a big part of it."

"Is she what you wanted to talk to me about?"

"No. What do you remember about those two years, Aaron?"

Ron shrugged. "Nothing. Only the months after the catatonia."

Andy sighed heavily. "Renée came to me in June of 1994 and asked a favor. She even gave me the tools I'd need to accomplish it. But I couldn't bring myself to do it for ten more months – not until Cody got knifed in Chicago and no one knew if he'd live. She was here in town visiting Bonnie and me when she got the call. I drove her to the airport, and while she sat white-faced and white-knuckled waiting for her plane to board, I realized how much she must have trusted me to tell me what she suspected. And on the heels of that I remembered Cody standing between me and evil men, being my shield.

"Three weeks later, on April 14, 1995, the night before the full moon, I went into the woods and laid in wait about a mile from the Wyckham House. Around midnight the beast caught my scent and came to kill me. I killed it instead. And do you know what happened then, Aaron?"

"No," Ron replied, trying to sound unconcerned and only managing to sound as though he was being strangled. He didn't *want* to know. That part of his lost years could remain in shadows.

Andy turned sideways in the pew to face him. "The wolf I shot turned into a man. And I found myself staring down at a man who'd gone missing eight months before you did. I carried him out of the woods on my back, and I dumped him on Harlan Michaels' desk. The look on Michaels' face told me that this was the werewolf that had bitten you."

That startled a laugh out of Ron, but it was bitter and devoid of amusement. "Werewolf, Andy?"

"Werewolf. Now I don't know what happened at that hospital you were in; you would have to ask those doctors who took care of you. But it's no coincidence your condition dramatically changed the day after I killed that wolf."

Ron could find nothing to say. First Kimberly, then Taryn, and now Andy, all stuck on the werewolf myth.

"Do you know why I tell you this tonight, Aaron?"

Ron had a sneaking suspicion it had something to do with indebtedness. "Because I owe you."

This startled Andy. "No, Ron, you don't owe me a thing. I went into the woods eleven years ago because it was the right thing to do. Cody did me a good turn and I wanted to help you. I know you love Anna, and she thinks the sun rises and sets on you. It's a glorious thing to see because Bonnie and I – well, we didn't know how you'd be when you came home from Philadelphia. We weren't sure if you'd lost your capacity to love when you lost Elizabeth and your friends."

"I can love," Ron replied softly. His thoughts strayed to Kimberly, waiting for him at home, trusting that he *would* come home.

"Oh, anyone with eyes can see that, Aaron. You were probably the last one to know."

"So what is it you want me to do, Andy? Go into the woods and shoot me a werewolf?"

Andy held his gaze without blinking. "That's the general idea. You see, my night vision isn't what it used to be. I can't be certain I'd get him this time."

Ron felt an unexpected rush of nausea. "Andy – " He licked suddenly dry lips as Andy continued to stare at him. "There's every possibility that I know the...the werewolf. I think it's Beth Fairchild's father. She came here to find him. I can't do this to her."

"Some people can't be saved, Aaron. If the Circle cursed her father, there's no out for him but death. Anna can be saved. All it takes is to kill the wolf that bit her."

"Oh God," Ron murmured. He covered his face with his hands. *Oh God, why me? Why does what's right have to be what's hardest?* Kimberly would hate him, but if he didn't put Anna first, he'd hate himself.

A long time later, he said gruffly, "I'll do it."

The tension flowed out of Andy. "I knew you would," he said quietly. "Do you need silver bullets?"

"No. I have my own."

"I thought you might."

Ron let the silence hang between them as the minutes crept onward, dragging them closer toward dawn, until he could put it off no longer.

"If you think she was attacked by a werewolf, Andy, we have to get her out of here before dawn."

"Why is that?"

"If the myths – the legends – are right, her wounds will disappear at dawn. Do you fancy explaining that to Reggie Spaulding or Paul Jacobs? Or any of the nursing staff?"

"Reggie will never allow us to take her out of here."

"Then we have to tell him."

Ron wished that Paul was on duty tonight; after Scott's miraculous recovery following Harlan Michael's unusual request, Paul would harbor few doubts about their sanity or their seriousness.

Andy stood, his expression resolute. "Let's go."

Morning broke, bringing dull gray skies and drizzling rain. Wind whipped through the town streets, driving before it crisp autumn leaves in swirls of scarlet and gold. A storm approached, promising rain and possibly snow. The clouds obscured the ghost moon hanging full and round in the sky.

Reggie had listened to them without interruption, but also with an expression of disbelief and disappointment. "You – I can understand *you* believing in superstitions and fairytales," he said to Ron, and then turned his disenchanted gaze upon Andy. "But *you* – this is your daughter we're talking about, and I can't believe a father would really want to remove his critically injured child from medical care."

Ron and Andy had exchanged a glance, conceding defeat. Their story would be substantiated by dawn; they could only hope Reggie didn't freak out completely.

Anna regained consciousness briefly as grey light colored the sky. Her fever spiked to 105 and her pain reached an intolerable pitch.

Reggie was forced to dose her with morphine, and decided to check her wounds before he went off shift.

He came out of her room, his black face ash-grey and his hands shaking. Ron listened, stone-faced and silent, to his whispered conversation with Andy and Bonnie.

Anna's wounds had completely vanished.

HOUSE CALL

The headache pulsed behind her eye like a warning beacon. Kim had tried to fend it off with aspirin and a nap – well, she didn't know if sleeping five hours constituted a nap or a night's sleep – but still the headache throbbed, worsening as the hours ticked by. Her belongings had been brought from Taryn's yesterday at some point in time she'd slept through, but her migraine medicine didn't seem to be among them – which meant both she and Ron had forgotten to pack it when they were at the cottage.

She didn't know where Ron might have hidden her car keys; for all she knew, he had taken them with him again to be certain she wouldn't go anywhere. She had to admit his ploy had worked; she'd been forced to spend her time resting, and she felt tremendously better, although her body was weak and quivery if she tried to do too much. Which was why she was sitting at the kitchen table; she'd made herself soup, and just the act of opening a can and microwaving its contents had done her in. Eating had pushed her toward exhaustion again. God knew when he would be home from the hospital; he hadn't said what had happened, only that Anna Malone had been in an accident and Jared Olmstead, her boyfriend, was dead.

Taryn's purse sat on the table; she pulled it close and lowered her head, using it for a pillow. She sat in the fog of semi-consciousness, the nearest thing to a state of sleep a migraineur without medicine can achieve, and didn't hear Taryn until she spoke behind her.

"Hey, have you seen my purse?"

Kim raised her eye, squinting against the grey light pouring in from the kitchen window. "Yeah, it's my pillow. I promise I didn't drool in it." She pushed the leather bag toward her friend.

Taryn grinned. "I'm so tired, I wouldn't care if you had." At Kim's cocked brow, she elaborated, "Couldn't really sleep. As soon as it got light, Scott drove me to the tavern to get my car. I'm gonna go sleep for a while, just as soon…as I find…my phone," she muttered, her hand feeling blindly through the obviously disorganized contents of her purse. Her hand came out with the elusive cell phone. "Finally. I'm hitting the sack. I'm taking the guest room, so if you need anything, just come on in."

"I'll probably just go back to bed myself. Maybe this headache will go away."

Taryn's critical gaze crawled over her face. "You were looking better last night."

"Migraine. I'll be all right. Go sleep."

When Taryn still looked reluctant to leave, Kim gave her a push toward the door, and at last her friend staggered away, yawning widely. She laid her head back down on the purse, listening to the quiet hum of the furnace, the whir of the icemaker filling the cube trays with water, the creak of the windows under the force of the wind. She thought about the morning she had awakened after the fishing gear arrived at her father's cabin, and about the dream she'd had of Ron before she'd ever met him. And realized that she hadn't had a precognitive dream in quite some time. Perhaps whatever she'd been drugged with – and Ron avoided answering her every time she asked if he knew what she'd been given and who had been giving it to her – had silenced her gift.

A stabbing pain like a spike through her eye derailed her train of thought. If she didn't get her meds, she would be in for at least twenty-four hours of agony, possibly longer. Her worst one had lasted four days – four long days of abject misery, vomiting, and boredom. No TV or radio because sound make her head want to explode. No reading or computer work because the words, although in English, made no sense to her tortured brain.

I could walk, she thought, and indeed she could, but she didn't know if she could make it to the cottage. While the town wasn't large, it sprawled over considerable distance. She estimated the cottage was about four miles from Ron's house.

The pain spiked again and she lifted her head, wincing. She pinched the web between her thumb and forefinger, numbing the nerve Caleb Schaefer had shown her in Mulberry's Grocery, and the headache faded to an inarticulate grumble. While this was a welcome relief, she couldn't sit here for hours waiting for the migraine trigger to shut down. She cast her eyes around the kitchen, hoping to find a convenient clothespin just waiting to be put to use, and her gaze fell on Taryn's purse. Taryn, who was asleep in the next room. Taryn, whose car was in the drive and whose car keys were poking out of an open side pocket of the leather bag.

Both hands reached for them before the idea had fully formed in her mind: right fingers pinching the webbing between thumb and forefinger on her left hand, which plucked the keys from the pocket of Taryn's purse and folded them into her palm to keep them from jingling. Her own purse hung from a peg on the coat rack by the back door, her sneakers beneath it; she retrieved her wallet and slid her feet into the shoes, still pinching the nerve to keep the headache at bay. She was fairly sure she could drive this way; she would find out soon enough.

It wasn't easy. For the sake of expediency and stealth, she let go of the nerve, needing both hands to start the car and guide it down the driveway and onto Stoneridge Way. The headache throbbed to brilliant life, a wave of nausea nearly convincing her to pull over. But it was just after eight in the morning, and she figured Ron would be home soon – had expected him home long before now, in fact – and she wanted to get back before he arrived. He'd be pissed if he found her gone.

As she passed the tavern, she slowed, her eyes widening as she took in the destruction of the service entrance door to the tavern. Scott, his back to the road, was busily fitting plywood into the opening to secure the premises. Kim accelerated slightly to get past before he noticed the car, and even went as far as jumping the stop sign, rounding the corner onto Willow Road faster than was wise. She breathed easier when she turned off the road and onto the driveway to the cottage.

The woods seemed hushed today, as though the events of the previous night had shocked all life into silence. Even the squirrel and the chickadee, who constantly quarreled in the maple outside the living room, were abnormally silent. Perhaps they knew of the supernatural creature that roamed the forest, the creature that existed outside of all natural order. The creature that wore her father's bracelet.

This thought made her pause on the bottom step of the front porch. Her father was a werewolf. A werewolf had chased her friends last night. Anna Malone had not come home on time. For a moment panic reigned and she couldn't draw breath, as though she had taken a blow to the solar plexus. The pain behind her right eye flared. She climbed two more steps and stopped again when she realized she couldn't get into the cottage. Ron had her keys and, not being the trusting kind, she had not hid a spare anywhere.

She smothered an impatient oath; unless she'd accidentally left a window open somewhere, she wasn't getting inside, and she didn't fancy staying out in the forest any longer than necessary. Already the hair on her neck and arms had stiffened with tension and fear; a werewolf ran loose in Mills, and who knew whether it had to be dark for the transformation to happen. The moon was full whether it was day or night, and a full moon seemed to be the only prerequisite for a werewolf to turn. She didn't want to be its next meal. God, she could think of nothing worse.

She circled the cottage, looking for a breach. Ah, there! Her entry inside: the window in the spare bedroom Ron had left cracked open after painting, and it would not be easy. She climbed onto the porch railing where it attached to the house, leaned around the corner, and pried off the screen. It fell with a racket, and she winced. With much difficulty, she managed to lever the window up, and then swung herself off the railing to hang off the sill. A feat of gymnastic skill vaulted her through the opening. She cracked her head on the sash as she sailed through and landed in a cursing heap on the bare wood floor of the empty room.

"Oh God!" The migraine sent spikes of debilitating pain through her head, and for a moment she lay on the floor, one hand pressing the knot on the top of her head, the other pressed against her pulsing right eye, wondering if she should have just driven herself to the hospital instead.

She didn't know how long she lay there before the headache backed off, but finally she was able to roll onto her knees, and from there she pushed herself to her feet. Her fingers were smeared with blood; the sash had scraped a chunk of her scalp away.

The grey daylight from bedroom windows couldn't reach the hallway. Her head swam as she stared into the gloom. The migraine pills had been in the night table beside her bed; she crossed the shadowed hallway and made a beeline for the table, fumbled it open, and breathed a sigh of relief. Just as she had thought, the small snap-open container that held three Maxalt-MLT tablets in sealed packets – four if she scrunched them in tightly – lay amongst hair clips, barrettes, and a cheesy sci-fi novel she'd been reading before she got sick. She freed a tablet from its factory seal, and she turned it out of the blister pack and onto her tongue, making a face as the slightly bitter orange flavor filled her mouth.

A splotch of blood from whacking her head on the window sash stained her tank-top and bra, so she shrugged out of them and pulled the only thing she could find: a button-up blouse that had been inadvertently left behind in her hasty packing. It would do until she could get a change of clothes from Taryn's, or until she could talk Ron out of a tee-shirt.

She paused in the doorway of her bedroom, the headache throbbing, blurring her vision. She needed water. Dehydration from her illness had, no doubt, triggered the headache in the first place. A quick glass and then she had to go; Ron was likely to have already discovered her absence.

She stepped into the darkness.

Pain exploded from her right cheekbone through her forehead and chin. For a stunned moment, she had no idea what had happened; it was like walking into a live power line. Then a rough shove pinned her against the hallway wall, her arm wrenched up behind her back nearly to the point of dislocation. Arms of steel held her in place and a warm, solid body pressed provocatively against her back. A delicious, sensual scent filled her space, muddling her thoughts.

"Nice and easy, beautiful," a low, deep voice crooned in her ear.

Her heart stuttered with panic, but she rotated her jaw, testing the pain, before managing to reply with a calm that amazed even herself, "Wow, you even make house calls?"

He chuckled, his lips still intimately near her ear. She shuddered and squirmed away. His hand bunched into her hair and held her firmly in place.

"Only when it's worth it, my dear. And this is definitely worth it."

"How long have you been lying in wait? You're a busy man – seems like you'd have better things to do."

"I didn't have to wait long because I knew you were coming this morning."

How could he have known something like that, unless he shared her gift for seeing the future? That was a sobering thought. "How is that even possible?"

"It's one of my many talents."

"Can you let go of my arm? I think you've dislocated it."

"Not a chance, darlin'. I know better. But too bad I can't dislocate that tongue of yours," he added under his breath. "Now I'm going to back away, and you're going to come with me, nice and docile."

"Where?"

"Just full of questions today, aren't you."

He stepped away from her and eased the pressure on her arm. The cloud of intoxicating cologne dissipated. He nudged her out of the hallway. Kimberly went compliantly until they reached the kitchen. This would be her only opportunity to break free of him and stand even a slim chance of escape.

With a move she learned from a personal defense trainer, she planted her feet solidly on the floor and drove her elbow with desperate force into his ribcage. In league with the devil or not, he had no immunity to pain, and he fairly howled with it. Stumbling backward, he collided with the counter and released her arm. She needed no further encouragement to bolt for the back door.

Acutely aware that every second counted, she fumbled with the deadbolt and yanked the door open. She had nearly gained the porch when he caught up to her, catching her by the hair. Excruciating pain flared through her scalp as he dragged her back into the house. She tried to trip him but he anticipated the move and sidestepped her. She

went down hard, landing with bruising force on the tiled floor. He
didn't try to break her fall.

"*I THOUGHT I TOLD YOU TO BEHAVE!*" he bellowed. His
expression transcended fury, and she was suddenly certain he was
going kill her right here in her own kitchen. *Ron's going to be really ticked
if this idiot stains the new tiles with my blood.* The thought struck her as
inexplicably hilarious, and she started to giggle.

His utter bafflement at her amusement only made her laugh
harder. And the harder she laughed, the angrier he became. She didn't
comprehend the mortal danger she was in until he straddled her
bruised body, his hands clenched around her throat.

He leaned in until his nose pressed against hers, hissing, "*Stop it!*"

She tried to suck in a breath. He squeezed harder, cutting off
virtually all of her air. No escape now. Her fingernails clawed at the
back of his hand, but he didn't release her. Her vision dimmed as her
lungs starved for oxygen.

The words came to Kimberly's lips unbidden, rasped out with the
last of her air.

"*Jesus still sees you.*"

He squeezed tighter still, and she fell into darkness.

WRONG TURN

If she didn't look too closely for it, Kimberly could almost see a
faint trail through the thicket. She followed it using only her peripheral
vision, until at last she pushed through the last snarl of brambles and
stumbled into the clearing. The cabin looked just as she remembered,
but this time she thought she could see the faint outline of a door. She
took a step closer and stopped when she saw a man standing in front
of the gate. Or – maybe *not* a man; she couldn't see him clearly.

"I've come to talk to Sarah. I have questions I need answered."

The figure moved closer, its features shifting until they became
recognizably human. Except his eyes. Pools of color swam across their
fathomless surface, flaring and fading like fireworks in an eternal
celebration. "You won't find truth with Sarah Bennett."

"And you are – ?"

"A messenger. You come to ask the fallen for truth, willing to swallow their lies as fact. You've taken a wrong turn, woman."

Kimberly stepped back, affronted. "I believe I'm on the right side. I certainly don't condone black magic."

He smiled sadly at her. "You see the devil's doorway now. Do you know why?"

"No." Kimberly turned to stare hard at the cabin. Ah yes, she could clearly see the door of the cabin this time.

"You asked Him to take back His gift to you. You said you didn't want it, in effect saying you didn't want *Him*. Do you still dream? Do you dream like you used to?"

"No. Not like...usual."

"Does it worry you?"

Kim's chin ducked toward her chest. She felt small and forlorn. He came to stand beside her, and now he was not human at all. A messenger, he had called himself. She knew him by another word: angel.

"Will He give it back?"

"It is your choice – free will and all it implies. Now you must wake up, Kimberly Owens. You must choose." He bent, his mouth covering hers, breathing life into her. *Wake up, Kimberly. Wake up and choose ..."*

* * * * *

He turned a slow, tight circle in the cell as if it would help him find an explanation for the incredible mystery confronting him. He had left Harlan Michaels's body in the near freezing cell until he could find the time to deal with it, not bothering to lock the door because he hadn't expected a dead man to walk away. The temperature ensured the body would stay well enough preserved he could put off disposal until after the full moon cycle. He couldn't risk burying the body in daylight, and he *wouldn't* risk burying it at night during the lycanthrope cycle.

The dilemma now facing him transcended ironic: Harlan's body had disappeared, leaving behind the remains of a slug, stuck to the floor in a puddle of dried blood. A very *large* puddle.

He had not reached the position of High Priest of the Circle by means of stupidity, and it took precisely three seconds for his mind to connect these dots.

Hands on his hips, he shook his head in utter disgust. Harlan had ended up with the last word after all and had pulled the bluff of all bluffs.

So one last preparation remained: loading his gun with the silver bullets he had taken from Harlan. He headed for his bedroom to swap out his rounds, his pace unhurried. He had several hours in which to deal with Harlan; first he had his guest to attend to.

He watched her sleeping for a long time after swapping the magazine in his pistol for one loaded with silver-tainted rounds. He reflected on the irony that the two most alluring women he'd ever met had both belonged to Aaron – and now to him. Elizabeth lay dead in an unmarked grave no more than fifty paces outside the clearing the Wyckham House occupied, where Kimberly Owens would eventually join her. Oh yes, he knew her now. Her real name, anyway. She'd hidden it well, but he'd found her real driver's license tucked into a tear in the cloth lining of her wallet. Why she was in Mills under an assumed name remained a mystery, but he would soon solve that as well.

Her breathing had been labored since he'd choked her on her kitchen floor, and she had not regained consciousness in the intervening hours. While on one hand he was grateful – the woman was definitely a challenge to his patience – on the other hand, he desperately wanted to know why she had said what she did.

Jesus still sees you.

In repose Kimberly's face lost much of its sharpness, allowing him to see the smoothness of the golden skin stretched over her cheekbones; the perfection of her small straight nose; the full, sensual shape of her lower lip. She seemed to glow in the dim light from his lantern, as though drinking in the beams and multiplying their luminosity tenfold. She entranced him.

Her chest rose in a shuddering breath, and she opened her eyes. He was doubly mesmerized as those eyes found his. The color and depth of fine whiskey, they held him motionless, quickened his breath, made his heart race like a schoolboy's.

"He's coming for me, Caleb." Her voice rasped. In the dim light from the bedside lantern, he could see the livid bruises from his fingers.

"Aaron? I'm not afraid of him."

"I'm not talking about Aaron."

"God? I'm not afraid of him, either."

She tried to sit up, only then realizing he had tethered her to the bed. The rope cut into her wrists painfully and when she tested her bonds, they held firm. Her furtive glance searched for places to which she could escape and found only the shadowy corridor over his shoulder. He had placed himself here deliberately, knowing if she got loose she would run him a merry chase through the dark corridors of the Wyckham House. She was fearless; the darkness wouldn't deter her flight.

"So this is how it's to be," she said. "Torture and rape."

"I've neither tortured nor raped you, Kimberly."

"Yeah," she agreed, "but the day's not over yet, right?"

Caleb couldn't help his chuckle. "It will be a shame to have to kill you, but unfortunately I can't have you carrying tales out of Mills."

She rolled her eyes. "It's the 21st century. No one would even raise an eyebrow at your black magic. Murder, however... But of course, I can't prove that, so you're more paranoid than the situation demands."

"You've no idea what the situation demands." He pulled his chair closer to the edge of the bed and turned it around so he could rest his arms on the back.

"I know nothing excuses murder."

"Not even immortality? Immortality with the added bonus of keeping your humanity?"

"Is that why you've already made an admirable attempt to kill me?"

"Is that what's troubling you? If I wanted you dead, you would be. No, my plans for you are much more intricate but sadly have the same end result. But imagine the possibilities...the progress I can make with your death...it's exhilarating."

"I don't want to imagine the possibilities," she replied hoarsely. "You're crazy. You have however many days God gives you. To try to steal more is ludicrous and to do it by stealing the lives of others is ghastly."

"Thank you for that moral newsflash. Now our time together grows short, and we have places to be."

Caleb stood up and shoved the chair aside. Kim watched him silently as he came around the end of the bed. She didn't cringe away from him. He leaned over her to untie her hands and heard her breathe in his scent. She would be hard to break in the few hours he had, but not impossible. He enjoyed a challenge.

She swayed slightly when he set her on her feet. He slid his arm around her chest and drew her hard against him. She was compact, firmly muscled, a contradiction of softness and steel. His pulse went wild. His lips brushed her ear.

"Don't try to run. You saw what happened last time."

"You don't really expect me to agree to that, do you?"

"Just remember, Kimberly: I can take your body or your life any minute I choose. Either one is fine by me."

His hand slithered over her shoulder and cupped her breast, his thumb swirling a sensuous circle over her nipple. Her heart jumped against his hand. Then his grip tightened with excruciating strength. She clenched her teeth to choke back her scream.

"Now I don't have the time with you that I had with Elizabeth. Three months of planning and two weeks of heaven. She was nothing but a whore at heart, you know. And she grossly overestimated her skill in playing games with me.

"But back to you. If you drive me to it, I will take what little time I *do* have and it will be utterly unpleasant. So let's have no repeats of our earlier altercation. Agreed?"

She nodded vigorously. He gave her one last squeeze; she arched away from the pain, her backside pressing against his groin with inadvertent intimacy. His pulse, already racing dangerously fast, leapt into a full gallop.

He guided her out of the room into a gloomy stone corridor, pausing long enough to take a flashlight out of his pocket and flick it on.

"Are there dungeons?" she asked, her voice steady.

"Yes."

"Is that where you have my father?"

"Your father? Why would I have your father? Who the hell is he?"

"Todd Garrett."

"That explains a lot," he murmured. Now it made sense – the timing of her arrival, the worry she seemed to radiate, her being at Aaron's other rental on Willow Road. Even her taking a job at the tavern had to have been with the ultimate goal of finding Todd; after all, the researcher had been a nightly patron.

They descended another full flight before she realized he hadn't really answered.

"It *is* where you keep him, isn't it?"

"I'm not keeping him anywhere."

"He's dead? You killed him?" She planted her feet on the hard stone floor. Walking too close behind her, he couldn't check his momentum in time and rammed into her, knocking her off her feet.

"Dammit, get up! I don't have ti – what the hell, woman!" He had yanked her up by the arm, and she came to her feet swinging, her whole petite frame behind her punch. Her fist caught him in the jaw, a left-handed roundhouse that would have been truly impressive had she been left-handed. But the blow was insignificant, all things considered, and barely rocked his head back.

He twisted her arm up behind her back, pressing in close again. "You're coming dangerously close to that promise of *utterly unpleasant*. Get moving."

She didn't come gracefully or cooperatively by any measure. Every step was a fight, every second an opportunity for her to catch him off guard. God, she was wild! The passion running below her calm, cool exterior was violent and unpredictable. He couldn't wait to stand in her storm and experience its feral power.

Down another flight of steps and into a dark corridor lined with stout, wood-plank doors. Her steps dragged as he dragged her past the cells to another set of steps that led upward. At the top of these, fire from old-fashioned torches cast the room in light and shadow, illuminating dark stains on the granite altar.

Her whiskey eyes locked on the flat stone, the mind behind them undoubtedly imagining all sorts of quite accurate reasons for those stains. Manacles dangled by stout chains to either side: a set for her hands and another for her feet. And then…then she would truly be at his mercy. He could be merciful for her; he was sure he could – for a time. Long enough to drive that reckless nature of hers past the point of reason and control.

A shove sent her sprawling on the floor beside the altar. He picked up the closest manacle and reached for her hand.

"No." She scuttled backward like a crab, but she was trapped between the altar and him. Being restrained meant the end of her life; her expression finally reflected her understanding. He wondered how far she would go to ensure her survival.

The iron cuff dropped from his hand to clank against the side of the altar. He lifted her to her feet. "What will you do to go free? Will you make an agreement with the devil himself?"

"No."

"That's regrettable. Ah well. Poor Aaron," Caleb murmured with mock-concern. "Always too late to save the women he loves. And I'll just keep taking them from him, over and over and over again." He reached up to brush his fingers against her cheek, and Kim recoiled with a grimace of disgust. "Tell me, Kimberly Owens, what makes a woman like you fall in love with a man like Aaron?"

"Why should you care? You don't understand love. I don't think you're even capable of feeling it."

His hand tangled into her hair again, yanking her head back with brutal force. But behind the pain in her eyes was defiance, burning brightly. She would fight him to the last, force him to take her when her surrender would be exquisite and so much more satisfying for them both.

He bent to her so swiftly she didn't have time to dodge. Her lips were cool against his. He stroked his tongue along them, the fingers of one hand pressing against the pulse in her throat. Her heart beat a wild, savage rhythm, betraying the war between her moral code and her body's craving. She tore her mouth away.

"That's not love, Caleb. It's not even sex; it's domination."

"But I promise to make it good, Kimberly. *Very* good." His fingers trailed from her hair, skating down the inside of her arm in a seductive caress. She jerked her arm away, and he secured the manacle around her wrist. He silently motioned to the altar.

She stared at the stone, her eyes riveted to the stain, which had resolved itself into a sticky puddle of blood. She began to tremble. Finally, he thought with relief, the true nature of her predicament had penetrated her fearlessness. For a long time he had been uneasy, Sarah's words – *anything is possible* – echoing in his mind. But Kimberly was only human, after all, and at the hour of death all humans desperately snatched at life with panicked, terrified hands. She was no different. She would cave, as they all did, given enough time.

"Don't mind the blood. Tiana Michaels had a slight...mishap."

"Oh my God," she breathed. Her shaking knees collapsed under her. He let her fall. "What have you done, Caleb?"

"Purely an accident, very unfortunate," Caleb replied indifferently. He leaned down and lifted her roughly to her feet. "Now here's the strange coincidence that you're going to explain to me. Tiana's last words to me were 'Jesus sees you.' And lo and behold, what does little Miss Kimberly say as the lights go out? Exactly the same thing."

Kim shook her head wildly. "I don't know – I don't remember anything – "

His hand shot out and grabbed her by the throat. She gasped for air, mindless with fear, her fingers scrabbling across the back of his hand. "Wrong answer."

"I don't know! I don't know! " Kim gasped. Her eyes on his were wide and guileless; he almost believed her. He eased the pressure on her throat. "Hop on up; I don't have all day."

"Caleb, please..."

"*Now*, Kimberly," he interrupted gently.

She climbed onto the altar gingerly, revulsion contorting her expression. She tried to avoid the sticky puddle, but he clamped the other manacle around her trembling wrist and slowly pushed her back until she lay flat in her friend's blood. She rolled onto her side, dry heaves twisting her body, but still she didn't cry. She was amazing.

Caleb pressed his searing lips to her forehead.

"Seems I've finally found something that rattles you. I guess you should have had the...ah...lemon bars with me after all."

He left her lying there on the altar of the devil, in her friend's blood, with no hope of escape.

SUCH A LIAR

Ron didn't make it home until after two in the afternoon. He'd stayed with Andy and Bonnie until the two had come to terms, as well as anyone could ever hope to come to terms, with the knowledge that Anna had been bitten by a werewolf...and survived. When Andy was driving him home from the hospital, he'd seen Scott working on the tavern door and had his friend drop him off to help.

The mangled steel door gave silent corroboration to Scott's and Taryn's story. It lay propped against the side of the tavern, the hinges bent and twisted. The wolf had done fair damage to the interior of the tavern as well; tables had toppled over and chairs had been smashed. He frowned as he thought of the bullets in a mason jar in his closet – bullets he himself had tipped with silver, following an instinct his subconscious had acknowledged. The gun case on the shelf beside the Mason jar held a Glock 19 with two 33-round magazines already loaded with his special silver 9mm rounds.

Yes, he'd always known, deep inside, what had happened to him and what he'd become. It had been easier to hide behind the self-induced amnesia, especially in the wake of losing Elizabeth, Peter, and Jason. There had been no need to remember what had happened – neither the events at the Wyckham House that night nor the many nights in Meadow Grove that followed – because remembering meant caring, and he hadn't. He'd only been waiting to die so he could escape the unrelenting pain. What a tale the doctor from Meadow Grove must have told Kimberly, and he marveled that she still wanted to be with him.

He cringed away from the thought of loading one of those 33-round magazines into his pistol and hunting her father.

"Let's get the hell out of here and go home," Scott said now.

They'd just finished sweeping up the last of the splinters from the broken chairs, as well as the broken bar glasses the animal had knocked from the back bar as it had careened out of the kitchen. He'd been oddly quiet while they worked, his brow furrowed in a troubled frown.

"Yeah, I want to be home before dark, and Kimberly shouldn't be left alone."

"Your house is a fortress."

"Even castles fall."

Scott was wrong; his house wasn't a fortress. It was just a house, with deadbolts on the doors and alarms on the windows – alarms designed to alert the occupants of the house to intruders but which weren't connected to an outside agency that could send law enforcement. He supposed he could have gotten that kind of security system even way out here in Mills, but every time he had even idly toyed with the notion, something inside him backed away from it. He knew what that something was now: a thirst for retribution. Let them come; he was prepared. Sixty-six 9mm rounds dotted with sterling silver waited for whatever they wanted to throw at him.

Whoever "they" were.

He contemplated this unknown entity as he cruised the Dart along Stoneridge Way several miles over the speed limit. He didn't need to worry – the constable appeared to have vanished; all attempts to reach him and his two deputies by phone last night had failed. Denny had gone strangely incommunicado as well; Ron's texts and voicemails had gone unanswered. When Reggie Spaulding left the hospital at the end of his shift, he promised to swing by the station and Harlan's house to see if he could rustle up the law. He left after a hurried conversation with Paul Jacobs, who came on shift after him. Ron saw Paul shoot off a hurried text message and wondered if more black SUVs were on the way.

Scott turned off Stoneridge Way without slowing. Ron winced as the car bounced over the rough driveway. He felt a sudden empathy for Kimberly when he was behind the wheel.

The cul-de-sac was empty when Scott parked in front of the house. "Taryn went home," he said unnecessarily.

"I wish she hadn't done that." His mind would have more peace with everyone under one roof: Taryn, Kimberly, Scott, Denny. Tiana, too, if she would answer his calls. "Have you heard from Tiana, by the way? I'm getting really worried. It's not like her to blow off work and not answer calls. And she wasn't home when I went by yesterday."

Scott got out and slammed his door, leaning against the car and talking to Ron over the roof. "I've heard from her. It's not good. I don't know where she is – I waited at her house night before last but she never showed up. Something happened there – a lot of blood on the carpet."

"For God's sake, Scott! Why didn't you say anything last night? Why didn't you call Harlan?"

"For one, you left with Andy to go find Anna almost as soon as we got here. Two, I don't think it was her blood. There were some bloody towels as well – looked like there'd been a fight. Three, Harlan's the last person who would run to her rescue."

"What?"

"You should read her journal this evening. Things are worse than bad, Ron. I don't understand a lot of what she's talking about, but there were some things in there about Elizabeth… I dunno if I believe it all, but after what I saw last night… Well, I guess it's not so far-fetched."

"What are you talking about? Why would Tiana know anything about Elizabeth?"

But Scott refused to say anything beyond "The journal's in my room. It explains everything. I'll go get it."

While Scott dashed upstairs to his room, Ron went to the hall closet and opened the Glock case, removing the pistol and slamming in a loaded magazine. He put the other magazine in his pocket, grabbed the mason jar of bullets, and closed the door, hollering up the stairs to Scott.

"Hey, I'm gonna get some mac-and-cheese going. I feel like some comfort food."

A slight movement on his left made him spin around, the gun raised and aimed in one fluid motion, his finger sliding onto the trigger. Taryn stopped, green eyes wide, the color leeching from her face as she stared into the barrel of the gun.

He lowered the weapon, sagging against the closed closet door. "You scared the shit out of me."

"Likewise," she replied, her voice shaking. "I didn't know you were that fast. What do you do, practice ninja moves while no one's home?"

"Something like that. What are you doing here?"

"Stayed here last night. Chased out of the tavern by a werewolf, remember?"

"Your car's gone. We thought you'd left." He eyed her with suspicion. "You didn't let Kimberly borrow it, did you?"

"Of course not. She's upstairs, asleep."

The words were barely out of her mouth before Ron was sprinting up the stairs. Taking them two at a time. Knowing he would find an empty bed and no note.

* * * * *

She thought the shadows moved in the corner behind her, darkness coalescing against a backdrop of charcoal stone, but she couldn't be sure. So she didn't look very long or hard; there were more things in this house of horrors than she would ever be able to bend her mind around. For the sake of her sanity, she thought it best not to dwell on the gruesome possibilities.

But still.... Kimberly moved her head slightly, peering into the black corner of the room where the light from the torch couldn't reach. Perhaps it was only a trick of her eyes, caused by the flickering firelight. The flames of the torch weaved and wavered, as though some source of fresh air caused currents to ripple past. The only other alternative – that the air moved because the stirring shadows in the corner had substance – was simply too much to bear.

Her breath drifted in a frosty cloud over her, and she shivered. She might succumb to hypothermia before her bladder burst; at this point she couldn't find the strength to care. The stone at her back, slick with blood, had failed to warm with her body heat. Instead, it seemed to leech away what little heat she had left. Her hands were cubes of ice, dead things that dangled at the ends of her arms. Tucking them into her armpits had only kept them warm when the rest of her had been warm.

"I need to use the rest room." Her voice shattered the silence, and echoed around the room in a sibilant hiss, making her flinch. She hadn't meant to speak; she had been determined not to ask him for anything.

Newspaper rustled, and the decrepit folding chair he sat in creaked under his weight as he shifted. "Feel free," he invited, his tone uninterested.

"I'm cold and hungry, too," she persisted.

Caleb sighed and rattled the paper again. "I suppose you'll become whiny and tiresome soon."

"Will it help?"

"Not at all."

"I should conserve my energy then."

He turned the page of his newspaper. "For what?"

"My escape."

A smile of genuine humor curved his mouth, and Kim felt her heart stutter. God, what a cruel trick of nature that this black-hearted man had the face of an angel. Five o'clock shadow darkened his jaw, leading her eyes upward to the sensual perfection of his mouth. His lips absolutely begged for kisses. She wondered if that's how he drew them in, his victims. If he charmed them – for certainly he was charming – and dazzled them with his heavenly looks, they couldn't see he was inexorably dragging them toward the open pit of hell.

"There are two ways off that stone, Kimberly. One is infinitely more pleasant than the other."

"I won't be anyone's whore."

He raised his head, pinning her with a narrow gaze. "So you say." He went back to his newspaper.

I won't! Kim thought fiercely. *Especially not his.* To remind herself of the mortal danger he represented, she forced herself to recount the minutes before she'd been brought to this death chamber. As though to help bring the memory into clear focus, her right breast throbbed. She could almost feel his fingers again, biting into her flesh in silent demonstration of what waited for her in the hours ahead.

But he had yet to touch her again in such an intimate way. She couldn't help but think he was only prolonging the inevitable because he enjoyed her dread, and that she would, indeed, find it dreadful.

"There's no sense in staying loyal to Aaron. He'll never love you. He's incapable. You're wasting your time."

"Doesn't matter."

"It will. Rejection can make a person reckless. And you know all about reckless, don't you?"

"Yeah, I know reckless. It walks hand-in-hand with regret."

He chuckled and gave the newspaper a last shake, folding it into a neat rectangle. A thoughtful frown tugged his smile out of place as he stood up and tossed the newspaper onto the chair. Quiet steps brought him to her side. Kim experienced a moment of the regret she'd just mentioned; she should have kept her mouth shut. He stared down at her for a long moment, and then leaned over her, bracing his hands on either side of her, seemingly unmindful of the blood.

"Are you certain? Say the word and I'll unlock the cuffs. I'll even let you bathe first, wash off all the blood."

"I'm pretty certain."

"Only *pretty* certain? That seems to leave room for doubt." He leaned closer, and she couldn't help it; her eyes were drawn to those perfect lips. She swallowed hard. "Choose wisely. I might not offer again."

"It would be very reckless," Kim said quietly. "And then I'd have regrets. Weren't you listening?"

"I was listening. I just don't believe you mean it." He bent yet closer until the side of his nose brushed hers. Kim dared not even breathe. Her pulse raced out of control, but she couldn't tell if it was from fear or anticipation.

"I meant it."

He shifted abruptly, his lips pressing a searing kiss on her forehead. "You're such a liar." A wicked smile curved his mouth as he straightened. She clenched her jaw, not sure if she was holding back a scream or her surrender.

He left her there without another word, his purposeful strides carrying him from the chamber. The torch light guttered, but Kim determinedly kept her eyes off the shadows in the corner. After a moment she began to shake; tears streamed from the corners of her eyes and into her hair, because he was right.

She was such a liar.

* * * * *

A fist of panic socked Ron in the heart when he palmed the switch and the overhead light revealed his empty bed. Down the stairs and into the kitchen where he'd hung her purse and deposited her shoes. The purse was there; the shoes were gone.

He lifted the small leather bag from the hook – spooking his cat from her perch on the extra chair kept near the door – and dropped it on the table, his hands shaking. Vaguely familiar with the ways of a woman's handbag, he was certain what it would contain. Twelve tubes of lipstick, maybe – and why did they always carry so many? They couldn't wear them all at once. Kleenex – both unused and smeared with lipstick. Combs and miniature hairbrushes and hair clips and sunglasses and powder compacts and perfume and a half-used roll of Pep-O-Mint LifeSavers thoroughly corrupted by purse lint. And all *that* would be in just one section. Though small, Kimberly's purse had three zippered compartments.

He unzipped the first one and dove in.

Perhaps she was the rare exception. Her purse was neatly organized and entirely free of clutter. One tube of lipstick called Sheer. *Why bother*, he wondered. A pair of Tommy Hilfiger sunglasses in a soft padded case. Expensive. Those must have set her back some. A tin of peppermint Altoids.

Middle compartment: Murine eye drops; a small bottle of generic aspirin; an Altoid tin requisitioned to hold a card of Benadryl tablets, full except for three mashed and empty blisters, and six berry-flavored antacid tablets.

Last compartment: a checkbook with a book of checks drawn on the Mills branch of Citizens Bank.

"Her wallet's gone, and so are her shoes," he said, numb with dread. How long had she been gone? How had Taryn not known?

"She stole my car?" Taryn brow creased in annoyance, but the corners of her mouth quivered like she wanted to laugh. "Why am I not surprised? She must have done it while I was asleep."

"Where would she go?" Scott wondered.

"Well, there are two possibilities," Taryn piped up before Ron could formulate an answer. "She could have gone to the diner for blueberry pancakes," and she sent Ron an irritated look, obviously remembering how he rudely interrupted their conversation to call the object of her great displeasure, "or she went to the cottage looking for her migraine meds. She said she had a headache."

"What time was that?"

"Before eight this morning."

They all turned to look at the kitchen clock. It was almost two-thirty. Ron supposed it was possible she had lain down at the cottage to let the medicine take effect and had fallen asleep. He muttered an imprecation under his breath and headed for the garage door, fishing in his jeans pocket for his car keys. Taffy leaped out through the cat flap in the back door to get out of his way.

"Where are you going?" Scott demanded, three steps behind him.

"To the cottage. Stay here."

"You shouldn't go alone."

"You shouldn't leave Taryn alone."

They stared at each other mutinously until Taryn broke their stand-off.

"You two sound like brothers."

"We are," Ron said, and slipped out the garage door, slamming it in Scott's face. He was in the truck and backing out of the garage as fast as the slowly rising overhead door would allow when Scott burst out of the house. The overhead door finally completed its journey. Ron gunned the engine and shot backward before his brother could reach the door handle. Through the cloud of dust the truck tires kicked up, he could see the garage door closing and was relieved that Scott wasn't giving chase. He had enough to worry about already.

The truck wouldn't go fast enough to satisfy his panic, although the speedometer claimed he was cruising through town at 50 mph. He barely slowed for the corner at Willow Road, and the truck fishtailed as he rounded it too fast.

No lights shone in the windows of the cottage. Ron fumbled through the keys on his ring until he found the one to the front door and slid it into the keyhole. He had the Glock ready as he pushed open the door and flicked the switch that turned on the closest lamp. The living room was empty. He closed the front door behind him and crept cautiously to the hallway, swinging around the corner in a perfect shooter's stance, the gun aimed, his finger on the trigger.

But the hallway was empty, too, as was the kitchen, the bathroom, and the spare bedroom. She wasn't here; he knew it before he entered her bedroom. He couldn't feel her presence in the cottage, like he had felt her since the first night she had walked into the tavern.

The bed was empty. A Maxalt wrapper lay discarded on the night table, confirming Taryn's suspicion that she had come for her medicine. The house was cold, another sign she wasn't here – he'd already learned she liked to be warm. A draft flowing into the room from the hallway reminded him that he'd left the spare room window cracked open to let the paint fumes dissipate. He crossed the hallway to the other bedroom to close the window, and stopped. The window gaped open, the screen gone. A smear of blood showed on the bottom sash. The crimson streak drew him across the room until he was close enough to see the few golden hairs stuck in the tacky blood. Kimberly's hair.

He closed the window and strode from the room, hitting light switches as he passed. There, on the hallway wall, a faint smear of red that had been lost in the gloom; a round print at face height. Bright light flooded the kitchen as he flicked a switch, and the scarlet streaks on the floor glowed like neon. Ron sagged against the doorway, suddenly terrified. Had she cracked her head and wandered off into the woods with a concussion? But no…Taryn's car wasn't here, so she had to have driven away. Good God, under the influence – however waning – of belladonna, migraine medication, and possibly a concussion, and she was driving around town. Crazy woman.

But he stood for a few moments more, his eyes crawling over the kitchen, looking for…he didn't know what. The blood on the floor indicated she'd fallen. The blood on the hallway wall indicated she'd hit the plaster with enough force to break the skin.

He retraced her steps from the spare room window, obviously through which she'd broken in, to her bedroom, to the hallway… If she'd had enough wits about her to find and administer her migraine medication, why would she suddenly lose them in the hallway so spectacularly that she'd hit the wall hard enough to break the skin? And come to think of it, if she'd started to fall, the blood would have been lower on the wall.

The scarlet splotch stared back at him from the plaster, offering a testimony he had no way of deciphering. He paced back into the kitchen, bending to touch the red streaks. They were tacky and misshapen, as though she'd moved – or been moved – enough to smear her blood.

And then he saw it, a small object no bigger than his fingernail that made his blood turn to ice: a strange hexagonal black button with a matte finish, lying against the toe-kick at the base of the sink cabinet. He'd seen buttons like that just recently.

His memory flashed up an image: a black-haired man with cold blue eyes, the strong lines of his handsome face marking him of the Schaefer bloodline, his hands clenching a black stone knife.

He straightened abruptly, pushing the image back into its crypt. But the vault had been breached, and the memories tumbled forth in a flood, driving him from the house and into the woods in frantic pursuit.

PRINCE CHARMING TO THE RESCUE

She must have slept, because she couldn't remember when he had returned to the ceremony room. She came awake to find Caleb standing beside the stone altar, murmuring what sounded like a prayer. The words were unintelligible; at first she assumed her sleep-numbed brain was just tracking slowly, but after a moment she realized he wasn't speaking in English.

He moved around the altar, stopping at intervals to murmur a phrase in the language of the ages. Thirteen times he stopped, and some quality in his voice terrified her enough that she didn't ask for explanations. From what she knew of his activities, she didn't need the details to know this was bad. Very bad.

Her eyes fixed determinedly on the flickering patterns of firelight on the ceiling; he'd lit another torch, chasing the shadows farther back and out of her peripheral vision. She didn't look at him when he stopped at the head of the stone, his hand resting on her head as though giving a benediction. He murmured the last of his prayers; she breathed a mental sigh of relief, but he wasn't done yet.

His fingers circled her right wrist, lifting her arm. She barely felt the obsidian blade of his ceremonial knife pierce the inside of her forearm. Her blood came thick, sluggish from the cold, yet enough for his purpose. The flat of the blade pressed firmly against the wound, first one side and then the other, and now she felt the pain. Near-hypothermia served as an acceptable anesthetic but not nearly as effective as morphine. Her teeth bit into her lip a second too late to muffle her whimper.

He prodded the wound, forcing more blood to flow and catching it in a small glass vial, which he stoppered when it had filled. At last he was done, but he didn't move away. He stood staring down at her for a long time, and then huffed out a breath, leaning close to her. His breath swept across her face, bathing her in peppermint. Her stomach rolled and she twisted her face away. Copper wafted through the air, and for a terrible moment she thought she would vomit.

"The rest of the Circle is making preparations. These things take time. I will grant you something I've never granted anyone before: a deadline to make up your mind and accept my offer. You have five hours. Once the Circle gathers in place around you, it will be too late."

Kim swallowed; the minimal saliva in her mouth did nothing to dispel the dry thirst at the back of her throat. Hunger gnawed at her stomach, held in check only by her nausea.

"No."

His eyes swept over her body, prone and defenseless on the altar. The frigid temperature had stiffened her nipples into hard nubs, which the thin cotton shirt did nothing to hide. His gaze lingered on the curve of her cheek, her blue-tinged lips, the swell of her breasts; then moved across her ribs, which stood out in sharp relief as though she'd been ill – and she had; he had made sure of it.

His hand followed in a whisper-light caress, his forefinger tugging on her lower lip, then traveling down over the small swell of her chin and the smooth skin of her throat, and jumped the collar of her shirt.

"How about now?" he whispered. The tip of his finger traced a lazy semi-circle around her left nipple.

She rolled away from him. He slammed her flat on the stone. The tender seduction was over; his palm pressed hard on her breast, his fingers cruel and punishing as they exerted enough pressure to build a scream behind her clenched teeth.

"Just remember I offered the easy way."

"The easy way isn't usually the right way." She gasped as his grip tightened, tears of pain spilling from the corners of her eyes.

He grinned. The torch lit his eyes, and what she saw in their glacial depths proved more terrifying than the impending ceremony and its probable, painful conclusion: incomparable desire, a blind quest to possess, driven by an animalistic need that was barely human. Dying – well, she could handle that, but she didn't think she could stand what came before it.

His fingers lifted the hem of her shirt, his hand hot against her cold skin as it inched toward her breast. Her mind shrank away from his intimate touch even as her flesh thrilled to it. She couldn't stop the sudden hammering of her heart or her quickening breath, but the essential part of her – the core of her soul – refused to surrender. He could take her body – indeed, there would be no stopping him – but she would not let him touch her mind.

"I feel your heartbeat," he murmured, slipping around to the side of the altar to give himself an easier reach. "It's going wild." His lips brushed her ear as he leaned in close to whisper. "You want me as much as I want you. Just give in. The whole ceremony can be averted."

With superhuman effort, Kim found her voice. It came ragged and breathless. "For a while."

"But that while can be glorious." His fingers moved again, heading south. Kim clenched her teeth, fighting back both a moan of pleasure and a shriek of horror. He popped the button of her jeans and slid his hand inside.

She violently bucked her hips away from his probing fingers, cracking their skulls together. He swore viciously. Kim lay dazed for what seemed an eternity, long enough for his reaching fingers to find their target.

His hand kept her pinned to the stone, his stroking fingers proving that she *did* want him, no sense denying it. She turned her face away in shame, silent tears streaking from her eyes. A moment later, he withdrew his hand and backed away from her, his expression hovering somewhere between dismay and uneasiness.

Without a word, he strode from the room. Kimberly rolled onto her side and curled into a ball, trembling in humiliation…and desire.

An hour later, the torches sputtered and flickered out, plunging her into absolute darkness. She would have thought she had crossed into the void between life and death but for her painfully full bladder and the ache in her bones from the cold.

Afraid to move, she lay as still as the stone altar beneath her, still curled on her side, hands tucked into her armpits. The ceremony room was too far below ground level to hear the noises of the forest outside, but the Wyckham House had its own sounds. No creaking floorboards, no branches scraping window glass – the floors of this house were ancient stone, and the glass, if there had ever been any, had long since been broken from the window frames.

No, these sounds were stealthy, sly, secretive. They floated through the darkness, echoing off the walls, surrounding her. Kim thought of the shadows she suspected had moved earlier and clutched her arms more tightly around herself.

There was no escaping the truth: she was going to die on this stone, and her time was running out. She could almost hear Bethany now: *"Reckless got you married to Mark Owens! Reckless got your mother killed! Reckless got you killed! Are you happy now?"*

The clatter of his footsteps on the stone stairs behind her made her heart hammer in dread. He had come dangerously close to breaching her resistance earlier. If he set his mind on seducing her, she would not be able to keep him at bay.

He didn't acknowledge her at first. He removed the expired torches and shoved fresh ones into the wall sconces. The large canvas bag he carried slid from his shoulder to the floor, and he began taking items from it: the black knife, neatly wrapped in black silk; a pewter chalice; the glass vial, dark with her blood; and thirteen blood-red pillar candles. She watched him move around the altar again, this time placing the candles into circular indentations she hadn't noticed on the floor when he'd brought her in. He uncapped the vial over each candle, letting drops of blood saturate the wicks. His lips moved, but she couldn't hear what he said. She didn't want to.

At last he straightened and came to the altar, the black stone knife balanced across his palm. He held it over her face for a long moment, his glittering eyes unblinking as they stared into hers.

"The blade is quite sharp. You won't even feel it going in."

She swallowed and instantly wished she hadn't: her mouth was parched, her throat sandpaper. "You mean I won't feel it at first."

His chin raised a fraction. "Of course."

A quick motion brought the handle of the knife into his fist. He held the point poised a mere inch from her eye, and then slid it into a bracket mounted dead center at the head of the altar. The blade scraped the stone and seem to ring like discordant crystal.

"Your time is running out, Kimberly. Only four hours left."

"My answer is the same as before." She turned her face away to stare at the torches, not wanting to look into the darkness.

He moved around to the side of the altar, filling her vision. "It doesn't have to be this way."

"You keep saying that, but I'm still chained to this stone."

"That's because you keep saying no." He smiled slightly as he trailed his thumb across the swelling below her right eye. His voice lowered, rough with desire. "Say yes, Kimberly. Go out with a bang."

"Pun intended?"

"Most definitely."

"I'll pass."

"Suit yourself. I'll just leave you alone for a while to consider your choices."

He moved away, taking with him the tantalizing scent of fresh rain in the woods that clung to his skin, and disappeared into the shadows.

Kim closed her eyes, sending up a silent thank-you for the strength that had let her resist him yet again. When a shadow fell between her and the torchlight, she thought she must have dozed and had missed his return.

A hand as blistering cold as arctic ice draped across her forehead. Exquisite pain spiked through her skull, the like of which she'd never experienced even while enduring her worst migraine. Every muscle in her body stiffened and seemed to petrify, locking her scream in her throat.

"Hush, sweet Kimberly," a voice rasped in her ear. Her mind reeled, frantically seeking escape, but she couldn't move from beneath that inhuman hand. Eyes above her, terrible eyes with mists of color that skimmed across their surface like clouds across a stormy sky. It hovered over her, stroking her hair, paralyzing her with its unblinking gaze. The scream built steam behind her frozen vocal cords, and with it swelled a torturous desire, a fountain of flame burning through her blood like lava.

The hand moved away, but no relief came. A throaty chuckle echoed in the room and seemed to reverberate in her pounding skull, amping the pain to an unbearable pitch. It left her lying in unrelenting anguish, wishing more than anything she'd accepted her captor's offer.

* * * * *

"Go on," Taryn said with wry amusement. "You know you want to. I'll be all right here – I'll lock all the doors and windows."

"Are you sure?" Scott, who for the past hour had been pacing in front of the fireplace – and annoying Taryn because he kept blocking the heat coming from the flames – paused in his circuit.

"I'm sure."

"But you'll be alone."

"I've got Taffy," Taryn replied cheerfully. "Wherever she is."

Still Scott hesitated. "He's gonna kill me," he murmured, knowing how Ron would react when he learned he'd left Taryn at the house alone. "Call Cody and let him know what's going on, and see if you can reach Denny too – he hasn't been answering his phone."

"I know." Her voice was hard.

He dug his car keys out of his pocket on his way to the front door, where he shrugged into his coat and hesitated again. "I wouldn't do this, Taryn, but I think I know where Tiana is."

"At the cottage?"

"No. Look…" He bit his lip uncertainly, and then plunged on before he could change his mind. "When my dad gets here, you need to give him Tiana's diary. It's in my desk drawer in my room. He needs to read it. And there's a key taped inside the front cover – he'll need that, too."

"What are *you* doing with it?"

"She left it for me. That's not important right now. I've gotta go." *Before it's too late.* But he couldn't think that way; negativity would only mire him in procrastination, and he feared he might already be too late. The bloody towels and stains in the carpet at her apartment didn't bode well.

"I'll call," she promised.

Still he hesitated, and on impulse retraced his steps, stopping in front of her. Before she could step away, he hugged her tightly, his face buried against her neck. "Be safe," he said gruffly, and strode to the door without looking at her again.

He had slid behind the wheel of the Dart and was pulling the door close when she burst out onto the porch; she had finally realized where he was going.

"Scott, stop! You can't go there!"

Panic raised her voice to a shrill tone he'd always privately thought of as "the nag tone." He threw the gearshift into reverse, backed up enough to turn the car, and sped away down the driveway as she sprinted down the porch steps after him.

At least he was certain she would call his father now.

The tires squealed as he rounded the corner of Willow Road at excessive speed, ignoring the stop sign at the intersection in true Schaefer form. He goosed the accelerator on the straightaway and slowed only when he approached the gravel driveway to the cottage, chaotic thoughts chasing each other around and around in his mind until he was finally able to grasp one long enough to examine it.

A black magic cult used an ancient, decrepit mansion deep in the woods as their base. Could he honestly believe the only way to that mansion was a narrow, switchback deer trail through the forest that took two hours to navigate on foot?

He stomped on the brake pedal and brought his Dart to a screeching halt in the middle of the road, where he sat for several minutes debating his next move. He knew the town and its surrounding woods like the back of his hand; there had to be a route closer to the Wyckham House than the one behind the cottage. Back past the tavern, behind Mill's one fine dining restaurant Sutter's Inn, a disused hunting track would take him within two miles, but the dense forest in that particular section of the woods would slow him considerably.

To the right, just visible from where he sat, lay the pitted road leading to the two abandoned mills for which the town had been named. It would take him closer than the hunting track – if he could get past the overgrown brambles at the head of the road. He was reasonably sure he could run the distance to the Wyckham House. Getting across the river was the only draw-back; there had once been a bridge, but it had washed away in a flood when he was in kindergarten.

He eased off the brake and nudged the accelerator, spinning the car toward the old mills road, stopping at the end of the blacktop where he got out to see what kind of shrubs blocked his way and if he could easily get rid of them. To his surprise, he discovered that he could see over the tops of them to a clear, well-maintained road. He poked around the brambles at the right side of the road. Ah, and what was this, camouflaged from view with leaf-green paint? A gate frame with a set of hinges. The gate itself was shrouded with silk vines and threaded through with maple branches dotted with dead leaves.

The Circle didn't have to make a two hour trek through the woods to the Wyckham House, because they could drive. No wonder so many people had offered to buy the cottage after Ron had purchased it; the Circle didn't want outsiders in any position to observe their movements.

The latch at the left side of the road released easily and swung the gate inward. The well-oiled hinges made no noise. He pulled the car past the gate, parked, and ran back to close it. He didn't want them knowing he'd discovered their secret. Confident the road ahead would be carefully tended, he sped the car along at nearly forty miles an hour.

The decrepit mills sat half a mile from each other, and just past the second one, the road ended abruptly in a large clearing. Scott parked, rummaged in the back seat for a flashlight, and again examined the shrubs blocking the way. This time they were real; the road truly ended here. A footpath along the river led deeper into the woods. He had to be close to the Wyckham House; the Circle wouldn't want to walk very far. He headed into the thicket.

Five minutes later, he came to a natural land bridge that crossed the river. He stopped, staring into the woods on the other side. An apprehensive look up at the canopy of trees told him daylight was running out fast.

He crossed the river.

The sky released a light patter of rain that disguised his less-than-stealthy movements. He caught glimpses of the Wyckham House through intertwined branches and shrubs, and shuddered. *The devil's mansion.*

He crept to the edge of the clearing and hunkered down behind a clump of filbert bushes, peering through a gap at the House. There was no sign of movement; no creatures roamed the meadow surrounding the house, as if they could sense its malevolence. Now that he had stopped making noise himself, he became aware of the absence of sound in the forest. No late season crickets, no scolding chickadees or chattering squirrels; just the rush of water over stone in the river, the gusting wind, the rain in the trees – but all were hushed, as though trying not to attract the mansion's attention.

"Okay, Scott," he whispered, gathering his courage around him like a cloak – albeit a threadbare one – and stood up.

Arms grabbed him from behind and a hand clamped firmly over his mouth. He struggled violently to free himself.

"Shhh! It's me." He sagged in relief, turning as Ron released him. "Scotty, what the hell are you doing here? I told you to stay with

Taryn!"

"I couldn't let you do this alone. There are things going on that you don't know, bad things."

Ron offered an ironic smile. "You think? How did you get here? You couldn't have passed me on the river path."

Scott pointed behind him. "There's a land bridge going across the river, and a short path to the old Rawlings mill. The mill road has been kept up pretty well; I think the Circle is using it. It's not a long walk from the mill to the Wyckham House."

Ron told him to stay put and vanished down the footpath, presumably to check out the land bridge. Scott waited impatiently, uneasy now that he was alone again. Ron wasn't gone long, and he looked grimly satisfied when he returned.

"That'll be convenient," Ron whispered, bending close to Scott.

"Where is Kimberly?" Scott whispered back. "What are *you* doing here?"

"She's gone. Taken from the cottage by force, if I read the signs right. And if my hunch is right, she's in there." Ron tipped his head toward the hulking mansion. "I'm going in to get her. I want you to stay here."

"No way. You don't understand what they're doing in there. They're breeding their own sacrifices to get more power – as in magical power. They will kill – they *have* killed – to keep that secret."

Ron glowered at him. "Are you finished? I need you out here in case I don't make it back out. Think about Renée and Cody. And Kimberly – if she makes it out without me, I'll need you to get her to safety."

"Nothing's going to happen to you," Scott argued. "And two of us are better than one in a fight."

"This isn't about combat, Scott," Ron hissed impatiently. "It's about stealth. I'm not interested in taking them on." He grabbed Scott by his jacket and brought him closer. "Will you do it my way, or do I have to beat you up?"

Scott grinned. "Go ahead and try it."

"Scotty – "

"Tiana is in there too. And hey, what about that wolf Taryn and I saw, and whatever attacked Anna Malone? You're going to leave me out here with that beast running loose in the woods?"

He watched Ron stumble for a logical dispute against this fair point. "I'll look for Tiana, too. He may be keeping them in the same place. Climb a tree; wolves can't climb."

"Are you kidding me? That's your solution?"

"Is yours any better? Listen, I know what happens to people who aren't supposed to be in there when the Circle catches them. It's not pretty. I can't take the chance of both of us dying here."

He knocked Ron's hand away and took a mutinous step closer. "So start beating me up, because it's the only way I'm not going in."

Ron wavered, casting a worried look at the house. "Will you please just stay here? I'll boost you up into a tree and give you my gun."

"Ron," Scott began, but Ron brutally cut him off.

"I mean it."

"How are you going to rescue anyone without a weapon?"

"I told you, I'm not interested in waging war. I'm only after my girl." Ron's hand dove into his jacket pocket and came out with the Glock. "It's loaded, so be careful. Now let's find a likely tree where you can keep watch for us."

Now Scott grabbed Ron by the front of his jacket. "You have an hour before I come in after you."

Ron covered Scott's hand with his own. "Don't come in at all. Whether I'm gone an hour, a day, or a year, don't come in. Now, I see a tree that'll work nicely."

Just at the edge of the clearing, Ron formed a stirrup with his cupped hands and boosted him into a sprawling maple. Scott climbed to a branch that afforded him both safety from a ground attack and a clear view of the Wyckham House. Ron passed the pistol up to him, and took Scott's flashlight in return.

"Stay relatively still; this tree is closer to the meadow than I like, but it has the best view. I want to be out of here before dusk. If I don't come out by twilight, get yourself gone."

"I won't leave you here. I'll be safe in the tree."

"Don't argue, Scott. Stay safe. See you in a while, or – well."

"See you in a while," Scott said firmly. Ron gave him a two-fingered salute and turned to go. "Wait!"

"What now?"

"About Tiana – I know you didn't do anything with her. I'm sorry I blamed you."

"I have no idea what you're talking about."

"You know, the whole thing with Tiana twelve years ago."

"Still don't know what you mean." Smiling, Ron lifted a shoulder in a careless shrug. "Take care of yourself, brother."

He vanished like a wisp of smoke, weaving through the thicket at the edge of the clearing to where the Wyckham House sat closest to the woods. Scott watched till he disappeared from view, and then settled into a comfortable fork against the trunk to begin his vigil.

STOCKHOLM SYNDROME

The utter loss of her ability to track time was perhaps worse than the pain itself. She had no clue how long she lay paralyzed, agony singing through her body. Its song was screaming metal, discordant harmonies, a throbbing bass that splintered her bones.

And then a cool, refreshing breeze through the desert of her pain: a cold cloth moving across her face, her neck, her arms. A trickle of frigid water dribbled between her breasts, and to her dying day she would think it had felt better than the best sex she'd ever had. At last the pain ebbed and disappeared altogether, leaving her weak and hyper-sensitive. Without warning, she started to cry, agonized sobs that racked her aching limbs. Caleb gathered her to his chest, his woodsy scent reminding her of a cool forest on a rainy day.

She was beaten, defeated. Too tired to fight. Too ill to escape. Too aware of his hand smoothing her hair and the beat of his heart, steady and strong, against her cheek. When her tears subsided, he wiped the last dampness from her face. A warning bell clanged somewhere in the back of her mind, ringing in the name of the Stockholm Syndrome, but its peal was made ever more distant as she hurtled toward slumber, lulled by the rhythmic rise and fall of his chest beneath her cheek.

When he suddenly set her away from him and unlocked the manacles around her wrists, she murmured a sleepy protest.

"I have to clean you up before the ceremony. Sit up."

That was enough to bring her fully awake. She'd forgotten about the ceremony. In fact, wrapped in his comforting embrace, she'd forgotten a lot of things, such as he was her enemy, her captor, her soon-to-be murderer.

"I don't think I can. I'll probably wet my pants. Gravity, you know."

"I'll give you five minutes with a bucket."

"A bucket?" She couldn't hide her distaste.

"This isn't exactly the Hilton, Kimberly."

His hand sliding beneath her shoulders startled her. He lifted her easily, and gravity had the effect she had dreaded. It took all her concentration to hold her bladder in check, so she didn't notice he had unlocked the cuffs around her ankles until he tugged her off the stone.

The bucket was an exquisite relief. She didn't even care that he watched her like a hawk waiting to pounce on a mouse. When she was done, he secured a cuff tight around one wrist and carried her makeshift toilet from the room. While he was gone, Kim scrunched her hand as small as she could, but she couldn't wriggle it out of the cuff. She sank to the cold stone floor and leaned against the base of the altar, hoping to warm it with what little body heat she had left.

"Up you come," he said, making her jump. She must have dozed, because she hadn't heard him come back in. "I'm going to wash the blood out of your hair, and I have a new shirt for you."

"Why bother?" she asked wearily. "You're just going to spill more – mine this time. Does it matter if I'm bloody already?"

"It matters very much. The ritual is complex; Tiana's blood will contaminate it."

He moved her to the other side of the altar, loosening her chain enough to bring her closer to the torches and their welcome heat. He managed to wash her hair with little difficulty in a basin of steamy hot water that he'd brought back with him, rubbed it with a towel, and even ran a comb through its tangles when he was done.

"Shirt," he said, and unlocked the manacle. She stared at him silently until he huffed out a sigh and yanked it open himself. The back stuck to her skin, crisp with blood; warm water sluiced down her back loosened it, and he eased it off. He freed her hand from the manacle to remove the shirt completely, fingers clamped around her wrist like a vise. She didn't attempt to run; she knew she wouldn't make it very far.

He cleaned her back with a large sponge, standing in front of her and reaching around rather than turning her away from him. The heat of his body warmed her icy skin, his scent filled her nose. She stared at the pulse in his throat, keeping her eyes averted from his, as he toweled her dry.

His hand replaced the towel, moving over her skin in light, tantalizing circles, exerting just enough pressure to slowly push her closer. Her body reveled in his heat even as her mind locked down, pushing all thought and feeling behind a wall.

His lips against her throat sent fire like ice through her veins. She trembled. He pressed soft kisses across her collarbone and the upper swell of her breast. Her head reeled, and she stopped breathing. Silent tears leaked from her eyes as his tongue swept liquid fire across her skin. His hand cupped her breast, gentle this time, caressing fingers starting a slow burn deep in her belly. Desire for him battled ferociously with her love for Aaron. She frantically erected more mental walls, slammed more emotional doors, until she feared she might never be able to find the core of herself again.

He yanked her against him roughly and crushed her mouth under his. His kiss was searing and cold, like kissing ice. Blackness stole into her, coiling through her blood, twining around her heart, tugging at the barriers behind which she had hidden the essential part of her being. Like the phenomenon when Aaron kissed her, his essence pulled her into him. But there was only darkness, a great void of nothingness that threatened to drown her. She knew then that he had no soul; he had sacrificed it for power, the power that now slid insidiously against her being, seeking a breach, determined to claim her, certain in its invincibility.

He wrenched away suddenly, as though she had burned him, and he stared down at her as though experiencing a jolting epiphany. He didn't explain his sudden retreat, just yanked a tee-shirt over her head and clamped a manacle around one of her wrists while he cleaned the altar and dried it with the towel, then draped it with a thick comforter, his movements hurried and angry.

"Why the blanket?"

"Can't have you dying of hypothermia before the ceremony, can I?"

It took a moment to find her voice. "No, that would be too merciful."

His lip curled. "Hop on up."

Kim glanced at the dark passageway to her left and then down at her manacled wrist. If she dislocated her thumb, she might be able to free her hand from the cuff, but he'd probably catch her before she made it to the hallway.

She climbed onto the edge of the stone, her legs dangling down. He secured her other hand and ankles and pulled the comforter up over her shoulders.

"Will you tell me something?" Kimberly asked. Her voice rasped in her dry throat like sandpaper over rock.

His glance was wary. "That depends."

"How did you get Elizabeth here? I can't believe she came willingly. Did you kidnap her too?"

"I didn't need to kidnap her. As incredible as it seems, she came here of her own volition. She just needed the right incentive, so to speak. And it was remarkably easy to do," he said, as though still surprised at how simple it had been to lure Elizabeth Peterson to her death. "A little bit of Ecstasy, a lot of alcohol, and she was ripe for the picking."

Kim was sorry she had asked. But at last someone would know the truth of Elizabeth's vanishing, even if that person didn't have much longer to live.

"It only took a week to make her pregnant, but I took an extra week just because she was so enjoyable." He flashed a grin at her, his eyes sparkling as though he'd shared a particularly humorous joke.

She shivered. Ecstasy had a reputation for making people hypersexual, and while under its influence, Elizabeth would have thrown inhibition – and Aaron – to the wind. But it didn't change the nature of the liaison; rape was rape.

"If you needed drugs to make her willing," she responded, her tone acidic, "then it was nothing more than rape."

"You're back to that, are you?" His voice was weary. "I didn't need to drug *you* to make you willing."

"No, you just drugged me to make me too weak to fight you off."

"You weren't fighting me off."

"And here it is, four hours since you kidnapped me, and we still haven't...."

His smile turned wolfish. "Is that an invitation?"

"No. Just an observation."

His smile widened but he didn't press the point. "It was ridiculously simple to get her to take the X. Of course, it helped that she partied with Jason while Aaron was out of town, and Jason wasn't particular from whom he bought his recreational drugs."

He paced around the altar, his velvet voice bouncing off the stones.

"When Jason passed out in the bar, no one thought anything of Fred offering to drag him home and give Elizabeth a lift as well. And there I was, waiting for her. She was...so sweet."

He stroked his finger across her collarbone as he passed in front of her.

"So eager."

His finger trailed over her breast as he rounded the altar to stand behind her.

"So much like you, although she didn't try to deny her attraction. And when I was finished, we left Jason in her bed beside her. No one ever would have been the wiser had she been able to keep her mouth shut. Now you know the truth about Elizabeth. As I mentioned before, she was just a whore at heart. I did Aaron a favor."

"That's your story, eh?"

"And I'm sticking to it."

"Your version of it."

He waved a negligent hand. "The only version of it. "

"Why would you think it even matters to me whether Elizabeth was a willing participant in your sexual interactions? It doesn't mean that I am."

"I'm just showing you that I'm not the hideous monster you're making me out to be."

"You think that because she was willing to have sex with you, that makes everything else you do okay? You curse people – you *kill* people."

He shrugged. "All true. Her willingness *did* end once she realized I was going to kill her. She thought she was in love with me. I didn't care because it made her willing, which made it easier to accomplish what I needed."

"Which was?"

"The child."

"You don't strike me as the paternal sort."

He stopped pacing and leaned against the altar, his mouth twisting in distaste. "I'm not in the slightest. Whiny children, snotty noses, messes everywhere. Drives me crazy. No, fatherhood is not what I was after. I just wanted a child."

Her gaze crawled around the ceremony room, noting the ancient spell-form carved into the floor, the candles in place around the altar, the obsidian knife sheathed at the head of the stone.

"You wanted a child to sacrifice," she whispered, bile rising in her throat.

"You say that like you're surprised." He straightened and turned to look at her. "You know what I am. You know what I do. You just pointed it out, didn't you? I curse people. I kill people. Where do you think that power comes from?"

"Not from innocent, unborn children."

He burst out laughing. His laughter peeled away the years and made him look much younger. "Of course it does. The blood of the innocent for the power of the damned. A heinous crime for glorious power."

"But you didn't do it, did you? You didn't go through with it."

His smile faded, leaving only the ghost of laughter upon his face. "You want so much to believe there's good in me. I wonder why that is."

"You didn't go through with it, right, Caleb?" she persisted, a rising sense of panic nearly suffocating her. If he had…oh, now she knew what he meant to do if she accepted his offer. He would still kill her…but only after he had made her pregnant. *The blood of the innocent for the power of the damned.*

He raised his hands, palms up. "Do you see a child here?"

She couldn't answer around the knot of horror in her throat. Worse, oh God it was worse than she'd ever suspected.

"When she realized she was pregnant, she couldn't very well tell Aaron she was sure it was mine. So she told him it was Jason's. She thought that first time with me had been a dream because she woke in the morning with him in her bed."

He paced around the altar again. Kim watched him warily, working her hands in the cuffs, testing their security under the cover of the blanket.

"She wanted more than one night – she wanted *me*. She said she was going to tell Aaron everything. I told her he would never believe her. So she scheduled a paternity test. Jason, the idiot, agreed to be tested to rule him out as the baby's father. Well." He slanted a smile at her. "I couldn't allow *that* to happen, now could I? The next step would have been a court-ordered paternity test for me, and the opportunity to gain power would vanish."

"So you kidnapped her."

"No. She came to me willingly."

"I still find that hard to believe."

"She said she wanted to talk to me. I pretended I was willing and anxious to sort things out. She came to the Wyckham House thinking to strike a bargain. Instead…"

Instead he had obtained the power he so greedily sought, and somewhere Elizabeth and her unborn child had lain dead all these years.

"I knew when they came – Aaron and his friends. They watched from the shadows, looking for a chance to rescue her."

He hoisted himself up to sit on the stone altar beside her, mussing her careful arrangement of the comforter. Almost absently, he tucked the blanket back around her leg, his fingers lingering on her knee.

"If you asked him, I doubt he could even describe what he saw – if he could remember, that is. Even to this day, my own brain can't quite comprehend what I'm seeing. An angel."

"A demon, you mean," she said, her tone a trifle sharp.

"You're way too smart for your own good," he murmured and offered a smile that made her shiver. "Demon, angel…there is no difference between the two except semantics."

"And whose side they're on."

"Oh, that's right; you're not a shades-of-grey kind of girl. It's all black-and-white and nothing in between. So here's some black-and-white, just for you, sweet Kimberly. Once I called the demon, Elizabeth knew there would be no escape. She finally realized I was serious." His gaze raked her face. "I see you understand. Once I call him, it's too late to change my mind – not that I ever have. Or ever will."

His warning was not lost on her. If she continued to refuse him, he would not hesitate to begin the ceremony. He would not spare her regardless of his desire for her. The bargain would be struck, and she would die.

"Do you want to see what's ahead for you?"

"I can guess well enough."

"I doubt it. They can show you. They can take you outside of time and show you Elizabeth's last minutes."

Kim turned her face away, bile rising in her throat. "Why would I *want* to see Elizabeth at the worst moment of her life? What the hell is the mat—"

He cupped her chin and turned her face back to him, his fingers biting deep into her cheeks, cutting off her words. His own were harsh, pelting her like cold little bullets.

"Of course you don't want to see it. No one *wants* to, unless they're—"

"Like you?"

His jaw clenched for a moment. "Yes. Like me. But you have no idea what's ahead for you. If you see what happened to her, you'll likely change your mind about my offer."

"What does it matter? You'll have me before you kill me anyway. Isn't that what you've been telling me for hours now?"

"I don't want to kill you!"

The words were bitten out reluctantly, with great effort. Kim didn't understand his internal struggle; killing came as naturally to him as it did to a wolf or a bear. He was primitive, uncivilized, cloaked in a suave, cultured façade that hid his true nature: a predator without conscience, a killer with no moral code.

"I'm no different than anyone else you've killed."

He grabbed her hand roughly, his other hand disappearing into his pocket and coming out with a ring of keys. A small bit of metal fashioned into a barrel released her hand from the manacle. Without a word, he freed her from her chains, slid off the altar, and backed away from her.

"What are you doing?"

"I assumed you didn't want to be torn limb from limb. I'll lock you back up if you'd rather." He took a step toward her, and she flinched away. The comforter dropped from her shoulders. If she took him by surprise, she might get past him, might be able to make it to the stairs and find a way out. It would be dark – pitch-black, in fact – but she'd crawl out of here if she had –

Without warning, they swarmed her, the ever-present shadows, engulfing her, drowning her in darkness, pulling her from the altar. She braced herself for impact with the stone floor, but instead she tumbled into free-fall, spinning, spinning, and his words came from a long way off.

"You *are* different."

IN THE HOUSE OF THE FALLEN

Some shadows have substance, as Aaron Schaefer discovered only five steps into the Wyckham House. His flashlight chased away most of the darkness, but some patches refused to be banished. These swallowed the light like black holes in space, and yet seemed not to be there at all; he could see the massive, pock-marked stones of the wall behind them, but it was like looking through a dark veil.

The air sighed through the house, strange currents that eddied and pooled around him. He thought if he listened closely, he'd be able to discern words, whispers of another dimension. So he tried to ignore them, because listening that closely might drive him mad.

He bypassed the horseshoe staircase and slipped down a pitch-black stairwell, the flashlight beam barely cutting through the darkness. What Caleb had planned for her was not something he would carry out in the odd, empty rooms of this mansion. He would want her in his killing room, on his killing stone, under his killing knife. Downstairs near the dungeons, in the room with the carved circle and its satanic symbols, lit with candles and torches and shafts of light that had life all their own...

His mind frantically pushed the memory away, but the ones that crowded in after it were, if possible, worse. So bad, in fact, that his mind would only let him see them in surreal flashes: a huge copper moon, brambles and branches slapping his face and arms, claws and teeth and a burning itch in his blood that turned to fire...

No. He wouldn't think of that right now. He would find Kimberly and they would get out of this hell house well before dark. Before moonrise.

The stairs curved to the left, a gentle winding that left him blind to what was ahead. The flashlight speared the darkness ahead, carving a thin path for him to follow. He pressed himself to the outer edge, his jacket scraping along the stone wall, his breath rasping and his heart thundering in his ears, loud enough he was sure the whole house could hear. Around and down...around and down...around and down...until at last it happened, the thing he had dreaded so much he had refused to put words to the fear: the flashlight hit shadows it could not penetrate.

Ron stopped, one foot still braced on the edge of the tread above the other foot. His heart skipped several beats and then zoomed along at a frantic pace, so fast he thought he might be having a heart attack. Cold sweat trickled down his neck and under the collar of his shirt, like icy fingers tracing feathery caresses on his skin, leaving frostbite in their wake as they moved upward into his hair.

His breath caught, jammed in his throat as solid as dirt. His body quivered, fight or flight instincts warring with his psyche's desire to simply lie down and die of fright. The fingers moved through his hair and down across his cheek in a frigid stroke.

His paralysis broke. He leapt from the step into the caliginous shadows, and fell into the blackness beyond.

* * * * *

The violent revolutions ceased, leaving her lying on the cold stone floor like flotsam, gripping the floor while her equilibrium continued to spin out of control. At last the vertigo passed. Kim pushed herself up from the floor and spun around to run.

She brought herself up short, at last realizing her hopeless predicament. Cloaked figures surrounded the altar, standing just outside the ring of candles that flickered light over the esoteric symbols carved into the stone floor. And surrounding them, swarming them, were hundreds of shafts of light, like stars brought to earth, too brilliant for the eye to bear and too glorious for words. Unseen by their human counterparts, they swirled around them, caressed and stroked them, whispered seductively into their ears.

And there he stood, her exquisite captor, enveloped by so many of them that he appeared to be a shaft of light himself. Younger, harder, more ruthless and cruel than she could reconcile with the man who had eased her migraine and traded sexual innuendos with her in the grocery store.

Light encircled her, lifted her up, bore her across the room to the stone altar. Panic choked her, stealing her voice and her strength. They hovered her over Elizabeth Peterson's nude body, restrained on the flat stone, the pregnant swell of her belly gleaming like opals in the torchlight.

And let her drop.

She fell into Elizabeth rather than on her, was sucked down and submerged in her soul. And in flooded Elizabeth's terror and betrayal like dark, bitter water. Her heart pounded painfully, fueled by adrenaline for which her body had no physical outlet. Caleb wouldn't meet Elizabeth's eyes at first, dismissing her as unimportant. And when she finally caught his gaze, Kim wished she hadn't. His gaze held icy indifference, a cold, soulless glance that neatly relegated her to nothing more than a tool to gain otherworldly power.

Elizabeth had loved him, the Caleb he had presented to her in order to seduce her and provide himself with an offspring for sacrifice. Had loved a beautiful, disastrous lie. And his betrayal killed her will to fight, to live.

But Kimberly, trapped inside her, a ghost layer from outside time, felt the baby kick and turn a lazy half-somersault. Her heart thrilled – her three miscarriages had occurred before she was far enough along to feel the babies move. She relished the thumps and stretches and sudden swirling movement of an unborn child moving inside her body. *She* wanted to live. She wanted the baby to live.

But it wasn't her body. And this baby's fate was dark and tragic.

Wind howled through the room and extinguished the candles. The Circle moved in closer, Caleb taking his place at the head of the altar. Firelight glinted off a black stone knife in his hand.

Ferocious protectiveness surged inside her, a tidal wave of aggressive emotion. She wanted to wrap her arms around them both and run with them, out of this time, away from the fatal danger, deliver them back to Aaron, who would love and protect them. What it would mean for her own life – and her heart – didn't matter.

But she couldn't move Elizabeth's body, couldn't interact with this time in any way because she was submerged under a layer of time or consciousness that held her paralyzed. Grief swelled, a bitter bile of the soul that choked her.

Caleb called, a guttural summoning.

It strode out of the darkness as though borne of shadow and took command of the light as though made from the sun. She recognized it from her dream, remembered it offering to make her dreams go away. And it had – she'd not had a precognitive dream since. She realized now what he had meant, the angel who had breathed life back into her: accepting the fallen's offer to make her gift disappear had been tantamount to telling God she didn't want *Him*.

"What do you offer me?" Its voice was wonderful and terrible, pealing like a beautiful bell slightly off tone, a sweet discordance that set off a compelling echo in the soul.

"The blood of an unwilling sacrifice," he responded.

"Is that *all?*" the being slyly crooned. "I've had plenty of those."

"The blood of the innocent: my unborn child for power." No emotion, no remorse. No mercy.

The angel leaped from the circle to the altar with the grace and speed of a giant cat. The torches flared and lit the flat stone. Quartz crystals threw back the firelight in flashes of white brilliance, flickering across Elizabeth's bare skin. It crouched over her, and she shrank back against the stone as far as she could. It stroked the gentle swell of her belly. Her terror swamped Kimberly's senses. Elizabeth's eyes locked on Caleb's, pleading and desperate.

"Please," she whispered.

But he turned away, waiting.

"You give your only child, human?"

"Yes."

"Do you understand how transference works?"

"Yes."

Elizabeth began to cry, great hitching sobs that echoed around the chamber.

"Bargain struck."

As fast as a striking cobra, its hand plunged into her chest. Her scream of agony pealed through the room, bouncing off the stones, an endless echo of horror. Her soul was a turbulent sea, tossing Kim on violent waves.

The demon murmured, peculiar words in an exotic language unknown to man. It yanked its hand from inside her chest, and Elizabeth fell instantly silent. Between its palms, it cradled the stolen soul, an essence of blue-white light and coalescing shadows.

Red-robed, hooded figures stepped forward from the shadows, supporting a scrawny woman between them. Another hooded figure stood beside them, holding a tawny cat by the scruff. The cat's eyes were wild.

The demon threw the light, and it passed through the woman. She shrieked and crumpled. They let her drop the floor; her head hit with a sickening thud, and her dead eyes stared up at the shadowed ceiling. The cat yowled.

Caleb swore bitterly as the blue light streaked back toward its body. He whirled around to the altar and brought his black stone knife down in a sweeping arc, straight into the pregnant swell of Elizabeth Peterson's belly, slicing upward into her chest.

The soul arced away from its dying body, seeking sanctuary. It passed through fur, flesh, and bone – and stopped. In a berserker fury, trying to dislodge the interloping presence, the cat howled and shredded the red-robed man holding it. He let go, bleeding from the flaying, and the cat shot into the darkness.

Elizabeth's hand, raised beseechingly, dropped into her pooling blood on the flat stone, and was still.

* * * * *

She dropped into the present, the world spinning in frantic revolutions, and rolled off the altar, thudding to the floor. The need to move, to hide, overpowered every other sense, and she scuttled backward until she hit the wall, mashing herself against it as though it would make her invisible.

Oh God. Oh God oh God oh God!

He'd killed Elizabeth and his unborn child with no expression at all, with no remorse, which was worse than if he'd been smiling as he hacked open her belly.

She clung to the stones, digging her fingers into the pits and pockmarks of age, finally grasping her true predicament. She was alone with a merciless, soulless killer, and there would be no reprieve. He would not stay his hand, no matter that he liked her, no matter that she liked lemon bars, because his killing was more than just convenient, it was for more than just supernatural power. It was a need, deep inside him, to twist and terrorize, to lay to waste and ruin every beautiful thing he touched.

"Now you know." His voice draped over her like velvet, soothing, lulling, a false security blanket.

"The cat…" She choked on the words. "I know that cat."

"Yes. You do."

"All this time, all these years, he never realized."

He shrugged. "That's no concern of mine."

"That's what you're planning to do to me? Why not just kill me?

Simpler, easier."

"Practice makes perfect. We have several projects aimed at finding the perfect immortality – one that allows you to keep your humanity and a human body. So far, we haven't been able to transfer human soul into human body, only into an animal. Our human subjects always die. The transference spell took us forever to even learn how to perform, and then we had a major setback when someone unexpectedly left the Circle. She had mastered the spell and was our only transference Caster."

"And you just let her go? I find that hard to believe."

"Believe what you will. Her freedom did not come without a price."

Kim grimaced inwardly. Of course there had been a price; he would have to ensure her silence, would he not? And she was sure the price had been cruel. She had to get out of here, before a cruel price was exacted from her simply because she'd captured a sociopath's fancy.

"What did you do to her? Put her soul into a cat?"

"We just convinced her six-year-old daughter to eat death cap mushrooms. Trust me, she got the message." He flashed a cold grin. "Aaron, however, wasn't as easy to shut up. Harlan tried to warn him, but he came to the Wyckham House anyway – and brought friends. Very brave, but – you'll appreciate this – very reckless."

"And you killed them."

She let her head droop, her hair forming a veil between them, through which her gaze surreptitiously swept the room. He paced around the head of the altar, slowly making his way toward her from behind, a casual maneuver meant to keep her from spooking. Four more steps and he would be in the perfect position: he'd lunge for her as she bolted, and he'd be unable to check his momentum, giving her an extra few seconds. Precious seconds.

He came two paces closer. "They didn't leave me a choice. They'd seen too much. I never expected Aaron would get away."

Because no one ever had.

He took another step. Kim tensed, shifting her weight from her heels to the balls of her feet, covering the move by pressing closer to the wall.

"It's time to get back on the altar, Kimberly. Only an hour until the Circle arrives."

She needed him on this side, so that he wasted precious seconds having to go around it to chase her when she ran. But he didn't take that last step.

"No."

He chuckled. "You'll probably spit in my eye and curse me as you die, won't you? No begging or pleading from you. Now get up, and get back on that stone."

"No."

He took the step and then another in rapid succession, moving so fast that she almost missed her chance. She shot forward, just missing his reaching fingers, and sprinted across the room to the dark corridor.

His pace was unhurried as he came after her. She thought she even heard him laughing. Without daring to glance back, she plunged into the shadows.

Reaching arms, grasping fingers, a solidity that she hit like a wall of quicksand; the shadows had substance. The harder she fought, the deeper she sank into their midst, and the less able she was to move. They held her in place, and still he came with that unhurried stride. His arms slid around her middle, and he lifted her out of the mass of dark beings.

She kicked and screamed, fighting ferociously as he dragged her back across the room. He moved one arm across her chest, trying to subdue her wildly flailing arms, and she bit him, buying herself freedom. She bolted for the other corridor on the far side of the room. He hooked his foot around her ankle, and she sprawled on the stones, scraping the scab off her cheek. Warm blood trickled to her chin as she pushed herself onto her knees. A solid weight knocked her flat to the floor again. His breath was hot in her ear, his body warm and solid against her back.

"That was a ballsy move. You have a lot of sass; I like that in a woman." His tongue traced the curve of her ear. Kimberly shuddered and tried to crawl away again. "Now as much as I enjoy a spirited wrestling match with a sexy woman, we simply don't have time. We're going to get up nice and slow, and you're going to lie back down on that stone, or so help me the last hour of your life is going to make you beg me to kill you."

He rose slowly, pulling her up with him, and any escape attempt she might have considered vanished when he grabbed a fistful of her hair, close to the scalp, and used it to guide her back to the stone. The manacles snapped around her wrists and ankles, the sound of death. She was down to the final hour of her life.

Strangely, what passed through her mind was not the highlights of her life but a single memory. Bethany, rocking her as she cried – her last miscarriage only weeks behind her, her marriage over only days before – whispering softly in her ear: *There's always hope as long as you have God. Always.* Bethany, always faithful, always believing, always praying for her. Kim hoped she was praying now.

You said I have free will, so I choose You. I want my gift back.

No bells, no fireworks, no fancy flashing signs to celebrate heaven's victory. Just a sense of peace that calmed her panic.

And hope.

DAMNED ANGELS

He was drowning although he could breathe, drowning in the spiral of time, in the eons that flashed by like mile markers on a dark highway. And there was no end to this road; he could travel it for eternity and never reach a destination, while in his own time, the minutes ticked past, and Caleb ended Kimberly's life.

His fingers grasped handfuls of nothingness, but his speed never slowed. His head whirled, giving the sensation of movement.

And it was just that – a sensation. A moment of concentration – a moment which might have lasted a minute or a year - proved it was nothing but smoke and mirrors, a cheap trick to confuse and disorient.

Because the spinning dark void of the spiral was actually shadowy beings circling around him, around and around and up and over, otherworldly vultures feeding on his terror and despair, while in fact he stood perfectly still, his feet planted firmly on the stone floor.

One of those vultures was going to help him, whether or not it wanted to.

He thrust a hand into the darkness, fingers grasping. The shadows scattered like startled chickens, only he was fairly sure he heard derisive laughter as they fled. He lunged at their retreating mass and caught hold, culling one from the flock.

"You're taking me to her."

The angel spun them around a quick revolution, and suddenly he could see. The corridor was filled with murky light, and the angel bathed him in brightness.

"I can fold you through layers of time until you end up in prehistoric times, when the beasts of the field reigned all but the Garden. How will you survive then?"

"Man will always be the most bad-ass animal on this planet. Take me to her." His tone rang strong and sure even as his mind reeled. He was talking to an angel, holding it by what would be the front of its shirt if it had a shirt. In truth, he couldn't quite tell what he had hold of; the creature was light with substance and mass, energy with solidity.

But still…my God, I'm talking to an angel!

"And if I don't?" It smiled slyly, fixing him with eyes that made his reeling mind slip another gear. Colors swirled and ebbed across those eyes, through them, as though they were of a depth that could hold infinite universes. And not just the colors his mind recognized, but every color, every hue in God's paintbox, colors he had never seen and for which he had no name.

"If you had a choice, you wouldn't be here talking to me," Ron replied reasonably. "Take me to her."

"There is no one here but you and me, and the rest of my kind. You're outside of time; you exist nowhere, and everywhere. She is in time, and she exists only in her time."

Ron clenched his hand tighter, although he was certain he could affect no harm to an angel. "I'm not interested in your riddles. Take me to her."

"You asked for it."

The angel seized him with no more effort than a man lifting a ragdoll. And flung him away, like a man hurling a Frisbee. Ron, his fingers losing purchase, saw the creature's triumphant, malevolent grin.

Damned angels.

And his fingers lost hold.

* * * * *

She lay in drowsy warmth, eyes closed tight as she basked in the after-effects of a dream. The warmth behind her shifted slightly, resolving itself into a distinctly male form. Aaron. Kimberly smiled in relief; it had all been a nightmare. No stone altar, no murderous black magic priest making sexual innuendos involving lemon bars, no imaginary clock ticking off the last hours of her life.

She tucked her hands more firmly under her chin. Chains rattled. Her eyes flew open, and there it was, like a night terror come to life: the same dark stone wall, flickering in the light from the torch. The air she breathed held the same biting chill, and the stone beneath her was the same stained granite slab.

Her head was pillowed on a distinctly masculine bicep, and as though he sensed her wakefulness, his elegant fingers tightened fractionally on her hip. He lay on the stone behind her, their body heat pooling under the comforter. She wasn't sorry for the warmth, but she couldn't help but think that dying of hypothermia would have been much better than this agonizing, inexorable seduction.

Both lay silent in their thoughts. She didn't want to know his; no doubt they involved dark and deadly matters. His disappointment that she still refused his offer of a temporary stay of execution hung between them like a black shroud. Her time was dangerously short; she could almost see the sand trickling through an hour glass, marking off the seconds.

After a long while, she spoke into the oddly companionable silence.

"Where does the smoke go?" Her eyes were on the flickering torches that had burned ceaselessly since he'd brought her to the ceremony room. There should have been a thick cloud of smoke in the room, burning her eyes and making her cough.

"Away."

"To where?" she persisted.

"Just...away. Didn't I tell you? This is a magical house."

"Not all magic is good."

"Depends on which end of it you find yourself—the giving end or the receiving end."

She let the silence fall between them again until, uncounted minutes later, she could stay silent no longer. *You never know until you ask*, her mother had always said, and so she asked because, however strange and unlikely, she was this man's greatest weakness.

"Caleb?"

"Mmm?" His breath stirred her hair at the top of her head. She was small enough that when curled together like spoons with a man his size, she fit neatly under his chin.

"Let me go. Please."

Her subdued request didn't bring the mocking laughter she expected, only a deep sigh. "It's too late for that. Bargains have been made. They aren't the kinds of bargains on which one reneges."

"It's not too late. It's never too late for forgiveness."

He was silent for so long she thought he wasn't going to answer. When he did, his voice was no more than a whisper. "I'm too far down this road to be redeemed, Kimberly. And I have no desire for it anyway."

The seconds stretched into minutes. Finally she whispered, "Liar."

He didn't challenge her accusation, but asked one last time, "Why won't you take my offer?"

"For reasons too many to count," she said softly. "There's God and there's Aaron, for starters. I won't betray them."

"Even if it means dying?"

She shrugged. "You'll kill me either way."

"It buys you a few months, at least."

"It's not worth the consequences. Did you really think I'd accept when it means you'll kill me once I'm pregnant?"

"Perhaps I'll let you live."

"You didn't let Elizabeth live."

"Yes, I did. It's only her body that's dead. Her soul...well, she's enjoyed many happy years with Aaron."

"Yeah, complete with Friskies and flea dips," she quipped caustically. "I'd rather die than be his pet."

"As I said, perhaps I'll let you live. I like you better than I did Elizabeth."

She couldn't help her bark of incredulous laughter. "Why on earth would you like me? I'm lying here damning you to eight kinds of hell, and given the chance, I wouldn't hesitate to plunge that black knife of yours into your heart."

His hand slid from her hip to splay over her stomach, pressing her closer. "How could I not like someone who likes lemon bars?"

"You're kid—" she began, but he shushed her, suddenly tense. He raised up on one elbow, his head cocked, listening intently, and then he slid silently from beneath the comforter. She lamented his warmth but not his proximity; it was disgustingly hard to refuse him when he was pressed so intimately against her.

"Someone's in the house," he said quietly.

"How do you know?"

"They told me."

They. The shadows that had become pillars of light when she was pulled outside of time. Angels. *Demons.*

Quiet as a cat, he moved fluidly across the room and vanished into the darkness of the stairwell.

Hope, that disgustingly optimistic beacon that refused to die, flared inside her. Hadn't she told him Aaron would come for her? And then terror bit at the heels of relief. He had tried to kill Aaron once, and he would be determined not to fail this time. If he got to Aaron before Aaron found her…

She bolted upright, working her hands in the manacles, scrunching her thumb into her palm to make her hand smaller. He hadn't fastened them as tightly after cleaning Tiana's blood from her and changing her shirt, but she still couldn't contort her hand enough to squeeze it out of the cuff. Too aware of the seconds ticking by, almost able to see them whizzing past, she banged one of the iron cuffs on the side of the granite stone; they were seemingly well cared for, but they were old. Parts within the mechanism had to be giving way to rust by now.

But they were solid and refused to spring. Her fear morphed to frustration, and she slid from the altar, slamming the cuff over and over against the edge of the stone until her wrist was bloody and her hand numb. And still she was trapped.

Despair fell over her like a noxious blanket, sapping her will to escape. She rolled back onto the stone, wincing as something hard and lumpy poked her in the hip. She fished around beneath her in the folds of the comforter, finally snagging a jingling ring and pulling it out from under the blanket.

Keys.

He had lost his keyring and hadn't realized it yet.

She was no idiotic damsel in distress, waiting for some damn man to come rescue her. Urgency made her fingers clumsy as she fingered through the ring, seeking the small, old-fashioned bit of iron that would free her from her chains. Ah, there… She slotted a small round key into the keyhole.

A primal scream from somewhere above her reverberated around the room, bouncing off the stone walls and building in volume as the echoes collided. Her head whipped up, and she voiced her own scream as Aaron Schaefer spun in mid-air, plunging toward the altar, his face contorted in a desperate grimace as he clutched a violently twisting shadow with both hands.

At the last second he flung his other arm around and grasped it by its back. It shrieked in fury, hurtling into its own disorienting free-fall. The light extinguished, and then lit again, this time in the form of a torch. And then was gone. On and on, through eons and eras, folding back through the layers of time to the present.

The angel twisted in his grasp, snarling and snapping, fighting to free itself and strand him in a time not his own. Scenes flashed by, the same room, different people, no people, no altar, then the granite stone he recognized from his

(memories)

dreams. And then came a scene he recognized: a woman with fiery hair and opalescent skin, stretched on the granite altar in offering, her swollen belly gleaming in the torchlight. *Elizabeth*.

He reached toward her, struggling to stay in this time, fighting the pull of the angel as it tried to fold him into another era.

"You can't enter this time. You're already here."

But still he fought to stay, until pain like lightning shot through him, hurtling him backward into the angel. They tumbled heels over head over heels until the angel pulled them through to Ron's present.

It grinned a spiteful grin and let go. Ron plummeted toward the ancient stone floor from a height of a hundred feet or more.

Its guard down in its moment of vicious triumph, the angel had given Aaron one precious sliver of a second to catch hold of it. Over and over they rolled through the air, hurtling toward the altar. He used the last of his strength and determination to twist the shadow so it was underneath him at the second before impact.

Kimberly screamed and flung herself off the stone, the chain around her left hand pulling tight over the granite. The angel hit with brutal force that would have killed a man. It cushioned Aaron's fall. He lost his grip on the shadowy being as it wrenched out of his grip, and he smacked onto the stone hard enough to rattle his bones. He groaned and slid off the side to the floor, where he lay stunned, the air knocked from his lungs.

The scrape of a shoe and the clink of chains. Whispers sighing on the air. Shockingly cold hands on his face. His lungs burning. Anxious words murmured lightning-fast in his ear. His cheek and shoulder throbbing. Shadows dancing before his eyes.

Not shadows. Spots. He needed air. Her voice chanted frantically in his ear: *Breathe, Aaron, BREATHE!* Cold hands gripped his shoulders, shaking him, trying to rouse him. His lungs were on fire, his vision black around the edges. And then the spasm passed, and he gulped air in desperate gasps, rolling onto his side, fighting back a sudden wave of nausea.

"Oh my God, Ron, what the hell was *that?*" Kimberly's voice shook, and her hands on his shoulders trembled violently.

"Trouble." He sat up, his head still spinning from his turbulent free-fall, amazed that he was alive. "Time to get out of here."

"You think? I was working on it when you fell out of thin air. I dropped the key somewhere."

A glance around told him it would be hell finding anything; the torches – torches? in the twentieth century? – lit only a small circle of the floor near the wall.

"Feel around with your hands as far as you can reach. I'll search where you can't." He hesitated before beginning his search. "Is Tiana here? Have you seen her?"

Her teeth caught her lower lip between them, and her eyes closed for a second. "He said she's dead. There was…a lot of blood. He made me lie down in it."

He swayed on his knees. Dead? He'd known Tiana Michaels all his life – how could she be dead?

"Did you see her yourself?"

"No."

Then there was hope that Caleb had been lying. He clung to it fiercely.

They wasted no time with cautious searching. Each frantically swept the floor around them, searching for the ring of keys that had flown from her hand when she had bailed off the altar. Kim's search was ordered by necessity, due to her limited reach; Ron's, although no less frenzied, followed an ordered pattern that ensured he wouldn't miss them.

And he didn't; his knee came squarely down onto the collection of serrated metal spikes. He swore vehemently, snatching them out from under his kneecap, which throbbed from the impact. It was as he crawled back across the floor to her, his fingers already searching for a round of iron that would free her from her chains, that he heard footsteps pounding down the stairs on the other side of the altar.

"Oh God." Kim's eyes were huge and panicked in her pale face, and she choked on the words. *"He's coming!"*

The iron key slammed home. He twisted it, freeing one leg, and then the other, and then her hands. His came away sticky with her blood. The keys clanked to the floor, and he dragged her to her feet to run.

Caleb leaped from the shadowy stairwell with frightening speed, vaulting over the altar before Ron and Kim had crossed the room to the alternate stairs. His scream of rage echoed around the cavernous room, seeming to come from the very stones.

"STOP THEM!" he bellowed at the shadows, which parted to let the fleeing humans pass.

"It is not our fight, human," one hissed in reply.

Ron chanced a look over his shoulder at the demon who had spoken. It grinned and lunged at him, hissing like a scalded cat. He flinched and yelled in alarm, and the angel fell back, its mocking laughter chasing them up the stairs.

He'd lost the flashlight when he'd fallen into the shadows. They ran up narrow staircases and down wide corridors, their hands skimming the walls to keep their balance and their bearings in the pitch-black mansion. The sounds of pursuit had faded, but Ron didn't kid himself about their situation. They were lost in a lightless house of confusing, random corridors, several floors up from ground level, if he had kept track correctly, and he was under no illusion that they were alone or that their unseen companions were friendly.

He groped in the dark for Kimberly's hand and stopped, catching her weight against him as she lost her footing.

"What – "

"I think I can find our way out of here, but we're going to have to go back down. We're on the fourth floor up from ground level, if I counted right."

"Ron, I've seen this house from the outside. There isn't a fourth floor."

"You've been in here long enough to know that this is no ordinary house."

The silence between them was pregnant with her uncertainty and fear. He imagined her chewing on her lower lip as common sense warred with terror.

"He's going to be waiting for us on the ground floor."

"We have no choice. Are you ready?" He tightened his fingers around hers, trying to reassure her even though he was ninety percent certain they were going to die here tonight.

"Yes." He started off again, but she yanked him to a sudden stop.

"If it comes down to it – let him have me and get yourself out. Renée and Cody have been through enough without losing you."

His fingers squeezed hers until she gasped in a breath at the pain.

"What the hell, woman? You think no one's going to care if you die? What about your father? What about Bethany – you think just because she's in Texas, it won't affect her? And Taryn – she thinks you're the greatest thing to walk through town in years." He paused. "What about me? Do you think I could go on without you?"

"You have to. Aaron, losing me will impact a lot fewer people than losing you will. You have to promise me – "

"No. We leave together or we die together."

"Aaron – "

"Let's go." She resisted again. "What now?"

"I don't suppose you have an extra layer on? I'm freezing."

He shrugged out of his hoodie, thankful he'd worn a thick flannel shirt and a tee-shirt under it, and helped her into it by feel. After that, she came along willingly with no more delays. He wasn't fooled. It didn't take a psychic to know she hadn't completely given up on her crazy idea; she would simply bide her time and spring it on him when it was most inconvenient to argue about it, because she was reckless and rash and stubborn and so damn courageous.

Random turns and unlikely stairs took them inexorably down toward the lower level. They passed through the house unimpeded. Every corner they rounded without confrontation amped his anxiety to a fever-pitch. With every stairwell that took them down, Kimberly's terror built until it was nearly a visible entity traveling with them. His gut twisted with his own fear and dread; what had Caleb done to her in the hours he'd held her captive?

Ron stopped, pivoted ninety degrees, and crossed the corridor, his free hand stretched out and feeling for the wall on the opposite side. When his fingers grazed the stone, skinning his knuckles, he turned back in the direction they had been walking and started off again, slowly this time, feeling his way along the wall.

"What's wrong?" Kim whispered.

"Nothing. I think we're close to the main staircase to the ground floor. I don't want to pass it by accident."

"I don't think we should go down it. He'll be waiting."

"We don't have a choice. I don't think there's any other way out."

"There has to be. How did you get out eleven years ago?"

"I don't know. It seems like there was a different door, but I can't remember it clearly. If there is, we passed it long ago. We have to go down where we can find a way."

"I'm scared."

Her admission was reluctant, dragged out of her with great effort. He stopped again, turning carefully, never letting go of her so he didn't lose her in the darkness. He pulled her close, leaning down to her until his forehead touched hers.

"Do I need to kill him?"

She understood what he was really asking. "No."

"What stopped him?"

"I don't know. It wasn't lack of opportunity."

His fingers clenched on her arms. "I should kill him anyway."

"I can't argue that he's bought his own death sentence with the things he's done."

There was a "but" in her voice, one he dreaded. "But you don't want me to."

"No one is irredeemable as long as there is breath and life in his body. Cody would agree with me."

"It's not Cody's decision."

"No. But it's not yours, either." He closed his eyes, drawing in a steadying breath. "Please, let's just get out of here."

"It means going down those stairs."

"I know."

He turned, his hand sliding down her arm to hers, fingers lacing together. They crept forward, inch by inch, slowly, pressed to the wall on their right to keep their balance.

And then suddenly the wall wasn't there. Ron stumbled, falling into the opening. He thought he heard laughter again, hissing from the darkness around them. Kimberly yanked him back, nearly dislocating his arm. He edged backward until he found the corner of the wall and leaned against the stones, muttering imprecations. Her arms slid around him, and she pressed her face against his neck. Her whole body shuddered against his.

He blew out a breath, gave her a squeeze, and pushed away from the wall. "Let's try this again."

The stairs were decrepit, decaying, and dangerous. He stepped carefully, slowly, feeling the next tread down with his foot to make sure it was stable enough to hold him before he put his full weight on it. The boards disintegrated as soon as his shoe touched, and he was forced to lean heavily on the precarious banister as he tested the next tread down.

Their torturous journey down the stairs seemed to take an eternity. In the absolute darkness, he couldn't see the bottom, and he had the unsettling feeling that these stairs never ended, that they were descending inch by agonizing inch into hell itself.

Without warning, he was ripped from Kimberly's grip and flung into space. In the scant second the demons folded him outside of time, he saw her on the staircase, arms outstretched, face streaked with tears, balanced on the edge of a precipice. The stairs below her had crumbled away, leaving only the feeble handrail trailing to the floor on one side.

And her foot was lifting to take a step into thin air, twenty feet above the unforgiving stone floor.

He was folded back into time, into darkness, and he shouted as he fell: "Don't move!" And prayed she would, for once, listen to him the first time.

"Aaron?" Her voice was thin with terror.

He pushed to his feet. Hands clutched him, hundreds of clawing fingers, spinning him around and around, until his head whirled so much he couldn't tell where the stairs were. The shadows snickered mockingly.

"Don't move. It's a trap. There are no – "

A wall of air slammed into his chest with bruising force. He flew backward and landed on his backside, skidding across the debris-strewn floor with enough velocity to rip the back pockets off his jeans. A shadow moved over him and weak twilight streamed across the floor; the angels had been gathered in front of the lancet windows, blocking the light from outside so that he and Kimberly could not see.

The shadow stepped into the light and bent close to his face, resolving into a being of such alien beauty that his breath caught in his chest. Kaleidoscope eyes bore into his, colors flaring and ebbing and flowing deep within. Its voice held a dissonant ring like flawed crystal.

"That one is ours. Agreements have been made."

Ron fought for breath, his mind scrambling for words in a suddenly blank landscape. "They weren't my agreements. She isn't his to give."

"And who are you in the scheme of things?"

"The man who loves her."

"Love?" The angel snorted. The sound of discordant bells echoed around the room as others chuckled. "That useless human emotion. *Love.*" It gave the word a derisive slur, and the angels all laughed again.

"Not just a human emotion. God loves, too."

"Ah, yes. For God so loved the world... Look what it's done for him: given him a race of mortal ingrates lacking morals."

"And who are *you* in the scheme of things?" Ron challenged, and the angel's laughter dried up. Names held power, all the more so in the angelic realm.

"An interested party."

"Certainly not a nameless one."

"Ron, who are you talking to? Get me the hell off these stairs!"

The angel snickered. "Your *love* is summoning. Go on, go save her. If you can."

It moved away from him, and Ron stood with difficulty; being flung around this house was hell on the body. He picked his way across the littered floor, one eye on the angel, one eye on the darkness ahead although he could discern nothing of the staircase until he tripped and fell over shattered debris. The angels hooted with amusement. Ron did his best to ignore them, picked himself up, and climbed over the obstacle.

"Where are you?" he called upward.

"Here."

To his right and a few paces forward. He moved forward and to the side.

"Say it again."

"Here."

Backward a pace. "And again."

"Here."

Above him and forward just enough. "Okay. You aren't going to like this, but I want you to jump."

"Are you out of your freaking mind?"

Probably. "I won't miss," he promised.

"You can't even see me – how do you suppose you're going to catch me?"

"Just do it. We don't have any time to waste arguing, unless you have a better idea."

"The banister…"

"…will break before you put all your weight on it. I *will* catch you, Kimberly."

"But – "

"Do you trust me?"

"Yes, but - "

"Then jump. Now."

A beat of silence, then an expressive sigh. "All right. I'm jumping. Now."

He closed his eyes, turning command over to his sense of sound and touch. A stair tread cracked and crumbled, sifting its splintered remains onto his upturned face as she stepped into the darkness. The rush of displaced air washed over him as she plummeted toward him. He reached out instinctively, catching her around the upper thighs, spinning them into a whirlwind to absorb the impact. He'd caught her too low; top-heavy, they tumbled to the floor, still spinning, and rolled over and over until her back hit the remains of a stair riser. The sudden impact knocked half the breath out of her.

Ron rolled to his knees, casting a glance toward the windows. Almost dusk. They had to leave now. Caleb seemed to have vanished; unless they ran into him outside, they were free and clear - provided the angels didn't decide to stop them.

"Can you walk?"

"I can't … even *breathe*. " But she pushed herself onto her knees. Grabbing his jacket for leverage, she managed to pull herself upright while nearly bringing him to the floor. But at least they were both on their feet.

He leaned close to her ear to whisper. "Let's see if they'll let us leave."

Taking the lead, he edged toward the windows, scooting his feet along to floor to locate debris before they tripped over it, their hands laced together tightly to keep from being separated. Four more steps and they'd reach the first pool of light slanting in through the tall Gothic windows. Three more. Two…

"Leaving so soon?"

The elegant, feminine voice came out of the darkness behind them, so unexpected that Ron paused, his manners kicking into gear instinctively, already formulating a polite apology. She walked around them and into a shaft of weak light. Sarah Bennett, herbalist and – if rumor pegged it right – practitioner of black magic of the highest order, chic in a matronly kind of way in a conservative black skirt, low-heeled black pumps, and a pristine white shirt with a lace-edged collar.

He clamped his jaw closed on his automatic response and drew Kimberly close up to and slightly behind the protective barrier of his back.

"You're free to leave, Aaron. But you have something of mine that I insist remains here."

"She doesn't leave, I don't leave." He winced mentally. Put like that …

"Oh, a two-for-one deal?" She chuckled. "I'm never one to pass up a bargain. All the same – " She waved a negligent hand at one of the narrow, glassless windows. "I'm afraid the door is swollen shut, but the window serves as an exit just as efficiently."

"Not without her."

Her face creased with irritation. "Oh, you humans are so annoying in your devotion to each other. You can find another, just as you replaced Elizabeth. I'm not asking, Aaron. I'm the teacher of enchantments; I made a bargain for my knowledge, and she's the prize. She belongs to us."

She strode out of the light, and like the shiny red skin of a beautiful apple peeling away to reveal a rotten, wormy core, her human guise faded, revealing a glorious, dreadful being. Ron's mind slipped its tracks once again.

"I see you understand your predicament now. No bargain was

made for you; you can leave. Just hand over Kimberly – "

"Pssst! Ron! Kimberly! Are you in there?"

The loud, rasping whisper speared through Ron like a knife in the heart. *Scott.* He didn't take time to weigh his options or ponder consequences. He tightened his hold on Kimberly's hand and ran, ignoring the closest windows because he would have to skirt Sarah Bennett. He sprinted toward the far end of the long, open hall from where Scott's voice had come, dragging Kimberly behind him.

The angels hissed and swarmed around them, clutching at Kimberly, wrenching at their linked hands. He reached the window, gasping air, trying to hear over his heartbeat slamming in his ears. Kimberly was trying to climb up onto the sill, but shadow hands yanked her back down each time she gained purchase. Ron lifted her by a belt loop and the back of her jacket and tossed her through the window.

Into the waiting arms of Caleb Schaefer.

THE OMEGA TEAM

Cody had gathered his team in Scranton the day before to brief them on the Mills mission; it would be a hard-and-fast entry, what his agency called a tag-and-bag because with cult leaders as extreme as Caleb Schaefer, someone usually ended up dead.

During these briefings, he turned off his cell phone so he had no personal distractions. Communication with his team and his superiors was handled through a "tactical device" no bigger than a cell phone and powered by a system created exclusively for them by Apple.

The apps on this baby connected him to maps of all kinds: geological, topographical, satellite imagery, and basic cartographical; to secure communication channels so he could receive and give orders, briefings, and – if need be – SOS calls; to encyclopedias of dark and arcane knowledge.

So to find, late in the day, that his cell phone was bursting with frantic text messages and voicemails from Mills was not a welcome – or comforting – discovery. And Taryn Ackerlin's latest text to him – just ten minutes ago – struck cold dread in the pit of his stomach.

I don't know why the hell neither you nor Renée answers your phone. But you need to get home NOW. Kimberly missing 7 hours. Ron went to find her 2 hours ago. Neither is back. Scott looking for Tiana at Wyckham. I DON'T NEED TO TELL YOU THIS IS BAD!!!!!!!

Cody swore vehemently and keyed out a quick reply: *ON MY WAY.* He offered no explanation for his or his wife's silence. Renée's charger had fritzed out and she had been hunting the cell phone stores of Scranton looking for a new one, which was proving more difficult than it should. As for himself – the only people he offered explanations to were his superiors, his teams, and his wife. In other words, those whose security clearances allowed them to hear those explanations.

He tapped a speed dial key, and when Denny answered, he said simply, "Find my wife. I'm preparing the team to mobilize immediately. There's trouble."

Denny wasted no time on arguments, not that Cody would have remained on the line to hear them. It would be no trouble for his second-in-command to locate Renée; she wore a GPS transmitter everywhere she went, disguised as an intricate Celtic interlace ring. She had accepted it with a thoughtful look after signing a ream of paperwork giving her a few basic rights and binding her to a boatload of restrictions. So many sacrifices she had made for his job; it pricked at his conscience more than he liked to admit.

Another key tap sent an alert to the rest of the team, advising them to grab all gear and prepare to mobilize. Cody didn't wait for a response; he didn't need one. This team didn't need to be babysat. He pocketed his device and began packing his and Renée's things. The car would be packed and he would be waiting in it by the time Denny returned with her.

The situation in Mills had deteriorated faster than he had anticipated, and he didn't like that he had missed the signs. He'd known Caleb was poised to strike; it had been more of an unshakeable hunch than it had been any clues or hints his brother had let drop – Caleb would never be so careless. He just hadn't expected him to move so soon. And that Taryn knew Kimberly Owens' real identity troubled him as well. What the hell had happened in the thirty-some hours he'd been out of town?

Denny found Renée quickly; Cody had barely got the car packed when they pulled up. Denny joined the team command car – one of the numerous black Escalades at their service – and Cody briefed Renée on the drive. The very fast drive. At times he exceeded the speed limit by twenty miles an hour, but he had no fear their caravan would be stopped; while the vehicles did not sport government plates, another tap on his keypad had alerted all state law enforcement agencies of his presence and emergency status.

He was a man with considerable power, who wielded it comfortably and responsibly, but right now he simply felt like a father teetering on the precipice of panic because his children were endangered.

Renée didn't fret or babble incessant reassurances; she spent the drive in white-faced, trusting silence, clutching the oh-jesus handle over her door as he guided the car at dangerous speeds through highway traffic and adverse weather.

Likewise, when they reached Mills, she didn't protest when he pulled over in front of Town Hall, handed her the keys, and told her to go to Aaron's and stay there with Taryn until she heard from him.

She was a good wife, a better wife than he deserved.

The mood in the command car was somber and serious, conversations kept to muted tones, and sometimes held without words. Denny was as silent as Cody unless instructions needed to be dispersed, and the drive down Willow Road took what seemed an eternity.

Cody was the first out of the Escalade when they stopped in front of the cottage next to Aaron's truck, impervious to the howling storm around them. Two quick motions sent the team around both sides of the house, while Cody and Denny slipped silently through the front door.

They conducted their search with meticulous efficiency, moving through the house from front to back rapidly and soundlessly. They inspected the kitchen the longest, scrutinizing the blood smears on the floor and the back door, which stood ajar.

Denny took a sample of the blood with a collection kit from his gear. After a minute of study and wordless speculation, Cody tipped his head toward the front door. They didn't speak until they were in the command car – where sophisticated equipment would jam any listening devices aimed in their direction.

"The blood on the window frame in the spare room – what do you make of that?" Cody wiped his face with a hand towel he pulled from the net pouch behind the passenger seat.

Denny frowned thoughtfully; even as he answered, he was making detailed notes of their search on his tactical device. "I can't see Caleb dragging her out the window, and Ron would have no reason the break in through a window – his key is on the ring with his car keys."

"The back door...I'm leaning toward Aaron having left it open. But the blood on the floor – Kimberly's?"

"More than likely. The blonde hair in the blood on the windowsill makes me think she broke in – didn't have her key with her for some reason."

"And Caleb was waiting."

"You can't tell me you're surprised. You even told her he was following her."

"I didn't expect him to make a move already. I was giving it until Thanksgiving, at least."

Denny finished his notes and pocketed his device. "He does seem abnormally fascinated with her. Ron's truck is still here; either she drove it and was taken away in another vehicle, or she came in a different car, which is gone, and Ron doesn't know about the old road or he'd have driven closer to the house."

Cody rubbed a finger over his upper lip. "I didn't see any reason to tell him about it. It's not like I wanted him to go there."

"Cody, you know Caleb is a sociopathic killer. Kimberly Owens is likely dead."

Cody heard the unspoken words behind what his subordinate said: *And if Aaron went after her, he's likely dead as well.* But he couldn't think that way. He never went into a mission believing the worst; to do so was likely to ensure the worst was handed to you along with your own ass. And he couldn't bear to think it about his own family.

Denny asked, "What do you want to do?"

A simple question, with a simple answer that posited enormous consequences. "We go, but no farther than the clearing. The weather is lousy; with the thunder, we'd probably be able to sneak up on them, but I don't want anyone going into the house. Taking Caleb alive would be ideal." Not because they were brothers, but because Caleb knew where all the missing bodies were buried. "But not required."

Denny keyed the command into his device, sending it to the rest of the team. In less than two minutes, they were bouncing down the drive from the cottage to the road, and turning toward the gate at the end of Willow Road.

Cody had discovered the camouflaged gate and the well maintained road beyond it eleven years ago after Ron had been admitted to Meadow Grove. He hadn't been part of the investigation; Guzman, his superior, subscribed to the same doctrine applied to the medical field: you don't treat your own. But it hadn't stopped him from probing into the events that had left his son catatonic and his son's friends dead. Knowing your ground – or your enemy's – gave you an edge, and he knew the area surrounding the Wyckham House as well as he knew his wife's face.

They paused just long enough to open the gate, and then just long enough for the agents in the last car to close it behind them. Each pause felt like hours to Cody.

It took no time at all to reach the end of the road, where Scott's Dodge Dart was parked. Empty. Half the team was dispatched to search the abandoned mill; the other half fanned out around Cody and Denny, a protective, watchful barrier.

They were drenched in seconds, but neither moved to open an umbrella. Umbrellas limited your field of vision, gave another layer of sound to filter. The rain pounded them, reminded Cody of a massaging shower head. After taking a splat in the eye, Denny wiped his face with a hand and slanted him a look.

"Why can't we go into the house? That's our best bet of finding Kimberly and Aaron. And Caleb."

"Our odds are drastically diminished in the enemy's territory."

"It's never stopped us before." In other words, it was different this time because it involved Cody's family and he was being more cautious. The implication that he was taking more care with his blood relatives than he ever had for strangers did not bother him; it was a justifiable assumption.

"We've never dealt with anything like this house before."

"That house in New Orleans was no picnic."

That mission had been full of traps, but they had been of human invention. In the end, they had rounded up the members of a nasty voodoo cult.

"No, it wasn't. But that house was just a house."

Denny digested this silently, and then remarked, "You'd drive Confucius crazy."

Cody grinned tightly but was spared further explanation by the return of the rest of the team. One stopped beside him while the others fanned out with their brethren.

"Sir, they're using the old mill as a garage. Five cars inside, including one belonging to Taryn Ackerlin – she works for your son, correct?"

"Yes." Ice flooded through him. The Circle was here; they were too late to save anyone. All they could do now was disband the cult and mete out justice. He closed his eyes for a sliver of a second. How was he to tell Renée that their sons were lost to this damned house?

"Your orders, sir?"

His eyes snapped open. "Invasion mode. Stealth please. Detain anyone and everyone, and we'll sort out identity and affiliation later. Take prisoners alive unless you're given no option."

"Your sons and the woman, sir?"

He swallowed hard to keep from choking on the words. "They are no longer the focus of this mission."

"Yes, sir." The agent moved off to disperse the orders to his fellow team members. Denny stood with him for a moment longer, his reticence heavy with what Cody suspected was disapproval. "What is it, Wallace?"

"We have no reason to believe – "

"I know."

"You said we weren't going into the house."

"I changed my mind."

A beat of silence held between them. "Yes, sir."

"Let's go."

* * * * *

Ron rolled twice and came to his feet in a crouch, but Caleb held her by the hair in an unshakeable grip. Pain ripped through her scalp each time he moved, and she stood up on tiptoe to ease the pressure. The other held a gun at midpoint between Ron and Scott, the latter of whom looked angry and embarrassed at having been caught.

"It's pretty handy, all of us sounding alike," Caleb said lazily. Against her back, his heart beat a wild, excited rhythm. Despite his rage that she had escaped from him in the ceremony room, he had enjoyed the chase, maybe even relished it.

Scott took half a step toward them, and Caleb took a firmer grip on her hair, pulling upward. Pain burned through her scalp and she yelled, clawing at his hand. Scott stopped, holding his hands up in a placating gesture. Caleb's grip eased slightly. Tears rolled down her cheeks, hot in contrast to the cold air outside. The sun inched below the tree line, taking with it any illusion of warmth.

"I believe this is called an impasse." Ron's tone was calm, but his eyes darted everywhere, taking in their surroundings, looking for an advantage. He shifted minutely but not randomly; some calculation in his head had told him he needed to refine his stance. Kim wondered how much wolf had remained in him after the curse had broken.

"One of us has to make a move." He brought the gun's sighting to bear on Ron's forehead. Ron made another slight adjustment as Caleb swung the gun toward Scott. "Which one of you, then?"

Kim raised her foot and in another move she learned from that personal defense trainer, she brought her heel down with all her strength on Caleb's instep, and followed the move with a sharp jab from her elbow to his chin, snapping his head back. He let go of her hair involuntarily as he stumbled backward from the force of her blow. The gun fell in the grass beside him, but she didn't dare dive for it; it was too close to him, and he would catch her again.

And then she was yanked forward, Aaron's lightning quick move snatching her from Caleb's suddenly grasping hand, and they were running for the cover of the woods, Caleb's roar of rage chasing them like a bloodhound.

Lightning rent the sky and the rain clouds burst open, soaking them in seconds. Thunder boomed, masking the gunshot. Kim didn't realize Caleb had fired on them until the bark of the tree directly in front of them shattered, shooting painful splinters into their faces.

Scott had outpaced them, his car keys in his hand, but when he cast a look over his shoulder, what he saw made him whirl around. His foot skidded in the wet grass, and then he leaped into the air, colliding with her shoulder and knocking her into a filbert bush. A loud crack shattered the night. He spun a quarter turn in the air and rolled into the wet grass, where he writhed like a snake on fire.

Sheet lightning lit the clearing and bleached the color from Ron's face as he skidded on his knees to Scott's side. Kim fought free of the shrub and crawled over to them, knowing it was bad, knowing the bullet had hit even before Scott coughed and a river of blood flooded from his mouth.

"Oh God." Ron's words choked off. His fingers trembled violently as he ripped open his brother's jacket. Blood stained his tee-shirt – too much blood. It poured over Ron's hands as he tried to pressure-seal the wound. "Stay with me, Scotty, all right? It's not that bad. Stay with me."

Scott's hand flailed wildly in the air; Ron caught it, gripping it tight. Kim watched, speechless with horror. This couldn't be happening. Other people died, not people she knew, people she cared about.

Gasping for breath, Scott struggled to form words. "…mom…" he wheezed. Blood bubbled and trickled from the corner of his mouth. A convulsion wracked his body, and then he was still. Rain pooled in his open eyes. Tears spilled from Ron's eyes and splashed on his brother's cheek.

"Dammit, don't you die on me!"

But Scott was already gone.

A perfect rage propelled Ron to his feet, consuming him, driving all thought out of his mind but that of retribution. Kim screamed at him, snatching at his arm as he sprinted toward Caleb, but he was too fast. Caleb raised the gun again, taking aim – not at his nephew, but at Kimberly. And then Ron launched himself through the air, catching his uncle in the midriff in a tackle that would make a veteran NFL pro envious. The gun flew into the weeds. The men tumbled through the mud, fists swinging and legs kicking, rain pelting them with uncontrolled fury. Ron gained the upper hand and used it ruthlessly, sorrow driving him to the brink of a murderous frenzy.

"I'M GONNA KILL YOU, YOU SON OF A – "

Thunder crashed its cymbals, drowning Ron's furious expletive. He pistoned his fist into Caleb's ribs over and over. Caleb gave back as good as he got. If she wasn't so certain one of them would kill the other, if Scott wasn't lying dead in the grass, she'd be able to appreciate the raw power and brutality of this flawlessly executed battle.

Over the violence in the sky and the violence on the ground, she heard voices, shouting to be heard over the roaring storm. Her hour was up; the Circle had arrived. Brawling with Caleb was one thing, but they wouldn't be able to fight off so many.

She scrambled over to the fight, skidding on the wet grass, feet squelching in the mud. Her feet flew out from under her and she fell hard on her hip. The oozing mud cushioned her fall, but she still landed with enough force to snap her jaws closed, sending an ache through her teeth. She crawled the rest of the way, grabbed the back of Ron's jacket, and pulled herself to her feet, at the same time trying to extricate him from Caleb's grip. He saw her over Ron's shoulder and snarled a smile, blood smeared across his perfect white teeth.

"We have to go!" she screamed. The crack of thunder drowned out her words. She leaned closer to Ron's ear to shout again – too close – and shared Caleb's next blow. The impact knocked her off her feet and into the mud again, rain pouring into her face. Ron's fury built to a firestorm of epic proportions.

"YOU MOTHERFU – "

Caleb's next blow cut off his expletive. Ron flowed with the impact and snapped back around, his hands sliding across his uncle's slick skin to fasten around his neck and squeeze.

Kim shook off her daze and found her feet again, wading back in to the fight. She wrapped her arms around his chest from behind and yanked him backward. Caleb became her unwilling ally as he fought free of Ron's murderous grip. The men pulled apart with a suddenness that sent them both sprawling backward.

Caleb crawled away toward the gun. Kim grabbed Ron's arm and tried to drag him.

"WHAT ARE YOU DOING?" he raved, fighting free of her grip. *"I'M GOING TO KILL THAT SONOFABITCH!"*

"THE CIRCLE, AARON! THEY'RE HERE!"

She tugged his arm again, and at last he seemed to understand. He staggered to his feet as the first of Caleb's black magic cronies spilled into the clearing. The members of the Circle didn't appear to understand what they were seeing at first, which gave them a precious few seconds to slip closer to the tree line.

"KIMBERLEEEE!"

Caleb's shriek of fury rose above the howling storm. Kimberly threw a look over her shoulder and stopped cold. He held the gun aimed at her head. She imagined she could see down the oiled barrel to the bullet that would take her life. She didn't know if he could hit her from so far away, but she didn't doubt that anything could happen near this house of the damned.

Their eyes met across the distance, and for a moment it seemed that he stood right before her, so close she could see the striations of grey and gold in his ice-blue eyes.

He pulled the trigger.

Ron flung her into the forest, throwing his body over hers. They rolled through the shrubs and ferns as the bark exploded off the trunk of the tree they'd been standing by. Muffled shouts came from the clearing; Kim climbed to her feet in time to see a group of men detach from the others in the clearing, running toward Ron and her.

"We've gotta go." She looked down at him. He didn't move, just lay in the leaves with a fern frond, brown at the edges, stuck to his wet cheek. "Get up, come on. They're coming."

Still he didn't move, so she knelt beside him and forced her shoulder under his arm. Hectoring and nagging, dragging and shoving, she moved him deeper into the woods, slowly, step by painstaking step, until at last his feet moved of their own

* * * * *

The team was expertly trained in covert forest maneuvers, and they moved like shadows over the land bridge and through the trees and shrubs on either side of the deer trail leading to the clearing. Cody and Denny took the rear, guiding men into place with quiet voice commands over headsets.

He'd never know if it was the crack of thunder or a gunshot, or something even more sinister. Over the clatter of the torrential rain, it was impossible to distinguish the difference. The team halted, waiting for Cody's command to keep moving. Denny scouted ahead to discern the situation. He was gone too long. Cody's anxiety had swelled to a nearly unbearable pitch when his terse "All clear" finally came over the headset.

The team moved forward. Cody followed. Denny was waiting several yards from the clearing. He let the team go past him but blocked Cody's path. His face was white.

"What is it?"

"Boss, you should fall back and let us handle this."

"Why?" A tidal wave of dread mushroomed from his heart through his entire body. His hands seized the front of Denny's jacket, but he couldn't feel them. He felt only an overwhelming terror that swamped all other senses.

"Cody, go back to the command car. Please, man."

Cody flung him aside and sprinted ahead, pushing past his team, ripping out of their grasping hands, until at last he broke from the cover of the trees and into a nightmarish landscape: Caleb's men running toward the woods, Cody's men in pursuit; Caleb himself racing pell-mell for the cover of the house; a still form on the sodden ground, rain-soaked hair black in the dying light.

His heart stopped. His mind scrambled to surmount a blank wall. He could just make out the tell-tale shape of the Schaefer jawline, and his memory refused to identify the clothing.

He didn't know which of his sons lay dead in the grass.

A stumbling step forward, and then another, and then he was skidding on his knees in the rain and the blood, and his heart was breaking, flooding with anguish and horror and an awful, bitter vengeance. He lurched to his feet, spinning around. There it was, crouched in the center of the clearing like a bloated, poisonous beast, gloating at what it had taken from him, daring him to bring his vengeance. The Wyckham House.

His teeth bared in a snarl, and a primal scream welled up from deep inside. Before he could give it voice, a blinding flash of light seared the clearing and the surrounding woods, and a violent concussion knocked him to the ground.

When the spots cleared from his eyes, the clearing was empty but for a litter of bones where the house had stood.

The Wyckham House had vanished to its very last stone.

THE TEACHER OF ENCHANTMENTS

"We made a bargain."

Clothed as Sarah Bennett, the teacher of enchantments strolled casually around the altar, trailing its fingers over the comforter the woman had discarded when she fled.

"Events occurred that I couldn't have anticipated."

"I'm not interested in excuses. You think I don't know that you let her escape?

"*Let* her escape? I chased her down! I almost had her in the clearing. I did everything I could to –"

"*YOU DID WHAT YOU WANTED TO DO!*" the angel bellowed. Its voice rang through the ceremony room, amplified by the very stones of the house. "*YOU ALWAYS DO WHAT YOU WANT TO DO!*"

Caleb experienced real fear for the first time since his thirteenth year, when he had stumbled upon Sarah's cottage deep in the forest beyond the Wyckham House. He backed away from the altar.

"You let her go because she's *different*." It slurred the word, ridiculing him. "You lost your keys through carelessness and arrogance, but you let her go in the clearing through mercy. Tell me, Caleb – when do we ever show mercy?"

"Never," he replied numbly. He did not argue his case; Armaros was right. He had deliberately fired above Kimberly's head as she escaped into the forest; he'd been honest when he'd told her he might let her live. Killing Scott had been entirely an accident, but not one he lamented. He held no affection for Cody's son – indeed, he held affection for very few of his fellow humans – but in the moment he'd had the gun sighted on Kimberly, he could not bear to take her life.

"I am Armaros, the teacher of enchantments, and I demand something in return for my knowledge. Since I can't have the woman"—its eyes, swirling with angry flares of color, beamed a glare at him—"I'll have you."

He screamed as it seized him and spun him until he lost all sense of direction, folding him outside of time. And then the Wyckham House imploded, trapping him, because this house wasn't really a house, it was a vehicle through the earth, *of* the earth, that existed outside the human realm.

Armaros' infernal laughter was the last sound Caleb heard as darkness consumed him.

IN THE FOREST OF THE BEAST

Two hours later, drenched and half-frozen, Kim allowed a small break. Ron collapsed onto a fallen tree, his face so wet she couldn't distinguish tears from rain. She felt hollow inside, sick with shock and loss, but she couldn't stop now. He had to know the score.

"Ron, we're lost," she said simply. "I don't have your sense of direction. I don't know these woods. But we have to keep moving."

He stared at her with dead eyes. "Does it matter now?"

Kimberly grabbed the front of his coat and shook him angrily. "It matters to me! We're still alive! Think of Renée and Cody – can you let them lose both of you tonight?"

Ron closed his eyes. She had found a flashlight in the pocket of his jacket shortly after they had run into the woods; she didn't know why he hadn't used it in the house, but it didn't matter now. She clicked it on and shone it directly in his face. Despair swelled deep inside; he had given up, and she had no hope of surviving without his help. She set the flashlight on the log, knelt in front of him, and cupped his face in her hands.

"Do you love me?" He turned his face away; she persistently turned it back. "*Do* you?"

Finally, he opened his eyes to stare into hers with such a blank expression Kimberly was certain he'd lost his mind. In a wooden voice, he said, "Yes."

"Then *help* me! I need you, Aaron. I can't get out of the woods alone, and I won't leave you." She shook him furiously. "We leave together or we die together!"

Ron closed his eyes again and drew in a shaky breath. "All right," he said faintly. "All right. I'm okay."

He reached out to embrace her and froze as a wolf's howl wavered on the night air. Its rising and falling tones carried on the wind, a paralyzing serenade that invoked not desire but dread, and produced an instant and dramatic reaction in him. He popped up from the log, knocking the flashlight into the leaves, his eyes wide and panicked.

"We need to find a tree, preferably a maple – they're easier to climb. The higher off the ground we can get, the better." He retrieved the light, staring at it for a long moment. "Where'd you get this?"

"It was in your jacket pocket."

"That figures." He laughed, but it was a bitter sound that frightened her. "Damned angels," he muttered, grabbed her hand tightly, and headed into the forest away from the howl.

Kim couldn't remember when she first noticed snow had mixed in with the rain, creating a slushy mixture that pelted her face and numbed her flesh when the wind changed direction. The moon vanished behind heavy clouds, leaving behind a palpable darkness.

Her feet moved by instinct, but she could no longer feel them. Her hand, clutched tightly in Ron's, felt dead. When he stumbled – and he often did – she checked his momentum and kept him on his feet, her reactions automatic. Weary and half-asleep, she followed faithfully, simple trust moving one foot after another. After another.

The hours passed, interminable, agonizing. Blisters raised and broke on her heels from the friction between her skin and her wet socks. Her lungs and the muscles in her thighs burned. It became a nightmarish chore to lift her leg over fallen logs and exposed tree roots and climb into and out of shallow ravines. More than once she lost her footing and crashed to her knees in the brambles. Ron barely spoke even as he lifted her to her feet and brushed her off. His heart had shattered, all happiness bleeding into the ground with his brother's blood. Kimberly's own heart shrieked her sorrow to God, but she was beyond tears.

Ron stopped suddenly, turning the flashlight so they could see each other. The snowy rain had deposited icy jewels in his raven hair; frozen diamonds that matched his colorless face. His cheeks and forehead bore scratches from the whipping branches of shrubs and conifers.

"There's one. I think it's just what we're looking for." He pointed ahead and to the left of the faint deer trail they traveled. "Thank God – I don't think I could go another fifty feet without a rest."

"Me either."

She followed him under the boughs of the huge maple, where he boosted her onto the lowest branch. She was exhausted, but she gritted her teeth and pulled herself into the tree. He jumped to grab the branch and swung himself up. He almost didn't make it, and knowing his second attempt would likely not be as successful as his first, Kimberly grabbed his leg and pulled it over the branch. He scrambled up the tree like a monkey until he found a sturdy perch. Kim followed after him, not as confident but willing to get as high off the ground as possible. They huddled together on the high branch, her back to his front, pooling their body heat to ward off hypothermia. Two branches, slightly lower than their perch, provided comfortable foot rests.

"I need sleep," he mumbled, pressing both the flashlight and the pistol into her numb hands. "Just an hour or two…"

"I'll keep watch."

Ron slept, the tree trunk at his back preserving and reflecting enough of his body heat that he could catch some needed rest without risk of freezing. His arms around her kept Kim warm enough, but she was thankful for the biting cold. She knew if they both slept, they might fall out of the tree, and God knew what might be waiting on the ground.

"Kim! Wake up!"

His whisper coaxed her out of disturbing dreams. She opened her eyes reluctantly to the soft glow of the flashlight. The storm had not abated during his watch; the wind gusted around them, driving freezing rain into the tree behind them. The maple's trunk blocked most – but not all – of it. The secret sound of rain in the forest should have been soothing, but the terror in Ron's eyes erased any comfort she might have found.

"What is it?" she asked, taking his cue and speaking in a whisper.

"I'm not sure." He moved closer to whisper directly in her ear.

"The howling has come closer over the last half hour, and now it's stopped altogether."

She nodded, unable to speak. She wanted to curl up, hide her face, and not look until morning, because she knew what stalked them: a werewolf. Her father.

He pressed his cheek to hers, his arms tightening around her. "It's after two in the morning. We only have five hours till sunrise. We can make it. We're safe up here."

"Ron, you know what's chasing us. And you know who it is."

"I know," he said quietly. "I'm sorry." He cocked his head, listening for a moment, and then pressed a finger to her lips. "Shush. I heard something."

He cocked his head, turning his ear in the direction from which he'd heard the sound. She fell silent, listening, but her heart thudded too loudly to hear anything over the roar of her pulse. She leaned forward to hear better.

It happened suddenly with no warning whatsoever. The branch beneath her right foot cracked and parted from the tree. Kimberly, balanced heavily on it to shift position, tumbled to the ground. Ron shouted in alarm and scurried down the branches as fast as he could move.

She managed to grab the lowest branch, but she gained too much velocity to keep hold of it. Several inches of humus cushioned her fall, and she lay stunned at the foot of the maple. Ron shone the flashlight down; the beam barely cut through the night.

"Give me your hand!" He leaned out of the tree as she stood up, extending his hand.

"I can't reach!" She stood several inches too short.

"I'm coming down." He lowered himself out of the tree and landed beside her, clumsy with exhaustion. "You all right? Come on, I'll lift you back up." He cupped his hands and bent down.

A low growl came from the shrubbery twenty feet behind them. They froze. Petrified could not even begin to define her state of being. She thought her very molecules would explode from fear.

"We're in trouble," he whispered, a newsflash Kimberly didn't need. "Slow movements. Maybe it won't attack if we move slowly."

Kimberly had a differing opinion, but she also had no alternative. She stepped slowly into the stirrup of his linked hands. The animal snarled a warning. Ron lifted her slowly. She grabbed the branch but before she could hoist herself onto it, the shrubs rustled and a nightmare sprang into their midst, a bulky beast like a timber wolf on steroids, with a smashed-snouted face and two-inch fangs.

Ron let go of her foot and reached slowly into his pocket for his Glock. Kimberly, lacking the upper body strength to pull herself onto the branch without his help, tumbled back into the humus, this time landing on her feet. The wolf took this as a menacing movement and sprang.

"*Run!*" Ron screamed. He grabbed her hand and sprinted down the deer trail. The wolf shot past where they'd stood, unable to check its momentum. It recovered quickly and gave chase for only a brief second before suddenly veering off into the thicket. Ron didn't for a moment think it had given up the hunt; it had simply employed an instinctive tactical maneuver.

Rivulets of snowy rainwater trickled down the back of Kim's coat and into the waistband of her jeans. Wind whipped the trees into a frenzy, which slapped and tore at flesh already aching and raw from the elements. She fought a rising panic at the odd form of déjà vu washing over her; her dream unfolded before her, second by horrifying second.

Ron led the way at a breakneck pace. His broad back kept most of the freezing rain from her face. He didn't fare as well; he faced the forceful gales of the late autumn storm that drove rain and snow into his skin like tiny bullets. The moisture froze to his eyelashes, and he squinted to protect his vision. He looked over his shoulder to check the path behind her and stopped abruptly, catching her as she ran into him. They danced around wildly for a moment before regaining their balance.

"What is it?"

"My dream – I dreamed this before I came to Mills! Ron, we have to stop running. We have to get into a tree again."

"We don't have time!"

"We can't outrun it, and we have five hours until dawn!"

He blinked as a sudden forceful gust of wind blew rain into his eyes. "In your dream...do we live?"

She shrugged helplessly. "I don't know."

Ron grimaced and took her hand again. "Come on. We'll find a tree."

The woods conspired against them. Trees grew closely spaced, and the sweeping boughs of massive conifers stole the sunlight from the deciduous saplings struggling to survive. Here and there a cluster of birch showed white faces in the dying beam of the flashlight, but no promising maples or oaks seemed to grow in this area. They came to the edge of a meadow, and Ron stopped again. The storm clouds broke apart, and moonlight flooded the clearing. Grass rippled as the wind swept over it, drenched stalks sparkling silver in the moonlight. The deer trail showed as a dark track winding its way to the other side.

"What do you want to do? Circle the edge and stay in the woods, or go across the meadow?"

Kim shrugged wearily. "I don't much care, Ron. Either way means more walking." They would have no cover if they crossed the meadow. Their progress would be slow and difficult if they stayed in the forest. She liked neither option but could not come up with any alternatives.

He sent her a worried look. Exhausted and limping, she looked as though she'd reached the end of her reserves. Fear and determination had kept her on her feet this long, but she badly needed food and rest or she would collapse. He had little hope she could remain conscious another five hours.

"Let's go across the meadow. Be alert; we'll have no cover." Ron took the Glock out of his pocket and checked the clip, and stepped into the clearing.

As though on cue, the ululating call of a wolf shattered the night. Every hair on Kimberly's body stiffened in terror. Impossible to gauge the direction from which the howl came, Ron broke into a run, his vision narrowing so he could see only his target: a maple with navigable branches on the other side of the meadow.

Kimberly's fight-or-flight instinct flooded her system with too much adrenaline, and she felt weak and helpless. Ron threw a look behind him to see if anything followed them, and the motion gave her an unobstructed view of the meadow. A dark form leaped from the forest into the clearing ahead of them. She screamed and Ron stopped abruptly. She barreled into him full-force, knocking them both to the ground. He skidded several feet closer to the wolf on the slick grass. Kim crawled toward him, certain she didn't possess the energy to rise this time. When she looked up, she knew she would have to.

The wolf stopped several yards from Ron, dropped into a crouch, and crept slowly forward, teeth bared in a growl they couldn't hear over the storm. Ron frantically searched the grass for the gun he had dropped when he fell. Kim saw it on the deer trail behind him.

"Behind you!"

Lightning flared like a nuclear blast. Ron stumbled to his feet and took a careful step backward. Thunder boomed. The wolf's lips curled back from its teeth. Kim tried to stand but couldn't make her trembling legs hold her weight.

As Ron dove for the gun, the beast leaped into the air, jaws open wide for a killing blow. Man and wolf flew through the night, over her head, and rolled through the grass mere feet behind her, Ron screaming, the wolf snarling.

Kimberly lunged for the gun, catching the eye of the beast. It released Ron's shoulder, blood dripping from its fangs. She couldn't look away from its snarling mouth; she'd never seen fangs so large. Its bloody snout rippled with a snarl, and it fixed her with a stare that glowed green with reflected light from the moon. Ron rolled onto his side, shrieking as the curse worked its torturous venom through his blood.

Her hands were too numb to grip the gun. She dropped it, and the wolf feinted an attack. She ducked down, her eyes never leaving the animal, and felt around for the weapon, yanking it out of the leaves as the wolf hurtled toward her. She was going to die.

She swung the gun up in a wild motion and pulled the trigger. It jumped violently in her hand, and the wolf plummeted to the ground, rolling several times. Kim fell to her knees, flinging the weapon from her numb fingers, curling into herself. *Daddy, oh God, Daddy, I'm so sorry. I'm so sorry!*

Ron, lying several feet away, groaned thickly, hands clutching the left side of his chest. She wiped her nose on her sleeve and crawled across the muddy ground to his side. Lightning flashed, allowing her to see the dark stain of blood covering his chest and shoulder. The wolf's fangs had missed his arteries by mere inches. His forehead was scorching against her icy hand. A curse-fever. She worried her lower lip; perhaps the myths were wrong and silver did nothing to end a werewolf's curse. Or maybe Ron's Glock had not been loaded with silver bullets after all.

Kimberly pushed to her feet and staggered to the wolf. It lay on its side, a neat bullet hole through the center of its forehead. Given the weather conditions, her numb hands, and the terror that had made her tremble violently, she should not have made this shot.

The beast's bones began to crack and shift. Fur retracted into stretching skin with a revolting shivery sound. Kim backed away in horror, unable to scream or look away, gripped by a queasy fascination as the wolf took human form.

And then she froze, bewildered, silently gaping at the tableau before her in the grass: a nude male figure with black magic marker letters scrawled hastily over his bony chest, giving her the only explanation she might ever receive – or ever need. *REVERSAL.*

Harlan Michaels lay dead at her feet, a bracelet of diamond-studded gold links around his left wrist.

COMMITMENT

Her stomach roiling, Kimberly knelt in the grass beside the constable. Her numb fingers scrabbled at the bracelet's clasp and finally succeeded in releasing it. She held the gold links to the moonlight, making the diamonds sparkle. Todd's bracelet, without a doubt. She pocketed it, wondering how Harlan came to be wearing it, and why, taking the curse upon himself, he hadn't made sure he was locked up so he couldn't hurt anyone.

She wiped tears from her cheeks before they could freeze. Her shaking fingers traced the ragged black letters on his skin. She could almost see him, chin bent to his chest, left hand stretching the skin so his right hand could form the scraggly, jagged letters. *REVERSAL.* Her father's salvation.

Kim drew a ragged breath and laid her hand over Harlan's still heart. "Thank you," she whispered. She stood with difficulty and staggered back to where Aaron lay unconscious in the grass. Kimberly stared at him blankly for a moment.

"Great." She didn't know how she was going to get him to his feet, but there was no one else to do it. Dropping to her knees beside him, she draped his right arm over her shoulder, and tried to lift. Predictably, she couldn't budge him.

A dip in the ground near his shoulder yielded a puddle of ice-cold rainwater. Kim eyed it balefully and huffed out a sigh, reluctantly dipping her hands into it.

He stirred at the cold splash on his face, but he could by no means be considered conscious. Pinching, slapping, and shaking him proved just as fruitless. Kim gazed at the ragged, bloody tears in his coat. There was nothing else she could do, so she gritted her teeth and pressed down hard on his wounds. Ron screamed his agony to the sky.

"I'm sorry! I'm sorry!" She took his chin in her hand, forcing his fevered gaze to her face. "Ron, *please*. You have to help me. We have to find shelter or we're going to freeze to death."

He blinked against the rain in his eyes, rolled onto his right side, and threw up. He dragged himself a few feet away and collapsed again, panting heavily. "Go on. I'm done for."

"Don't you say that!" Kim shouted angrily. "Don't you dare give up! You get on your feet, Aaron, or so help me – "

"All right, all right!" he interrupted weakly. He held his arm up, and Kimberly crouched down, wedged her shoulder beneath his armpit and circled her arms around his waist, and pulled him slowly from the ground. His feet scrabbled on the wet grass to gain purchase, skidded, and he spilled to the earth on his injured shoulder.

Kim flinched as he screamed, but she couldn't afford to pamper him. She positioned herself again, and with the last of her strength lifted him to his feet. He swayed dangerously, and she eyed him with growing trepidation. *Infection is the biggest worry with field wounds,* Kim could hear her father saying. *Keep it clean and keep it dry.* Having returned from two weeks in the wilderness with an Air Force survival instructor, Todd had been bursting with knowledge he couldn't wait to impart to his less than enthusiastic daughter.

I wish I'd listened more closely now. I could use an Air Force survivalist right about now. She could keep Ron neither clean nor dry in their present environment.

"Which way do I go?"

"Home," he mumbled. "I don't...can't see the trail..." He slumped heavily against her, and she struggled valiantly to balance the shift in weight. He clearly clung to consciousness through superhuman effort, and with a sinking heart she realized he could offer no help. He probably couldn't string a coherent sentence together.

"I'm a city girl," she muttered heavenward. "What were You thinking?"

Lightning flared across the sky, lighting up the meadow for a brief but illuminating second. Less than a hundred feet away at the edge of the clearing stood a huge hemlock, with graceful, sweeping boughs that brushed the forest floor. It would do.

She prodded Ron in the ribs, making his eyes spring open. "No sleeping on the job, big guy. I need your help."

One foot after another, after another became Kim's mantra as they crossed the meadow at a snail's pace. The effort cost Ron everything he had. When at long last they reached the sanctuary of the hemlock, he tumbled to the ground, gasping for breath.

Kim shone the flashlight around to get a sense of their shelter. A thick layer of fragrant needles would provide a comfortable enough bed; she shoveled a large drift of them around him to preserve his body heat. His feverish gaze found her in the gloom.

"Not…a normal wound," he said through gritted teeth. "Did you…know?"

"Yes." Kim didn't know what could be done for a wound inflicted by a supernatural being. The werewolf lay dead, its curse on its victims ended, but what damage had the injuries already caused?

"Should I try to find wood and build a fire? I don't know if there's any that isn't soaking wet."

"No way…to light it," he muttered, pain tightening his voice.

"Don't you have a lighter?"

"I quit smoking."

Kimberly smiled a little. "Why did you go and do a thing like that?"

"You," he said simply, and closed his eyes again.

She laid down close to him, gathering needles around herself, and let him sleep, keeping a close ear on his breathing in case it became labored. She didn't know what she would do if it did; they had traveled miles into the forest and were good and lost. It could take days to find their way out. By then infection could have poisoned his blood. Her mind sifted through the bits of herbal lore she'd come across over the years, but she couldn't come up with a single natural antibiotic other than honey. She doubted she'd find any here.

Don't let him die! Oh God, please don't let him die, not now, not after we made it this far!

The night rolled unhurriedly toward the dawn. Sunrise blushed the sky with muted tones of gold and mauve; the storm had passed, leaving behind a clear, cold day. Kim took careful note of a distinctive tree where the sun ascended, and roused Ron.

In too much physical discomfort to sleep deeply, he woke easily.

Shocked at his gray pallor, Kim pulled his coat aside to examine the wounds. His tee-shirt stuck in the gashes, so she collected icy rainwater to soak it off. Once the fabric gave way, Kimberly gasped, bile rising in her throat, propelled by panic.

Four diagonal slashes, angry red and inflamed, ran from collarbone to breastbone. Livid puncture wounds from the werewolf's teeth lined his shoulder. Blood crusted the injuries, dried to a thick, red coat across his chest and down his back. A *lot* of blood.

"I have to clean this. You have two choices: now or later?"

"Now," he said, clenching his teeth against her poking and prodding.

She found a small rock with a sharp edge and cut a large strip from the hem of the hoodie he'd loaned her. A puddle not far from the hemlock gave her clear, cold water. She soaked the cloth strip and set to work. The blood came away easily enough except directly around the wounds, where it had coagulated in thick, black-red clumps. Kim dabbed at these and let the cloth soak the blood loose for as long as he could stand the icy water. White-faced, he bore the pain, imprisoning his scream behind clenched teeth. Finally, he grabbed her wrist to stay her hand.

"No more."

Kim stared at the crusted gashes uncertainly. *Clostridium tetani and staphylococcus are just two of the bacteria found in dirt,* her phantom father enthused. She looked up at him, taking in his fever-bright eyes. Sweat stood out on his face despite the cold, and he trembled from head to foot. Shock would be his worst enemy now.

"All right," she agreed reluctantly. "But I'll have to do this again later. It has to be clean." She cut another swatch from her hem to bind his wound. "I hope this jacket wasn't one of your favorites."

"Not...anymore," he replied weakly.

She wound the damp material under his arm and over his shoulder to pad the wounds as much as possible, and tied it on with the drawstring from the hem of her coat. She stuffed his arm back into his tee-shirt and jacket and let him rest for a few minutes.

"It's serious damage, Ron. We have to get you to a doctor. Are you going to be able to guide me?"

"We'll see."

Fabulous, she thought. I'm on my own. *Moss grows on the north side of the trees,* her memory offered. She saw several specimens nearby completely encased in light green moss. *This whole freakin' forest faces north then.*

There was no reason to procrastinate; they had no food and sleeping would be impossible in the cold, so Kim ducked under Ron's good arm and helped him to his feet. He leaned against the tree trunk, dizzy and sweating, while Kim selected a course.

They headed into the forest, the sun at their backs. As she walked, the links of the gold bracelet clinked in her pocket.

She thought she had done a fair job of not following the sun as it completed its journey across the sky, but shortly after noon Ron made her stop to rest by the simple expedient of tumbling to the ground. He propped himself against a tree on a cushion of soft damp moss, panting heavily, and judged their location from the position of the sun.

"We should be going that way – west. You're heading northwest, toward the mountains."

Kim shook her head in self-disgust. "I'm no good at this."

He didn't respond; he had spent the hours unable to offer any real help as he wandered in and out of delirium, fever burning through his body.

"Do *not* take that as an accusation," she said sharply. "This isn't your fault. It's mine."

"Not your fault you were blessed with precognitive dreams and not a sense of direction," he argued reasonably.

Kim nodded. No, not her fault, but a sense of direction would have been more useful in their present circumstances. He wouldn't make it much farther today; if they didn't find a road, they would spend another night in the cold. Wounded already, it would be a miracle if he didn't end up with pneumonia. She looked up toward the sun and couldn't help thinking, *A little help would be useful down here!*

"I'm hungry," she said a little while later. He opened his eyes; sweat stood out on his blanched face and his gaze was fever-bright.

"Me too."

"Do you think we'll make it out of here?"

He shrugged with his good shoulder, wincing as the movement pulled at his crusted wounds. "We leave together or we die together, Kimberly."

She smiled. "That's not a bad motto."

He smiled back and corrected gently, "That's not a motto. It's a commitment."

SANCTUARY

Just past three o'clock, they came upon a stand of Virginia creeper cascading from a large oak tree in a preening display of crimson. Kimberly stared at it for a long moment through a haze of exhaustion and pain, and then turned and headed toward it. Ron, virtually asleep on his feet, did not rouse as she aimed them into the thicket.

The sun dipped low in the sky to her right, telling Kimberly they traveled more or less south. She felt certain they would eventually stumble upon a road if they continued to move in this direction.

The creeper became her beacon; she searched for its blazing color against the green backdrop of the gloomy forest, moving from one glorious display to another. Ron murmured incoherently, and she knew his condition deteriorated every minute he didn't receive medical care. She prayed she had chosen wisely; following the red vine through the forest seemed a whimsical, frivolous thing to do when she thought about it logically. When she set logic aside, however, it appeared to be the only sensible choice.

Just before the sun set below the treetops, he slid from her grasp and fell into the mud, unconscious. She checked his wounds as she had every hour since they left the shelter of the hemlock that morning. The gashes and punctures had grown worse as the day progressed, becoming inflamed and filled with pus. Infection had set in, and the close proximity of the wounds to his heart deeply frightened her.

She settled him more comfortably and took stock of her surroundings. This patch of forest had not grown as thick as the area they had traveled through last night. In fact, the way had grown easier, the deer trail wider, as though well-used by efficient trailblazers.

"I'll be right back," she murmured, touching his cheek.

Kim could see the next swatch of crimson through the murky light, no more than ten yards away. She made her way carefully to it, scuffing decaying leaves and pine needles into piles so she could navigate her way back to Ron.

The trail curved to the left just past the creeper. She peeked around the bend, and gasped in shock. Expecting to see the forest stretching endlessly before her, instead she found a small hunting cabin. She blinked, then closed her eyes and pinched herself. Afraid to look in case the cabin proved to be a mirage, she reluctantly peeled open one eyelid. Not a hallucination, then. The cabin nestled in a small clearing, tidy and well kept. Split tamarack logs formed two neat rows along the side of the small structure. The gurgle of water from a brook close by almost made her cry.

She hurried back to Ron, laying her cold hands on his face to rouse him. He blinked at her blearily, but she didn't believe he was coherent.

"I found a cabin. Come on, you have to help me."

He couldn't provide much help. Weak and feverish, he staggered and nearly fell once she got him upright. The last leg of this day's journey became the most difficult. Half an hour later, she pounded on the cabin door.

No one answered, and she could hear no movement inside when she put her ear to the door. She raised her hand to knock again.

"Kim," Ron panted. "Just try the door and go in if it's unlocked. I can't stand much longer."

The knob turned easily, granting them entrance. She guided him into a sturdy wooden chair at a small dining table and closed the door. Shadows filled the cabin, but it didn't take her long to find a lantern. The strike of a waterproof match, a huff of igniting propane, and light banished the darkness to the farthest corners of the room.

Decorated in no-frills Spartan style, the cabin nevertheless provided their every immediate need. Canned food, MREs, a sealed plastic bag containing books of waterproof matches, propane for the lantern and the camp stove on the kitchenette counter. A wood stove occupied the corner to the right of the door, a stack of split tamarack and chunks of seasoned maple conveniently stacked nearby.

Heat topped her list of priorities. She filled the stove with wood and kindling she found in a half-whiskey barrel and set it aflame. Ron slept upright in the chair, his cheek pressed against the wall. Kim left him there while she found a large stock pot and a plastic pitcher and filled them at the brook.

A large cedar cabinet in one corner yielded plastic-wrapped blankets and pillows and, wonder of wonders, several pairs of well-worn sweats and thick, clean socks. Kim eyed the bedding, perplexed, until she realized a bed folded down from the wall.

The stockpot heating on the camp stove, she pushed her exhaustion aside long enough to accomplish the necessities. The Murphy bed came down easily on oiled hinges, revealing a feather mattress encased in plastic to keep bugs out. She made the bed and laid out clean clothes and first aid supplies, then woke Ron again. He needed help to strip off his wet clothes and don sweat pants and dry socks; Kimberly assisted, her face flaming. She'd envisioned undressing him any number of times in her daydreams but never under such drastic circumstances. His tee-shirt had dried to his seeping wounds and had to be soaked off, a chore which proved as bad as she had suspected. At last she had him stuffed into bed; fed and watered, dosed with aspirin, clean and dry, wounds disinfected and liberally coated with antibiotic ointment and fresh bandages, Ron slept.

Finally able to tend her own wounds, Kimberly stripped off her own wet, dirty clothes. Her socks were a mess of blood and dirt but since they had been wet all day, they didn't stick. The blisters had broken and rubbed raw until they'd spread into large patches of bloody flesh. With a glance at the bed to make sure he was asleep, she examined the gash in her arm where Caleb had taken her blood and the spreading stain of purple bruise in the shape of a man's fingers on her right breast. Those would heal and fade, but what he had done to her psyche was something she feared worse than the physical scars he had given her.

Although she wanted nothing more than to lie down and sleep, she soaked her feet in warm water for twenty minutes, bandaged her feet and arm, and pulled on sweats and socks with a sigh of pleasure.

An MRE quieted her rumbling stomach, and a cup of instant coffee warmed her insides. The wood stove had warmed the room nicely, and at long last she allowed herself to relax.

Firelight played off Aaron's face as she watched him, her teeth gnawing her lower lip. Thoughts of home brought more matters to worry over: Scott's death, her father's whereabouts and condition, the tawny cat that housed Elizabeth Peterson's soul.

And how was she going to tell him that the love of his life had not been lost to him all these years but had lived in his house in the body of a cat?

Exhaustion bowed her shoulders, and she pushed the worries away for the moment. Tomorrow would bring whatever it would, and she could not stop it. Time now for rest and renewal.

She stoked the fire, blew out the lantern, and crawled under the covers next to Ron. His fevered skin threw off waves of heat that kept her warm, and she fell asleep to the comforting rhythm of his breathing.

Kimberly awoke well into the morning, cozy and comfortable, her back pressed snugly against Ron's side and his good arm circled round her, his hand resting on her ribs. He was still too warm. Kim frowned, worried.

"Mmmm. You make it difficult for a man to be a gentleman," he murmured into her hair, erasing her frown.

"Just watch it, mister. No Russian hands and Roman fingers."

"Ruin all my fun," he said. He kissed her ear and sat up, grimacing.

"How do you feel?"

"Like I was attacked by a werewolf. Hurts like Hades, but I feel like a new man today – fangs, fur, curse and all."

"Oh, stop." She rolled onto her back and stared up at him. He looked positively dangerous, like a landlocked pirate, his hair unkempt and two days' beard coloring his jaw. He turned and smiled, catching her watching him, but she thought there was a certain reserve in his manner. And so it began, the breaking of her heart.

The morning passed in relative silence as they prepared to leave.

Kim put away the bedding, stocked the woodpile by the stove, and scattered the embers of the fire while Ron prepared their meal. With no idea of how long they would have to travel, she filled a pillowcase with MREs and a couple of plastic bottles of water she had found in the cupboard. It would tide them over for a while, at any rate.

Her last task, once the cabin had been restored to its original condition, was to change his dressings. She gazed with concern at the torn and bitten flesh, still inflamed and oozing pus.

"It's bad, isn't it?" Ron asked quietly. He could see the slashes, but not the bite wounds.

"Bad enough and getting worse. I'd better take some medical supplies with us. I don't know how long we'll have to walk."

"Not long, I'd wager. This cabin is obviously well-stocked and frequently used. I doubt its owners would want to walk too far to get here. We'll probably find a road a mile or two from here provided we take the right trail."

She smoothed the last strip of first aid tape over the gauze bandage and helped him maneuver back into his sweatshirt. As she bent near, his good arm slid around her, pulling her to him. She didn't realize she was crying until he brushed his fingers across her cheek, smearing her tears.

"Kim, don't cry. It will be all right."

"He's dead because of me. How can you not hate me for that?"

"I could never hate you," he whispered. "None of this is your fault. Now stop." He let her go, trying a smile that turned into a grimace of pain. "Let's get out of here. I want out of this damn forest."

The trail proved easy to find; it was the only one sporting four-wheeler tracks. Kim didn't know how far they would have to go until they reached the road; if the cabin's owners came in by vehicle, she and Ron might be in for another marathon walk.

He retreated into grim silence, holding his pain – both physical and emotional – behind clenched jaws, forcing himself to keep moving despite his exhaustion. She wished for rain so she could cry and not worry him.

Their walk ended abruptly four and a half miles from the cabin at a two-lane, blacktop road. She stared at the dark ribbon winding into the distance, unable to quite believe what she saw. Ron sat down hard in the grass by the shoulder; he might have felt renewed when he woke this morning, but the journey, though short by recent standards, had sapped any strength he had gained overnight.

She sat down beside him, watching the road in both directions. Birds chirped and whistled in the trees around them, and she thought if they could remain suspended in this moment, she would be happy enough.

A car passed, heading west, but the little old lady driving either didn't see them or didn't want to stop. Kim couldn't blame her, although she felt disheartened to see the taillights of the old Impala fading in the distance.

They passed the next hour and a half in complete silence. Ron eased himself down onto the grass, his head resting on her thigh, and lapsed into fevered sleep. Immersed in sorrow and exhaustion, she didn't even hear the vehicle approaching. When a woman's voice called out to her, she stared at the minivan as though seeing a mirage.

"Do you need help?"

Kim looked at Ron's pale face, at the blood seeping through his bandages and staining his sweatshirt, and burst into tears. Need help? Did they ever.

* * * * *

Todd Garrett turned his face to what would have been a glorious sunrise had he not been so cold, tired, and hungry. He stretched his stiff limbs and shifted on his branch, wincing at the pain in his backside. He'd spent thirty-two of the last forty-eight hours tied to this tree, safely off the ground. If he became a werewolf, he didn't want to hurt anyone. If he *didn't* change, he didn't want to *be* hurt by anyone.

A careless boater had unknowingly provided him with everything he needed to stay dry and secured in the tall oak tree he had selected. A tarp, a yellow ski rope, a wind-up flashlight, and three Baby Ruth candy bars seemed like a king's ransom to a man on the lam from murderous occultists.

When he woke the first morning and found himself still tied to the tree, he figured he must have judged the moon cycle incorrectly or he had changed in his sleep, couldn't get free, and didn't realize it. He rather doubted the latter; what he understood from Alonzo Stafford's book, so kindly provided to him by Tiana Michaels, the transformation into werewolf form proved extremely painful. So he had tied himself up a second night and kept himself awake through sheer force of will. Todd knew now he had not transformed; therefore, either he had been lied to about the Circle's curse, or the spell itself had failed.

It took him nearly two hours to untie the complicated knots in the ski rope. His fingers were numb and when he had tied them, he had meant them to hold.

Finally free, Todd climbed out of the oak and set off on a deer trail toward civilization.

AFTERMATH
November 3, 2004

Aftermath.

Kimberly contemplated the various applications of that word to the current situation. Was aftermath the devastation Cody and Renée were weathering at the loss of their son? Was aftermath the horror of finding Scott's body in the Wyckham House clearing, a horror Cody would live with for the remainder of his days?

Or perhaps aftermath was the shadow of the supernatural that lurked in everyone's eyes, the scars Aaron Schaefer and Anna Malone would bear on their bodies and hearts for the rest of their lives, the twitchy paranoia that made her father jump when startled, the arrests and the impending trials for those of the Circle who had been discovered with blood on their hands.

Maybe aftermath was Harlan Michael's body lying in a remote meadow, slowing becoming a permanent part of the landscape – and her father, who wrestled with his conscience over the man who had sacrificed himself to a wicked curse in order to return Todd to his daughter unscathed.

Or aftermath could be the young witch with silver-blonde hair whose black magic had backfired, addling her brains. There was not much he could tell her, but Cody had confided that Nadine had *seemed* to be all right until the precise moment the Wyckham House had vanished from sight. Now she raved and sobbed and shouted nonsense, tearing at her hair and clothes until she had to be restrained. She would not be leaving the top-secret medical facility to which she'd been sent the night she attacked Kim.

Aftermath was all of these, but most of all, for Kim, it was the unfathomable relief of seeing her father, starved and tired but whole, limp into her hospital room in Scranton; and at the same time, it was the silent breaking of her heart as she watched Ron struggle to accept what had happened to him so many years ago, and how that cataclysmic event had spilled over, with tragic consequences, into his life today.

The cat was dead. Its fluffy body, matted with blood, had been found in the clearing with those of Scott Schaefer and Tiana Michaels – and piles of bones like driftwood, some so old it would take a forensic anthropologist to date and identify them. Kim had no idea how or why Taffy had been at the Wyckham House, but because she had, Elizabeth Peterson was finally free.

Caleb Schaefer had vanished like smoke. This, perhaps, was the most perplexing event other than the Wyckham House itself disappearing. The roads into and out of Mills and the clearing the Wyckham House had occupied had been under careful surveillance by Cody's team. Nothing should have been able to get past them, and yet Caleb was gone without a trace.

The front door opened and a large shadow fell between her and the porch light. Aaron claimed the empty space beside her and awkwardly handed her a steaming mug. A sling held his left arm immobile so he wouldn't pop his stitches. He had strict orders not to use the arm at all until the stitches came out, not even to carry a mug of –

"What's this?" Kim asked, smiling.

"Tom & Jerry, courtesy of your manic friend." He patted his stomach. "If she doesn't go home soon, I'm going to weigh three hundred pounds."

Kimberly snorted and sniffed the air experimentally. "There's peach cobbler in the oven, by the way. I know that smell anywhere."

Infuriated by Kim's silence, Bethany Fairchild – the *real* Bethany Fairchild – had descended on his house two days ago – the day he'd discharged himself from the Community Medical Center in Scranton against all medical advice. Kim, Cody, and Ron had arrived back at the house to find her fuming in the kitchen, preparing a massive pan of spinach manicotti and muttering imprecations under her breath. She'd had full command of the Schaefer abode since her arrival, freeing Renée to grieve in peace and Cody to handle the enormous task of investigating the Circle and its members. Kim didn't know where he found time to grieve; the circles under his eyes grew deeper with each passing hour as he worked tirelessly to hunt down every last member of Caleb's cult, and it had been days since she'd seen even a ghost of his smile. He was working himself into exhaustion, the investigation his vengeance on those who had stolen his son's life. Those in the Circle who came under his brutal scrutiny came to fear him nearly as much as they had feared his brother.

"What are you going to do now, Ron? Somehow I just can't see you reopening the tavern."

"I'm going to sell it." He sipped his drink and grimaced when the hot liquid burned his lip. "I have a degree in horticulture, and I own a lot of land. I think I'll open a greenhouse. Sell plants."

"That'd be nice," she agreed. "Although you seem a little manly to be cultivating flowers."

"You and Denny," he growled, setting his mug on the porch railing. He stared out at the twilight sky – a sky colored the exact shade of blue as his eyes. "I'm just a romantic at heart, I guess. I'll grow you roses and lilacs and honeysuckle. But no tulips."

She frowned. "Why no tulips? I like tulips."

"Because." He lifted her hand and kissed the back of it. "These two lips are all you need."

"That was very corny," she said, laughing, but a slow flush heated her body, and her heart thrilled at the touch of his lips.

"Yeah, I amaze even myself sometimes." He set the swing in

motion, his socked foot pushing against the railing. Kim pulled her own socked foot up under the blanket. Neither could comfortably wear shoes yet, although tomorrow Kim would have to suffer through. She and Todd were scheduled to fly out of Scranton in the early afternoon.

He had tried to talk her out of it, and God knew she was tempted. She couldn't seem to make him understand her belief that he needed time to come to terms with everything they had learned. She had no clue how you wrapped your mind around becoming a werewolf or around the bizarre phenomenon of the soul of your fiancée being trapped in the body of a house cat for eleven years. But she did know you didn't come to terms with such events in less than a week.

"You're still leaving tomorrow?" he asked after a moment. She nodded, unable to voice her answer. He drew in a breath and let it out in a sigh. "I feel like you're not so much leaving Mills as you're leaving me."

She looked up, startled, catching the sad twist of his lips. "No, not ever. I just...I can't even begin to comprehend how you must feel with everything that's happened, everything we've learned. And this thing between us..."

"I believe it's called love," he said with amusement.

"When I'm with you, it's like your presence overwhelms my senses. I forget to breathe, I forget everything but you."

"It's no different for me."

"I have to learn how to manage it."

"How are you going to do that three thousand miles away from me?" he demanded, exasperated.

"I don't know," she admitted crossly. "I just feel that it's the right thing to do."

"Running is what you're doing. And everyone expected me to be the one doing it."

"I'm not running. I'm...I'm learning to cope."

He smirked, and she could clearly see his thought. *Yeah, coping by running.* She decided a change of subject was needed.

"Dad brought up an interesting point yesterday."

"Oh yeah?"

"He wondered why we didn't run into the woods toward the cottage. We didn't have to go through what we did."

Ron stared at her silently. For his part, he wouldn't change a thing as he thought back over the two days they'd spent slogging through the woods, lost and cold and hungry. From the headlong flight into the forest to the moment Kimberly killed the werewolf and finally to her obstinate refusal to give up until she'd led them out of the wilderness – it all blurred in his mind. He'd made a promise to Andy Malone, and that alone would have taken him into the forest.

But in the end, the only thing clear centered on Kimberly and him. God had woven them together with every kiss they shared, had shown them each what lay at the core of the other so trust would grow and fractured souls would mend. The hours spent slogging through the rain and muck, huddled together for warmth in a maple tree…those events created the ties that bound him to her, joyfully and irrevocably.

He replied softly, "Yes, we did."

Kim took his hand and squeezed it. Ron laced his fingers through hers, savoring the contact. Tomorrow she would leave, and God knew when he would see her again.

He tugged her over to lean against his uninjured side, releasing her hand to put his arm around her. She snuggled in, and he wished they never had to move from this spot. *If wishes were horses…*

As though reading his thought, she murmured, "We'll sit out here every morning, drinking our coffee. And every evening for the sunset after the kids go to bed. And when we have summer thunderstorms, we'll be safe and dry right here while we watch."

"And we'll eat blackberries from the garden over homemade vanilla ice cream," he whispered. "I'll cut you bouquets of roses and lilacs – "

"But no tulips," Kim finished.

He turned her face up to his. "Because these two lips are all you need," he whispered back, and sealed the promise with a kiss.

"Do you have everything, sweetie?" Renée fretted.

Kim set her suitcase down at the head of the porch steps. "I think so."

"Beth's sweater? And her curling iron?"

"In my suitcase." Bethany had returned to San Antonio that morning, leaving behind various items for Kim to keep track of.

"If I find your bracelet, Todd, I'll send it along."

Kim had managed to keep track of it through dozens of miles of wilderness, only for Todd to lose it within hours of it being returned to him.

"Please do." Todd hugged Renée and shook Cody's hand. He paused before Ron. "Thank you for taking care of my daughter."

Ron flushed. "I didn't do such a great job, Todd." His blue eyes skated over Kimberly, resting on the bulky bandage visible under her shirt sleeve, her black eye and the raw scrape on her cheek, the fading bruises around her throat.

Todd didn't see his daughter's battered appearance; he saw a change in her eyes, in how she held her head high, in the way she spoke and smiled with confidence. He hadn't seen that in years. Nothing short of divine intervention could have led Kimberly to the very family who could keep her safe and change her life.

"I think you took very good care of her," Todd disagreed, smiling. He shook Ron's hand, his grip firm. "I'll be seeing you…son."

Renée reluctantly gave up her hold on Kimberly, wiping her eyes as she passed the younger woman over to her husband. Kim held Cody at arm's length for a moment.

"I'm sorry about Scott. Had I done things differently, I would have been able to save your son."

"But you *did*, " Cody whispered, and slanted a look at Aaron. "We'll be all right, Kimberly."

She stood up on tiptoe to kiss his cheek. "Your wife's a lucky woman."

He grinned. "I'm the lucky one." He shunted her over to Ron, knowing that delay would not make their goodbye any easier. Subtly, he moved Renée and Todd farther away and engaged them in conversation.

"Well," Ron said, scuffing the toe of his sneaker against the floorboards.

Kim had no idea how to proceed, so she started in a brisk,

business-like manner. "Don't forget to go see your mother in Utah," she instructed, although she doubted it likely that he would forget. He had been thrilled to hear from her after news of the Circle's demise and Caleb's disappearance had reached her.

"You have my addresses. I'll be in San Bernardino for a week or so, as long as it takes to arrange for my things to be shipped to Dad's. Then I'll be at Dad's house in Forest Falls, until – "

He leaned down and kissed her, cutting off her words. Kim felt it begin, that familiar ebb and flow, the giving and receiving, the combining of one soul in two bodies. She reflected it was not entirely unlike the Circle's transference spell, only no one had to die.

"Da mi basia mille," he whispered against her lips.

"Then a hundred, then another thousand, then a second hundred," Kim whispered back. He obliged by bestowing on her the first ten.

"I'll put the rest on account until you're home," he promised and she smiled brilliantly.

"I'll see you soon," she whispered, and kissed him fiercely.

She watched him in the rearview as Todd guided the car down the muddy drive to Stoneridge Way as he leaned against the pillar of the porch, his hands shoved deep into his pockets. The morning clouds had given way to sun and bright patches of blue skies; a stray sunbeam lit his hair with red fire. Kim gripped the edge of her seat with both hands, trying to still a sudden swell of panic.

"Are you all right?" Todd asked with concern.

"Fine. Just drive." He turned away, but not quick enough to hide his grin. "And for God's sake, Dad, do you have to drive like a ninety-year-old man? Put some gas in it."

Smothering his grin, he goosed the accelerator as he guided the car onto the main road. They rounded the curve and the tavern flashed by on the right. She clenched her teeth together as they approached Willow Road.

Sunlight spilled over the road, turning the tar patches on the blacktop into rivers of molten gold. Todd would always claim these had blinded him to the stop sign, but Kim knew better. He blithely jumped the stop, cruising through the intersection without slowing.

This final reminder of Aaron Schaefer shattered her resolve.

"Stop the car, Dad! Stop! *Stop!*"

Todd stood on the brake and the car skidded to a halt. She sat in silence, trying to quell the rush of anxiety that raced her pulse along at heart-attack speed. Her breath came short, and her fingers dug deep indentations in the padded dashboard.

"So you'll be staying then?" Todd asked. To his credit he managed to stifle his grin of delight. She nodded convulsively. "Should I turn the car around and go put that boy out of his misery?"

"Yes!" she hissed.

Todd might have trained for NASCAR the way he drove back through town. Kim thought it was just as well that Harlan Michaels was dead or Todd surely would have earned the mother of all reckless driving tickets.

They bounced off the road and onto the driveway. Maples whizzed by in a blur. A cloud of dust kicked up behind the car, but Kim had eyes only for the man who leaped off the porch and raced toward them.

"Stop! *Stop!*" Kim screamed, but Todd had already brought the car to another skidding halt, tires spitting gravel. She popped the door and jumped out, sprinting toward Ron, her aching feet slapping through puddles and sending sprays of muddy water into the air.

He caught her with his good arm, the impact swinging them around in a circle. She pressed her face against his neck and breathed him in. He smelled like soap and limes and her tears, which he wiped from her cheeks. He smelled like home.

His eyes met hers, immeasurable blue like a fathomless sea, and when he smiled she thought the sun had exploded.

"I forgot to ask," she said breathlessly, holding her hand against a stitch in her side. "The lilacs – will they be purple or white?"

"Both," he murmured. "And yellow. I can get those from a specialty greenhouse."

"But no tulips," she reminded him.

"Just these two lips," he agreed, and bent to kiss her.

Todd cleared his throat behind them, and they turned to find him setting her luggage on the gravel road on high spots between puddles.

"I'll just be leaving these here. I have a plane to catch." He grinned.

"I'll take care of her," Ron promised.

"I've heard this before." Todd grinned. "If you find my bracelet, keep hold of it. I'll be back for the wedding." He tipped them a wink, climbed back into the car, and sped off toward the road.

"What do you think?" Aaron asked, tugging her back around to face him. "Think you could spend the next sixty or so years with a reformed werewolf?"

She slanted a wicked smile at him. "I'm sure it will be beastly, but I think I can manage."

"Then let's go tell Renée she can finally plan my wedding."

Somewhere, Kim felt certain, God grinned at His own brilliant matchmaking

EPILOGUE

No one knew from where the house came; it seemed as though it had dropped from the very sky one day and over the next hundred and fifty years was immortalized in Heron Bay's history.

Its gray stone face and soaring lancet windows gave the house a graceful, stately façade. It took one's breath, inspired dreams of living in splendor and riches.

But no one lived there. Uninhabited since 1945, when the last family fell victim to a murder spree, the structure fell into disrepair. Rumors abounded of hauntings and demons, and psychics in the little Washington town created gruesome visions of child sacrifice and blood oaths to the devil.

Bayview Manor stood empty to the ungifted eye, yet the fallen walked its halls. The devil's mansion went where the devil traveled, and the devil had come to Heron Bay.

ABOUT THE AUTHOR

Sharon Gerlach was in training to be a ninja, but a dismaying lack of physical grace and balance--not to mention the inability to keep her big mouth shut--ended her ninja career before it had

 really begun. Now she writes. She doesn't write about ninjas because that's obviously a sore subject. But she writes about other really cool things and figures someone else will cover the ninjas. Life's really not all about ninjas, anyway.

Sharon lives on the dry side of the Pacific Northwest with her husband (who must really be fond of her as he hasn't left her yet despite her ninja failings); her three kids, and a grandchild (none of whom possess ninja qualities either); and a Border collie who suffers the presence of six cats. Yes, you guessed it--ninja cats!

Blog: sharongerlach.wordpress.com
Twitter: twitter.com/SharonGerlach
Facebook: www.facebook.com/AuthorSharonGerlach

OTHER RUNNING INK PRESS BOOKS

NEMESIS — N.L. Gervasio

After the last prince ran off without any notice, breaking her heart and their engagement along the way, Nemesis Mussolini swore off men and passed the time kicking ass and slinging drinks, something her mafia father would never approve of. But, when her boss Clancy ups his flirtations, it's difficult to remember she's not interested, especially when he gets that delicious evil glint in his eye that makes her melt.

OFFICE POLITICS — Sharon Gerlach

Malaria is nothing a good dose of quinine can't handle, thinks Frannie Freeman when her vile office manager Malia—aka Malaria—marries their boss Sam, whom Frannie has loved for years. When Sam suddenly confides that he believes he was roofied the night of his surprise Las Vegas wedding, Frannie prepares to battle for her man with a woman's three best weapons — a loyal heart, a willingness to fight dirty, and the strongest margarita money can buy.

THE SECRET DREAMS OF SARAH-JANE QUINN — Sharon Gerlach

Self-confidence and social skills have never been Sarah-Jane Quinn's strong suits. So when two men – as different as night and day – vie for her affection, she's both flattered and mystified. And then Sarah is brutally attacked by a violent stalker. In the aftermath, she must re-evaluate her priorities and decide which man reaches deepest into her heart – and let the other go forever.

MALAKH — Sharon Gerlach

He hunts, silent and unseen. The string of mutilated bodies points to a madman, but biological evidence yields no DNA—

human or animal. Suzanne Harper had once been the lover of an angel. The evidence points to him and tells a terrifying tale: he's working his way to her. Now she must reconcile her longing with justice and honor, and she must do it fast...for the next murder could be hers.

CONDEMNED — Sharon Gerlach

Tools that relocate themselves. Shadows glimpsed from the corner of one's eye. The feeling of being watched when no one's there. It's all in a day's work for the crew renovating Bayview Manor, a dilapidated mansion overlooking the Pacific Ocean on the Olympic Peninsula. Interior designer Rachael Payne doesn't believe in ghosts, but owner Geoffrey Windsor wonders if her faith protects her from the forces within his mansion — or blinds her to them.

www.runninginkpress.com